Praise for the novels of Rosalind Noonan

PRETTY, NASTY, LOVELY

"Suspenseful . . . A world of blackmail, bullying, and lies. This quick read will keep readers guessing." —*Booklist*

TAKE ANOTHER LOOK

"Noonan grips readers in this suspenseful novel . . . worth picking up." —*RT Book Reviews*

AND THEN SHE WAS GONE

"A story of optimism and encouragement, despite the heart-wrenching subject matter." —*Chatelaine*

ALL SHE EVER WANTED

"Noonan has a knack for page-turners and doesn't disappoint . . . a readable tale." —*Publishers Weekly*

THE DAUGHTER SHE USED TO BE

"An engrossing family saga and a suspenseful legal thriller. Noonan covers a lot of narrative ground, with a large cast of characters whose situations involve morally complex issues, as well as knotty family dynamics. This novel would fuel some great book-club discussions."
—*Shelf Awareness*

Please turn the page for more praise for Rosalind Noonan!

ONE SEPTEMBER MORNING

"Written with great insight into military families and the constant struggle between supporting the troops but not the war, Noonan delivers a fast-paced, character-driven tale with a touch of mystery."—*Publishers Weekly*

"Noonan creates a unique thriller that is anti–Iraq war and pro-soldier, a novel that focuses on the toll war takes on returning soldiers and civilians whose loved ones won't be coming home."—*Booklist*

"Reminiscent of Jodi Picoult's kind of tale . . . it's a keeper!" —Lisa Jackson, *New York Times* best-selling author

THE
SISTERS

Books by Rosalind Noonan

ONE SEPTEMBER MORNING

IN A HEARTBEAT

THE DAUGHTER SHE USED TO BE

ALL SHE EVER WANTED

AND THEN SHE WAS GONE

TAKE ANOTHER LOOK

DOMESTIC SECRETS

PRETTY, NASTY, LOVELY

THE SISTERS

SINISTER
(with Lisa Jackson and Nancy Bush)

OMINOUS
(with Lisa Jackson and Nancy Bush)

Published by Kensington Publishing Corporation

THE
SISTERS

ROSALIND NOONAN

KENSINGTON BOOKS
www.kensingtonbooks.com

KENSINGTON BOOKS are published by

Kensington Publishing Corp.
119 West 40th Street
New York, NY 10018

ISBN-13: 978-1-4967-0804-5
ISBN-10: 1-4967-0804-0
First Kensington Trade Paperback Printing: December 2018

ISBN-13: 978-1-4967-0805-2 (ebook)
ISBN-10: 1-4967-0805-9 (ebook)
Kensington Electronic Edition: December 2018

10 9 8 7 6 5 4 3 2 1

Printed in the United States of America

For my sisters, Denise and Maureen,
The best examples I know of genuine love.
And to my sisters around the world,
Here's to freedom.

PART 1

THE LAST TIME I SAW YOU

PROLOGUE

You can't do this. You cannot do this!

The voice in her head wailed at her like a repeating siren as she pushed the stroller onto the wide porch of the fire station. Glory Noland summoned all her strength to tune it out and stay composed for Ruby's sake. It would be wrong to share her panic and paranoia. Her babies were going to a better place, happier and healthier than Glory could ever make them.

This is best for your girls. You're doing the right thing.

The right thing.

Swallowing back a swell of stormy emotions, Glory moved the stroller to the side of the door and adjusted the eyelet edge of her baby's cap. Lulled to sleep by the walk, Aurora was still, her pale brown face was angelic, her steady breath a whisper. Whenever the baby was asleep and quiet, Glory longed to swoop in and nuzzle those chubby cheeks and drop light kisses over her dark, smooth brows. Her baby smell, her smooth skin. In the quiet interludes, she was heaven.

But those moments were rare. With Winston gone, Glory had no time to love on her baby. No time to read with Ruby.

No time to sleep, eat, think, breathe.

So hard to breathe. She needed air.

"Mommy, can we go home?" Ruby pressed into Glory's thigh, her little arms holding on as if Glory were a tree in a flood.

Glory was too choked up to answer. Besides, what would she say? *No, little bug, you can never go home again. We can never . . . but you'll have a new home. A better, safer place than I could ever give you.*

The creak of one of the weathered wooden doors startled Glory as a stocky man with dark eyes and a short handlebar mustache appeared in reflective green trousers with suspenders over a T-shirt with the emblem Portland Fire and Rescue 99.

"Hey there," he said. "How's it going?"

"Fine. Good." Her voice was pitched so high, it was obvious that she was overwrought. "We just stopped by to . . . to see the firehouse."

"Is that right? Well, sorry about that, but we don't do tours."

"Really?" She touched Ruby's shoulders, looking down at her to avoid eye contact with the fireman. Her face had to be red, her eyes puffy, from all the crying. "This one is going to be disappointed."

She dared to look up and saw that his dark eyes studied them intently. Was he on to her? "Maybe she could sit in one of the trucks? She loves trucks."

Ruby turned to Glory and sneered at her as if she'd lost her mind.

Don't ruin this! The last thing she needed was for her daughter to correct her now.

"If you don't mind, sir." Glory fed the lie. "We walk by here every day, and I keep promising her that we'll stop in."

He tilted his head, reconsidering the plea from the obviously rattled woman. "You're killing me, ma'am. Okay, I guess we could take a quick look. Come on around here, young lady, and I'll get you situated," he said, leading Ruby around the side driveway to the two tall garage doors.

Glory followed with the stroller as things began to fall into place. This man was going to make the most difficult task of her life more bearable.

"I'm Bob Candida. You can call me Fireman Bob," he told Ruby. "And what's your name?"

"Ruby Noland."

"Okay, Ruby. I'm going to get you to help me open the fire-house door." He opened a box on the wall, tapped a code onto the keypad, and then lifted Ruby in his arms so that she could reach the panel. "You press this button here, the one that says 'enter,' and we'll see what happens."

The sight of Fireman Bob with Ruby in his arms, trying to teach her the way that her father had, brought tears to Glory's eyes.

Ruby gasped as the huge door began to lift.

"See that? You got the door to open," Bob said encouragingly, and Ruby granted him a smile.

Inside the cool shadows of the garage Bob talked about how they needed the big trucks to put out fires. He explained a few parts of the truck, but Glory was unable to hear over the roar in her ears and the noise of her own heart, thrumming in her chest. The physical consequences of a broken heart that would never be mended.

And now she was crying again, and Aurora was awake and fussing, threatening to spoil the plan.

Glory ducked beneath the awning of the stroller, hiding as she swiped away tears and took one last look at Aurora, stretching and kicking at the blanket. Only four months old, still a baby.

How can you do this?

In one movement Glory picked her up and jostled her gently, soothing her complaints. *Who will know how to settle you down? You'll have to make the switch to formula, and what if you resist? What if you won't take the bottle? I wish I could have gotten you bigger and stronger, but that's for your next mother.* She brushed her fingertips over one chubby cheek, trying to memorize Aurora's features in this moment. *Your next mother . . . she's a lucky woman.*

It was after Bob hoisted Ruby up high into the driver's seat of the truck that Glory made her move. While Ruby counted the little lumps in the grip of the steering wheel, Glory motioned Bob away from the cab.

"I need your help." She extended Aurora toward him.

With a squinty look of surprise, he took the baby. From the way he one-armed her, Glory suspected he had kids of his own. *Good.*

"Cute kid. Do you need to find her bottle?"

"Her name is Aurora, and she's a good baby. She hasn't had solid food yet, and you can usually soothe her with her Huggy Bear toy." She hated the catch in her voice, but she pressed on. "I need you to take care of her, and her sister Ruby. I heard that I can leave them here, that you'll do the right thing."

"Oh. Wow. Hold on." Bob shifted the baby and held her out, giving her back.

"No." Glory stood her ground, arms folded across her chest, a living skull and crossbones. She was dying inside, but she could not touch her baby again.

Aurora whined, not enjoying the suspension, until Bob pulled her back to his chest.

"Hold on now, ma'am. What's your name?"

"I get to leave her, no questions asked. That's the law."

"The Safe Haven Law applies only to infants under thirty days old. This one is older than that. And Ruby must be four or five."

"Four, but they need to be together. They're sisters."

He squinted in disbelief. "You can't do this. Ma'am, this is a firehouse. We're not set up for something like this. You'll be wanting them back in a hot minute, and you're the best thing for these girls. There's no substitute for a mother's love."

"You have to take them. That's the law."

"Not really. Look, I want to help you, but we're in the business of fire and rescue. If you hold tight, I can find someone from Child Services to work with you. A social worker."

"I have one of those." All those days Glory had been ducking Juana Lopez, fearing the social worker would take her kids away, when that would have been the best thing for everyone. She fished Ms. Lopez's card from her pocket and handed it to him. "You can call her, but I need you to take them. Now."

"If you need a place to go, there are family shelters—"

"No." Glory had a place to go, but the girls needed something more. A family. Two parents. A home. With their mocha-colored skin and spring water blue eyes, they would be challenging to place, but somewhere in the state there was a family with love in their hearts. There had to be. "Please," she pleaded, "please, help me. I'm dying inside, but still, I know that this may be the only right decision I've ever made. The only right choice."

Outside the garage it began to rain and a wind gust brought them the smell of wet concrete and tiny, furious pellets of moisture.

"All right." There was resignation and annoyance in his eyes, but also commitment; he would do the right thing for her girls. "I'm going to give you my contact information for later." He placed Aurora in the stroller and fished a card out of his pocket. "For when you change your mind and want them back. In my experience, mothers never give up on their sons and daughters."

Not me. You don't know me, she thought, sliding the card into her pocket. Once she got across the street, she would tear it up into a dozen tiny pieces and watch them flutter into a trash can. "Sever all ties to the outside world," he'd told her. That was the only way to start over.

When he turned away to fetch Ruby from the truck's cab, she wanted to stop him. She'd been hoping to slip away, avoid the good-bye. It was always best to skirt around the wound.

But now Ruby was on the floor, taking her hand. "Can we go now, Mommy?"

Time for the deepest cut.

Glory squatted down to her daughter's level. "Mommy has to go, but you're going to stay here with Fireman Bob."

"I want to go home," Ruby whined, tugging her hand.

"Remember patience, like we talked about?"

"I don't like patience. When are you coming back?"

"Soon." Glory had to choke the word past the thickness of tears and emotion.

"Not soon!" Fear clouded Ruby's blue eyes. She had learned that sometimes "soon" never came.

"I need you to be a big girl, Ruby. You need to listen and take care of your little sister, okay?"

"Okay, Mommy. But can't I go with you?"

Unable to face her anymore, Glory stood up and pressed her daughter against her in a hug. "Be good and patient and always remember how much Mommy loves you."

Ruby mumbled something, her voice cracking with a whimper as Glory rubbed her back, and then quickly turned and stepped out of the garage bay and into the rain.

She didn't look back, not when Bob called for her to wait, not even when Ruby's pathetic sob carried across the street.

She kept walking, fueled by a mixture of guilt, sacrifice, and a sense of relief that surprised and shamed her. She had done it for her girls, but it felt good to be free. Even at a high price, freedom tasted light and sweet.

CHAPTER 1

Three Months Earlier

Four-year-old Ruby stood in the doorway, watching her mother watch the man on television. Everybody on the television was laughing at the man, but that was grown-up stuff.

"Can you switch to cartoons?" Ruby asked.

Mommy lifted her head from the couch. "It's too late for cartoons. You're supposed to be in bed, love bug. It's after midnight."

"Aw. I'm not tired." What she really meant was that she wanted to stay up until Daddy got home.

"You fell right to sleep two hours ago."

"I'm getting a snack. I'm hungry." Not really, but it was a way to stay up with Mommy for a while. Ruby went into the kitchen and opened the cupboard beside the oven. Mommy put the cereal and crackers there so Ruby could do it herself. Like a grown-up, except smaller. Something was bubbling on the stove as Ruby took out two boxes and lined them up on the floor.

Life cereals were squares. Cheerios were circles. Ruby was going to teach squares and circles to Aurora when she got bigger. Right now Aurora was a baby, and babies didn't know anything. Ruby knew things. She knew that grass turned green from drinking the rainwater. But people didn't turn green from water. She knew that Daddy was gone to 'Laska. Life cereals were Daddy's favorite. Ruby put two handfuls of those into a plastic cup and pushed the boxes back into the cabinet.

At the couch Ruby pressed against Mommy's knees, wishing she could sit in her lap. She used to snuggle with Mommy all the time, but now Aurora was always in the way. When Mommy's eyes opened, she wasn't mad. "Good girl." Ruby smiled when Mommy pulled her into her lap, and Ruby found her familiar spot. She tried to look into Mommy's eyes, but they were closing. Mommy's eyes were full of blue sparkles, like something magic under the sea. "You have my eyes," Mommy always told Ruby, and Ruby always said, "I'll give them back," and Mommy laughed.

"Don't forget to brush your teeth again."

"Okay, Mommy."

Ruby closed her eyes as her head rested against Mommy's chest. This was what she'd wanted, the hunger that had pulled her out of bed. She missed her mommy and her daddy, too. She wanted Mommy to put the baby down and play with her. She wanted Daddy to come home and give her a ride on his shoulders or play jungle forest with her. He was the elephant and Ruby was the little lost lion cub that he carried back to safety. Then he would tickle her with his trunk, and she would feed him peanuts. He was a good elephant.

Mommy let out a big breath and it was extra loud to Ruby, with her ear to Mommy's chest. Mommy didn't play jungle forest, but she liked to snuggle and read books to Ruby. But Mommy didn't read anymore because of the baby, and sometimes Mommy fell asleep in the middle of a snuggle. Like now. Sometimes that was boring, but tonight Ruby just waited and stroked Mommy's hair, winding the dark threads through her fingers until the ends sprang out.

Not ready to close her eyes, Ruby stared at the people on television. Talk, talk, talk. Grown-ups didn't know how to play. Their television was boring, but Mommy said there were no children's shows on at night. After a while she wriggled out of Mommy's lap and munched a few pieces of cereal. Mommy was still sleeping.

"Quiet," Ruby whispered. Holding the cup in both hands, she walked carefully on the floors, one bare foot in each square, until she was in Mommy and Daddy's room. Sometimes Aurora slept in here, but tonight she was in the laundry basket near Ruby's bed.

Propping her cup on the bed, Ruby climbed up and crawled to the middle. Facedown, she wriggled between the two pillows and pretended to be asleep. She pretended Daddy was on one side of her, Mommy on the other, like before. When Ruby sneaked into their bed, she was always the middle of the sandwich.

She squeezed her eyes shut, but she couldn't sleep. Maybe Daddy would come home tonight?

Ruby waited. She tried to breathe Daddy's smell from his pillow. She scrunched her ears, listening for the squeak of the front door, his heavy steps, the songs he sang to himself without moving his lips. No. She couldn't hear him.

Rolling over, she noticed the cup of cereals toppled onto the bed. *Oops.* She picked them up and scooted over to Daddy's side of the bed, where the table held only a tissue box. When Daddy got home, he was going to be hungry. "These will be a good snack for you." She began lining up the squares of Life, stopping to eat one occasionally when it was too crumbled or broken to be a square anymore. When she finished, the line of cereals curved around in a funny shape. Like an elephant trunk.

"I left you some peanuts, Daddy Elephant," she said, smooshing the side of her face into his pillow. Eyes closed, she pretended that she was waiting for Mommy and Daddy to come to bed. Soon. Things were always going to happen soon.

CHAPTER 2

Half a dozen cars remained in the parking lot of the Montessori school as Tamarind McCullum approached the one-story building with tinted windows and a river stone façade. Although the school wasn't really on her route home from the bus stop, Tamarind frequently took a detour to walk by and monitor the mood of the place, a potential school for her baby.

Our baby.

She slowed her pace, enjoying the walk after a long day at her desk, knowing the exercise was good for the baby, too. In the years that she and Pete had been trying to conceive, she had just about memorized those books on the "how to" of pregnancy and infant care. She knew that personal care during the first weeks and months of a child's life were important for bonding, but after that early-learning centers were an excellent way to nurture a child's independence and social skills. It took a village, and she and Pete wanted their baby to soak up culture, skills, and knowledge from the world around her. The Montessori school was the closest, but Tamarind had also heard great things about the Little Red Schoolhouse, which was ten minutes' drive from home.

Which to choose . . . This was how she rolled, planning and researching in advance to make careful, informed decisions. As she'd already learned that the baby couldn't be enrolled until he or she was born, there were still six months to decide.

She turned toward the school as the front door opened and a little boy scampered out, racing across the deck. You could tell a lot by the attitudes of kids and their parents as they left the building at the end of the day. This dark-haired kid paused at the banister to wait for the man following him out.

"You forgot your collage, Brandon."

"Oh yeah." The boy lifted his arms to take the small poster. "See, Dad? You have snow in the winter, and then in the spring the snow goes away and flowers pop out of the ground."

"That's right. How many seasons?" the father asked.

"Four," Brandon said, waving his collage in the air.

Tamarind smiled at the boy's enthusiasm. *Score points for the Montessori school,* she thought as she moved ahead and the school disappeared behind the hedge of the neighboring house. She had been leaning toward this school, but she would tour both facilities before she made a choice. One of the trickier things would be testing how the administration and parents of the schools would react to having a family of color in their community. The Portland area was primarily white, with a small percentage of Asian residents. There would be no student exactly like their baby, no other children with an African-American and Indian heritage. Tamarind could accept that, as long as the school community could accept her and Pete's child.

That worried her sometimes. "What if kids are mean to our son or daughter because his skin is browner than theirs or her food smells different?" Tamarind had asked her mother, Rima, who was thrilled about the prospect of a grandchild.

"Some kids find reasons to pick on their classmates. Others will be more accepting. But every child has challenges. This is part of life."

"That scares me," Tamarind admitted. "My heart will break if I have to watch my child suffer."

"The heart is stronger than we think," Rima told her. "Your kid will be fine. Everyone has problems. We figure them out. But every child is different, like a snowflake. That's the beauty of variety in this world."

Her mother's confidence, which often came out in the form of bossiness, had been reassuring to Tamarind in the years that she and Pete had been trying to conceive. Now that there was a baby on the way, Rima was already laying out the plans for Tamarind and their newborn to come and live with Rima and Karim for a few weeks after the birth. It was an old-fashioned Indian tradition for a daughter to return to her mother's home during that time.

"For how many weeks?" Pete had asked, reluctance in his voice.

"Six weeks. It's enough time for me to take care of Tamarind and that gives her time and energy to take care of her new baby," Rima had explained.

"Wow. That seems like a long time," Pete had said. "Maybe too long. I'm going to miss her, and you know, I can take care of her, too."

"You can visit on weekends," Rima had agreed. "The rest of the time, you go to work while I nurture Tamarind back to health. This is a mother's job—the boring things like feeding and cleaning, the important things like lifting the spirits. This is what mothers do for their daughters."

"I see." Pete had been wise enough not to argue with her mother, though he'd expressed his concerns to Tamarind in private. He was concerned at having his wife and baby so far away in Seattle. And what about his family? Didn't they deserve a chance to see the baby, too?

"They can visit the baby in the hospital," Tamarind had said, pointing out that most of his family lived in the Portland area. "And we'll be in my parents' house, under my mom's care. Is there anyone more capable in the world?"

"Your mom is a dynamo. She's great," Pete admitted. "I'm just not sure I'll be able to share you and the baby."

"Please. I know it's asking a lot of you, but this is one of the old traditions I want to keep. After a woman gives birth, no one can take care of her like her mother. At least that's what my mom and the aunties have told me."

"I'll think on it," he'd said. She had planned to give him a week or two before nudging him, but the next morning he'd slipped his arms around her waist while she'd been sipping from a mug of herb tea.

"You're carrying our baby," he'd said, his lips brushing the sensitive lobe of her right ear. "You've been going through the nausea. Your body is changing. Once the baby is here, the least I can do is let you recover with your mom."

"Thanks, sweetie." She had melted against him, her eyes tearing up at the goodness of her man, her Pete. He would be a wonderful daddy.

As the blue Honda pulled out of the school parking lot, Brandon glanced at her through the window of the back seat and smiled, revealing two missing teeth in the front. *Stinkin' adorable.*

She smiled back. There was a good chance that she would see Brandon and his dad again. A very good chance.

CHAPTER 3

The gray shroud of sleep clung stubbornly to the air as Glory Noland opened her eyes in a panic. What was that awful shrieking sound? And the acrid smell, the dull blur of smoke that hung under the ceiling—

The smoke alarm. Fire. Her babies!

Clawing her hair from her eyes, she shot up on the couch and turned toward the kitchen wall.

The stovetop lit the dark apartment, flames licking a pot that glowed red.

Oh, God!

On her feet, raking back her hair, Glory wasn't sure what to do first.

Someone was banging on the apartment's front door, adding to the shrill screech of the smoke detector as Glory hurried from the sofa to the horrid glow of the stovetop. Heat seared the air as she reached for the knob to turn the flame off. Smoke leached from the black disk in the red-hot pot. Ruined.

Glory coughed and swatted at the smoke as she stepped back from the heat. She could have burned down the house, killed them all. Even now, this putrid smoke was probably damaging their lungs, seeping under the door of the kids' room. Her little ones.

First, protect the girls. Glory shoved open the wimpy window over the sink and turned on the fan in the range hood.

Swallowing hard over the dry grit in her throat, she used a potholder to pick up the pot. The heat radiating from the hot metal made her wince. She knew she had to get it out of here, but where? She cast about, looking for a place to put the searing-hot metal.

"Open this door!" Ellen's low croak thundered at the door.

Glory crossed the small living space in four steps and used her free hand to open the front door. Her landlady blocked the vestibule.

"What the hell are you doing? It's the middle of the night." Ellen gathered her fleece jacket closed as she glared at the pot. "Are you cooking meth?"

"My breast pump. I was sterilizing it. I fell asleep." Maneuvering around Ellen, she stepped out into the damp, cool night. The patter of rain on the rhododendron bushes was a welcome relief from the alarm. Glory held the hot pot out to collect some rain. It steamed as she placed it on the concrete porch. Cool drops landed on her head and shoulders, leaving dark slashes on her T-shirt and jeans. She had fallen asleep in her clothes again. Again and again.

"That smell." The smoker's voice drew her back from the garden escape. Ellen raked her gray hair away from her face as she sniffed. Most days it was combed and sprayed into a gray cloud around her head, but sleep had broken the hold of hair spray, making it jut out in disarray. Kind of goth, or very Einstein. "Is that toxic smoke?" Ellen began swinging the door, fanning the smoke. "Was it plastic? The PCBs are going to kill us all."

"I hope not." Lingering in the rain, Glory wondered if it could be true. Most of the smoke had hung at the ceiling, and she doubted it made it past the closed bedroom doors. Funny that the girls hadn't woken up. Some nights, a sneeze could do it; other times, they slept like tiny boulders.

"And why were you cooking this pump?"

"Sterilizing it. You have to keep it clean."

"And why would you need a breast pump? You got no husband to feed the baby."

But I do, Glory wanted to argue. *I do have a husband, a man who fires my soul and shares my dream for our daughters. Love of my life, I need you here!* But right now, it was not to be. Winston needed to be in Alaska, working in an oil job to make enough money to pull them out of debt and build a nest egg. Despite Mom's warnings of unreliable men, Glory had found a gem. A man with a big heart and the desire to provide for his family.

"What would you even do with breast milk?" Ellen couldn't back off a topic until she had chewed her way through.

"It's for day care. So I can get a job." Glory hated having to explain herself to Ellen, who always pushed too far, asking how much things cost and criticizing Glory's decisions. "I've been interviewing at the mall."

"The mall? And you're paying someone else to watch your kids? Don't you know the money you pay for day care is gonna eat through your paycheck?"

"I need to work."

"You need to make money someway. You're behind on the rent."

"I know. We talked about that." Inside the smoke alarm ceased its ear-piercing alarm, a huge relief. Glory swiped a splat of rain from her forehead and scraped her dark hair back, tying it off with a band from the pocket of her jeans. Now that the topic of money had come up, this conversation was doomed.

"Being a little late is one thing, but now you owe two months, and we're coming up on June. I don't think you understand how it feels to be kept waiting."

Waiting? Glory's whole life was a waiting game. Waiting for Winston to call. Waiting for him to return. Waiting for the baby to arrive. Waiting for the kids to drop off to sleep. Waiting to hear about a job.

Waiting for life to get better.

"I'm sorry. I . . ." If only they could catch a break. Winston had been searching for a new job since the refinery he'd been working for went off-line a few weeks ago. He said the low price of oil was hurting the industry. Now the little bit of cash Glory had made as a barista before Aurora was born was running out. "I'm going to pay you, Ellen."

"Of course you are, but when I don't get rent on time I'm in a predicament. You know I need the money to pay the mortgage on this place." Ellen lived upstairs in an updated version of Glory's apartment with shiny wood floors, fancy brushed-copper faucets, and granite counters in the kitchen and bathroom. Ellen had insisted that Glory see the place, taking her through like a museum tour guide. "This is what you get when you work hard," Ellen had said smugly. Although Glory had complimented her landlady, a fancy kitchen wasn't her idea of a happy life. She wanted Winston back, their family together in a home they could afford. A little house with a lot of love.

The first time she encountered him, she realized that he understood about real love. It had been in English class, sophomore year, and though she'd been dating Lance Pitt at the time, she had been amused by the lean, black football player with his serious voice and insights and smoky eyes that had melted the heart of every girl in that class, and maybe Ms. Feathers, who was old enough to have crow's-feet wrinkles at the outer edges of her eyes. "When you get down to it, the play's really about love and hate," Winston said of *Romeo and Juliet*. "If the Montagues and Capulets hadn't hated on each other for all those years, then Romeo could've married Juliet, no problem. But these two families were like in the middle of Mafia gang wars."

"Exactly," Ms. Feathers had agreed, prompting the class to discuss factions of hatred in their everyday lives.

Glory had thought of how her mother had hated her father, but that seemed too personal to bring up in class. Instead, she watched and listened as Winston just about led the conversation, talking about the divisiveness of hate and the power of love. "Divisiveness" . . . he actually said that word. O.M.G. He was a man in a class of annoying, groping boys. He made

Lance look like a ten-year-old. Glory knew right then and there that she wanted to be near Winston Noland, to get to know him better. She wanted to know that warm-honey feeling of having his soulful eyes take her in as she nestled against his hard, athletic body. Winston promised the right combination of sex appeal and play and rebellion. She knew her mother and stepfather would freak if they ever caught her with an African-American guy, but that was their problem—or so she'd thought at the time. And months later when her and Winston's paths had crossed on the football field, Glory hadn't been disappointed.

She still loved him like the first time she saw who he was. More, now that they had these babies together. She missed him so much it hurt.

"So." The landlady's sharp voice jarred her back to the present dilemma. "When will you have my money?"

"I'll call Winston in the morning and see what's what," Glory said, knowing it was a hollow promise. She hadn't been able to reach Winston for days—five days now—and she was sick with worry. Last she'd heard, he'd been driving north from Fairbanks to check out some maintenance job near the Arctic Circle. Horrible scenarios of his car going off the road or getting slammed by a truck played in a loop through her mind, haunting her day and night. *Come back to me, my love,* she prayed whenever she had the chance.

"If you can't pay on time, I need to find a renter who will. You know I have the utmost sympathy for what you're dealing with. You and your babies."

Not really, but you didn't argue with a woman like Ellen. "You've always been fair." Glory edged toward her door, wanting the conversation to end. "I'm sorry about the rent. I'll pay you soon as I can."

"I don't understand why you don't just go home to Roseville. Let your mother take you in. Doesn't she want to see her grandbabies?"

Glory teared up at the thought of home. Her little room

under the eaves of the attic had seemed like a jail when she was in high school, but now Glory longed to climb into the lumpy twin bed and close her eyes. She would slide under the worn quilt that smelled of Downy and sleep for days.

But that wasn't going to happen.

Glory couldn't bring her children back to Roseville, not without them attracting curiosity and disapproval, even from their own grandmother.

Besides, the little attic room was lost to her, home to some other teenage kid or a storage space to house Christmas decorations and snowboards. Katherine Halpern had sold the old house and gotten a new place with Ray. *"It's very freeing to downscale,"* her mom had insisted during one of their rare phone conversations. *"And I had to get out of that neighborhood. People never forgave us for what you did."*

The unforgivable—falling in love with a black man.

Glory still prickled at the existence of racism in this day and age. And from people who had been her coaches, her Sunday school teachers, and scout leaders. Even her minister had counseled her to end her relationship with Winston because she should "stick with her own kind."

There was no going back to Roseville.

No going back to her mother, whose prejudice and fury had surprised Glory the most. Katherine Halpern had raised her daughter to be a good Christian, to be kind to people and help the needy. To "do unto others as you would have them do unto you." Every night Glory had knelt on the attic floor, leaning into her bed to say her prayers, just as her mom had taught her. She'd thought her mom truly believed everything she preached.

Then came the day that Katherine had come home in a bad mood. "I had a rotten day at work, and it started when Nella Miller told me that you're dating a black boy. Everyone was looking at me, as if you'd been locked up by the cops. I told her she was mistaken, that my daughter would never take up with a black person."

"Mom, just calm down, okay? His name is Winston Noland, and I'm not doing anything wrong. He's a really nice guy, Mom. A good student, and he plays on the football team."

The fury that flashed over her mom's face made Glory's pulse race in fear. "I don't care if he's president of the United States. You're not going off with some black man."

Glory couldn't believe her mother was acting this way, so smug and bigoted. "I'm not going off anywhere," she had responded in a low, controlled voice. "I'm just going to hang out with my boyfriend."

Malice flashed in her mother's blue eyes as she lifted her hand and slapped Glory's cheek. Stunned, Glory pressed a hand to her cheek, though the sting of humiliation burned Glory more than the actual pain. Disapproval cut deep, but shoves and pinches emphasized a point.

Coming back to the moment, Glory looked up at her landlady, realizing the woman was waiting for a response.

"See that?" Ellen jabbed a finger in the air, having mistaken Glory's hesitance for agreement. "I've hit on a good idea. If you take those babies back to see your mother, she'll take you in. There isn't a woman on earth who can turn her own child away."

"You haven't met my mother." Glory stepped into the shadows of the vestibule to hide her thoughts. There had been a time, back when Ruby was a newborn so many moons ago, when Katherine would have held the door open as Glory carried her first baby inside. Glory would have paused for her to catch a breathless glimpse of Ruby's sweet baby face, and maybe that moment would have sparked a care inside her, a pang that ran deeper and swifter than the currents of disapproval from the neighbors or the ladies in the church choir.

Maybe. Maybe not.

Glory liked to think that it wasn't cruelty in her mother's soul, just cruel behavior. A fingernail pinch. A stinging slap on the cheek.

Not for her babies.

She and Winston were going to raise their kids on love—

that was the dream. Holding on to the dream. A poet himself, Winston had captured Glory's attention when he rapped Lewis Carroll's poem "Jabberwocky" in the high school talent show as if it were the coolest lyric ever created. He once quoted a Langston Hughes poem on a birthday card, that poem about clinging to your dreams or else you'd be a wounded bird who couldn't fly. "Hold fast to dreams . . ." Glory wasn't giving up on their dreams just because they had hit the tough stage, Winston working on an oil rig up in Alaska and her being a single parent caring for two little ones. This bitter trial would make the good times together that much sweeter.

"Make sure you take care of that pot in the morning." Ellen's voice pulled Glory back to the here and now. "If you can't move in with your mother, you'd better get looking for another place." The landlady's mouth was a grim line as she pulled the outer door closed and threw the bolt. "Because you can't stay here."

Fear spiked the exhaustion that she was always trying to keep at bay. Ellen didn't mean that; Glory knew the woman had a heart beneath her splintered exterior. "We'll talk tomorrow."

"You bet," Ellen said, making a threat and a promise.

Glory clasped the doorknob of her apartment and leaned her cheek against the wood door. Ellen would be kinder in the morning. Everything would be better in the morning . . . if Glory got some sleep.

Summoning the energy to move with a deep breath, she closed the door and tiptoed to her dark bedroom, stripping her clothes off along the way. A movement in the dark told her that Ruby had climbed into Glory's bed and was awake.

"What was that noise?"

"The smoke detector, but it's fine now." Glory kept her voice at a whisper, though that suddenly seemed ridiculous. If Aurora hadn't been awakened by the blasting alarm, a quiet conversation shouldn't bother her. The baby was due to nurse in an hour or so. One hour. Glory needed at least an hour; her body craved the dark cocoon of sleep.

Something stiff jabbed at her midriff as she reached toward

Ruby in bed. A book, Ruby's favorite, *Harold and the Purple Crayon*.

"That's my book, Mommy."

"I see."

"I was reading."

"That's good." Glory stroked the tight dark curls away from Ruby's face as she nestled in beside her and fell off into sleep.

CHAPTER 4

Winston Noland sensed heads turning as he made his way through the Fairbanks electronics store. Nearly a million people in the state of Alaska, but barely 1 percent of them were African-American. Which made him a novelty wherever he went. A scary, menacing novelty.

Don't worry, folks, he wanted to announce with a cool smile for the curious mom in tight jeans and a hockey jersey and her two kids, whom she pulled closer. *I'm not holding up the store. Just buying a cell phone. You can put your eyeballs back in their sockets.*

The hockey mom plucked a credit card from her wallet with shiny red nails that somehow reminded Winston of home. Glory was into that stuff, changing colors at least once a week. She had perfect hands, small but strong, and she always, always wore her wedding ring. He liked that she let people know she was his. He'd been damn lucky to fall in love with a beauty who loved him back.

As the woman mindlessly placed items on the counter her daughter stared up at him. The DVD of a Disney movie. Some HDMI cords. Her brother helped the mom lift the small box fan from the cart.

Winston could use one of those for the room he was renting in the back of the Cougar Saloon. Nights had been cool, but a fan could divert the smell of cigarette smoke and sour beer that seeped in from the bar in the old log cabin building. Still, it was lodging. Better than some had up here. Better than sleeping in his car, which he'd done the first night of the job in Livengood. With a population of thirteen, now fourteen, with him staying in the saloon, Livengood was barely a blip on the Old State Highway 2 as you drove north from Fairbanks. Most places wouldn't list a place that small on maps, but in the interior of Alaska if two guys with a dogsled camped out for the night it seemed to be enough to name the spot and call it a town.

Winston glanced back at the man in line behind him and saw the two revolvers riding his hips, hanging low on a belt like a gunslinger. That was some Wild West gangsta shit. People in Oregon didn't show off guns in stores, but then Winston was a long way from home. And this was the civilized part of the wilderness in Fairbanks proper. He'd driven down here at first light to deposit his paycheck and replace his cell phone, which had died when it flopped into a puddle on the job site. There were no banks in Livengood, but now, with his check deposited, Glory would be able to have some cash. And once he activated this cellular device, he would finally be able to talk with her. Five days of silence seemed like forever in this beautiful empty scrub country.

"Will that be all?" the cashier said by rote, staring down as she scanned the cell phone's box. Without waiting for an answer, she told him the price.

Winston took his credit card from his wallet and inserted it in the chip reader. The machine processed it, then flashed "Approved." As he removed the card, the cashier held out her hand. "Can I see that? And two other pieces of ID, please."

The hockey mom in front of him hadn't shown any ID to use her credit card. Whatever. He handed the cashier his Oregon driver's license and his bank card, and she studied them with skepticism, her nose wrinkling. "Oregon," she said in disgust.

"Yes, ma'am." She was a teen, too young to be a ma'am,

but he had learned that quiet respect could expedite things. He waited, annoyed that she was keeping him from getting the phone charged, his data switched over, so that he could call Glory. She was going to be pissed at him. On fire. But he didn't have many options, stuck on the job up in Livengood, with the closest store an hour and a half away. Working twelve-hour shifts, he wasn't going to risk that drive till his day off.

Trying my best, Morning Glory, he thought. *All for you and the girls.*

One night he'd been about to ask the saloon owner Bear to let him use the saloon's landline, but the big guy was quiet and weird, with a wandering eye that made Winston feel like Bear was watching him. No, better not to push the guy who'd relented on giving him a room that wasn't a legal rental. If Bear snapped, Winston would be without a bed and looking for another job in a few days. He knew when not to push.

"Mm-kay," said the cashier, finally handing back the ID cards.

He signed the receipt, then forced himself not to dash to the car, knowing that a black man on the run might alarm some people. At the door he paused to keep it open for an older man walking with a cane. His mother had been gone a decade, but she'd been diligent about instilling manners in him when he was a kid. "It's one of the things I love about you—that you're polite and kind to people," Glory used to say back in high school. "Actions reveal a person, and you've got a kind and generous heart."

She gave him more credit than he deserved, but that was "Gullible Glory," always looking for the good in people. Sometimes she was naïve that way. Like when they first met on the football field that hot August night before junior year. She'd been on a practice field working out stunts with the cheerleading squad, and he'd been at the fifty-yard line going through the paces for the offensive line coach, a prick of a man who hated his weak players and detested his token black running back. It had been a hot Oregon day, with blue sky and a raging sun that made the grass sweat. Coach Legion had worked the offense hard, then dismissed everyone but a handful of players: the sophomores and bench warmers. And Winston.

"Form a circle!" Coach called, pushing back his trucker's cap. "That's right, boys. We're going to play a little game called Pit Drill. Noland, you git in the middle. That's right. Noland's in the pit, and you boys are gonna take him down."

Winston couldn't believe it as the other players gathered around him. Racist much? Besides, the drill had been banned a few years ago. Too many hits. Too many concussions.

Winston pushed out his mouthpiece, trying to maintain respect. "Coach. This drill's dangerous. How about we run some laps?" While a few laps might make them all lose their lunches in this heat, anything would be better than this.

"Are you actually crossing me, Noland? Do you think your opinion matters? Or are you just too tired to practice?"

"Sir, I'm just saying that—"

"Noland here wants to be a running back." Coach Legion pointed at Winston. "He's gonna have to learn how to take some hits. Show me what you got, boys."

A tense stillness overtook the field as the coach backed away and the players sized up Winston. This was bullshit. Stupid for all of them to chance getting hurt. There were enough risks in football without doing a stupid practice drill that upped the odds of turning your brain to jelly. But the air was thick with fear and challenge—the coach's challenge. Try it and you might be a hero. Say no and you'll ride the bench for the season.

Winston put his mouth guard in, lowered his chin defensively, and braced for attack. The first two hits were okay, shoulder-to-shoulder practice tackles.

But the third man, Drew Kelso, came in like a Mack truck. Helmets smacked together, and Winston saw stars. "Easy, Kelso," he muttered over the block of mouthpiece. "It's just a practice."

Kelso reared back with a snort, his eyes cold, soulless beads under the curve of his helmet. "Shut the hell up." Kelso lunged at Winston again.

This time the thunder of helmets knocked Winston off his feet and into blackness.

Sweet rest.

He woke up to Glory: eyes as blue as the summer sky and a pale face with a few freckles on her nose that made her look like a kid. Most white girls didn't get this close to him. But she was scared . . . a sense of alert buzzed around them.

"Are you okay? Can you hear me?"

"Yeah. I'm just . . . just dizzy."

"He's awake!" she called to someone. "We were worried about you. We were practicing over there when you went down." She touched his arm, her cool palm pressing the biceps under his shoulder pads. She cared; he could feel that.

He started to get up but realized he was on a stretcher in the parking lot. "What happened?"

"You were out. Another player crashed into you, and you were unconscious. The coach said to leave you, that you would wake up, but I couldn't." She leaned close to him, her eyes slivers. "That coach is an asshole."

"You're preaching to the choir, girl," he said.

"My name's Glory."

She wasn't a diva, but there was something sexy and fresh about her. Those pink lips and blue eyes in a heart-shaped face . . . She was real, not one of those fixed-up girls with hairpieces and layers of makeup. She had shiny dark hair, long, curvy legs, and a smile that made people smile back.

"Juicy lips and eyes so blue, baby, you know that I love you," he sang the stupid song under his breath as he finished changing the data over to the new phone. Finally, with the new cell plugged into the running car, he could access his information. Twenty-three missed calls from Glory. He felt like a dick, but it couldn't be helped.

When he called her cell, she picked up on the first ring.

"Glory, babe, I'm so sorry."

"Oh my God, Winston! Win!" Her voice was crystal clear; it was hard to believe she wasn't a few blocks away instead of two thousand miles. "I've been sick about you. Where the hell have you been?"

"Sorry, babe. My phone died, and I couldn't get away from work till now to get a new one."

"Work? Where are you working that you can't take a break?"

"I get breaks, but just not enough time to make it to town. The job's in Livengood. Only it's not so good. A one-saloon town almost two hours north of Fairbanks. The only thing it's got going for it is the pipeline runs there, so there's a few jobs. I got me a summer position as a pipeliner. The boss says he'll see how that goes, maybe extend me through the winter."

"That's good, right? A pipeliner. That's great. It could be a long-term thing. The girls and I could come up and join you."

"We'll see. Not sure how I feel about bringing you and the girls just south of the Arctic Circle in the wintertime. It's in the middle of nowhere, and they say it gets only worse in winter. It's no place for the girls, and you would be bored."

"Not like I got a lot going on here. But I'm so relieved you're okay. I was freaking out, Win. You're killing me, here."

"I know. You've got your hands full, but I'm trying up here. I just couldn't leave the job till my day off, and there's no phone stores out on the tundra. They're working me like a dog, but the pay is good. Gotta look at the positive."

"I get it." She sounded tired now, her voice wavering. "At least you're all right."

"And we got money. More than a thousand bucks in the account."

"Woo-hoo. I guess I can pay Ellen. She's been bugging me."

"Give her one month's rent for now," he said. "There's going to be a bill for the new cell on the credit card. But that'll come in next month. If I keep pulling in a grand a week, we'll get ahead again." He scanned the parking lot, just to make sure no one was alarmed that he was sitting in the car, talking. "How's my girls? Put Ruby-doo on for me."

"She's still asleep, Win. So's Aurora."

"Did I wake you up?"

"Sort of, but that doesn't matter. I miss you so much."

"Yeah, it sucks here without you. How about we do Face-Time when I get back to Livengood? I want to get a look at Miss Ruby. I feel like she's growing up without me, and Aurora, I've never been in the same room with her. That's just wrong."

"I know, but it's the only way. You need to get that welding experience any way you can. And the money is a plus." She was making sense—a role reversal for them. Usually Glory swung with her impulses, while he was the rock, the practical one.

"You're right. If I can make it through the winter, we'll have enough to get me through the welding program at the CC."

"Sometimes you have to wade through the mud to get to the clear water."

"That's my Roseville girl talking," he teased. "Someday we'll take the girls to that old swimming hole at Miller's quarry."

"Not likely. Unless a new age of enlightenment suddenly hits Crescent County, Oregon."

"You're right," he admitted. Although he wanted his daughters to experience the joys he'd known as a kid in the country, he couldn't dismiss the barbs that two mixed-race girls might encounter in that rural area. Not that Portland was a bastion of black life, but in between the old school and the leftist elites there was a middle range of tolerance. Portland, Fairbanks, Roseville—every place had its dark corners. He and Glory would have to teach their girls how to deal, how to choose their battles, how to step up when it was time to be counted.

"Are you writing?" Glory asked. "Send me some poetry."

"Soon," he promised. Right now his words were too raw, soaked in longing for home. He didn't want to make her cry. "I'm losing it up here, babe. I'm like one of those astronauts who's broken loose from his tether."

"That's why I'm here to talk you down." He could hear the old Glory in her voice: the sense of humor, the confidence, the hope. "I got you, Spaceman. What's his name? The guy in the song."

"Major Tom."

"That's it. Wherever you go, whatever you do, you've got a lifeline that leads back to me."

"Back to you," he said, thinking about the long road home and wishing that he were driving south right now. Back home, back to Glory.

CHAPTER 5

Maybe it had been a mistake to keep the pregnancy a secret from Pete's family. As Tamarind scanned the landscape of the state park dotted with McCullum aunts, uncles, siblings, cousins, and their offspring, she wondered how she was going to keep this a secret throughout the picnic when it consumed her thoughts. Granted, it had taken her and Pete so long to get pregnant that they'd agreed to keep the fertility details to themselves, and it seemed too soon to broadcast the announcement through his large, loving family. But sitting here in the center of the McCullum patchwork quilt, Tamarind longed to sing out the coming of the new family member.

As she reached for a floret of raw cauliflower, she smiled at Cousin Mary's three kids who knelt in the grass, plucking at flowering weeds as they talked over their juice boxes. Sibling companionship. Growing up as an only child, Tamarind had longed for the camaraderie of a sibling, even one who fought with her over the last piece of creamy *kulfi* sprinkled with pistachios. Sometimes she felt that she'd missed out on the support, the laughs, the responsibility. Marrying into Pete's large, loving family had seemed like hitting the jackpot. Everyone in West Green knew the McCullums—had gone to school with one of the kids, been a patient of Doc's, taken art lessons with Janeece. But Tamarind, whose family moved to the Portland area from New Delhi when she was seven, had learned the hard way that you couldn't walk into an instant attachment.

Back then, the kids at school didn't know what to make of a little brown-skinned girl who spoke Hindi as well as English. It didn't help that Tamarind's family followed the Indian customs of their ancestors. Tamarind brought roti bread in her lunch sack and celebrated Diwali instead of Halloween. When Tamarind finally brought two classmates home, she'd been embarrassed when they wanted to know the source of the smell in the kitchen, where her mother was preparing curry and *subzi*. One of the girls, a willowy blonde named Olivia, had refused to try Rima's curry. But the other, a rangy girl with a deep curiosity and the climbing skills of a monkey, had pronounced Mom's curry delicious, and a friendship had been born. They were still close friends, though Sidney and her husband had moved to California for job opportunities last year.

Relationships took time; Tamarind knew that. Although she had veered away from many Indian traditions to fit in with people at school and work, she had learned that the only way to truly be accepted was to stand up and be yourself. But that didn't make it any easier as an outsider among some members of Pete's family. His father, Doc, was a brisk, tough nut to crack. And in the three years she and Pete had been together she hadn't found an effective way to deal with the bossiness of Pete's sister, Kaysandra.

"Delicious, aren't they?" Kaysandra rested one knee on a nearby picnic table, watching as Maisie dished up some baked beans.

"Out of this world," Cousin Maisie agreed.

"It's a foolproof recipe. You use five cans of beans. I always add fava beans, but it doesn't really matter what kind." In her crisp white shirtdress with the slimmest pink pinstripe and matching pink leggings to the knees, Kaysandra looked cool, with just the right hint of summer casual.

Seated at the next table, Tamarind questioned her choice of khaki shorts and a black print top with an empire waist as she crunched on a carrot and pretended to focus on the hummus and veggie platter. She'd chosen the top because it hid her thickening waist, but it was so bland. Unlike the McCullum women, who knew how to pull an outfit together, whether it was a gem-toned summer dress, bold print kaftan, black tights topped by a long-line tank top, or jeans with a T-shirt boasting the name of a college. The McCullum women had a certain swagger and style that Tamarind admired but hadn't yet acquired. Big-boned and square, Tamarind was the girl who fell in love with colors and patterns until she saw how they clung or draped from her body in the unforgiving light of a dressing room. But soon she'd have a new wardrobe. For the next family effort, Tamarind would be decked out in a flowing maternity dress.

The biggest downside of the McCullum family Memorial Day picnic was that the touch football game consumed the men, leaving Tamarind to fend for herself amid Pete's loud, boisterous family. It wasn't that Tamarind was shy; there simply had never been an incident before or after the wedding that solidified her place in the family.

"My kids love 'em," Kaysandra went on, "and I haven't broken the news that they're actually good for them." She put a lacquered finger to her lips as she lifted her chin toward the picnic table in the shade where nearly a dozen kids sat eating.

The kids' table.

Kids were plentiful at McCullum family gatherings. One of the things that usually poked at Tamarind's sensitive spot at functions like this. But not today.

Today Tamarind had a secret that brought her such euphoria she didn't care about the kids' table or the adorable baby nursing under the pavilion or the fact that her sister-in-law was proclaiming herself Queen of Beans. All the sacrifices, the ten grand, the month of shots and nausea, swelling and vomiting, had been worth it. She was going to be a mom. This time next year, she and Pete would have a little baby.

The knowledge of the life inside her made Tamarind so secure and happy that she felt able to tolerate her sister-in-law. Leaving the noble veggie platter behind, she pushed away from the kids' table and approached the mighty Kaysandra.

"I'm going to have some of those famous beans I keep hearing about." Tamarind dished a spoonful onto a paper plate. "Is this a secret family recipe?"

"It is, but I can share it with you. How you doing, Tam?" Kaysandra asked, using the shortened name that used to make Tamarind bristle. Back in grade school kids teased her in music class, calling her "Tam-tam-tambourine."

"We're good."

"You two still trying?" Tact was not in Kaysandra's toolbox. She floated the bald question out into the spring afternoon in front of God and children and the entire family.

Tamarind looked around to see who was listening, but the other women and children were eating and chatting and milling around and did not seem to be paying attention. "We're always trying," she said, forcing a devilish smile. "Isn't that the fun of being married?"

"I guess. You guys got a great attitude." The pity in Kaysandra's eyes made Tamarind look away. *Don't be feeling sorry for me,* she wanted to say. Instead, she focused on chasing some garbanzos and butter beans across the plate with a spoon.

"I'd be a little cranky if I'd been trying for that long. What's it been? Two years? Three?"

In lieu of an answer, Tamarind pushed the spoon into her mouth. "Mmm. These are heavenly. I would love to have your recipe."

"I'll email it to you." Kaysandra touched Tamarind's forearm for emphasis. "And you know what else I'm going to send you? I've got some brochures from work about being a foster parent that you two should take a look at." Kaysandra was a rock star in the world of social work. A strong advocate for children in foster care, she had placed foster kids with a few members of the family. "Pete and I were chatting about fostering a child as a way to adopt, and I think you two would be perfect."

"You're so sweet, but . . . foster care isn't really in our plans." *And I can't believe Pete rolled over for you that easily.* Tamarind could just imagine him being cornered by his older sister, the bully of the sibling group.

"Lot of kids out there, and children of color are hard to place here in Oregon," Kaysandra said.

Tamarind was tempted to ask how many children of Indian descent were in the program, but she knew the answer already. A big fat zero, since Oregon did not have a diverse population.

"You and Pete would be awesome as mommy and daddy," Kaysandra said, continuing with the sales pitch. "You two could make a huge difference in some kids' lives."

A flicker of maternal joy heartened Tamarind. At least Kaysandra was pushing for a good cause and she believed in Tamarind's and Pete's parenting skills. Tamarind was tempted to share their good news. That would stop the pitch, the hard sell. But her sister-in-law was not one to keep a secret, and Tamarind couldn't deny her husband the pleasure of telling his family. *Just suck it in and smile.*

"It must be very satisfying for you," Tamarind said, "helping all those kids. I know everyone in the family admires that."

Kaysandra batted the notion away with a swipe of her hand. "Sheesh. I try." She touched Tamarind's wrist. "I'll get you those brochures. Just something to think about."

"You are a formidable advocate."

"I gotta look out for my babies. My helpless babies," she said, scanning the picnic area. "My flesh-and-blood kids should be able to fend for themselves, but I don't know where they've gotten to." She shielded her eyes from the sun and shouted: "Anyone seen my kids?"

"I saw them!" Janeece McCullum called to Kaysandra as she headed toward them across a wide swath of grass. Her sister Rosie walked beside her, both women stepping carefully amid clods of fresh-cut grass and fallen fir cones that looked like something much worse.

"You did?" Kaysandra turned to her mother. "Are they behaving?"

"I saw Isaiah and Jason. Missy is minding them. Doing a good job."

"Where're they at?"

"Over by the pond. Watching the cutest family of ducks."

"Something amazing, the way those babies follow their mamas," Aunt Rosie added. A plump woman, she wore a fire-engine red shift, denim jacket, and sunglasses that hid her eyes. "My kids never listened that way."

"Tell me about it." Janeece looked majestic as usual, her hair braided in a smooth crown atop her head, her willowy figure accentuated by a flowing caftan, an abstract spray of color against a sapphire background. Probably hand-painted by Janeece.

Tamarind tilted her chin up at her mother-in-law, grateful when Janeece placed a hand on her shoulder and graced her with those eyes, wise and serene. In Janeece's big round eyes she saw all the light of amber in the sun.

"Children." Janeece chuckled. "You can only pray that your little ducklings will follow along half as well."

Resisting the urge to press a hand to her belly, Tamarind smiled. Her mother-in-law had confidence in the future, insight into Tamarind's potential as a parent. *Thank you, Janeece,* she thought, letting the silent message float on the summer breeze. *Thank you for believing in me.*

CHAPTER 6

Life is good, Glory thought, agreeing with the cute graphic poster she passed as she pushed the stroller through the mall. She had a husband who loved her, money in the bank, and two amazing daughters to fill her days.

Rolling over the fake cobblestones of the mall's interior, she let out a lazy yawn. She had nursed the baby after talking with Winston, then had dozed off again. Although she'd caught just a few spotty hours of sleep, the haze of exhaustion and stress had been eased by Winston's phone call. Winston was okay. Now the other details would fall into place. The gray mist of depression seemed to be dissolving as she moved through the mall atrium to the elevator.

"Mommy, can I throw a penny in the fountain?" Ruby peered over at the old fountain, three circles of water spouting in front of a pile of rocks where the water cascaded down. The smells of chlorine and Cinnabon mingled, not unpleasantly.

"I don't think I have a penny," Glory said. "And they don't want coins in the fountain. It can break the water system." In truth, she was anxious to get upstairs to the food court for cheap eats and good company. She'd recently made friends with a group of sisters who met for lunch at the mall after they finished work each day. Women her age who didn't judge Glory for her life choices.

"Aw-w-w." Ruby stretched the sigh out to three syllables.

"But I want to make a wish." She tugged on Glory's dress for her to stop the stroller. As Glory was putting on the brake, Ruby jumped out of the rear basket and spun toward the fountain. "I want a wish, Mommy. Daddy lets me make a wish." Before Glory could grab her, her eldest was headed down to the water.

The East Center Mall's builders had constructed steps leading down to the water in what had to be a moment of idiocy, and Glory always worried that her adventurous daughter would be the one to wade in. Now she bumped the stroller down two levels and left it parked while she corralled her oldest daughter.

"Ruby, stop! You can't run off like that."

"Okay, Mommy. I just want to make a wish." She held her little hand out, her lips curled in a hopeful smile.

Her combination of innocence and determination melted Glory's heart. "Oh, little duck, let me see if I have change." Back at the stroller, she dug in the diaper bag and managed to scrape out a lone nickel.

She brought it back and leaned down to press it into Ruby's palm. "Here's a nickel for you."

"Ooh!" Ruby's blue eyes glimmered. "How many wishes in a nickel, Mommy?"

"Five. Or one big wish."

"One big wish, Mommy. That's what I want."

"Good." At least it wouldn't take long, Glory thought as she pointed her daughter toward the quivering water. Ruby hopped down the last two steps, Glory's breath catching each time. Pausing at the bottom level, Ruby held the fist with the coin to her mouth and paused, as if praying over it.

Winston was the adventurous parent, while Glory worried about every bump in the road, seeing every concrete surface and sharp object as a potential hazard. The stroller was still safe a few steps up; the only people nearby were moms and an elderly couple sitting on a bench facing away from the fountain, which was oddly ugly and refreshing at the same time. The basin of the pool was so blue, and the purple and yellow flowers flourishing along one edge gave it a lush look. The statue atop the waterfall was of a Native American man, kneeling down to catch the water gurgling through his hands, and though Glory liked the idea of honoring native people, the innocent look on his face said he had no idea of the ways white civilization would marginalize and torture his descendants. She had overheard someone in the food court saying that the tribal man rose to his feet after the mall closed at night and went outside to smoke a pipe. The statue was definitely creepy.

A few feet away Ruby cast the coin into the fountain and clambered up the steps in an excited little dance. "I made a big wish, Mommy. I wish for Daddy to come home."

"That's a sweet wish. And the best part is, it's going to come true."

"Today?" Ruby pleaded.

"Not today, honey. But soon." She took Ruby's hand and led her up the steps.

"When is soon?"

"He's coming back as soon as he can. Daddy has some work to do in Alaska. He needs to finish his job up there."

"Is he almost finished?"

Glory felt guilty that the concept of time was lost on a four-year-old. Even a smart kid like Ruby. "I know you miss him, love bug. I miss him, too. But he just started a new job, so he's going to be there a while longer."

"No, Mommy. I wished him back."

There was no arguing with four-year-old logic, so she tried distraction. "I'm hungry. How about you?"

"No, Mommy." Ruby broke away from her clasp and ran across the atrium. "I want Daddy!"

So do I, Glory thought, tamping down her annoyance as she kept her eyes on her daughter. "You'd better come with me if you want to ride in the glass elevator."

Ruby stopped in her tracks and glanced back over her shoulder. That bait got her every time. "Okay, Mommy," she said, climbing onto the back of the stroller once again.

Up on the second level Glory headed to the food court,

where she ordered two kids' meals from the taco shop—cheese quesadillas with rice, beans, and a side of applesauce. Best deal in town, and one of the meals along with Ruby's leftovers was more than enough for Glory.

The baby began fussing while they waited in line, and soon after Glory ordered, her whimpers accelerated to a screeching cry. Feeding time again. Glory held her on one shoulder while she paid, but Aurora would not be soothed. Glancing toward the tables, Glory caught the attention of one of the sisters, Laura Lemon, who waved her over. Quickly, Glory hustled her kids and the stroller over to the petite young woman with a ring through her nose and short lemon yellow hair, which had earned her the Lemon name.

"Sit with me!" Laura was wrapping up the paper from a burger she'd just finished eating. "No one else is here yet."

"Thank you. And would you mind picking up our food? This one needs attention."

"No problem." Laura took the receipt from her and leaned down to peer at Ruby. "Hi, Ruby. How are you?"

Suddenly shy, Ruby pressed her face to the back of the stroller, as if that would make her invisible.

"It's polite to say hello to Mommy's friend," Glory said, her voice a bit louder to be heard over the baby's crying.

"Hello," Ruby muttered into the fabric of the stroller.

"She's so cute. I'll be right back." While Laura went to fetch their food, Glory draped a light blanket over one shoulder and started Aurora feeding. By the time Laura returned with two plates of food, Glory felt calm, almost sleepy, lulled by the baby nursing at her breast.

The kids' meals caught Ruby's attention. "Mommy, is that applesauce for me?"

"Yes, it is if you eat some of the other food."

Ruby took a seat beside Glory. "I like applesauce."

"I know, love bug. Thank you so much, Laura. This one was so hungry. Say thank you to Laura."

"Thank you," Ruby chimed.

"No worries," Laura said, lifting a plastic spoon. "Do you want me to feed her?"

Ruby scowled at the little bird of a woman. "I can do it." She spoke slowly, as if Laura would have trouble comprehending.

"Mind your manners, Ruby," Glory said, turning to Laura. "If you just open the applesauce, she can do the rest. She's pretty independent." Winston had worked with Ruby every day to teach her little things. He'd gotten down on his belly to encourage her to crawl and patiently worked with her until she could pick up Cheerios. He'd coached her constantly, building her vocabulary and a spirit of independence.

With Aurora nursing, Glory decided to wait to eat her meal. "Thank you for helping us," she said. "You're a godsend."

"No worries. I find children fascinating. Maybe 'cause I can't have them."

Please, take mine, Glory wanted to say, though she suspected the joke would be lost on the ever-so-serious Laura Lemon. And it was a joke. Glory loved her girls—Ruby with her hungry, inquisitive mind, and Aurora, with her cherubic smile, her baby Buddha belly—but these past few days they'd been pulling at the roots of her frazzled nerves. Aurora had her crying time—at least an hour a day at dinnertime—and Ruby had a tendency to venture off and whine and ask a million questions. But Glory couldn't imagine life without her little family.

And they said we'd never make it, Glory thought as she watched Ruby capture a spoonful of rice and beans and carefully lift it to her mouth. When Glory had left home to marry Winston on her eighteenth birthday, she'd been pregnant with Ruby and counting the days until she could escape her mother's control. Winston had more freedom at home, but Glory didn't meet with his family's approval. His mother, Bernice, had died when Winston was in high school, and the aunt who took over caring for Winston and his brother believed that Glory was trying to cash in on Winston's football skills. His father, Tom, a long-haul trucker whom Winston rarely saw, worried about his son having to support a wife and child without a job. Most of their high school friends had abandoned them, too, though some of that was to be expected after Glory and Winston left their hometown for Portland. The guys had thought Winston was a fool to tie himself down at a young age, while the girls were horrified at the prospect of giving up their shapes and their social lives to have a kid. "You guys will never last," Glory's friend Elizabeth had told her.

Ha! Proved you wrong! Glory thought as she looked past her girls and focused on Laura Lemon, one of her new friends, who was talking with Ruby. Although Glory didn't know Laura well, she knew the young woman could be trusted. Laura was part of a group that frequented the mall, congregating at the food court with the enthusiasm and spark of long-lost family members. The sisters, as they called themselves, usually stopped in to eat a late lunch after they finished their jobs at a nearby hotel. They filled the food court with smiles and goodwill before heading home to a house they shared within walking distance of the mall.

Back when she was still pregnant with Aurora, Glory had silently observed as the young women swept through the food court, cleaning off tables and delighting over a new flavor of frozen yogurt. At first she'd been skeptical. How could they be so cheerful all the time?

Months later, she still hadn't figured the sisters out, but she had gained a few insights on their pasts. These women were licking their wounds, recovering from bad situations, and the owner of the house, a man named Leo Petrov, provided a place for them to heal. Although the women rarely talked about themselves, they shared sad details about their sisters. Rachel was a professional cellist who had sought sanctuary after a breakdown left her with a terrible case of stage fright, and Georgina had escaped a violent marriage. There was Natalie Petrov, Leo's beautiful sister, who was confined to a wheelchair, and Laura Lemon, daughter of millionaire parents who had tried to confine her to a mental institution. Julia had been tortured by her own mother in a small town in eastern Oregon, and Annabelle now felt loved for the first time in her life after years spent in foster homes.

Lost souls who had found happiness—that was who the sisters really were. Despite Winston's cautions, Glory welcomed their help and enjoyed the company of women her age who weren't supermoms looking down their noses at Glory for everything from marrying a black man to buying the cheaper inorganic produce. Let the stroller brigade down at the park criticize Glory all they wanted. These days one of the few things that recharged Glory's battery was her trips to the mall, a chance to be a part of the energy that swept around the sisters like a fizzing, glimmering aura.

"Your daughter is so cute." Laura's pale eyes soaked up Ruby's gestures like a scientist observing a creature who had just landed in the mall from another planet.

Ruby frowned up at the woman and continued counting out corn chips from her plate, counting only the unbroken triangles and popping the crumbs in her mouth. "Mommy? Can I save these for Daddy?"

"I'd rather you eat them now."

"That's sweet," Laura crooned. "Is your daddy at work?"

Ruby nodded. "He'll be home soon."

"He's been gone for months." Glory blinked, embarrassed by the tears that suddenly stung her eyes. She was so hormonal lately, and though she was getting tired of telling her story, sometimes it helped remind her that she had a good man who loved her. "He's never even met Aurora. She's named after the aurora borealis. You know those lights up north, in Alaska? Her daddy says they're amazing. That's where he's working, on the pipeline in Alaska. He adored Ruby when she was a baby, but he's never met this one. Aurora was born after he headed north."

"And it's hard for you," Laura said slowly, as if trying to piece things together, "but it sounds like a great story that will end happily. Like a romance novel. You're so lucky. I'm lucky, too, having Leo and the sisters."

"Your group seems to be very happy. How did you come to join them, if you don't mind my asking?"

Uncomfortable now, Laura began gathering wrappers onto the tray. "Leo saved me."

"And what did he save you from?"

"My parents. They wanted to lock me up forever." Laura arose and lifted the tray. "But let's not talk about the bad things. Only the good. Your husband will be home soon, I'm sure. A happy reunion." She carried the tray to the bussing area and dumped the trash into the bin. "And there they are!" She waved toward the food court entrance. "My sisters."

They moved as a casual group, only a handful of women today. Glory recognized Rachel, Annabelle, and Kimani, followed by Natalie, being pushed in her wheelchair by her brother, Leo. Glory gave a casual wave, then lowered Aurora to her lap to quickly refasten her bra and button her dress. It was one thing to breastfeed in front of the sisters, quite another to feel exposed in front of the gorgeous, ageless Leo Petrov. With honey blond hair, eyes as blue as the sky, and a well-toned, solid body, he possessed a mix of charm and good looks that made Glory feel a bit nervous around him. Not that he was her type, and even if he were, she was a married woman who was very much in love with her husband. Winston was the light of her life, her soul mate. But Leo Petrov was a sort of celebrity, a bright sun, and when he was near, everyone seemed to draw closer, warmed by his glow.

"Hey there, Glory," he said, coming to the head of their table as someone else wheeled his sister over to the kebob shop. "Did you get food? How about you, Laura?"

"I already ate, and Glory has a quesadilla here," Laura answered.

"Excellent. No one will go hungry on my watch." His eyes gleamed as he smiled.

It was a small gesture of kindness, but Glory was touched that someone in the world cared if she ate today. "Thanks for asking."

"It's what I do. I like taking care of my sisters. I could take care of you."

"You're so sweet." She pulled her plate closer and bit off a corner of the quesadilla. Sometimes breastfeeding made her voraciously hungry.

"It's my calling," he went on, "taking care of women who need help. It started with my sister when she had the accident that put her in that wheelchair. I learned that I could offer a safe home. Protection. I could protect you, Glory."

"It's tempting sometimes," she said lightly, "but I have a husband and these two." She nodded toward Ruby, who held Laura's hand as they waited in line for frozen yogurt.

"Beautiful children." He looked away, as if something else in the food court had caught his attention. "I love kids, but we're not set up to handle them. Just the sisters. It's sort of a primal thing. Man protecting woman. It works."

The way his eyes sparked when he smiled made something flutter inside her. Okay, maybe she did have a little crush on him, and she was drawn in by the fantasy of nearly a dozen women living as sisters, working together to love and support one another. Glory knew that the reality wouldn't quite live up to her ideal of young women having an extended sleepover in a sorority house setting—something she'd missed out on by having a baby while her friends were attending college. Glory knew the sisters would have their issues and annoyances, but they would always have one another, someone else to share the burden of paying the bills, cleaning the house, and locking the door at night.

Someone to talk to. Sometimes that was all a person needed.

CHAPTER 7

After the football game, Tamarind assisted Pete in conducting an awards ceremony of sorts—a McCullum family tradition that everyone enjoyed. Taking a seat, she tried to ignore the slight pain in her belly. Probably too many baked beans. She should have stuck with the veggies and the burgers that Doc had been tending on the grill. Tamping down the discomfort, she looked up at her gorgeous husband and tried to focus on what he was saying.

"For the most botched receptions of the game," Pete said from his spot at the head of one of the picnic tables, "the Oven Mitt Award goes to my brother James." He extended a hand to Tamarind, and she handed him the hideous pair of quilted oven mitts made from brown fabric with autumn leaves in the design. "James, we know you're an OB, but we're all wondering how you manage to catch so many babies when you drop everything on the field."

Chuckles skittered through the crowd as Pete's older brother, James, came to the front and stood beside his younger brother to accept his award. Both men had soulful brown eyes and smiles that lit their faces, though Pete was leaner than his brother, probably from all that running he did.

"Now, for the most promising player, we have the Silver Cup Award." On cue, Tamarind handed Pete a paper cup that she had covered with aluminum foil. "This one's for the man who's got the most potential in real football, and I'm proud to say that goes to Young Bozie, who you all know is going to be playing for the Huskies next season."

A cheer went through the crowd as Bozie, a broad, solid young man with tree-trunk thighs, jogged up to Pete.

"To you, my cousin, the Silver Cup." Pete handed it over with a flourish. "Make sure you always wear one to protect the family jewels."

Without a hint of a smile, Bozie held the cup up and waited until the applause died down. "I want to say thanks to Cousin Pete and everyone else for organizing this. Good to see everyone come out. But I'm afraid I can't accept this award."

"What?" Pete feigned offense.

Shaking his head, Bozie frowned at the cup. "I don't know about you, brother, but this thing's way too small for *my* family jewels."

People burst into laughter and applause. Tamarind laughed but found herself bracing against the tug of pain in her abdomen. Kaysandra doubled over and her husband, Ed, slapped the table as he leaned back and roared with laughter.

As Pete and Bozie razzed each other and the afternoon heat seemed to swell around the group of people, a wave of light-headedness washed over Tamarind. The sick feeling reminded her of the fertility process, the days and weeks spent giving herself injections that caused nausea and cluster headaches. Funny how a wave of nausea could bring back the past so vividly. With one palm flattened on the picnic table, she used the flat surface as an anchor and coached herself to take calm breaths.

When the ceremony finally ended, Tamarind wanted Pete to walk with her to the restrooms, but he was surrounded by men who wanted to continue the jokes. She was not the kind of wife to break that up with a dramatic demand.

Maybe the walk will help, she thought, swinging her legs around the end of the picnic table. She arose slowly, holding on, maintaining equilibrium. Bracing herself against the dizziness, she started walking, following the mulch path dappled with sunlight. They'd gotten a beautiful day, with a broad blue sky, a cool breeze, and the blessed sunshine that made Portland summers magnificent.

A perfect day, until now.

Something was wrong.

By the time she reached the ladies' restroom she could barely breathe with the tightness in her chest and the rapid thud of her heartbeat. Tears filled her eyes when she saw the deep red blood staining her underpants and shorts.

Oh, please God, no.

She used the thin toilet paper to clean up as best she could, all the while going over what she'd read about pregnancy and miscarriage. Sometimes there was blood—spotting—and everything turned out fine.

That could be me. Maybe our baby is okay.

But right now nothing felt okay, as the cramping was getting worse.

Locked in the booth, she waited until a group of girls, probably around nine- or ten-year-olds, judging from their conversation about kickball and ice cream, left the restroom, and then she called the OB clinic and left a message for the doctor on call. Time dragged on as she sat there, trying not to cry. Stress wasn't good for her or the baby.

As she waited, she texted Pete, telling him she wasn't feeling well, sharing her symptoms. She added that it wasn't an emergency, as she knew that nothing could stop the worst-case scenario.

Dr. Bergen confirmed that when she finally called back. "There's nothing we can do to prevent a miscarriage," she said, "but you should come in this afternoon or tomorrow and we'll try to get a sense of what's going on. We can do an ultrasound and check the levels of pregnancy hormone to see if the fetus is still viable."

"Okay." Tamarind's voice was a croak, her throat thick with emotion. "Can I come in now? I need to know."

"The clinic is closed today, but I can make arrangements for the tests to be run at our urgent-care facility."

They set up the appointment, and Tamarind ended the call and stared at the screen saver on her cell phone—a photo of Pete and her kneeling beside a wooden bassinette that her grandfather had made so many years ago. It was a family tradition to place newborns in the cozy structure. The day she and Pete had taken that photo, they had been so happy. Thrilled. But life had a way of knocking you to the ground when you least expected it.

A sob slipped out, and she rested her face in one palm. Someone else was in the restroom, and she didn't want to alarm the owner of the scuffling feet. *Keep it in; hold it back. At least for now.*

"Is everything all right in there?" asked the other person.

"Fine," she said, trying not to show the strain.

"Why don't you come out? You sick in there?"

"Kind of."

The feet came closer, pausing in front of the door. "Is that you, Tamarind?"

Just her luck. There was nowhere to hide. "Yes."

"It's Kaysandra. Do you need help?"

"No. Thanks."

"Okay, then. I just can't ignore someone locked in a bathroom. In my line of work you see people trying to live in restrooms, bathing in the sinks and all that. Drug addicts shooting up and overdosing in coffee shop bathrooms before anyone knows they're in there. I've seen it all; some of it I wish I could unsee."

"I'm just sick. Cramps."

"It's that time. I get it."

No, you don't! Tamarind wanted to scream. *You don't have a clue about what's going on with me and Pete and our baby.* She tried to take a calming breath, but the air puffed in on a string of sobs.

"Girl, you don't sound right to me." Kaysandra moved behind the panel, trying to peer through the slit. "You need an ambulance?"

"No, I just—"

"Open up. Come on, now. Don't make me crawl under the door on this pee-stained, smelly floor. Open up, Sistah-girl."

The use of the affectionate term softened her resolve. Sniffing back tears, Tamarind pulled up her shorts and opened the door to face her sister-in-law, who looked up at her with sympathy warming her amber eyes. "Well, you don't look as bad as you sound."

"I'm afraid I'm having a miscarriage."

"Oh. Oh no, honey." The news registered in Kaysandra's eyes like a stone settling in a pond. She rubbed Tamarind's shoulder, her expression softening. "You going to see a doctor about that? Or you want Pete to get you home?"

"I called the doctor. I need to head over for tests, but I'm kind of nauseous and the cramps keep coming, and I don't want to walk around with this stain on my shorts."

"Okay, then. You still feeling punky? You want to wait here while I get Pete?"

Tamarind nodded.

"All right, then. I'll get my brother and be back in a flash. You stay put."

"Thanks."

Kaysandra waved her back into the booth. "You just sit and rest. And you know what? This could be a false alarm. That's what I'm praying for."

"Me too," Tamarind agreed as she watched her sister-in-law head out. She would keep the dark predictions to herself as she went through the tests at Urgent Care, but in her heart, she knew.

She had lost the baby.

CHAPTER 8

"*Winston, where are you?*" It was getting late and Glory wanted to put both the kids to bed, but not before they had a chance to see their father.

With her cell phone on speaker Glory let it pulse on and on, waiting for Winston to pick up as she walked the baby around. She stepped over Ruby, who had lined up stuffed animals against the couch and was systematically feeding them with a plastic spoon from the food court. Ruby could entertain herself for long periods of time now, but Aurora was at a stage where she couldn't self-soothe and she wanted to nurse all the time. Poor little sweetie. Walking her around was the only thing that calmed her when she couldn't feed, but Glory was exhausted from wearing a path through the carpet. Her shoulders ached and the baby's warm body seemed glued to her chest.

"I know a girl; her name is Rory. Hey, Rory, Rory, roar. She makes everything a story. Hey, Rory, Rory, roar," Glory chanted as she paced across the small room and tried to interest the baby in her Huggy Bear toy. "Of course, we'll never call you Rory, sweet pea. Not when your mom is named Glory. People will think we're weird." She laughed at herself. Of course, she and Winston were weird. They prided themselves on traveling a different path, listening to a different song, grabbing ahold of life by living. When she got pregnant and

Winston got injured, they'd both realized that their education wasn't going to come from college, but from the real world. "School of life, babe," Winston liked to say.

Sometimes it was a harsh school, spending your days and nights taking care of two little girls. Aurora's eyes were open wide, her gaze latched on to Glory's face. "I know, you find me mesmerizing. But where's your daddy?"

The baby gurgled and Glory caught a glimpse of the photos on the built-in shelves. "Here's a picture of your dad." She held up a framed photo of Winston, her favorite, where he was wearing a white hard hat and showing off his biceps with a fat snowcapped mountain on the horizon behind him. A chubby-cheeked scholar, Aurora studied the photo with the eyes of a skeptic. "And this is us." The photo of the two of them, arm in arm, was a selfie taken on the bricks of Pioneer Courthouse Square when Glory was pregnant with Ruby. "Must have been four or five years ago." Glory and Winston looked so hopeful and happy, she in her favorite black raincoat, he in his letter jacket from high school. All hormonal, she had given five dollars to a woman who claimed that she'd run out of diapers for her baby at home. "You're an easy target," Winston had claimed. "Gullible Glory." He was always on her about being easily swayed by people, but she couldn't help it if she had a big heart. Really.

"What do you think, little one? Is your daddy the best in the world?" Glory asked.

But Aurora had already turned away from the photo; the man pictured there struck no spark of recognition in her infant mind. She'd never even met Winston. Unlike Ruby, who'd spent the first two years of her life being carried around in her father's arms. Those two had bonded like peas in a pod. When Winston returned, he and Aurora would have a lot of catching up to do.

There was a click on the phone followed by his voice. Winston! "There's your daddy."

She hurried over to the table to prop up her cell phone and position its camera. As the screen opened to Winston's face,

Glory had to bite her lower lip to keep from crying. The streamed video made him seem so close, it was like a sick joke, dangling a picture of the bait without the tangible flavor. He was a beautiful man, with bold cheekbones, bronze skin, and amber eyes. She missed his calm, his humor, his sanity. And the safety and comfort of his arms.

"Hey, baby. You look tired. "Did I wake you up?" she asked.

"Nah." He rubbed his eyes. "I was in the saloon, talking with the owner. Just to give you a sense of how things are up here, people call him Bear. A weird dude, but he's renting me a decent room."

"Day drinking?"

"Maybe I had a few." He tilted his head, giving her that slow smile. "It's my day off, babe, and I waited until I got back to Livengood. But let me see my girls. Hey, Ms. Ruby!"

While Winston made a fuss over Ruby and the baby, Glory backed out of the image frame and dropped the happy face. This was the first she'd heard of Winston drinking alone up there. He had never been an alcoholic or anything like that, but he'd gone overboard a few times back in high school after big football wins and he'd drunk by himself after his knee injury, when he'd lost the chance to play college ball. But she'd pulled him out of that. He always said that she was his compass, helping him stay on course. How would he navigate temptation without her?

Would it help him to know how much she missed him? Probably not. It wouldn't help for her to go all Hallmark Channel on him while he really wanted ESPN. So far she hadn't confessed, but before he'd left for the job in Alaska she'd snagged one of his old T-shirts. The shirt had been washed dozens of times, its fibers worn soft and full of his scent. Glory kept it folded and tucked under her pillow, except at night when she curled up with it pressed to her face and neck.

Six more months . . . that's all they needed to build up their savings and get Winston some welding experience. She could hang on that long.

"Have you been counting things out for me?" Winston asked Ruby.

"Daddy, Daddy . . ." Ruby reached for the phone, and Glory had to caution her to leave it be or else they all wouldn't be able to see him.

"I'm feeding the babies," Ruby said.

"You are? Feeding Aurora?" he asked.

"Feeding the stuffed animals," Glory explained, "but she's been counting away. I got her signed up for preschool, but you won't believe the list of supplies they want her to have. It's crazy."

"You're going to school, Rublekins?" Winston said.

"No . . ." Ruby hesitated. "I'm gonna stay with Mommy."

"But you got to go to school to learn more things."

"No, Daddy. I'll take care of Rora."

Winston thought her resistance was adorable, which irked Glory. Who would have to coach their daughter through these fears and leave her crying in the classroom? Sometimes Winston didn't understand that his long-distance parenting was making the situation worse for Glory.

I'm tearing my hair out here, and you think it's all cute?

"Stop it!" she snapped at Ruby. "If you don't leave the phone alone, you are going to have a time-out in your room."

CHAPTER 9

Ruby used to like FaceTime with Daddy, but not anymore. She didn't want to talk to him on the screen anymore. She wanted him to be here.

"When are you coming home?"

"Soon."

"Tomorrow?"

"No."

"The next tomorrow?"

"No. You need to be patient."

Be patient. Be patient. Ruby was sick of that. Patient was boring.

She grabbed for the phone to get a better look and Mommy kept yelling at her to stop.

"Bye, Daddy!"

She ran into the big room and jumped onto the bed and burrowed under the covers. No one would find her here until Daddy got home. She was a fish swimming, swimming in a river. Then it was hard to take a breath, so she pushed the covers down and hugged Daddy's pillow.

She hunched on her belly, gripping the pillow, and she saw herself becoming a little turtle on a rock in the sun. But the turtle was so lonely without any other turtles in the pond. She imagined little turtles swimming toward her, baby turtles who were struggling in the water. "I'll save you!" she called to them. "Give me your flipper!" Holding tight to the rock, she reached into the water and pulled a baby turtle to her rock. She saved one, two, three, four little turtles! The turtles were so happy to be together that they made up a little song and huddled close together as they sang it.

Ruby felt so cozy with the other turtles gathered around her that she closed her eyes and sat listening to their cute turtle voices.

When Mommy came in and sat in the bed beside her, she opened her eyes and the turtles were gone. It made her want to cry, she missed them so much.

"You found your own bedtime." Mommy smoothed down Ruby's hair. "You must have been tired."

"I was playing, Mommy. I saved baby turtles."

"That's nice. Let's get your jammies on and get you to bed."

"I wanna stay here, Mommy. I'm tired."

"I'm tired, too." Mommy bowed her head. "Fine. But when you start school, you need to have a more regular bedtime, in your own bed."

Ruby crinkled her nose. None of that sounded good. "I don't want to go to school."

"Just for half a day. And I know you're going to love it. Look." Mommy picked up a book from the nightstand and opened it to the middle. "If you go to school and learn a little bit every day, you'll be able to read this to me."

"I can read it. It's about poor Pepito. He loves to dance, but everyone makes fun of him. Except that one man."

"You know the story, but after you go to school you'll know how to read it yourself. Soon you'll be able to read any book you want. You're going to love reading. You'll be getting the key to open a new door."

Ruby wanted a key. Aurora liked to play with Mommy's keys.

But you didn't need a key to open a book.

"What's the key for?"

"To open new doors."

"But what's behind the door?"

"A whole new world."

"Like the moon?" Ruby didn't want to go to the moon. Mommy said men went there on a rocket ship, but then they came home. There was too much night between her home and the moon, which was farther away than 'Laska. "I don't want to go to the moon," she said.

"That's good, silly, because you're stuck here with us." Mommy leaned close and kissed her cheek.

"And I don't want to go to school, Mommy. I'll stay home with you."

"But you like the school. It's got a playground with swings."

Ruby wasn't so sure about school. They passed the school building on their way to the park, and it had a loud bell that rang for no reason, and the girls and boys in the school yard thought she was invisible because no one ever noticed her walking by with Mommy and Aurora. And Mommy and Rora were going to leave Ruby there, and if she was invisible they would never find her again.

Ruby wasn't going to the moon and she wasn't going to school. She was going to stay right here and wait for Daddy. Even if she had to be patient.

CHAPTER 10

Juggling the roses and the takeout box, Pete turned the key and tried to push through the door without disturbing Tamarind or dropping the almond French toast that she always ordered for Sunday brunch at Tucci's. She hadn't eaten since early yesterday, and he was determined to get her on the road back to health with good food and TLC.

But it would be a slow process; he was beginning to see that. He dumped the box and keys on the kitchen counter and placed the bouquet of flowers beside the sink. Where did she keep the flower vase things? He wasn't big on that stuff. He'd gone to two markets to find her favorite color—bright coral roses, a flaming orange, the color of a sunset or a tandoori oven. Would she see them through the haze of grief and pain?

Last night she had been suffering both emotionally and physically. Pete had felt hollow and sick himself, but he didn't have to deal with the physical stuff, the cramps and dizziness and all those other plagues that women suffered. She'd had a rough night, and he'd lain awake, his hand on her shoulder, just being there, because there was nothing else to say or do at that juncture. Earlier in the doctor's office they had passed through limbo, the not knowing, to hell as the doctor on call had told them that they'd lost the baby.

"I'm sorry," the female physician had said, taking a moment

to sit with them and talk as a human being while Tamarind sobbed and he had rubbed her shoulder, holding back the rise of bitter sorrow in his gut. The doctor waited a full minute, surprisingly comfortable with giving Tamarind time to wail. "Was this your first pregnancy?" the doctor asked.

"Yes, and we've been trying awhile," he answered, aware that Tamarind was too overwhelmed to find the words. "We went through in vitro. Tamarind's been through a lot, but we wanted this baby. Do you know why it happened?"

"That's a question I can't answer. Based on what you've told me, it's nothing you did or didn't do, nothing you ate. Miscarriage is a natural event that usually can't be prevented."

Although the doctor's statement had been clear, Pete had replayed the afternoon in his mind, scouring the day for anything that might have set off the terrible end of the pregnancy. Maybe he shouldn't have left Tamarind alone while he played football. Maybe he shouldn't have dragged her to the picnic at all. Though she tried to make the best of McCullum events, he knew that she didn't feel a strong attachment to his family yet. Maybe he should have stayed out of hot tubs. Maybe when he was an idiot college freshman he shouldn't have bet his friends that he'd never have kids. Never was a dangerous notion; he knew that now. He could spend the rest of the week second-guessing his actions, but it wouldn't change what had happened.

The roses looked kind of bushy in the vase, too much green, but if he messed with it he'd only make it worse. Pete slipped his shoes off by the kitchen bar and quietly carried the flowers to the bedroom, peeking into the shadows. Facing away from him on the bed, she was a study in dark and light—black hair, white cotton T-shirt, and a white sheet drawn up to her waist, clamped down by one cinnamon-toned arm. Her beautiful form exuded pain, and he wished he could take it on for her.

He couldn't tell if she was awake. *"Dilnashi?"* He whispered the endearment she had taught him, the Hindi word that meant "one who lives in my heart." When there was no re-

sponse he circled the bed and saw that her face was a mask of
sleep, her black eyelashes emphasizing the ridge of cheekbones
shimmering with the dew of sweat. At least she'd found sleep
at last. He set the roses on the nightstand and slipped out of
the room quietly, closing the door behind him. Sleep mattered
most; the French toast could wait.

He brewed himself a single cup of coffee and stretched out on
the couch with his cell phone. Maybe a short nap, then he would
scramble some eggs and check on Tamarind again. There were a
few messages from their Realtor, who'd lined up condos and
small houses for them to look at today. That wasn't going to
happen. He dashed off a quick message declining, saying that
Tamarind wasn't feeling well. Maybe next week.

Or maybe not. If their family wasn't going to be expanding
in a few months, the mad search for a new place might be off.

He took a sip of coffee, mulling that one over. Tamarind
would have something to say about that. And much as he liked
the low overhead of this place, it had the feel of a collegiate
apartment, thin walled and temporary.

A new wave of sorrow was sinking in when there was a tap
on the door. Pete sat up, wondering who would tap and not
ring the bell. The short, dark-haired woman was still knocking, her face stern with a grimace, when he peered through the
peephole.

He opened the door to his mother-in-law. "Rima! I wasn't expecting you. Tamarind said you didn't need to come." Tamarind
had been emphatic that she was fine when she'd talked to her
mother this morning, but it was just like Rima to pick up on the
nuances of her tone.

"She always says that. She thinks she's independent, but I
know." Rima wheeled in a rolling suitcase, propped a fat tote
bag on top of it, and slipped off her shoes. Dressed in a teal
sari with a matching blue-green bindi on her forehead, Rima
Singh looked the role of a modern Indian woman. When Pete
had first met Tamarind's mother, he had asked Tamarind
about the meaning of the dot that seemed to be tattooed on

Rima's forehead. "Traditionally it's a sign of respect and blessing for the Hindu woman who wears it," Tamarind had explained. "But here in America, it's also a fashion statement for Indian women."

"Where is she?" Rima placed her gray pumps neatly in front of the hall closet.

"She's asleep now. She didn't get much sleep last night."

Rima picked up Pete's shoes from the kitchen floor and lined them up beside hers with a disapproving expression. Pete bit his lower lip, wanting to laugh in the awkwardness. In less than sixty seconds his mother-in-law had corrected him in his own home, but he wasn't going to get annoyed. He'd been around strong women all his life, negotiating childhood with a handful of sisters who had taught him that every man and woman had to stand his or her ground with strength and humility.

"Has she eaten? I brought some peppermint tea, very good for calming the stomach. And bananas."

"She does need to eat. I brought her French toast for when she wakes up." When Rima eyed the takeout box with suspicion, he added, "It's one of her favorite things."

"Then maybe it will help," she conceded.

Watching her unpack the grocery items from her tote—fruits and tea and a jar of chutney—he realized a nap would be out of the question now. Part of him wanted to flee his own home and leave his wife to her mother's care while he went off to lick his own wounds, but that was only because Rima had a way of taking over, reorganizing drawers, as she was doing now, and criticizing their lifestyle. In truth, he knew Tamarind wouldn't mind. But she was his wife, and the sad loss belonged to both of them. He would stay and own the situation.

"I was just about to make some breakfast for myself," he said, taking a pan from the hanging rack and placing it on the burner. "Would you like some eggs and toast?"

"No, but I'll make it for you." When he started to object, she pushed him away from the stove. "I'll do it. It's what I do."

"Why don't you relax?" Even as he said the words, he knew it was a ludicrous request for her. "You had a long drive down here. I can scramble my own eggs, Rima."

"Of course you are able; I know this. But when you go to work, do you expect someone else to do your job?"

"No."

"Of course not. So this is what I'm saying. This is what I do, taking care of my family. Please, allow me the satisfaction of doing my job, Pete."

"All right then." He surrendered the kitchen, moving over to a barstool. "This is great. I'm not very good at making scrambled eggs, anyway. Tamarind says I put too much heat on them."

"I'll make you poached. Less fat. Better for you."

"Poached is great." Pete smiled as she switched the skillet to a pot and started water heating.

Although his mother-in-law sometimes played to a stereotype, she was as complicated and textured as a rich tapestry. Rima had grown up in New Delhi, in a family with some privilege. Her fluency in Hindi and English had helped her land a secretarial job at the U.S. Embassy, where she had met Tamarind's father, the son of a New York City cabdriver. To hear Tamarind tell the story, you'd think it was a fairy tale with the noble diplomat Karim Singh lifting Rima from the squalor of New Delhi, Prince Charming to her Cinderella, but having picked up on the details, Pete knew it was more complicated than that. Life always was. Karim was not a prince, but a hardworking young man whose ambitions had driven him through grad school at NYU and then to a series of positions at the State Department. And Rima, the daughter of a prosperous exporter, was no maid sweeping cinders, though it must have been challenging to leave her family and her safe world behind and come to America.

"Later, I'll make roti," Rima said as she cracked two eggs into a bowl. "That will make her feel better. When we're sad, it's good to be surrounded by familiar things."

He nodded, wondering what familiar things could bring

him comfort. To slip on his old, torn Nike shoes and go for a run by the river? To slip into the sterile hallways of the office and settle into his cubicle in front of the monitor . . . the screen that held past, present, and future in its infinite codes?

"You are sad, too," Rima observed.

"I am, but in a different way, I guess. I can't imagine a future in which we repeat this pain. I can't imagine Tamarind going through all the things she's endured all over again, the headaches and cramps. The shots. The entire insane dance."

Rima turned away from the stove and positioned herself across the island from him. "She wants to give you a baby, a family."

"And I appreciate that, I do, but I love my wife, and I can't see why she should sacrifice so much for something that doesn't have to happen. We are a family, with or without a child. I love your daughter, Rima, and she's enough for me."

Her brown eyes welled with concern as she pressed her palms to the countertop. "You're a good man. I know this. But you need to understand what matters to a woman. My daughter, she's a mix of old and new, traditional and modern woman. She wants to be a proper wife to you, to give you a son or daughter as a woman should."

Pete knew it would be a waste of time to argue the vast changes in gender roles for millennials. There was no persuading this dear, devoted woman that he could be happy without children. He reached across the counter and placed his hand over hers. "Look at the toll this is taking on her, on both of us, but mostly her. The injections and mood swings, and now the pain. The physical pain and the emotional, too. Our hearts are broken over our baby."

"Yes, yes, yes." She patted his hand. "This I know."

"People think you just dismiss it and move on if the baby isn't born, but there's still grief. You feel the loss. One minute you have a baby on the way. The next, the little thing has died, and it's so tiny and undeveloped and hidden away that it may as well be in another universe. It's that far out of our control. We had a kid who died before it even made it into the world.

I'm not sure I have the hubris, the selfishness, to do that again and again just so I can have the family I want."

"I understand your sorrow." Rima shrugged. "But maybe this isn't all about you and what you want right now."

Although she turned away to tend to the eggs, her physical retreat barely diminished the zinger she'd just landed. *Oh, snap!* Like her daughter, Rima didn't pull her punches.

"This is about me and Tamarind, about what's best for both of us. I love your daughter, Rima, and we have a wonderful life together. We both like our work. We go to shows and concerts. We can jump in the car on Saturday morning and drive to the coast if we want. Life is good."

She turned back to him. "When you die, will you be thinking of walks on the beach and concerts? No, I don't think so. It's your children who will fill your heart in those last living moments. Your children. Your legacy."

"But what if—"

"No." She raised the slotted spoon, interrupting him. "No more talk now. You need to eat."

As if she'd dosed him with her magic wand, Pete shut up. Rima hummed a meandering tune in her birdlike vibrato voice as she propped each egg on a slice of buttered toast and served it up to him. Pete knew he was being mothered, although he wasn't the one who needed it.

Or maybe he was. In any case, he recognized there was no stopping Rima when she was on a path.

CHAPTER 11

"Another beer?" The bartender pointed at Winston, who nodded. What else was there to do on his day off in the middle of nowhere?

"So how long you been up here?" asked the guy sitting next to him at the bar.

"This is the seventh week," Winston said.

Seven weeks in hell, he thought as the guitar solo from "Hotel California" twanged on the jukebox.

"You like it?" The beefy guy wore black glasses, a lumberjack plaid shirt, and a quilted vest that was puffy as a marshmallow. A white guy, of course. Everyone in Alaska was white. But the lumberjack and the bartender hadn't seemed fazed when a black man came through the door.

"The work is good," Winston said. "But I'd rather be back home." He would have told the lumberjack that he missed his family, but he didn't want to sound like a candy-ass. You couldn't go round crying to strangers in saloons, showing them photos of your wife and kids, unless you wanted to be rolled in the parking lot. But that was the truth. He missed Glory and little Ruby. He felt like a dick that he'd never even seen Aurora in person.

What kind of a father was he?

A responsible father—that was what Glory always said when he brought up the problem. And then she'd go into the progression of how their life was supposed to go. After his ACL injury in college, he'd had to give up the dream of playing pro football. With his scholarship pulled, he'd dropped out of school and tried to get a job in construction. Welding or plumbing seemed to be the way to go, with plenty of jobs, though he needed training. Since he hadn't been able to get into the welding program at the community college, they had looked to Alaska, where he could be trained as a pipeliner and eventually get some welding experience on the job. And then he'd go back to Portland, start raking in decent money as a welder. Kaching.

Winston still liked Glory's plan, though there'd been some obstacles. Jobs on the pipeline weren't that plentiful, and some of the refineries had been shutting down. And now that he was here, the days dragged on, whether he was working or on a day off. The endless vistas of tundra and wild grasses depressed the hell out of him, and people told him that got worse once winter set in. He had that to look forward to.

He had driven thirty minutes to escape the mind-numbing boredom of the log cabin saloon with its mangy moose head hanging on the wall and the stale music from some Pandora station that seemed to favor Led Zeppelin. Thirty miles south of Livengood, he'd found a different saloon, this one a brick building with a couple of neon beer signs in the window. Same sour beer smell, same canned music, and a bartender just as detached as Bear.

Yeah, he was definitely breaking new ground here.

He stared up at the TV screen—a baseball game that seemed to be holding the lumberjack's interest.

"This time of year, someone somewhere is playing baseball," the lumberjack said. "Come November you get a lot of dark days between football games. My money's on Atlanta for this one. I lived there once."

"How was it?"

"Too much traffic. You follow baseball?"

"Not much. Portland doesn't have a team, and football's

my game. I like the Seahawks. I used to play football in high school."

"Really? Everybody's got a story."

In his pocket Winston's phone buzzed. Probably Glory, and he wasn't going to be the wuss husband who interrupted a conversation to text his wife from the bar. She would want to Skype, knowing it was his day off. But she didn't need to know he was spending the afternoon in a saloon. He would call her when he got back to Livengood.

"So what position did you play?"

"Running back, until I blew my knee out."

"And now you're stuck here. You like Portland?"

Winston shook his head. "Too much traffic. But I got my girls back there, so it's preferable to this place."

"Everything is preferable to this shithole." The lumberjack eased off his stool and headed to the men's room.

Winston took a sip of beer and pulled out his cell phone. Yep. Two calls from Glory and four text messages. He could go out to the parking lot and Skype her from the car. The sound of her voice would help take the edge off the uneasiness welling in his chest. But then she'd have a million questions, and she'd be pissed that he was out drinking, when it was his right. The only way to kick back when you lived thousands of miles from any sign of home.

I'll call you soon, he typed, then sent the message. *There. Can you leave me alone now?* he thought.

The saloon seemed to be darker as he glanced toward the parking lot. The door was like miles away. The flashing beer sign in the window caught his attention and held it, thrumming on and off, making the room teeter like a ship on the waves.

What the hell was the ABV on this beer? He didn't remember ordering anything too potent. He shoved the half-full mug onto the bar, sloshing the liquid onto the shiny wood.

Suddenly the bartender was there, his yellow eyes like sour onions in a meaty face. "Time to go, Kanye."

The jab stung, but it was nothing compared to the tight coil of nausea strangling Winston's body. They'd drugged him. *Bastards*. He flung a twenty at the bartender and held on to the bar to steady himself for the long walk to his car.

"You'd be smart to stay with your own kind."

"Right." Winston knew that. He'd lived his life avoiding situations like this. How had he been so stupid to think that a neon sign that said OPEN only applied to certain types of people? *Stupid*.

For a second the doors at the rear of the bar confused him, and he wondered if his room was back there. He could make it. Just a few steps.

But then the lumberjack emerged from the shadows of the back hall, his grim smile a reminder that Winston didn't belong here. He had to get out. Now.

Bracing himself against the darkness licking at the edges of his vision, he moved toward the door. The parking lot. His car. He had to get there. Swaying and listing like a damaged ship, he started the hardest journey of his life, out to his car.

CHAPTER 12

"Where is your daddy?" Glory said aloud as she paced across the living room juggling a fussy Aurora and an endlessly ringing cell phone. No one answered, of course, though Ruby would have said something about him coming home soon if she weren't in the bedroom, lining Goldfish crackers up on the nightstand. That girl came up with the oddest games sometimes.

After a text message yesterday, Winston's day off, he hadn't called or gotten in touch at all. That was Monday, today was Tuesday, and he was back to work, though she didn't know his hours. The worst scenario that came to mind was that something terrible had happened. Her second fear was that he'd gone on a bender. Winston could usually control his drinking, but sometimes, when things were bad, she'd seen him go off the deep end. Not that things were that bad, with his job and the regular money, but in recent conversations she'd picked up on his loneliness. Much as she tried to get across that they were "two lonesome stars stuck in distant parts of the sky," she wasn't sure she'd been reaching him lately.

When he dried up like this, Glory saw that her life was an empty shell without him. She tried to maintain a stable environment for her kids. She tried to engage in adult conversation, though she worried that she seemed needy. That morning she'd lingered at the classroom door, wanting to engage the teacher, Miss Mandy, who greeted them every day with a cheerful smile. Mandy Reynolds seemed to be in her twenties still, with streaked brown hair that curled to her chin in a precision haircut. She favored bright, flowered dresses and dusky pink lipstick that reminded Glory of the pale roses in her mother's garden. Standing beside her, Glory always felt a bit goth in her worn jeans and black T-shirts.

"How's Ruby doing?" Glory asked.

"She's adjusting well," the teacher said. "It's quite a change for all these children, but they're more flexible than they seem."

"I was worried about Ruby because she can play alone for hours. She makes up her own little worlds, with toys or crackers, and—"

"We'll have time to talk more at parent-teacher conferences." Miss Mandy's voice was cool, maybe even a bit stern. "We don't want to discuss the kiddos in front of them."

"Of course," Glory said as a boy let out a wail in the corner. Some dispute over a toy truck. While the teacher intervened, Glory's attention shifted to Ruby, who was lining blocks up at the edge of a bookshelf, talking to herself, probably counting. Was that normal? None of the other kids seemed to be doing it. She would ask Miss Mandy about it at the conference. Hitching the baby higher on her hip, Glory wished she were allowed to stay and chat with Miss Mandy, who seemed eternally cheerful and in control. That was the kind of friend Glory needed.

"We'll see you at pickup time, Mrs. Noland," the teacher said, obviously trying to get Glory out the door. Women like Miss Mandy didn't need to make new friends, and no one wanted to listen to a poor, lonely mom whose husband wouldn't even answer her text messages.

But she did have the sisters. Their company was limited to afternoons at the mall, but it was better than nothing.

Glory was about to dial Winston's number again when Aurora let out a wail, her pinched face turning bright red. "Oh, it's not that bad," Glory said, rocking her gently. They'd already been out in the stroller twice as they'd walked Ruby to preschool and back. How did you soothe a baby who'd napped and eaten and was being walked around like a princess?

"Why are you a cranky pants, Rory?" Ruby asked, appearing at the bedroom door with the paper sack of crackers.

Glory laughed. "She *is* being a cranky pants. You're a good big sister to understand that."

"Do you need Huggy Bear?" Ruby picked up Aurora's favorite comfort toy and jiggled it in front of her. "Huggy, huggy, huggy!"

The baby let out a crisp cry, perplexing Ruby.

"Let's get Rory some fresh air. Leave the crackers here, and let's find your jacket." Grabbing some hoodies for the girls, she corralled them outside, maneuvered the stroller down the front porch steps, and set the baby inside. The pale sunshine of the late afternoon held some lingering warmth, though the breeze was a reminder that autumn was on its way.

"Hi, Miss Ellen!" Ruby called to the landlady, who stood talking with a young woman at the front gate. The stranger seemed semi-professional, wearing khaki pants and a dark blazer and holding a notebook. Probably some city planner or pollster or solicitor whom Ellen had snagged. As the self-appointed neighborhood watch, Ellen Carlucci seemed to enjoy shooing away people who did not live on the block.

"There they are." Ellen held her arm out in an awkward wave.

Glory nodded before ducking under the stroller awning to buckle in Aurora, who had gone silent and wide-eyed with the first blast of cool air. "That's better, isn't it?" Glory soothed, grateful that she wouldn't have to push a crying baby past the landlady. Ellen claimed to love children, but she seemed to enjoy complaining about Aurora's crying time in the afternoons.

"Glory?" Ellen called.

Glory stood up, glancing toward the gate.

"Come join us a second."

Thank God we've paid most of the rent, Glory thought as she shrugged on her own jacket. It had been awkward trying to avoid their landlady when they'd been so far behind, but now Glory could come and go with her head held high. With next week's paycheck, they would have enough to pay the remainder of their October rent.

With Ruby standing in the rear of the stroller, Glory pushed toward the gate. "Looks like a beautiful afternoon," she said, returning the smile of the woman with the clipboard. A forced smile on both sides.

"Glory Noland. That's her legal name, not a nickname for 'Gloria,'" Ellen said, always a stickler for detail. "And the children are Ruby and Aurora."

Glory nodded. "We're just heading out for some fresh air."

"Not so fast," Ellen said dramatically.

"I'm Juana Lopez, from Portland Child Services." The woman extended a hand, making Glory scramble to switch Huggy Bear to her left hand so she could shake. "I'm wondering if you have a few minutes to chat?"

This woman was a social worker? Trying to process the situation faster, Glory pressed Huggy Bear to her chest, then tucked it in beside Aurora. "What do you want to talk about?"

"I called DHS to investigate the fire. I was worried about you burning the house down," Ellen said peevishly. "Of course, that was weeks ago. It took them that long to get someone out here. It's a wonder we're not all burned to a crisp by now."

"Ms. Carlucci, we're overworked and underfunded. It takes a while to process nonemergency complaints."

"What are you talking about?" Glory asked indignantly. "I would never set the house on fire."

"But you almost did with that stove fire." Ellen frowned at the social worker. "Smoke was everywhere—the toxic kind, I think. The smoke detectors went off, thank God, but this one almost slept through it. Might be postpartum depression, or worse. All I know is, I worry about the safety of my house and these little girls."

Glory's fingers tightened on the bar of the stroller as she pulled it back toward her. Ruby stared up at her, blue eyes lit with fear. "We're all fine here," Glory insisted. "It was an accident, a pot left on the stove when I dozed off."

"I think she would have slept through the smoke alarms if I didn't come downstairs and wake her up," Ellen insisted in a sour tone. "We'd all be dead."

"Let's not exaggerate." Glory appealed to the social worker. "Ms. Lopez, she's blowing this out of proportion."

"Please, call me Juana."

"We're all fine, Juana," Glory continued, "and this was a onetime accident."

"Still, I need to file an incident report, and I'd like to discuss this more in private. How about if we step inside your apartment and talk about this off the street?"

Glory looked back toward the house, wanting to clear this all up. She was happy to talk with the woman, but what would Juana Lopez think of their home, with cereal and crackers spilled here and there, stains on the carpets and sofa—the perpetual mess of being alone all day with babies? Sometimes it was a marvel that Glory found time to shower, let alone clean the apartment. But she doubted that any social worker would understand that.

"We've got to get going. We have an appointment." Glory hoped they weren't able to see through the lie.

"It will only take a few minutes," Juana insisted.

"Sorry. Gotta go."

"Some other time, then." Juana handed Glory a business card and peeled a sheet of paper from her clipboard. "Here's a copy of the complaint. My name and contact info are on both of these. You need to call me and make an appointment for a formal interview."

Glory swallowed, her dry throat starting to feel sore. The social worker made it sound like she was in trouble, which was the last thing she needed. At the back of her mind she thought of stories she'd heard about children being removed from homes that were deemed unsafe. "Okay, then. We have to go."

As she wheeled her girls away, she was conscious of the two women watching her, judging her, thinking that they could do better.

I have a husband! she wanted to shout at them. *A man who loves me. A man who would help take care of his children.*

If only he were here.

CHAPTER 13

Determined to escape the social worker, Glory made her way to the mall under a sky that was rapidly turning from clear blue to pewter. By the time she reached the outer ring of the parking lot, raindrops skittered over the pavement, pelting her head and shoulders. She pushed the stroller in through the mall doors just in time to avoid a soaking.

Today she longed to tell her friends about the social worker, the accusation of her landlady, and the crazy fear that these women might try to take her girls away. Glory was dying to get the words out, but these women at the mall wouldn't understand. They weren't mothers and none seemed to have an aggressive bone in her body to strategize a counter-strike. What was that expression they loved to say? "Leave the bad; focus on the good."

Sometimes their talk reminded her of the girls' lunch table at high school, where the smallest stories burst into huge moments of delight. Today Annabelle was the storyteller. Glory was lost in the weary trance of breastfeeding when Leo joined the group, taking the empty seat directly across from her. Annabelle was telling them how she spit her pickled beets into a napkin and tucked it into a crevice under the table to make her foster parents think she'd eaten her vegetables. Eyes closed, Glory imagined the little trick and smiled. She opened her eyes to see Leo sitting tall, his broad shoulders braced against the back of the seat. Although he said nothing, he commanded the table, the kind caretaker of the women gathered there. In that moment, Glory wished he were her protector, too.

She turned her head away, not wanting him to see the longing in her eyes as she tried to conjure an image of her husband, the lines of his body, the curve of muscle and bone. His flat, smooth stomach, the ridges of his abs. It was all there in her head—Winston in totality—but the memory grew fainter with each day that he was away.

When she lifted her chin she discovered Leo staring at her, though he wasn't making eye contact. Maybe she should have been offended, but instead her blood heated as she felt his gaze on her bare breast. A tug of sweet sensation rippled deep down inside her, a visceral desire. She wanted him, and she wanted to think that he wanted her, too, just for this crazy moment.

Of course, it was not meant to be.

Glory stroked back Aurora's curly hair as people chuckled over how Annabelle had tricked her foster parents.

"Were they horrible people, your foster parents?" asked Laura.

"Not really. But I thought they were so bossy after living with my mom, who had no rules. Really, the worst parent of them all was my mother, with her bouts of paranoia and violence. She's addicted to crack, but I didn't understand that until I was a teenager."

"So foster care saved your life," Natalie said. "We have to be grateful for the kindness of good people like that."

"I see that now," Annabelle admitted. "But all those years, I would have gone back to my mother in a heartbeat. I think I would have been better off if she'd just given me up for adoption, but she refused to let go. So I went from one home to another, waiting for the day that Mom would come rescue me. A day that never happened."

"And there's the lesson." Natalie sat back in her wheelchair as if it were a throne. "When a parent gives up their child, they need to let go completely. Not that any of us will ever need that bit of advice," she said, looking around the group. "Oh, maybe you, Glory."

"Not me," Glory said defensively. It was as if they knew about the accusations of the social worker in Glory's front yard.

An image of Juana Lopez, her silver hair and stoic eyes, loomed in Glory's mind as a giant of a woman blocking the walkway to their little apartment. Maybe the woman wasn't that evil, but Glory didn't trust her. She couldn't take a chance of getting tangled up with the department of child welfare or anyone who might try to take her girls from her. Eventually, Ms. Lopez would give up and just close out the report.

Go away, Glory thought. *Leave us alone.*

CHAPTER 14

"Maybe we should buy a little house here and leave the pressure cooker behind," Pete said, imagining beach walks like this every day with the glimmering blue Pacific a backdrop to his beautiful wife. This afternoon she'd forgotten her baseball cap and the waterfront breeze lifted her dark hair behind her. Between the wind effect and her classic black sunglasses, Tamarind looked like a model at a shoot in the islands.

"Run away to Neverland?" Tamarind cocked one eyebrow. "Will we live on love and fairy dust?"

"Fairy dust might get a little dry. But I could telecommute, and you could find something out here." He turned and started walking backwards so that he could face her. "Actually, with my promotion, you wouldn't need to find work right away. You could take that ceramics class you've always wanted to try."

"I doubt there's much work for paralegals out here. And the coast is no place to raise a kid, *dilnashi*. Half of the year it's gray and rainy here. It just about shuts down in the winter, and when the big quake comes, everything from here to I-Five is supposed to be decimated."

"That's harsh."

She shrugged. "I'm becoming more of a realist."

"And what about the other harsh reality?" He hadn't wanted to bring this up on their weekend at the beach, tucked into the cozy inn at Manzanita with a hillside suite overlooking a beach dotted with evergreens. But they'd made progress here. Each time the orange sun slid into the silvery blue line of the ocean was a measure of recovery from the pain, a day closer to getting back to normal. They were ready to discuss the elephant in the room. "The doctor was pretty straightforward." They were not going to have kids, at least by the usual methods, and even if they tried in vitro again, it was unlikely that Tamarind would carry to full term.

"I feel so inadequate."

He pulled her hand to his lips and kissed it. "You are more than adequate in my book."

"Just this once could we not joke about it?"

The steely look in her dark eyes took him by surprise. "Yeah. Of course."

"Seriously, my body has failed the one thing it's supposed to do to propagate the species." She sidestepped around a mound of seaweed. "You know, when I think back to all those years of birth control pills. All that awkward fumbling for a condom, so freaked out about getting pregnant. What a waste of time and effort. A big cosmic joke."

"Yeah, but we had some fun trying. At least until the IVF. I'm glad that part's over. From now on, no more pain. No more shots and hormones."

"I'm still getting over the disappointment. I'm still angry with myself, but I'll get over it. What matters is that we will have a family, not how we get it."

"We could be a family of two." That morning when they were in bed, his lips pressed to Tamarind's neck and his palm on the taut skin of her abdomen, he'd wondered if they were teasing fate. "Maybe it's enough that we have each other," he said. "It seems that's meant to be."

"We are meant to be, *dilnashi,* but we're destined to have children. I saw it in my tea leaves."

"You read your tea leaves?" It was a thing for Tamarind and her mother, sitting together and chatting as they tried to see the future by looking at the dregs in a teacup. Intriguing, yes. Interesting, definitely. Reliable, no way. But the idea of decoding brown shit in a cup seemed hinky to him. Besides that, the methodology was flawed. A dagger meant a warning against using sharp words and a door meant opportunities were coming, but to his eye a rectangular dagger could look a hell of a lot like a door. Pete preferred the guarantees of hard science. One plus two was always going to equal three, whether you saw a dagger or a door in your cup. And if he was looking for help to navigate his life, he wasn't going to rely on some soggy tea leaves. "So when did you do this reading?" he asked.

"This morning, while you were taking a shower. You saw the teapot they brought to the room. I saw a fish, which means good news, and a crescent. That can mean rebirth or something feminine. Maybe we'll have a daughter. Or maybe it's about the rebirth of motherhood for me. I've been feeling so wounded. You know that."

"I know." He swallowed back his skepticism. Tamarind knew he wasn't into the tea leaves, but it was one of those things about which they had agreed to disagree.

"But the best part was, in the bottom of the cup, the more distant future, there was a basket. For me, that means only one thing: a new baby."

Staring ahead at the whitecaps breaking in layers parallel to the shoreline, Pete worried that she'd lost her mind. He trod carefully. "Are we talking about adoption now?"

"I know, I said I'd never do it. But I've been humbled by life. If I can't bear children, we'll find a child who needs us."

"So you changed your mind? Really?" It threw him off, especially since Tamarind was not one to back off her convictions. Adoption. Her sudden change of heart gave him pause; it seemed kind of forced. "We don't have to rush into anything."

"You could hardly call it a rush. We're already in our late thirties. If we don't get started soon we are going to be geriatric parents. You'll be tossing our son a ball from your wheelchair."

"Easy now. I'm only two months older than you."

She pressed up to his side, walking in tandem as she slid her arms around his waist. "And you wear your age well, old man."

He lifted her and swung her around, a maneuver that used to make her laugh. Nothing much had amused her since the miscarriage, though he now detected a spark of hope in her eyes.

So it was going to be adoption. He lowered Tamarind's feet to the ground, then stared off at Neahkahnie Mountain. All along Pete had pushed for adoption to save his wife the discomfort of IVF. Now that she had come around, a new set of worries occurred to him at the prospect of an adoption really happening. What if he didn't bond with the kid? Although he usually liked messing around with his nieces and nephews, he didn't have to take those kids home and shower them with love. What if he wasn't able to be a good father to this kid? It was his own fault, and now his big idea was threatening to bite him in the ass.

"You're scared," she said.

"Just trying to change gears. You were so dead-set against it; I thought it was off the table."

"I have a new angle on adoption. I've been thinking about it a lot, and there are kids out there who don't have families. Kids who need love. Adoption's not for everyone. Actually, parenting isn't for everyone. Many adults don't possess our mad communication skills and amazing talents."

"And modesty."

"My point being that it takes a special couple to parent children. And you and I, my husband, we are it." She tipped her chin up to him, one dark brow cocked in a smile.

"Look at you, all confident and proud."

"You love that about me." It was true. Her iron resolve and faith in people kept him in the game, grounded and hopeful. Before he'd met her, Pete had been quick to make people laugh, but his humor had been based on a stoic sense that anything that could go wrong would go wrong. She had changed that.

"I love everything about you," he said, breathing in her

dark, soulful eyes, her glossy black hair, her rich cinnamon-colored skin. "And I'm glad you've got enough confidence for the two of us."

"Don't worry. There's plenty of that."

"Have you talked to my sister?"

"About that . . . You know I love Kaysandra. I do. But she's always ramming her agenda onto the table. Always pushing her business around."

"She means well, baby, and this time, I think she can help us."

"There's no doubting her passion and connections. But I worry about our privacy. If we go through Kaysandra, our personal and financial business is going to be out there in your family."

"She would never expose us. Kaysandra's got a big mouth, but she'll take care of us. She'll be professional about it."

"All right, then. We'll keep it in the family."

CHAPTER 15

Tuesday, Wednesday, Thursday . . . three days without word from Winston.

The knot of worry grew inside Glory's chest like a ball of yarn growing larger as doubts and suspicions were twined around the core of fear. Had Winston been binge drinking? Had he had an accident working on the pipeline—a fall or a piece of heavy equipment knocking him out? Or maybe it was something worse. Maybe he'd met someone. She knew he'd been struggling with loneliness and isolation. Maybe the dark, cold nights alone in that wilderness had become too much for him to bear.

On Friday morning while Ruby was at school, Glory tracked down the phone numbers for the two main hospitals in Fairbanks, Alaska, and called their emergency rooms. It took a while to get to the right person, but she was finally able to confirm that Winston had not been brought into either hospital's ER.

She was grateful and pissed that he would put her through this silence. And it wasn't even the first time. Did he think she was just chillin' down here, taking care of the kids 24/7 and dodging the landlady?

Miss Mandy seemed especially warm when Glory arrived for the Friday pickup. "I want you to see Ruby's art project— a jack-o'-lantern face. I thought she did an especially good job." She pointed to a goofy-faced pumpkin pinned to the bulletin board amid a sea of orange construction paper. "See how the facial features are in the right proportion? That shows a level of development that's more advanced than most of my students."

"That's great." Glory had to rein in her reaction for fear that she might burst into tears of relief. At least something was going right in her life.

"Keep up the good work, Mom, and have a nice weekend," the teacher said as Glory and her girls headed out the door.

Just as Glory rolled the stroller down the ramp beside the steps, black dots of rain began to appear on the pavement. "Put your hood up, Ruby," she said, pausing to arrange the waterproof blanket over Aurora's legs. The rain was a steady patter on Glory's hood for the next block. And then her phone buzzed.

Annoyed, she paused under the cover of some trees that still had their leaves and checked it. A number from Yukon, Alaska.

Winston. He probably broke his phone again and was using a friend's line to call her. Quickly, she tapped the talk button and pressed the phone under her hood as she tried to keep walking. "Hello?"

"My name is Kip Wyman and I'm with the Alaska State Troopers. I'm calling for Glory Noland. Is that you?"

"Yes." Dread rushed through her, heavy, sullen, and icy cold. Was Winston in trouble with the law?

"And you're related to Winston Noland?"

"He's my husband." A frightening pause as wind rattled the branches overhead, sending leaves and water cascading down on them. "Is he okay?"

"I'm sorry, Mrs. Noland, but your husband is dead."

She didn't believe him. He couldn't have said that. She wheeled the stroller around and hurried back to the cover of the school awning. "What did you say?"

"Your husband was found deceased in his vehicle this morning."

Deceased. A chill came over her as she turned the word in

her mind, feeling as if everything was happening from a distance, at the end of a cold, vacant tunnel. Her legs kept moving, the rain kept falling, but something inside her froze. Plunging under the cover at the school entrance, she parked the stroller against the brick wall and turned away. "What . . . what happened to him?"

"His car went off the highway, down into the ravine. It's an isolated stretch of road without guardrails. From what we can see, he'd been there awhile. Maybe a few days."

"Days?" So he'd been gone—dead—all this time that she had been getting aggravated with him for not returning her calls? "All that time and no one stopped to help him?"

"We don't get much traffic up that way, especially this time of year when the tourists and snowbirds have headed south. And you couldn't see his car from the highway. I figure it took a few days for someone to drive by slow enough to notice the tracks going off the road."

As her hands gripped the brick wall, digging into the jagged edges, she imagined Winston suffering alone . . . in pain. No. It couldn't be true.

"How do I know you're who you say you are?" she asked in a shaky voice. "This could be some terrible joke."

"I wish it weren't true," he said in a quieter voice. "As I told you, I'm Kip Wyman, from the Yukon Division of the State Troopers. Listen, I can give you a number to call back after you've processed this. That way you can confirm who I am, too."

"I have your number in my phone," she said coldly. "I'll call you back."

"Mommy, I'm cold," Ruby complained. "The wind is making me wet."

Glory waved her off, staring into a dark tunnel of death matters such as funeral arrangements, legal notifications, and spreading the word to family and friends. She'd never done this before, tucking away all the loose pieces at the end of someone's life. Never before, and she didn't want to do it now.

"All right then, Glory. You take care, now." Officer Wyman sounded sad. "Call me back soon with your questions, 'cause I know you'll have a bunch and I'm here to answer them for you. I'll help you through the details with his body and personal effects and such."

Personal effects. Hearing that phrase made it real. Winston was gone. A tiny whimper escaped her throat, but she forced herself to take a deep breath and stay focused. "Okay. I'll call you back," she said. She cut the connection and stared at the old brick building, the walking path she had ventured down countless times with the stroller, the play structure Ruby liked to climb. Everything looked the same as ever, but that was an illusion. Everything had changed.

This was her ground zero.

Moving like a zombie, Glory got the kids home, hung the wet items over the tub, and cut up an apple for Ruby to snack on. Sometimes to celebrate Fridays they got an early dinner at the pancake house, but not tonight.

Glory couldn't see that she'd ever have an appetite again.

In a trance, she nursed Aurora and stared at the cartoon characters on the PBS show she'd put on to keep Ruby occupied. Any way to delay calling Kip Wyman back. She closed her eyes and tried to make it all go away, but there was no escaping the cold, hard knot of dread inside her, a frozen stone that would never thaw. This would not go away.

Finally, she called the number and a woman answered, confirming it was a branch of the state troopers. Wyman came on the line quickly, his voice warm as an old friend. "How are you doing, Glory?"

"Not well. I feel numb."

"That's a normal reaction in situations like this. I'll help you out on this end as much as I can. Right now, you should get a pen and paper and take notes, because you've got too much on your mind to remember all this."

Glory started writing on the backs of envelopes for junk mail. First there was the matter of Winston's body, which she couldn't afford or handle. She told him she would contact Win's father for those decisions. Or maybe his aunt Rosalee would want to travel up to Alaska to retrieve her nephew's body. A trip like that would be impossible for Glory and her girls.

"The vehicle was totaled," Wyman said. "Did you have comprehensive coverage?"

"Just basic liability," she said. The car hadn't been worth that much, but now Glory was left with no transportation.

Wyman would help her donate the wrecked car for scrap and would send her papers so that she could get a refund on registration from the DMV.

"I guess I should have asked you in the beginning if your husband had a will. Do you know if he had one?"

"He didn't. We knew we'd need something when the kids were born, but we thought there was time. He was young, not even twenty-four yet."

"We all feel like there's time." The trooper had been in touch with Winston's employer, who would send Glory his final check. Did she want Winston's belongings shipped to her via UPS? Only his wedding ring. His other possessions—his shoes and shirts, the warm parka they'd picked out before he'd headed north—she couldn't bear to see the remains of who he'd been. She would keep his wedding ring and the T-shirt he'd left behind. That was all.

"I'll have the coroner send you the death certificate," Wyman said. "You'll need a few copies for legal purposes. If I were you I'd make some copies and hold on to at least one original, as they're difficult to replace."

She thanked him, though the idea of keeping the documents in her and Winston's home chilled her to the marrow. Before he ended the call, Officer Wyman reminded her that she needed to let Winston's family know.

Call the people she didn't know. She promised to do it. Wyman would call back in a few hours to check on her and retrieve contact information for Winston's father.

Between scraping together macaroni and cheese, feeding Aurora, and walking through her crankiness, Glory tried to hear his voice, imagine him here in the apartment, carrying

Ruby around or sitting at the head of the table. How could she be drawing a blank?

The contacts on her phone listed his aunt's information: Rosalee Noland. It seemed like a friendly name, but Rosalee had never approved of Glory enough to spare a smile. Bracing herself, she called the number and listened as it rang on and went to voice mail.

It seemed like a crummy thing to leave a message, but what if Rosalee was screening the call? What if she never answered? Glory would be doomed to call her every day from here to forever.

When the voice mail beeped, Glory left a message. "This is Glory, and I'm sorry to leave this in a message, but I have to tell you that Winston is gone. He was killed in a car crash near his job in Alaska." She included Officer Wyman's phone number, suggesting that Rosalee call him for the details. That would take Glory out of the mix and save her from the harsh words Rosalee was likely to have for her. There'd be blame, for sure. All those "if our boy hadn't married you, he'd be alive" scenarios, which Glory just couldn't take right now. After she hung up, Glory felt a stab of regret. It was so cold to leave a message like that on voice mail, but what the hell? She'd never done this before, and she was drowning here.

She wasn't surprised that his father didn't answer. A long-haul trucker, he was probably on the road, driving north through California or east through Wyoming. She left a similar message, though maybe her voice was a little softer this time. The one time Winston had brought Glory up to Springfield to meet his father, Tom Noland had been personable, with smiling eyes and a chuckle that chugged along. He'd bought them lunch at a local diner and asked Glory questions about her family. Afterward she told Winston that he seemed like a nice man. "Yeah," he agreed, "but he was never around. I'm not going to be that kind of father."

But now you are that kind of father, and it's not your fault. No one to blame but life and death.

If there was some other thing she was supposed to do, it would have to wait until morning. Leaving the television on, she plodded into her bedroom and found that Winston's side of the bed had a tiny lump under the covers. Ruby slept there, tidy rows of Cheerios on the nightstand beside her.

You have to tell her in the morning.

Oh, God. Maybe morning will never come.

She slid under the covers beside her daughter and fell into a dark, restless sleep.

CHAPTER 16

I'm dying.

Glory had always believed that a person could die of a broken heart, and now she knew it to be true.

In the days after she received the news about Winston, Glory felt her life break apart in pieces, like a tree that was being systematically taken down, one limb at a time. She was physically ill, unable to eat or sleep, tenderly sipping water to soothe a scalding sore throat. She was worn down by the infernal noise in her ears, the chorus of things unsaid, the memory of interactions that would no longer be repeated. The simplest actions like making tea or climbing into bed seemed like a betrayal of Winston because he would never enjoy them again.

The sickness came in waves, roaring in her ears, dulling her brain. The flu? She would have thought so if her heart didn't physically ache in her chest. Twice she passed out on the way to the bathroom and ended up crawling. If the illness swallowed her up, she would go in peace, except for her girls. She needed a plan for her girls, who weren't being fed or bathed properly. Her milk seemed to have dried up, and she'd had to coax Aurora into taking a bottle with chalky formula, while Ruby seemed to be surviving on cold pasta and applesauce. She needed help.

In desperation, Glory called her mother. She pulled a blanket over her shoulders, slipped on her clogs, and stepped out into the gray drizzle to tell Katherine about Winston. The girls were in the apartment, and she hadn't told Ruby yet, didn't have the strength to deal with that.

Katherine couldn't resist gloating. "I told you it wouldn't work out. What did he do? A street fight? A drug overdose?"

"No, Mom." She sank onto the porch, sitting on the top step where it was dry. "It was a car accident."

"DUI?"

Glory didn't know about that, but she insisted that it wasn't his fault. "He was working hard and supporting his family. Why can't you respect him for that?"

"Well, he didn't succeed!" Katherine snapped. "And now I guess you want money."

"That would help, so I can get a sitter, and get to a doctor. And pay some rent."

"Oh, my baby girl, you have got to grow up. I've already given you half of my savings, and that wasn't enough?"

"We needed a car."

"Lot of good that did you. Listen, Ray doesn't know I sent you money, and I'm afraid of what might happen if he finds out. He'd be gone with the wind. I can't send any more. I don't have it, anyway."

Glory believed that. Her mother had retired from her job as a school lunch lady with a meager pension. "What about the girls? Can you take them for a while, just till I get back on my feet?"

"You can't be asking that. We live in a one-bedroom trailer, and I've never even met your kids. You can't pass them off on strangers, Glory."

"You're their grandmother."

"In name only. You made your choice when you decided to disrespect my opinions years ago. The damage is done. You can't expect me to fix your life now that things with your husband have soured."

"He died, Mom. Why can't you understand that he didn't do anything wrong? He was killed, and now my heart is broken and I'm sick and I need your help."

"I feel for you. I really do, Glory. But I got problems of my own. You need to grow some gumption, girl. Pick yourself up and move on."

Move on . . . as if she had anywhere to go. With a groan, she arose from the cold porch as her mother rambled on about things that didn't matter. "I gotta go feed the girls."

"Okay, Glory. You take care now. Let me know how things work out." As if she cared. Katherine just didn't want Glory to hate her.

Inside the apartment felt stuffy and warm, the heat pumping. Pushing open one of the windows in the front, Glory collapsed on the fat chair near the screen and sucked in fresh air. What would happen to her girls if she died in this little apartment? Maybe she should write down a will, asking Miss Mandy to take both her girls. She'd read somewhere that if you write something down, even on the back of a napkin, the courts have to honor it.

It was hard to imagine Miss Mandy, in her pretty flowered dress and pink lipstick, trying to keep her two girls happy. She'd have formula on her dress, and no time for those gold highlights at the hair salon. Or maybe Miss Mandy would train them well, like pets. The girls would sit at their little desks all day and go to their little beds each night right on time. Tears stung Glory's eyes as she realized Miss Mandy might be a better mother than she could ever be.

Resting her chin on the worn brocade of the chair, she noticed someone coming in through the gate out front. A woman in a black raincoat with the hood up. A flowered skirt beneath the hem of the jacket. For a moment she thought Miss Mandy had come, but that was wrong.

It was the social worker, Juana Lopez, coming to the door.

Her heart thudded in her chest as Glory ducked down. Had Ms. Lopez seen her? She scrambled down to the floor, pressing her face to her palms.

Please, don't take my girls away.

Had she heard about Winston? Maybe she knew that Glory hadn't gotten Ruby to school all week. And Glory had never called her back about that fire report.

Ms. Lopez thought Glory was an unfit mother.

Glory crawled under the window and rose to shut the curtains just as the doorbell rang. It was her!

"Mommy," Ruby called from the bedroom, "there's someone at the door!"

"Shh!" Glory hissed, standing frozen behind the door.

Now there were footsteps on the stairs, and Ellen's voice in the vestibule, calling.

Glory backed against the wall, hugging herself as Ellen spoke with Ms. Lopez.

"I know she's home. I heard her talking down here."

"Glory?" Soft knocking on the inner door. "It's Juana Lopez, from Portland Child Services. Do you have a few minutes to talk?"

Aurora was fussing in her playpen, awakened by the noise. Glory crossed the room to retrieve the baby and duck into the bedroom, where Ruby had arranged a family of rubber duckies in a circle on the bed. She spoke to them quietly as she gave each one a moment in the center next to the mommy duck. "Don't worry. You'll get a turn. You will, too. Soon."

Thank God Ruby didn't feel her mother's panic. The doorbell rang again, twice.

"Someone's at the door, Mommy," Ruby said without looking up.

"I know, I know." Glory pushed Rory's hair from her face and clipped it back with a baby barrette. At least she was quiet now. "We're just going to sit here quietly until they're gone." She changed the baby's diaper and put her into a onesie that wasn't as dirty as others. They were running low on diapers and needed a trip to the laundromat, but Glory couldn't imagine that happening. She had been ready to bag the dirty clothes and put them into her mom's car for a trip down to Roseville, but Mom wasn't going to drive up to rescue her and the girls. Now there was no hope in sight.

The mail slot opened and a business card dropped to the rug. Glory left Aurora on the bed with her sister and crept out to the living room, where she could hear Ms. Lopez and Ellen talking in the vestibule.

"At this point, I just need them out," Ellen was saying. "They're behind on the rent, and I can't afford to take the hit. I'm a single woman with a fixed income."

The social worker's low voice was harder to understand, but Glory heard her promise to "find them a place."

She *was* trying to take the girls away.

Weak and trembling, Glory went to the kitchen, poured herself a glass of water, and forced herself to drink. She had to get better, get hydrated, get some food in her. If she didn't pull herself together, she would lose her girls.

The answer had come to her by accident. It was Ruby who'd asked if they could go to the mall to get a quesadilla. The inclination to say no was strong. Glory had been saying no to most of her requests, including going back to school. The daily trip to school and back held too much of a risk of Child Services swooping in and grabbing the kids.

Maybe it was crazy to hope they would change the rules, but Glory had to give it a try. She took the extra time to wash her hair and put on the black dress she saved for special occasions. She put the girls in outfits purchased for Aurora's baptism, an event that had been postponed until Winston's return. "Sometimes you need to put a little sparkle on," she told the girls as she straightened the white eyelet trim on Aurora's cap.

As soon as they stepped off the escalator on the second floor, the sisters waved and called to her from a large table in the food court.

"We've missed you!"

"Where have you been?"

"So good to see you."

"I need my little munchkin fix," Julia said, rushing over to the stroller to pick up Aurora.

Kimani gave her a hug and Laura guided her into a seat at the table.

"Mommy, can I get a quesadilla?" Ruby asked.

"Is that okay, Mom?" Annabelle asked. "I'll take her over to the Mexican place."

"Sure." Glory sent them off with one of her last five-dollar bills and turned back to the group.

"Where've you been, Glory?" Leo asked, his blue eyes wary. "We've been worried about you."

Their support and enthusiasm was like a cushion around her, saving her from untold injury. Trying to keep her voice from getting ragged with emotion, Glory told them about losing Winston and getting too sick to function.

"It's a good thing you made it here. I wish you had told us," Laura said, patting Glory's shoulder.

"I wanted to," Glory said, "but I didn't know how to reach you without coming here, and I was too sick to go out." Glory wasn't sure of their address, and none of them had cell phones. Natalie had explained that cells were an unnecessary expense when they lived in the same house with the people who mattered to them.

"But you're here now, and we can help you."

Georgina nodded. "We take care of our sisters."

"Thank you," Glory said. "Though I'm not a sister, you've always been so kind to me."

"You're a sister of the heart; that's as good as it gets," Kimani said, pressing a palm to her chest.

"Have you eaten today?" Leo seemed genuinely concerned. "You seem a little shaky."

"I haven't been able to eat much since we heard. I've been sick."

"Your heart was broken," Laura said dramatically, making it all sound like a poorly acted play.

"Laura, go get her a protein shake from the fruit bar. And

something solid. White rice from Bamboo Gardens," Leo said, turning to Glory. "That should be gentle enough for you."

A wave of exhaustion hit Glory as Laura hurried off; the journey here had taken it out of her, but she needed to stay focused. This was her only chance.

"Do you want to talk about it?" Leo asked.

She did. It was rough, but she hadn't had a chance to tell anyone what had really happened. She told them about the phone call from the Alaska State Trooper. The unpleasant phone calls with Winston's aunt and sisters to make arrangements for a funeral Glory would not be able to attend. She didn't have the money or the nerve to put her babies on an expensive bus and haul them down to Roseville, especially after she heard the lack of welcome in Rosalee's voice. "I guess we could find you and the girls a motel room on the interstate," Winston's aunt had told Glory. A motel room! Like Glory had money to burn. The two final checks mailed by his employer— a little more than six hundred dollars—would not last her and the girls a lifetime. And the sickness. She was used to overcoming obstacles, but this dizziness and achiness and nausea was too much.

"When our spirit is suffering, it manifests in our bodies," Leo said. "You've had a traumatic loss. It will take time to recover. Time and love."

"And we love you, Glory." Kimani linked her fingers through Glory's atop the table. "We want to help you. Can we help her, Leo?"

"Of course we can," he said. "We have a place for you to live. We'll keep you safe and protected and well fed. But you will have to work like the other sisters. We can get you a job at the hotel, cleaning rooms. It doesn't pay much, but it will cover your room and board."

"That would be wonderful." Glory's heart was singing. "And I'm happy to work. I don't care what shift, as long as someone is around to watch my girls."

"Oh, wow." Leo tilted his head sympathetically. "Sorry, I thought you knew."

"We can't have children in the house." Kimani squeezed her hand. "We're not set up for it."

Glory had heard of the policy before, but they had to make an exception for her girls. "They're good kids. Ruby is polite and independent, and Aurora is a smart little thing. She'll learn fast. And I know how to keep them both quiet."

"They are good kids," Laura said.

"Everyone here adores them," Kimani agreed. "But the house wouldn't be safe for them."

"Please," Glory begged, looking from Kimani to Leo. "Please. We won't be any trouble. You'll never know we're there, and we won't stay long. A few weeks, maybe a month . . . Just until I can get back on my feet."

"We don't want you for a short stay," Leo said. "We're not a halfway house. We're a family, dedicated to each other. If you join us, we want it to be because you're committed, too."

"I am committed." Tears stung her eyes, and she hated the whimper in her voice. "I do want to stay. I need you in the worst way." The kind faces watching her were too much to bear; she let out a sob and covered her face with her hands.

It was too much, coming so close to being saved and then being set adrift again. She tried to muffle the sound of her crying with her hands as she sensed something shifting around her.

"I'm sorry, Glory." Leo's voice was close, his hand rubbing her back. "I thought you understood that joining us is a way of starting over. We sever all ties with the outside world and create a new life, a good life."

When she looked up, the sisters were heading toward the food vendors and she was alone with Leo.

"I want to start over, I really do, and my children won't hold me back. Can't you help me out? Can you bend the rules, just this once?"

He shook his head. "The truth is, your kids would be better off in an environment that's designed for them. You wouldn't send an old man to kindergarten, right? And you wouldn't send a five-year-old to work at a job. We're talking about the welfare of your kids. You love your daughters. I can see that."

"I do."

"Is there anyone who can take them for you? Someone who's good with kids. This would be the best time to make a switch, when the children are young and flexible."

"I tried my mother. She said no." And maybe it was lucky. Katherine had been petty and mean when Glory was growing up.

"No one else? No aunts or sisters?"

Glory shook her head. It was useless. They would have to go back to Ellen's and hang on in the apartment until the police came to evict them.

"I do know of a place you can take your kids. One of our sisters had a baby, and she left it at a hospital. There's a law, I think it's called Safe Haven, and you can leave an infant at a firehouse or hospital, no questions asked."

She sniffed, wiping her eyes with some stiff brown napkins from the table. "And what do they do with the babies?"

"They find them a safe home. With loving parents." He sighed. "I don't know about you, but that's a better upbringing than most of our sisters had."

The sisters' stories had reminded her of the cruelty in the world. There were the extreme cases, like Georgina's husband, who had left her chained to a bed for a week. And the more apathetic predators like Annabelle's string of foster parents. Sometimes people were simply not fit to be parents.

While others were made for the role. Cheerful, kind women like Miss Mandy. If only Glory could be that way. If only. But she wasn't that patient or organized.

"I know what to do," she said, scanning the food court for her girls. There they were, at a distant table, Ruby finishing her meal while Julia played patty-cake with Aurora. "I need to get my kids, but I'll be back." She looked up at him, her gentle hero. "Will you still be here?"

He gave a nod, his blue eyes holding her, bolstering her. "We'll wait. I'll always be here for you, Glory."

* * *

Afterward, as Glory hurried back to the mall through a rain that smelled of wet cement and chalky soil, she thought of how good this would be for her girls. Ruby would never have to know the tragic circumstances of her father's death, and she would have a bright future ahead. Miss Mandy had thought she was developmentally ahead of her class, so she would have no trouble switching to a new school. Aurora was so young, she would adjust easily to another mother's loving care.

Leo had been right; the timing was perfect. The switch had to be made now, while they were young and able to bounce back. He was right, despite the voice that wailed deep inside her like a repeating siren telling her to go back. Go back. Go back.

This didn't feel completely right. When she misjudged a curb and flew to one knee, smacking her hands on the pavement to stop the fall, she wondered if it was a sign to go back.

Gathering herself, she caught her breath and looked around. No one had come rushing to help her. No one cared.

But Leo and the sisters, they would pick her up and protect her.

Everyone needed someone to watch over them. Right now that was the most powerful gift she could give to her daughters.

PART 2

THE SHAPE OF TEA LEAVES

CHAPTER 17

Twelve Years Later

*P*olynomials are your friends, Ruby had texted to her friends, trying to help them with the algebra homework. *When you're factoring them, just look for the "a,b" and you're home free.* She had even gone over the first three homework problems with Delilah Thorn, who hated asking questions in class and counted on Ruby to explain things to her. Algebra wasn't hard for Ruby. She got it.

But now the numerals and variables seemed indecipherable as she stared at her open book on the kitchen island. She pretended to be working while Dad emptied a bag of greens into a bowl and tossed in some cherry tomatoes. From what she'd seen, dinner was going to be weird, but no one really cared if Dad made a grass salad and burned the pizza. They were all sick over the news.

She pressed the sharp edge of her polka-dot notebook under the nail of her thumb, worrying it there so that the pain alternately stabbed and abated, a tidal surge of sensation. Better that than the raw pain of Aurora's jagged sobs from the bedroom, or the sad resolve in Mom's eyes, or the awkward beatbox sounds Dad made as he moved about the kitchen.

"I wanted to talk to you alone," Mom had said, taking a seat on the stool beside Ruby. It was strange enough for Mom to be home from work when Ruby got out of school, let alone changed from her work clothes into jeans, thick socks, and a fleece jacket. But for Mom to sit down in the afternoon, when there was a dinner to be prepared and mail to sort through . . . Ruby had known something was wrong. "You're a lot more stoic than your sister," Mom went on, "but I know you've got a huge heart under that façade. I wanted to give you a chance to ask questions. Dad and I just met with the doctor and found out I have breast cancer."

After hearing the word "cancer," Ruby had struggled to process the details. Head down, she had let the curtain of crimped curls fall over one eye, trying to hide her fear while Mom had put her usual positive spin on news.

A silver lining! They'd caught it early. She had the best doctors in Portland. The prognosis was good. They'd moved up her surgery date to November, after they celebrated Diwali, but before Thanksgiving. Mom's mother, Rima, would come stay with them while she was recovering. Mom kept saying how fortunate she was, having a supportive family and great medical coverage.

Ruby didn't think she was lucky at all, getting cancer after she ate healthy, mostly fruits and vegetables and a few Indian dishes with meat, and went to Zumba classes and walked all the time with Dad. Tamarind McCullum was in better shape than most of the moms in West Green. Strong and tall and more beautiful than any of the stars of the Bollywood films that Ruby had seen at Nani Rima's house. Ruby had to work with a flatiron to make her rippling hair as silky and straight as her mom's. Which made sense, since Ruby was adopted and didn't have the same genetics. Ruby and Aurora knew the facts of their births, and yet Aurora often whined about how much she wished she were a real McCullum, half-Indian so she could look more like Mom, and with the lithe athleticism from Dad's side of the family. Aurora acted as if their parents could magically rearrange her genes to match theirs and hand it over in a box with a bow for Christmas. Plus Aurora was too self-centered to see that it bugged Mom, who always insisted that the girls were real McCullums. Aurora could be such a brat.

"Is there anything you want to ask me about?" Mom had said. Her dark eyes had been round as quarters, her tone thick with encouragement that rang false to Ruby. She could feel Mom's fear radiating like a sunburn beneath her clothes. And if Mom was scared, how was Ruby supposed to feel?

"Are you going to need chemo?" Ruby had asked. It was a fake question meant to replace the bazillion questions she couldn't ask. Like, *What if you're not okay, Mom? What if you can't beat the cancer? What will happen to Aurora and me?* Sure, there was Dad, with his Men's Wearhouse "dress casual" shirts and slacks, his cool squint when he stared at the computer screen, his goofy attempts to make his daughters smile. He was good for a father, but he didn't really know what was going on in the house or in their lives.

"I might need chemo after the surgery," Mom had said. "That's down the road a bit. Right now I'm going to focus on the surgery, okay? Any other questions?"

Ruby shook her head. She didn't think she could talk anymore without her voice cracking, and she didn't want to fall apart now, in front of Mom. The least she could do was pretend that everything would be all right.

Mom had given her a big hug and told Ruby how proud she was to have two smart, caring daughters. "Don't be afraid to talk to me about this anytime you want. I love you," Mom had said. That made Ruby's mouth pucker.

"Love you, too."

"Now. I'm counting on you to calm your sister down after she hears the news. I'm afraid she's going to freak out."

"She's such a drama queen."

"Your sister is fire, and you are ice. Someday you will come to appreciate each other."

Ruby didn't think so, but she didn't argue with her mom. After another hug she turned back to stare at her algebra homework while the family drama unfurled. Aurora blew in the side door, yelling, "Mom? I told you I needed new soccer cleats."

"What's that?" Mom headed toward the laundry room as Aurora held up a muddy cleat with the toe flapping open. Mom laughed out loud. "Oops."

"I told you! It opened up halfway through practice and I had to sit out because Coach Kazz was afraid I would trip." Aurora disappeared again to strip off her dirty clothes.

"Sorry about that!" Mom called after her. Ruby thought Mom was way too nice to Aurora. "I guess there's a shopping trip in your future."

"Tonight?"

"Maybe tomorrow."

"But I need them for practice tomorrow night. What's for dinner?" Aurora asked, reappearing in her Under Armour shorts and top.

Dad came in behind her, carrying a grocery bag. "I told you, I'm making a homemade pizza. I got the dough at the store."

"Are you putting vegetables on?" Aurora lamented.

"Only on half. Your half will be pepperoni. It's gonna be great." Dad's enthusiasm only highlighted the weirdness of the day. He was trying too hard. Beatboxing something about rolling in dough, Dad washed his hands and got started.

Mom followed Aurora back to her bedroom while Ruby stayed in her spot at the kitchen counter, pretending to do homework that was probably not going to get done tonight with this crushing news and the fear stabbing through her chest. She allowed herself a dark fantasy of failure. What would happen if she showed up to class without her homework done? It made her tremble inside to think of getting an F on anything. When you were a straight A student, people didn't understand how close you came to falling off a cliff every time you made a mistake. Fighting failure was a daily battle.

"Oven preheated," Dad said aloud. "We are ready to load the pizza." He opened the oven door and stole a sliver of cheese before gripping the pizza tray.

Ruby could feel the blast of heat from where she sat behind the island. "You should use an oven mitt."

"I got this, honey." He slid the tray in, flinching as one hand nearly grazed the side of the oven.

"Oh my God, Mom, no!" Aurora's voice seeped down the hall, followed by the sounds of her sobs.

"You know, Rubes, I'm proud of you for keeping your cool," Dad said. "Mom's going to be fine, and Aurora will pull herself together, too. She's just got a different way of processing things."

"I can't!" Aurora's wail from down the hall underlined Dad's point. "I just can't, Mom!"

"Honey, wait. Let's talk about this." Mom's voice was elevated now.

"That's what I'm doing!" Aurora whined.

"I wish she would shut up," Ruby muttered to her father. "She always makes everything about her."

"It's annoying, I know, but it's her way of venting."

"I'm going to finish in my room . . . where she's not venting." Ruby gathered her books just as Aurora stormed into the room, tears streaming down her cheeks.

"Mommy is sick!" Aurora whined. "What's the matter with you guys? Am I the only one who cares about this?"

"Of course we care." Dad came out from behind the counter and put his hands on Aurora's shoulders, as if she were a rising bubble he needed to push back to earth. "We share your concern, Rory. We're all worried about your mom, but we're going to do our best to support her and nurse her back to health when she needs us."

"But it's awful!" Tears glimmered in her eyes as Mom appeared in the hallway. "Cancer! It's so scary. My friend's mother had cancer. Gia's mother. I think it was breast cancer, too. She died."

"Would you shut up?" Ruby couldn't believe her sister would say that.

"I'm the only one here who's talking about it, while you guys sweep everything under the rug." Aurora pressed a hand to her chest, as if she were miming heartbreak. "What's wrong with you?"

Ruby hugged her books, tempted to throw one at Aurora. "You are such a moron."

"Oh my God! You're the moron!"

"Don't call her that!" Dad snapped, but Mom was standing between them, holding her hands out like a referee separating two brawling players.

"Okay, we need five minutes of quiet time." Mom's dark eyes were fierce; she was in disciplinarian mode. "Both of you, off to your rooms. When you come back for dinner we will speak like civilized people. And no cancer talk until after the dishes are done. We're going to talk about this and then let it go for the time being. I'm not going to let this disease consume our lives. Now go."

It was a relief to escape and think about anything but Mom having cancer. Ruby went down the stairs to the daylight basement, glad that hers was the only bedroom on this level. She dumped her books on the bed, went straight to the shelves Dad had built into the wall for her brightly colored collection, and scooped up her favorites, the family of five baby rubber ducks.

"She *is* a moron," she told the little yellow ducks in her hands before carrying them to the bed. She stretched out on her side and began to arrange the ducks on the comforter in a starburst pattern, as if the five of them were kissing. This was her therapy since she was little, the arrangement of rubber ducks to line up the things that were askew in her world. The ducks soothed her, and something about the hopeful expression in that upturned orange beak brought her comfort. For a time in middle school she'd tried to downplay it, but now that kids were making tons of money selling original Pokémon and Star Wars figures on eBay, her rubber duckies were considered cool.

"Slightly retro and adorable," Maxi always said when she gave the purple duck with the blue polka dots a squeeze. Maxi's favorite.

Ruby had ducks in various bright colors and identities. Officer Duck, Cowboy Duck, Dr. Duck, Captain Duck. There was a mermaid with a bikini top and a fish tail, a nurse duck, and a queen duck. Maxi had brought back a Statue of Liberty duck from New York City, and a few years ago Delilah had given her a rainbow duck before any of them understood that it stood for LGBTQ freedom. "I just liked the colors," Del said recently, "but now that I know what it means, I like it even better."

Ruby lined up the ducks on the edge of her textbook, and one by one they dropped off the edge into the water. *See that? You can swim. You'll be fine.*

The ducks were confident and supportive, unlike real people. They would never talk about death in front of someone who had gotten a cancer diagnosis.

Pushing off the bed, she brought over Mama Duck and gathered the little ones around her. *Oh, Mama, don't be sick. Wake up, wake up! Rora is crying.*

Aurora thought Ruby's ducks were stupid. She didn't understand why they weren't in the bathtub and didn't care that water would make them fill up with yucky black mold. She didn't understand the comfort the ducks brought Ruby in the ways that she could squeeze them like stress balls or assort them in organized patterns. Aurora didn't appreciate organization.

And Aurora didn't appreciate their parents. Tonight had proven that more than ever to Ruby, who remembered bits and pieces from when she was four years old. She remembered crawling into bed between her parents. She recalled being hoisted in the air and carried around, floating in her father's arms. Her daddy, who had gotten down on the floor with her and made a game out of counting crackers and Cheerios. Her daddy, who read her books and taught her silly poems. Her daddy, who had been a football star in high school, which Ruby could picture, though it had to be before she was born. Her daddy was magical and ethereal, while Mommy was real, reliable, the everyday parent. Sort of like her current mom and dad. Her original mother used to take her to the duck pond and to some Mexican restaurant for tiny quesadillas and applesauce. Mommy, with her hair that smelled like vanilla cookies and her starry blue eyes and instructions for Ruby. "Say thank you. Don't forget to brush your teeth. Take care of your sister."

Ruby had been old enough to remember, but Aurora was a lost cause. If Aurora had any memory of being left at the fire station on that rainy day, she would be thankful for what she had now. She wouldn't be manipulating Pete and Tamarind now as if it were their job to smooth over every little bump for her.

Not Ruby. She loved her parents. She knew Mom and Dad loved her and she was grateful to be their daughter. Even if she was curious about the woman who had left her behind, she wasn't going to jeopardize her parents' happiness by making them pay some investigator to find her birth mother.

Without much time before dinner, Ruby called her smartest friend, Maxi. Maxine Ellison Cohen was Jewish and kind of wild but nerdy, too. She didn't fit the normal profile for West Green High, either, which made it easy for Ruby to be friends with her. Back in junior high they'd been the outliers who'd been chosen last for dodgeball in PE class. More recently, some kids gave them props for varying from the white-bread path. Some kids thought it was cool to be Indian, mixed race, or Jewish, cool to be different, which Ruby thought was a little weird. Designer genetics? It wasn't as if she or her friends had any choice in the matter.

"Wassup?" Maxi asked.

"Hey. Can you send me a picture of your algebra homework?"

"You mean, like, the answers?"

"Yeah."

"Sure, but I can explain it to you if you want. I thought you got this chapter?"

"I'm just too distracted right now. We had a bomb drop here." Ruby wanted to hold back, but if she didn't tell Maxi, her head would explode. "Don't say a word to anyone, but my mom has cancer and she needs surgery."

"Oh my God. Ruby! I'm so sorry."

"I know. Don't tell a soul, because I wasn't supposed to tell you."

"I won't tell anyone, I swear. That's awful. Is she okay? I mean—"

"She said they got it early and that's good. I don't know." Her parents weren't beyond lying to keep things calm. Reframing the truth, her history teacher called it.

"Well, that's something. So I guess you didn't tell her about the search."

"I didn't. I can't. How can I? This is no time to be stabbing her in the back."

"You wouldn't be stabbing her in the back. The search doesn't involve Tamarind and Pete."

"The search is going to hurt them both, and I can't take that chance right now."

Ruby remembered exactly how the idea of searching for her biological mother had started. It was one of those drowsy latenight sleepover conversations with her friends.

When Delilah was annoyed with her parents and wished she were secretly adopted and had cool movie star parents, the whole adoption issue had been cracked open. "Do you think about your biological mother?" Delilah asked. "I mean, maybe she rocks it like Pink. Or maybe she's really in touch with her inner self like Selena Gomez. You must wonder about that all the time."

"Sometimes. My aunt Kaysandra says I suffered from separation anxiety when the social workers got me. I was convinced my mother would come back."

"Aw . . . that just breaks my heart."

Ruby shrugged. Most times she felt that she'd left that sad little girl behind. "But I realized how lucky I am. I've got a great mother and father. I'm luckier than a lot of kids. And from the stuff that I remember, I think my birth mom was kind of sad. Definitely poor. At least that's what my aunt Kaysandra says. She helped my parents with the adoption." A social worker, Aunt Kaysandra had always been the person Ruby went to when she had questions about what had happened back then. "It was so hard for you. Do you remember how torn up you were about it, sweet pea?" Ruby usually shrugged those questions off, though she soaked up any information she could get on her birth parents. Somehow, it was easier sharing her memories with her friends.

"What else do you remember about your birth mother?" asked Maxi.

"It's embarrassing, but I remember stupid things, like feeding the ducks at the pond or playing with Cheerios on my father's nightstand. Aurora was just a baby, so she's got no memory, but I was four, so I remember . . . images. Like old photos that keep fading every year."

"That is so intense," Delilah said. "Do you remember what your mother looked like?"

"Blue eyes, and she was white, with shiny dark hair. She seemed so brave, pushing my sister and me all around the neighborhood in a stroller. We went everywhere with her, and that made me feel so grown-up, like I was her best friend."

"That's so sweet that you felt close to her," Delilah said.

"What about your dad?" asked Maxi.

"He's not so clear. I kind of remember him as one big laughing hug. He was a big guy, like a football player, but he would get down on the floor and play with me. He used to recite poems. Silly poems, like Shel Silverstein's stuff and that Lewis Carroll poem." Back in middle school when Ruby was practicing kicking on goal with her friends, she had begun to recite a silly poem she knew from childhood:

> " 'Twas brillig, and the slithy toves
> Did gyre and gimble in the wabe:
> All mimsy were the borogoves,
> And the mome raths outgrabe."

Delilah had chuckled, saying that she didn't know what the heck Ruby was talking about, but it made her feel "mimsy." Maxi had recognized the first stanza from Lewis Carroll's poem "Jabberwocky"—totally impressed that Ruby could recite the entire piece. Her voice became a low growl as she clawed at the air, reciting the lines:

" 'Beware the Jabberwock, my son!
The jaws that bite, the claws that catch!' "

Had she learned it in school? No. It came from her daddy. The man who went away somewhere to work in Alaska. And Ruby kept waiting for him to come home. But he never did.

Waiting. Waiting. So patient. Mommy had promised that he would be home soon.

Soon.

Mommy also said she would be right back when she left Ruby and Rory at the fire station.

Right back.

Ruby was too embarrassed to admit that she remembered the fire station. It was such a pitiful memory. The giant table. The men, with their dusting of mustaches and distant smiles. They gave her ice cream, an orange Creamsicle. A dreamsicle, that was what her real mom, Tamarind, called it. As if ice cream on a stick could transport you to your destiny. Well, in a way, that day at the firehouse, it had.

Last year, the prospect of the girls getting their driver's licenses seemed to open up a new chance for Ruby to dig into her roots without upsetting her parents. Her friends were convinced they could make it a secret mission, and they were eager to help her find her biological mother.

"We'll help you," they insisted. And Ruby secretly delighted in the chance to find out more, just as long as no one said anything to Tamarind and Pete.

"Yo." Maxi's voice brought her back. "You still there?"

"Yeah."

"So what are you going to do?"

"Right now my mom is all I can think about. I mean Tamarind, not the other mom."

"I knew that."

"So I don't know about the search. Maybe I'll do it without

telling them. I'm sixteen. They don't have to know everything
I'm doing."

Dad called her up to dinner. "I gotta go. Send me the homework."

"So you're giving up the search?"

"For now." Someday she would find her birth mother, Glory.

And if her parents found out about it?

She would figure out a way to reframe her story.

CHAPTER 18

The footsteps on the attic stairs were light and cautious, the sound of a person not wanting to bother anyone else in the house. The familiar pattern, the step and step, step and step, was Mama's sound, the plodding climb she had to make because of her bad left knee.

Taking no chances, Luna switched off her flashlight and shoved it, along with her book, down into the sleeping bag as the lock was popped open and watery silver cut a swathe through the small attic cubby. Light washed over the plywood walls and floor, the corner bucket, the dusty boxes she had stacked in a peak like a capital A as a memorial to Annabelle. She was relieved to see the silhouette of Glory, a blanket swaddled around her shoulders like a shawl over her nightgown and bare legs.

An angel with long brown hair—that was her mother.

"Mama, it's getting cold up here. I guess fall is really—"

"Hush, now. We don't want Leo to hear that I'm letting you out."

"But he's asleep," Luna said. His room was two levels down; he wouldn't hear them even if he was awake. And the sisters had probably gone to bed, too.

"The walls have ears, and I don't want to give him reason to punish you again. Come on, love bug. Let's get you downstairs to our room. Not a word till then."

In the shadowy light of a hanging bulb, they walked down the wood stairs, taking care to keep their footsteps soft, "like you're walking through balloons," Mama always said.

As they crept through the quiet house, Luna opened her left palm and smiled at the secret message Hazel had drawn there in purple ink. Purple, like Harold's crayon.

I love you, with a drawing of a heart for the word "love."

Luna pressed her fist to her chest, hoping that it didn't wash off too soon. Even with all the trouble she'd gotten in for pushing through the hole in the fence to go next door, this secret message made it worth it.

It was so unfair that she had to be punished, locked in the attic just for visiting her friend. Hazel Hanson didn't get punished for having friends. She got to see her friends every day at school, which Luna imagined to be a magical place chock-full of friends, where you could hold hands and learn together all day long. "I wish I could go to school," she always told Hazel.

"But homeschooling works better for some kids," Hazel's mom had said. She said it was definitely working for Luna, who had read all the Harry Potter books herself. "You have excellent reading skills," Hazel's mom had told Luna one day when the Hansons' cable went out and they had chosen to read a book together for fun. That had made Luna glow inside. But still, she would rather go to school and make lots of friends.

Once inside their room, Mama placed the rolled-up towel under the door to muffle their voices. Sitting cross-legged, they faced each other on Mama's bed by the window that overlooked the backyard with its two tall yew trees and sagging lawn. Leo's room was at the front of the house, on the other side, but they had made a habit of whispering to each other when they were alone.

Mama leaned forward and took her hands. "My brave girl, are you all right?"

Luna nodded. The attic was less terrible now that there was a sleeping bag, a light, and a book to read. If she was stuck up there during the day, she could clean off a spot on the grimy little window and watch for Hazel, coming home from school, so easy to spot in her cherry red rain slicker. Luna could do some of her normal stuff up there in the attic, but she didn't like being punished. "It's so unfair," she whispered.

"When we got back to the house and Leo told me you were locked in the attic, I was just sick about it. I knew it was serious when he wouldn't let you out for dinner. Tell me what happened." Mama had been out of the house, working at the hotel with most of the other sisters.

"I was in the backyard and I heard Hazel on the swings. That creaky sound. I peeked through the loose board and she asked me if I wanted to come over."

"That loose board that you removed?"

"It was already rotten. And I had done all my reading and writing assignments. So I squeezed through the fence and we hung out." Hazel had taught her to say "hung out" instead of "visited," the way the sisters talked about getting together. Plus she'd seen it on a bunch of shows she got to watch at Hazel's house. Kids' shows. Hanging out at Hazel's was like time traveling to the planet of Happy. When Luna said that in front of Hazel's mother, Nicole said that it was "just about the most adorable thing I've ever heard." And she had a big smile that made Luna feel warm inside. "Why does Leo get so mad when I go over there?" Luna asked her mother.

"It's against the rules, and Leo was upset when he couldn't find you."

"He should just let me go and he doesn't need to worry. Hazel's my friend." Luna loved Hazel. Every time they saw each other Hazel gave her a hug, and when they had to part Hazel said, "*Love you!*" That was what good friends did. "Hazel's mother said I'm welcome anytime. She wants to meet you, Mama. Won't you come over and talk to her sometime? I think maybe she would help us."

"No, Luna, this cannot happen. You can't go over there."

"Why not?"

"You are not to leave this house, ever." Mama's mouth stretched in a frown and little creases appeared in her forehead. Her mad look.

"Why can't I hang out with Hazel, Mama? Girls my age like to hang out and have friends." Luna had seen enough of Nickelodeon to know that much.

"Who takes care of us?"

"Leo."

"That's right. He feeds us and gives us a place to live. He's our protector, and we need to follow his rules. For now."

"But Mama—"

"I can't stop him from locking you in the attic. I can only . . ." Tears were in Mama's eyes as she pressed a hand to her mouth. "I think of Annabelle, and I can't help—"

"That's not going to happen to me," Luna assured her. She'd been little when Annabelle died and it was a foggy memory, though sometimes she talked to her ghost in the attic. Luna didn't really believe in ghosts, but when there was no one else around to talk to, a ghost was a good listener. "Leo doesn't understand how important friends are. That's why he doesn't have any friends."

"He has the sisters."

"That's different." Luna couldn't say how, except that the sisters only pretended to like one another.

"I know you want to visit with your friend. I have friends, too."

Luna squinted in the dim light of the bedside lamp. "You do?"

"I think it's a good thing to have a friend outside the house."

"But it's against the rules. You just said—"

"I met my friend at the mall, when I was shopping alone. Leo doesn't know. Neither do the sisters, and they can't know. That's the thing about having a friend outside the house. It has to be a secret. Do you understand?"

"Yes!" Luna rushed to give her a quick hug, adding, "Love you, Mama!"

"You can't tell anyone about it. It'll be our secret."

"I won't. I can keep a secret." Luna knew that was another

thing friends did for each other. "Can I meet your friend? What's her name?"

"Maybe someday you can meet. Someday when you're allowed to leave the house like the other sisters."

"Do you think . . . Will Leo ever let me out?" Luna looked out the window into the blue-black night punctuated by a few squares of light from the windows of neighboring houses. She ached to get out of this house. Sometimes she recognized that there would be danger beyond these walls. She had seen violence in movies, and occasionally she heard the squeal of a car's wheels or an ambulance's siren to remind that things could go very wrong. Leo said the world was full of Voldemorts. He'd had the sisters watch all the movies so that they could be grateful that he protected them from all the bad things. But Luna saw the world beyond their house as a Hogwarts academy where most of the students had good hearts and only a few were mean and devious. At least that was what she wanted to believe.

Mama was also staring out the window, watching, as if the blue darkness soothed her. "Your time will come. He can't keep you in this house forever."

"He says I'll never leave. That I'm going to be next in line to take over the housekeeping chores here."

"What?" Mama's spine straightened as she drew in a breath. "You're only ten years old. How could he say that?"

Luna shrugged. "That's what he told me. Next year, he's going to start sending Sienna to work at the hotel, so I can take over—"

"Listen to me." Mama's breathless whisper scared her, though she wasn't quite sure why Mama was suddenly alarmed. "If he ever says that again, you just nod and go along with it. Let me work it out with him. But I promise you, that's not going to happen. I won't let it. Do you understand?"

Luna nodded.

"Things are changing." Mama slid off the bed and pulled the blanket closer around her shoulders, though the room wasn't cold. "Changing too fast. I need to think." Staring at the floor, she walked to the wall, turned, and paced back.

"So when can I hang out with Hazel again?" Luna didn't really care about taking over the chores, as long as she was allowed to have a friend.

"Not for a while. You can't get caught over there again. I can't protect you when I'm not here, and it breaks my heart when he locks you in the attic and I can't help you. Promise me you'll behave while I'm at work."

With one last look at her friend's house beyond the fence, Luna turned away from the window and went back to her own bed in the corner. "I promise."

"Now go to sleep." Mama huddled under the blanket like a guard, her gaze moving from the window by her bed to the bedroom door. "You need to help with breakfast tomorrow."

Most mornings Luna set the breakfast table and sometimes made toast or poured juice. Natalie insisted that everyone pitch in around the house, and Luna didn't mind if she wasn't too sleepy. "Okay, Mama." Luna slid in under the comforter. Most nights she didn't pull down the sheets because it was too much trouble to make the bed in the morning. She felt under the pillow to make sure it was in place, its worn corners and smooth cover a comfort to her. Although she was too old for the book now, sometimes she read it over when no one was watching. Harold reminded Luna of the possibilities beyond her window. Right now, if Luna could draw one thing with a purple crayon it would be a giant slide that would take her straight from her bedroom window to Hazel's side porch.

Opening her hand in front of her face, she took one last look at Hazel's message before closing her eyes. Hazel loved her. Somehow, Luna would find a way to hang out with her again. And if Mama met Hazel and her mom, Nicole, she would realize how a friendship could save you. Maybe, if Mama came over one day, Hazel's mom would let them stay, not just for lunch, but overnight, for a while. Or forever. Hazel's mom was so nice, she would definitely say yes.

One small purple crayon could draw a million possibilities.

CHAPTER 19

The next day as she made her way briskly through cleaning her rooms at the hotel, Glory Noland carried the seed of worry that had been difficult to swallow in last night's whispered conversation.

On the desk in 218 a five-dollar bill was wrapped in paper from the hotel notepad with a child's drawing of a duck saying: *Thanks!* So the woman with the two little boys had checked out. Glory rolled the bill into a thin coil and tucked it deep down in her bra. Perfect timing. She was going to need to make a purchase at the mall today and every dollar helped in her Luna fund.

In more than nine years of cleaning hotel rooms, Glory Noland had learned a few tricks of the trade. If she cleaned the same rooms and left little prizes behind, people were sometimes shamed into leaving her a tip. That meant giving them extra coffee packets, little creamers from the front lobby, and especially a washcloth shaped like a duck, a sort of washcloth origami, along with a note that said: *Have a ducky day!* That was usually the clincher—the duck—since it made people think she'd spent extra time for them, which she had. And sometimes it was a big hit with fans of the Oregon Ducks, one of the state university teams.

Of course, she would have gotten in big trouble if Leo or Natalie ever found out what she was doing. Wasting money on coffee and Mini Moos and clean washcloths, which she snuck home in batches and crafted in her room, sometimes getting Luna to pitch in.

The housekeeping tips were the only funds she had for herself and her daughter, and though she had to give some up to Natalie to get away with skimming away the best tips, she was saving up for the next adventure. With Luna turning eleven in a few months, things were changing way too fast for Glory to control. The changes had alarmed Glory at first—Luna's rounded, firm bottom, her swelling breasts. Glory hadn't seen it coming, but in the blink of an eye her little girl was turning into a woman. The other night, Glory realized her daughter needed to start wearing a bra. In a few months, she would no longer be safe.

Worry brought a sour taste to Glory's tongue, and she swallowed hard and tried to switch gears. She would have liked to fill one of the plastic cups on her cart with water and wash down her worries, but it wouldn't be good if someone saw her slacking. She'd be done soon enough, climbing into the van specially outfitted for Natalie to drive, then filing into the mall for a late lunch. She needed to think positive. Leave the bad; focus on the good—one of the mantras of the sisters.

There had been good things, so many good things, that came out of the house. Leo and the sisters had lifted her up when she'd been at her lowest, providing food and shelter and company. And love. In their way, they had tried to love her.

When she'd first joined the sisters, they had brought her back to life. Although she hadn't realized it at the time, she'd been dehydrated and probably malnourished, suffering from sleep deprivation, grief, and stress. Georgina had fed her chicken broth and homemade dumplings. Laura had read to her. Rachel had played her cello, filling the air with classical music that pulled Glory's mind from her personal pain to the collective consciousness of sorrow. Natalie had signed her up for the SNAP program—food stamps—and put her on the payroll of the hotel. "But I don't know how to get food stamps. Don't you have to wait in line or go for interviews?" Glory had asked. Natalie had assured her that there was nothing to worry about. "We'll handle all of it for you, your food stamps, your paycheck. You'll always have food and a wonderful place to live; we'll see to that." Grateful, Glory had burst into tears, and the kind but stern Natalie had patted her hand as she waited for her to calm down and sign the papers.

Working quickly, Glory balled up the linens, snapped a fitted sheet open over the bed, and moved around the mattress. Top sheet and pillowcases, blanket and comforter. She had to move methodically, staying in step to finish on time. Although Leo rarely came to the hotel to manage, Natalie was usually in the office, doing accounting, and she was a numbers person, expecting everything to tick like a clock. Glory usually managed to finish her rooms by three, unless she had to clean up after a very piggy person.

Although Leo was the hotel's housekeeping manager, he usually stayed back to go grocery shopping and supervise the cleaning of the house while his "team," most of the sisters, worked at the hotel. At least that was what everyone said. But Glory knew differently. It didn't take long for Leo to take care of maintenance and small repairs while his favorite sister cleaned the house; those tasks could be accomplished in the first two hours. After that, there was time for other activities.

Glory knew, because she had been Leo's favorite sister when she joined the house. Later she had learned that she'd pushed Laura out of that spot, but at the time she naïvely believed that she was Leo's first and only. In that heavenly year, she had felt loved and protected as they'd made love in the twin bed of the room he shared with his sister. "I need to be close to Natalie so that I can help her get around during the night," he'd explained. "The sisters take good care of her during the day, but it's too much to expect one of them to assist her all night long. I'm her brother, and I need to take care of her."

Glory had loved him a thousand times more to know of his loyalty to his disabled sister. It didn't matter that their time together came only during the day while the others were away, and she didn't mind sharing him with the sisters when someone was home sick or Natalie needed help getting to a doctor's appointment. There was contentment in knowing that she would find her way back to his arms. On a normal day the basic cleanup didn't take her long. She would scrub the bathrooms, mop the kitchen counters and floor, vacuum, sweep, and then search him out. Sometimes she would find him outside in the sun or cold, raking leaves or reinforcing a fence post. Other times he would be inside, replacing a broken hinge or a washer in a faucet. Leo was good with his hands, and he generously applied those skills when the two of them were alone. Most times they didn't have intercourse; Leo thought that was wrong without marriage. But he'd shown her ways to find pleasure with hands and lips, feather touches and firm pressure.

At a time when she mourned the loss of her husband and her girls, a time when she had not expected to have life again, he had lit the spark of joy deep inside her. They had been the perfect complement for each other, yin and yang, night and day.

But their perfect union was short-lived. A year or so after Glory's arrival, Natalie was furious to discover that Glory had become pregnant. Natalie demanded that Glory go for an abortion, but at four months it couldn't be done. In front of his sister, Leo had claimed innocence, turning the blame to Glory, who was accused of breaking the rules and engaging with men outside the house.

Outside the house! Glory pointed out that she rarely left the premises and when she did it was for shopping trips with Leo or the other sisters. In a tense meeting with Leo and Natalie, Glory had stood her ground. "Leo is the father of this child," she said, her voice croaking with emotion. Maybe it was hormones or maybe it was the memory of being pregnant before—her baby girls!—but in those days she had been constantly on the verge of tears. "We're going to have a baby. That's a beautiful thing, a miracle of life. You should be happy about this."

"*You* are going to give birth to . . . to some creation of sin. Some dirty thing. No one is happy." Natalie's voice was steely and clipped. "We will continue to provide for you, but no one will ever be happy about this."

"Leo?" She begged for his support. "Please..."

But he stared down at the floor, his silence deafening.

She had learned two things that day. (1) Leo wasn't the man she had thought he was. (2) Although Leo appeared to be the patriarch and great protector, Natalie was the mastermind of the house, the wizard behind the curtain.

The bedside clock indicated that she had seven minutes till the van would leave. Glory vacuumed her way out to the hallway, pulled the plug on the vacuum, and fluffed the pillows on the bed before leaving the room. As she stowed the vacuum and rolled her cart to the storage room, she tried to clear her head of hurtful memories and worries about Luna. Natalie tended to pick up on disturbances, wheedling her way into the tender spots.

Downstairs Glory went out through the hotel's rear entrance, stepping into a misting rain. She found the van with its door open in its usual spot in front of the hidden camera; it was Natalie's way of keeping track of sisters who were finished with work and ready to go. Georgina waited inside, slumped in her seat with her eyes closed, her lips moving in a troubled silent dialogue. A ghost of a person, Georgina was said to have escaped a violent husband, though sometimes Glory thought that the poor woman was still suffering his abuses, still recounting terrible encounters in her mind.

"Looks like I made it with some time to spare," Glory said, climbing in and taking a seat in the back, giving Georgina some space.

Laura appeared at the doorway, smiling. "Hello, sisters. Oh, there you are, Glory. Natalie is looking for you."

"Me?" Attention from Natalie was not usually a good thing.

"She wants to see you in the office."

Had the guest mentioned leaving a tip? The origami duck made out of a washcloth? There were so many things Natalie could pounce on her for. *Please, let it not be the money.* Natalie didn't seem to really like anyone, but Glory knew the woman had a dark corner of her heart reserved for Glory and the child who wasn't supposed to be added to the sisterhood.

Glory approached the reception area cautiously, prepared to defer to any guests. The sisters had been ordered not to congregate in the common areas or spend too much time talking with guests. "Remember that you're here to clean and serve," Natalie reminded them every few weeks. Fortunately, the only guest in sight was an older man browsing the rack of tour brochures by the window. With a nod to Rachel, who was on the phone at the reception desk, arranging a reservation, Glory skirted around the counter and peered into the open office door. The small room was sparsely furnished with file cabinets and a single desk to give Natalie space to navigate in her wheelchair. As she sat there, her eyes focused on the computer, Natalie's face and golden hair seemed to glow in the light. With her blossom pink lips, true blond hair, and bold cheekbones, she was a beautiful woman if you didn't know how speckled her heart was. "Dirty thing." When Natalie had first started using the name for her baby, Glory had been stunned. Later she forced herself to adopt it in her mind every time she looked at Natalie. *Dirty thing. My baby is innocent; you're the one with the charred black soul.*

Glory straightened her spine, summoning inner strength. "You wanted to see me?"

"I need you to clean Two-Oh-Seven. Julia is running behind and she won't be able to get to it."

"I'll do it right away, but I'm going to be a little late finishing."

"That's fine. You and Julia can walk to the mall when you're done."

It was a fifteen-minute walk, and Glory wanted that extra time at the mall today. Besides, it was raining. "Can you wait for us? I'll be quick. And I'll help Julia finish whatever she's working on."

"We need to leave on time. I have things to do." Natalie clicked the mouse, closing screens, shutting down.

"But it's raining," Glory said, trying not to sound whiny.

"A little rain never hurt anyone. We'll see you at the mall." When Natalie turned her chair toward the exit, Glory hurried out ahead of her. No use pushing the argument. Natalie always won.

Forty minutes later, Glory and Julia joined the sisters at the food court. With a smile she didn't feel, Glory declined to take a seat, saying she was too soggy. She got her lunch money from Leo and headed off, saying she was going to dry off in the restroom first.

As soon as she was out of sight of the group she dashed down the escalator, purchased a hot pretzel at a food cart, and shoved large gobs into her mouth as she headed toward the far end of the mall. She was so hungry that the smell of cleaning fluid on her hands didn't even bother her as she downed the nuggets of dough. Her meager supper of Crock-Pot stew or a sandwich was still hours away, and she had no time for real food if she was going to take care of her errand and see him. Shawn. Her new boyfriend.

Her heart melted a little as she passed by the elegant window of Victoria's Secret, with its wispy angels holding delicate bras in pink, ivory, and red satin and lace. Some of the bras were adorned with beads and sequins, as if to be worn by royalty. Glory wished she could purchase one for her angel, but they cost way too much.

Glory made her way into a tween store, where she found a section for "bras and bralettes." It was difficult to judge without Luna here, but she decided on a two-pack of bralettes, one pink, one white, for $17.99. The clerk said they were returnable if they didn't fit—"Just leave the tags on"—and Glory handed over a chunk of her savings with the ever-present glimmer of worry that she was not saving enough, not fast enough. Not that she received a salary. Natalie doled out a small bit of spending money each week to cover meals from the mall, but the stipend was so small that, even without eating, it didn't add up quickly. She checked her watch. Just enough time to say hi. Then she had to scoot back to the sisters, before anyone noted her absence.

Leaving the store, she felt a twinge of sadness for Luna, who would have loved this place with its cheerful signs about "Tween Power" and "Clothes Tweens Love" surrounded by brightly colored hearts and flowers. But Luna had never been inside this store or any store. The house was her home, school, and prison, at least for now.

But Glory was going to get them out, and this time she was taking her daughter with her.

She had a plan.

She'd found a man.

Their way to freedom.

CHAPTER 20

It was her.

Ruby backed up into the window of Foot Locker and pretended to stare down at her phone as the woman walked by. Dark brown hair tucked behind both ears hung loose over her shoulders. Pinkish skin the color of Ruby's salt lamp. Blue eyes that gazed right past her, focusing on a distant light in the future. Worn jeans and a black fleece and short black boots that made her resemble every other mom in the mall.

But no, this one was different.

She's mine. My mother.

Even in the quick glimpse, Ruby saw the resemblance, the features she and Aurora shared with Glory—round, high cheekbones and sapphire eyes. Ruby knew she should stop her, go after her, talk with her. This was Ruby's big chance. But she couldn't move. All the questions and insecurities of twelve years seemed to swell up into her throat as she watched the woman walk away.

"Oh my God." Desperate to tell someone, she opened the screen on her phone, clicked on recent messages, then paused. It wasn't really textable information.

Guess who I ran into at the East Center Mall? My birth mother!

What a weird thing to text her friends. And Aurora, who

was inside Foot Locker buying new cleats . . . should she run in and grab her?

I just ran into our first mother! Leave the stupid cleats and come on; I'll show you!

God, no. Aurora didn't care about the woman she didn't remember, and even if sworn to secrecy she would spill the truth to Tamarind and Pete once she realized she could look more loyal and loving than Ruby. When Ruby had been recruited to use her brand-new license to drive her sister to the store for cleats, no one suspected that they would have to make three stops, winding up here, a mall on the east side of Portland, to locate the perfect pair of soccer cleats for Princess Aurora.

The East Center Mall. What were the chances of finding Glory here?

Moving into the path in front of the stores, Ruby crept forward, advancing just enough to keep track of Glory as she cut in front of a sunglasses cart and crossed over to the opposite stores. Not wanting to lose sight of her, Ruby crossed behind a jewelry kiosk. When she rounded the kiosk's corner, there was Glory, just two yards away, smoothing her hair, straightening her jacket, as she stared up at the illuminated sign of the House of Shoes.

Ruby ducked back, her heart beating way too fast as she peeked out again and saw Glory enter the shoe store. Was she shopping? Or maybe she worked there—

"Can I help you find something?" the woman from the jewelry shop asked. She had the bored confidence of a twenty-something who felt sure that Ruby wasn't a buyer but was venturing way too close to the merchandise.

"No, no, thanks," Ruby said, edging away from the kiosks and taking up a spot by a fake tree, a safe distance from a gray-haired man with a rolling oxygen tank who sat with a younger woman on the bench.

Months ago when Ruby had told her friends about her plans to search for her birth mother, they had tried to help her organize the mission. Delilah had pumped Ruby with a million questions and made notes of all the answers as if there were going to be an exam at the end of the interview.

"So your father died in Alaska, and your birth mother is still living in Portland?" Delilah repeated, tucking her vanilla blond hair behind her ear with her left hand while she wrote with her right. Delilah had three sisters, each with the same pale hair that lots of the girls at school admired.

"That's what my parents have told me over the years. The social worker said Glory was local. But that was twelve or so years ago. She might have moved."

"If she's still poor, like you said, she might have moved to a cheaper area, or to another job market," Maxi pointed out. "Poverty limits people's options and social mobility."

Delilah and Maxi suggested that Ruby dig deep into her memories of her life with Glory. "If you can remember where you lived or places you used to go, maybe we can find someone who knew your birth mother," Delilah suggested.

Maxi had helped by coming up with an article from a science magazine about long-term memories and how childhood memories faded like old photographs, though some details remained strong.

"You're telling me to remember things I've worked hard to forget." It wasn't that the time before Mom and Dad, Tamarind and Pete, had been terrible. It was the way it had ended, with Mommy taking her and Rory to the firehouse and promising, *promising* that she'd be back soon.

"Just try. Think back to the earliest things you can remember. Things you liked to do. Things you hated."

Ruby had promised to think about it, but it was a struggle to get beyond the wall of her memory. She remembered sitting in the apartment waiting for Daddy to come in the door. She remembered how Mommy didn't have time to play once Aurora was born. Mostly she recalled the crushing disappointment of waiting for "soon" to happen. She had bought the package on "soon." After Glory had dumped them at the fire station, Ruby kept insisting to social workers and psychologists that her mommy would be back soon. It still broke her heart that her younger self had believed that. So instead of details leading to her mother, Ruby mostly remembered what a stupid little kid she'd been.

Until one day, as she was walking to school, a memory sparked when she passed a small playground where a young mom was there with her two kids—a baby in a stroller, and a little boy in a sandbox, who had lined up a dozen Matchbox cars and was running them down a sand hill.

The playground . . . Glory used to take them to a playground next to a school and a park with a duck pond. Aurora had still been a lump in the stroller, but Ruby had liked the swings. And she had organized the toys left in the sandbox and sometimes collected rocks and leaves. And they had watched the ducks in the park but couldn't feed them because that made them mean. Ruby could picture that little playground by the school.

Her school.

And her teacher . . . Ruby had both feared and adored the woman with flowered dresses and a kind smile. Preschool had been a succession of tasks, from art time to reading time to nap time to recess, but those patterned grooves had been reassuring for Ruby. What had been the teacher's name? Miss Annie? Miss Mandy. That sounded right, but Ruby didn't think she'd ever known the woman's last name.

The plan had been to check out small preschools in East Portland to see if Ruby recognized any of them. "From there, maybe we can find the house you used to live in?" Maxi had suggested. They had been set to start once Ruby turned sixteen and got her license in March, since it was hard to get to East Portland from their suburb south of the city without a car. But things had gotten in the way. Homework and papers for all of them. Ruby and Maxi went to Salem for Model United Nations and volunteered at the dog rescue. Delilah played basketball in the spring league. Life got in the way.

But now, with Glory just yards away, talking to some man in the shoe store, the search had just kick-started itself.

The shoe store's glass window featured some low displays of shoes and sale signs that allowed Ruby to see inside, which was good, because Ruby would have definitely been noticed in the nearly empty store. How long had Glory been sitting there beside the man, both of them facing away from the door? He had slicked-back hair and wore a shirt and tie, and though Ruby couldn't see his face, she did notice the way he gently brushed Glory's hair away from her eyes. Their hands touched, linking fingers, and then there was a quick kiss before they both stood up, as if to end the visit. Glory began to leave the store.

From observing the silent scene, Ruby could tell that they liked each other. He was her boyfriend or maybe her husband. It seemed weird, but she shouldn't be surprised that Glory's life would have changed over the past decade. In a way the most surprising thing was that her location hadn't changed; she was still here in Portland, probably living in the same neighborhood where Ruby had started school.

Inside the store Glory lifted a hand to say good-bye. Time to hide. Stepping back behind the potted tree, Ruby waited for Glory to exit the store, again walking quickly with a purpose.

Ruby followed, not too close, and rode up the escalator behind her.

At the top, Glory headed straight for the food court, where diners were sparse. Too late for lunch, too early for dinner. Mostly stragglers, some employees on break, sat sipping or munching and staring at their cell phones. But over by the window two large booths held a bunch of women, who waved Glory over when they saw her.

So, she had friends.

Pausing behind a bussing station with napkins and packets of ketchup and mustard, Ruby shuddered as the group in the food court aligned itself to a memory. Like a new photo being imposed over an old faded one, she saw a younger version of herself trundling into the food court with Glory.

The stroller. Ruby used to stand on the back of the stroller, clinging with gritted teeth when they hit a bump.

Ruby liked the Mexican place because the meal came with applesauce. She still liked applesauce.

And the women had clustered in a group, just as they were now. With one woman in a wheelchair, a vinyl chair with big wheels.

Ruby wasn't sure how to absorb what she was seeing. So Glory had been involved with these women, for twelve years? Were they some kind of club?

The women had been nice to Ruby, doting, buying her ice cream and frozen yogurt. But she hadn't trusted them. When she and Mommy got to the food court, Mommy didn't pay attention to Ruby anymore, except to correct her.

"Did you say 'please' and 'thank you,' Ruby?"

"You need to be polite to Mommy's friends."

Now that seemed ridiculous. She'd been four years old! What kid that age had perfect manners?

Suddenly angry, she glared at Glory, who was folding up the plastic bag with her purchase, her head lowered. Somber and silent as she took a seat with her friends. A band of women . . . like overage sorority sisters.

This is what you left us for? A flock of mall queens and a shoe salesman?

Ruby hated that this woman could hold any power over her, but Glory was a mighty figure in her world.

Why? Why didn't you come back for me?

She would get her answer. Not today, with Aurora texting her, wondering where she was. But soon, when things with Mom settled down, she would find Glory and confront her. Finally, she was going to get her answer.

CHAPTER 21

Tamarind lifted her margarita to the woman who had done so much to help her fulfill her dreams. "Here's to life, love, and good health."

"I'll drink to that, girl." Kaysandra clinked glasses with her and leaned forward with a conspiratorial look. "So how are you really doing? Are you scared about the surgery?"

"Hell, yeah." Tamarind took a sip of her drink, staring at a colorful sombrero on the wall of Tio Pedro's Mexican restaurant as the sweet liquid went down. "Staring down the barrel of a gun at the big C, part of me is shaking in my boots. The other part is just trying to hold on to my family and pretend it's going to be fine. Necessary denial."

"That's good. At least we know you're not delusional."

Tamarind smiled and took another sip. After a day at the office with her coworkers tiptoeing around her, she was glad to be relaxing with someone who wasn't afraid to fling out the truth. There was no manual on how to tell people you had cancer, no greeting card to announce it gracefully, and though Tamarind knew everyone handled things differently, she just wanted the information out there so she could move ahead without feeling she was hiding something. Transparency was important to her, but not everyone could handle the truth so well. "I put the word out at work today, just so everyone would know what was going on with me."

"How'd that go?"

"A mixed reaction. Carla in Accounting couldn't stop crying, which was awkward. I barely know her."

"Chances are, she's battled cancer in some way, maybe lost a loved one or a friend." Kaysandra reached for a tortilla chip. "She's probably scared."

"She's not alone. Fear is a real pain in the ass." That morning while the shower was heating up Tamarind had stepped up to the bathroom mirror and taken an honest look at her tall, broad-shouldered body. For so many years she had struggled to come to terms with this body. Her light brown skin that made her not black and not white. Her height that made her feel graceless as she towered over her mother and most of the other girls her age in school. Her flat butt and small breasts. It had taken her nearly three decades to love and appreciate this body, to come to terms with who she was, and now that she was going to lose her breasts she wondered if she'd have to redefine herself, or was her soul big enough and strong enough to overlook those physical changes?

"I shouldn't complain," Tamarind said. "I've got one of the best surgeons in Portland. He's got the hands of an angel— that's what my gynecologist says. They've got this reconstructive surgery thing down. At last, I'm going to get a perfect set of breasts. Here's to that." She lifted her glass in a small toast and drank deeply.

"Good on you for looking at the plusses. Did you try the salsa? I can't stop eating these chips." Kaysandra pushed the bowl away, then grabbed one more corn chip. "So what are you afraid of? Something specific, or more a general feeling of dread?"

"I have a list. First, I'm worried about the anesthesia, about going to sleep and never waking up."

"That one's a piece of cake. These anesthesiologists put people to sleep all day, every day. They know their stuff. I've been under so many times. Don't you worry about that part."

"Then there's the question of the cancer spreading. What if

it takes me down systematically so that I spend the rest of my life being a burden on Pete and the girls?"

"A scary thought." Kaysandra nodded, dipping another chip in salsa. "But you know, you're lucky you've got people who love you who want to take care of you. They want to share your life, whatever shape that takes. And you'd do the same for Pete or your girls. We're blessed, girl. But I don't blame you for worrying. Sometimes you've got to think through all the angles."

"And what about my girls? What about the effects of my illness on their stability? What if they have to live the rest of their lives without a mother?" Tamarind rubbed her thumb over the cold frost on her glass as she imagined her girls forging ahead without her. "Aurora took the news really hard. She's been quick to cry and voice her fears since I broke the news a few days ago. Aurora has always been that way, emotional and unfiltered, but at least she's expressing herself. Ruby is another story. She seems calm and competent, a tough soldier, but you know she must be hurting inside."

"Ruby can be hard to read." Kaysandra frowned as she rubbed salt from her fingertips. "Those quiet, independent ones, you never know what's going on in their heads. And Ruby has those abandonment issues. I know she hasn't acted out for years, but she was so crushed when her mama left her. Those things can play out later, yes, but Ruby has a strong support system. She's got parents who love her, a good sister, and close friends. I know she seems closed off, but I got my eye on that girl and she's learned how to vent in her own way. She's doing fine, but when things go wrong, she's got a safety net."

"You're part of the safety net, too." The margarita was working with Kaysandra to warm her to the prospect of hope. Their family would come through this, scarred and reconfigured, but united in love. The stubbornness of the woman sitting across from her who had once annoyed her to no end now held her upright like the frame of a house. "Pete and I have talked, and if something happens to me, he knows he could work with you raising these girls."

Kaysandra's eyes, usually so smoky and confident, became earnest and shiny with tears. "It's not going to come to that, Tamarind, but I'm honored, and you know I'll always be there for the whole damn crew."

Tamarind reached over and squeezed her arm. "You know we love you."

"Love you more."

"And please, if the worst-case scenario happens, promise me you'll keep my girls away from motorcycles and blue eye shadow."

Kaysandra bit back a smile. "That goes without saying."

CHAPTER 22

The music from Rachel's cello rose through the air like an eagle, wide wings flapping, beating to a peak where it leveled and soared high in the sky. It told a story, maybe a frightening story of flying through a furious storm, but it made Luna want to keep her eyes closed to fly along with the giant bird. She didn't want to be reminded that she was in the sitting room, gathered with Leo and the sisters for one of Rachel's Sunday evening recitals. The music could make her forget she was stuck in the house, but only for a minute.

She peeked at the group to make sure no one was staring at her. No one was. Lips moving and eyes closed, Georgina was off in her mumble world. Kimani swayed her head in time to the music while Sienna sat picking at her cuticles. Leo sat back with a gentle smile, but his eyes swept the room, always in control. Laura and Julia stared at Rachel as if they could burn her with a hot look. Probably jealous, or maybe they couldn't understand the music. Sitting next to Luna, Mama had her hands clasped as she looked down at her lap. Maybe falling asleep? She was always tired now, all because of her secrets. Luna wished they could hold hands, but Leo wouldn't allow it, so Luna closed her eyes again and tried to get away in her mind.

Even though she'd made a promise to Mama, Luna couldn't stop thinking of her next chance to hang out with Hazel.

Rachel's recitals were nice, and community time was one of the best things that happened here in the house. Leo always reminded the sisters how lucky they were to have classic literature to read and DVDs of so many movies to enjoy together. Sometimes Natalie recited poems, but they were stories of death and dried-up blood and shells and bones. But Luna didn't want to sit with the sisters. Old women and crazy birds.

Over at Hazel's house there were beads to string into necklaces, glitter glue and paints and easels for real artwork, and a whole shelf full of kids' books to read. Hazel got to watch Nickelodeon on television, which had shows about real kids. About girls with superpowers or the ability to fill a room with a song and make sad people happy again. Luna knew they were made-up stories, but she couldn't stop thinking about them. Sometimes at night she wondered what she would choose as a superpower if given the choice. And the snacks . . . chocolate puddings in small cups. Yogurt in a tube. And sometimes Hazel's mom made them their own little pot of tea or hot chocolate that they poured into dainty blue cups with gold rims.

The song ended, and the house was flat and boring again as Luna opened her eyes to the very dull room of clapping women. Rachel could pull some amazing music from that cello, but Luna would rather be at Hazel's, listening to Pandora or watching Nickelodeon.

"Very nice," Leo said. "Thank you, Rachel, for sharing your gift with us. That's why we keep those hands protected and away from cleaning fluids." Everyone knew Rachel got to work the reception desk at the hotel to save her hands from getting injured. Some of the sisters were jealous, but Luna would have taken any job at the hotel, just to get out of this house.

"And I've become quite good at orchestrating the front desk," Rachel said. Her eyes stared away when she spoke, and her hair, a drab brown mixed with silver streaks, was always scraped back tight. Luna wondered if she slept that way, too. Dressed in her usual long black skirt and white blouse, Rachel looked like a member of the orchestras Leo made them watch on television because classical music was "good for the mind." Mama said that Rachel had once played in a symphony orchestra on a big stage.

"I'm glad we're utilizing your talents," Natalie said, "but we're not here to glorify any one person. We all work hard so that we can eat and have a roof over our heads. That's all."

The light faded from Rachel's eyes. "I know that." A deflating balloon, she gave a little bow and shrunk into her seat again.

Most of the sisters were staring down at the floor now. Natalie had a way of dimming the hope inside everyone.

"Do you want to play another piece?" Natalie asked.

Rachel shook her head without looking up.

"Thank God," Sienna muttered. "Nothing puts me to sleep like a cello solo."

Everyone turned to the new girl, as if she'd just lit fire to the house.

Big trouble for her.

"In our house, we focus on the good," Natalie said. "And I thought you'd been here long enough, Sienna, to learn how to support the sisters who work to put food on our table and keep us warm and dry in the Oregon rain."

"Chill, sister. I'm just being honest." Sienna looked to Leo for support. "Like I tell your big brother, sometimes the truth hurts."

"Many things in life hurt," Natalie said flatly. "But here we focus on good things."

"Good things . . ." Sienna pursed her lips and pressed a finger to her chin. "If I could just think of one. What's good about a house of zombie women listening to a squealing cello? The place smells like boiled barley and old farts and you've got more rules than a prison."

"Sienna!" Leo glared at her.

Kimani leaned over to whisper in Sienna's ear, but Sienna snarled and pulled away. "Remember Annabelle? I never even met her and I could give a crap about some bitch who starved herself in the attic."

Her comment sucked the air out of the room. The sisters were frozen in place, stunned by Sienna's outburst.

But Sienna was wrong. Wrong, wrong, wrong, Luna wanted to tell her. She wished the ghost of Annabelle could be here to speak up for herself.

Get the legend right, okay? I wasn't poisoned and I didn't starve myself. He did it. He locked me in the attic without food and water because I went to the police. I missed the food, but in the end, it's the water that will kill you. You can't go without it. People worry about starving, but it's the water. Always the water.

Of course, Luna only imagined the ghost. She barely remembered Annabelle, but sometimes when the old house was creaking or sighing she imagined it was Annabelle, longing for a tiny sip of water. Mama had told her what happened to warn her about Leo and the attic, and she knew it was true.

Always the water.

"This is just too bad." Natalie's stern voice brought them all back to reality. "I'm very disappointed that you put a damper on our music time by acting out, Sienna. I had thought you were ready to socialize with the sisters, but if you can't follow the rules, you can't enjoy the benefits. Come with me." Natalie turned her wheelchair and moved out toward the door.

"You heard her." Leo nodded after his sister, his eyes on Sienna. "Go."

She rose and stuck her spiky fingers into her long, curly hair. "Aren't you coming?" she asked Leo. When he shook his head, she squinted and made a disappointed *Kah!* sound, like an angry bird. But she followed Natalie out of the living room. She would be taken into the big bedroom on the ground floor that Leo and Natalie shared. Luna didn't know what went on in there during grown-up meetings, and she didn't really want to know. It was bad enough that she got Natalie's cold fish eyes and the stinging comments that made Luna feel bad. *Dirty thing.* As if Natalie couldn't remember Luna's name.

And then there were Leo's lame punishments that he insisted she brought on herself.

One of her earliest memories of him was being carried roughly up the stairs in his arms and lowered to the attic floor, where she was locked in the dark for hours and hours. The punishments always came with stupid explanations like: "I wish you didn't make me do this," and, "Maybe you'll learn," and, "This hurts me more than it hurts you."

Luna had spent many hours crying in that attic cubby. The darkness used to scare her, and the small space sometimes grew hot in the summer and cold in the winter. When Mama first told her that a girl had died there, she had huddled against the brick, afraid of the dead girl's ghost. But over time she had found little comforts there. A glass octagonal window that overlooked Hazel's yard. A vent that brought her fresh air from between the trees outside. She pretended that the rectangular ridges of the chimney bricks were healing stones that pressed peace into her palms. She recited the "Jabberwocky" poem, reminding herself that she could conquer the monster of fear. Sometimes, if you pretend often enough, you begin to believe.

After a while she started talking to Annabelle, and though there'd never been an answer, she imagined the voice of a girl like her sharing her sadness. On bad days, Luna dug her fingers into the sharp edges of the bricks and pretended that the cutting pain was the worst pain she would ever know in her life. On good days, she pressed her palms to the brick surfaces and imagined that the earthen clay baked into each brick had a story to tell her. Luna loved stories. She'd been reading at age four with lessons from Rachel and Laura. They still tutored her from workbooks Mama bought at the Goodwill stores.

But Luna's favorite part of lessons was writing stories with Mama, who told stories of Luna's father that were disguised as fairy tales. Yesterday Luna had written down the story of a knight, Sir Winston, who died in battle. His wife lost her home and was forced to give her babies to a fairy for safekeeping.

She found work in a castle, where she had another child who was forced to hide in the castle tunnels because the king and queen hated children.

"That's me, right?" Luna had asked, and Mama just said, "Maybe."

The story work had started as part of her schoolwork when Luna was learning to write, but Luna loved the task of putting the adventures on paper. One day, she was going to tie them all together with ribbon and make a book.

"Was my father really a knight?" Luna had asked Mama.

"No, pumpkin. He worked in the oil industry. He was learning to be a welder."

A *welder*. It was something Luna would have to look up in the dictionary. She wished she could go upstairs and do that, but Leo still wanted together time.

"Let's watch something educational," Leo suggested, fueling Luna's hopes. Although Leo had blocked Nickelodeon and most kids' programs, some adult things interested Luna. Maybe he would choose one of the Harry Potter movies. They owned all of the DVDs because Leo claimed it matched the story of his life. He was the original Harry Potter, savior of the world, and he was thrilled that J. K. Rowling had told his story.

But instead Leo clicked through the stations of basic cable to the History Channel. A story about Vikings who hacked at each other with their swords and let out a holler as their dragon ships sailed through the sea. Why did they always shout and drink and fight?

"Can't I go read?" Luna whispered in her mother's ear.

Mama gave a stern shake of her head.

"Because we don't allow children in this house," Natalie said all the time, glaring at Luna. As if it were Luna's fault for existing. "But children grow, and someday you will be old enough to work for us. Earn your keep. Then you will be a real person in this house. Until then, you are your mother's problem."

When Luna asked Mama what that meant, she was told not to worry. "I'll take care of you." And Mama did. She brought Luna clothes when the sisters went shopping at Value Village or the Goodwill store. And just this week, she'd brought Luna beautiful soft underwear to wear over her breasts. Bralettes, Mama called them. "To give you some privacy, so, you know, you don't show through your shirt."

Luna didn't know that she'd been showing through, though she had noticed Leo looking. There was a kind of mad look on his face when he stared at her chest. It made her want to curl up like a wilting flower. She turned and caught him staring now, instead of watching the Viking ships cross a map of the Atlantic Ocean.

Folding her arms protectively across her chest, she leaned close to Glory and whispered, "Can we go upstairs?"

"As soon as this is over," Mama whispered back.

Luna let out a sigh, impatient to leave the circle of sad faces. But those were the rules. The stupid rules.

CHAPTER 23

"Look, I'm crazy about you," Tyler said as he put a twenty-dollar bill on the bar. He had a way of lowering his voice and watching her that made Glory feel like she was as amazing as a sunrise. "But we both know this is an adult relationship—a social thing. No strings, no commitment."

"Is that what you think?" Glory's voice was playful, but she had to struggle to keep her hand from shaking as she took a sip of her lemon drop. Nothing was working out for her. Tyler had been her best prospect, her shining star, but she'd failed again.

For weeks, she had been scouting men at the mall and meeting them at night, after she snuck out of the house in the dark. It was a difficult role to play, buttering men up, pursuing kindness, loyalty, and enough generosity to get the offer of a place for Luna and her to live while Glory saved some money, got a job, and hooked on to any government assistance she could get. For weeks, she'd been failing.

Shoe salesman Shawn had seemed promising. A sweet kisser and a romantic at heart, he had seemed ready to pledge his undying love to Glory until she suggested they go to his place.

"It'll have to be your place, since I'm between apartments." Turned out Shawn was living with his mother, who had stringent rules about what would go on under her roof. At first Glory had been devastated when that didn't work out, but she'd learned from it. Shawn had shown her that she had the courage and ingenuity to escape from the house at night, circumventing double-bolted doors locked from the inside that only Leo held the key to, as well as Leo's "laser-light security system." Shawn had helped her purchase a very basic cell phone for which she had been able to pay for six months' service in advance. It wasn't a smartphone, but she was able to text, which gave her a way to reach people outside, and it was small enough to stash in her bra. And Shawn had helped her realize that she still had a power over men. After a decade of hiding her light in a house of badgered slave women, Glory still knew how to shine and lead a moth to the flame.

Prospective hero number two managed the Cineplex at the mall, a step up, she'd thought, except that they had never made it out of his car in the parking lot of the Crescent Bar. Back in high school, her friend Kendall had called a guy like that "a human octopus." Not that Glory would have minded having sex if it were folded into a commitment. At thirty-four, she was ready to end the dry spell and release some of the demons that had been locked inside her. But Glory wasn't out for a good time. She needed a path of escape. When it became clear that Mr. Cineplex's car was not going to take her down that road, she declined his invitations.

And now Tyler Engle, a guy with a real job designing cabinetry for a major Northwest home builder, was rejecting her. He had shown her some of his designs the first night she met him at the Crescent—computerized maps of kitchens that he could open on his phone, with tiny measurements and three-dimensional models. A little bit of art and a lot of math. Tyler was a smart guy. She needed him to be her guy.

"Why don't you take some time to think about it," she told him. "Because we do have a good thing going. I hate to toss that away just because it's a little bit out of your comfort zone."

Tyler sucked air in through his teeth. "I'm afraid we're looking for some very different things."

"But that might change if we give it a try. Maybe you could just give us a place to stay until I get back on my feet."

"Sorry, Glory. I feel your pain; I really do. But that's not who I am. I'm meant to be single."

"So maybe it wouldn't be forever," she pleaded. "Please, just for a few weeks . . ."

"My apartment is tiny, and I've already got two kids. At least that's what my wife says." He grinned, but his pointed chin and gray bristled cheeks fell short of a roguish look. "That was a joke. She's my ex-wife."

"But I'm not laughing. It's hard to joke when your life is at stake."

"You're being overly dramatic. I realize living in a group home probably sucks, but it's a roof over your head for now. So why don't you stay there while you save up and get back on your feet? It's as good a plan as any."

Staying in the house was no plan at all, but Tyler couldn't know that from the limited information she'd given him. He wouldn't understand that her salary went directly to the house account, as did her food stamps from the state. He wouldn't believe that her girl was undocumented. He didn't comprehend the risk she took on the nights that she climbed out her window and slid down from the roof of the shed so that she could meet him. She had never mentioned how difficult it was to navigate the stunt with her bad left knee.

He didn't understand that she and Luna couldn't just leave; they needed to escape.

Not that she hadn't tried to get Leo and Natalie's permission to leave with her daughter. After Luna had been sequestered in the attic yet again, this time overnight, Glory had begun to wonder if Leo and his sister were annoyed enough to release them and be done with the hassle of hosting a mischievous ten-year-old.

She decided to appeal to Natalie, the numbers person, by presenting the prospect of saving Natalie money. As the bookkeeper for the hotel and the house, Natalie tended to reduce everything to what it cost her. "I can't pay that kind of money," was Natalie's line for anything from an overpriced piece of clothing from Goodwill to a repair that Leo had called in an electrician to handle. It wasn't just that Natalie did the accounting; she actually owned the hotel and house.

"She got rich in a lawsuit," Annabelle had explained in secret soon after Glory had joined the sisters. The two women had shared a room when Glory first arrived, and Annabelle had been happy to fill her in on the culture of the sisters or, as she had called it, "The Ballad of Leo and the Gnat." The Gnat had been her nickname for Natalie, a cruel nickname for a disabled person, Glory had thought, until she got to know Natalie better. With her unrelenting drive to burrow under your skin and find fault, Natalie was quite the irritating pest.

"Once upon a time there was a beautiful brother and a sister who wanted to rule a kingdom." Annabelle had paced as she told her story. "But, poor them, they didn't have any money and no one wanted to be in their kingdom. So they got lucky one day when the princess got hit by a car. I know, that doesn't seem to be so lucky, but the car was driven by this rich lady, and the princess wasn't hurt too bad. But she played up her injury and said she'd never walk again. And they sued the rich lady and got a big payout to get the kingdom rolling. So they bought a van and a hotel and a house. And they filled the house with broken women like us who were desperate enough to be their slaves and keep the hotel running for cheap. And the princess spent her days counting their money, and she was so happy. And the prince, well, you know how he spends his days, getting a lot of happy endings for himself. So they got their kingdom, King Leo and the Gnat."

A young woman with hair the color of ginger and a fiery temper, Annabelle was so convincing she appeared earnest even when you knew she was telling a lie. As a girl she had been kicked along through the foster care system until she'd found the gumption to stop kicking back and simply escape. She was the most defiant of the sisters, and Glory knew to take her story with a grain of salt.

Still, the tale had spurred a dozen questions. What about

the rest of Leo and Natalie Petrov's family? What was the truth about Natalie's spine injury? Hadn't they taken in all these women out of charity? "And why don't they just hire a staff to clean the hotel so that we can get our own jobs?"

"Because it's not about money; it's about power. Control. Don't you know anything?"

"I know that I'm grateful to have a place to live," Glory had replied, a bit defensively. Back then she'd been in the newly minted shine of being Leo's favorite, the chosen one who worked in the house and acted as his wife. At the time, she'd hoped to one day become his wife. A foolish hope. Young and foolish.

"I've lived in strangers' houses enough to know that there's always a price tag. They want your body, your scratch, or your soul. Some of them want a double dip. Everybody wants something from you."

Had Natalie Petrov gotten what she wanted out of Glory?

The questions echoed in her mind as she locked up her cleaning cart and moved swiftly down the hotel steps, following the festive diamond-patterned carpet to the front office to make her plea. It had been a good morning for Natalie, who had joked at the breakfast table about buying a cow to keep a steady supply of milk for the sisters. Later in the van she had said something about the power of the rain to wash the world clean. "See how the drops glitter on the windows?"

Glory had hurried through cleaning her rooms, wanting to take advantage of Natalie's rare good mood. In the reception area, Rachel was talking with a guest, a wispy gray-haired woman who was trying to hold back a tall, slender greyhound on a fat pink leash. Glory skirted around the desk and paused in the open doorway.

"Do you have a minute?" she asked.

Natalie's upper lip lifted in a sneer that made her pretty face seem broken. "Is there a problem?"

"All good," Glory said, remembering the first rule of the sisters: Leave the bad; focus on the good. She stepped inside the office and leaned against the framing of the door. "I've been thinking about how to smooth things out in the house since I caused a few ripples with Luna."

"You did. You flat out broke the rules." Natalie removed her glasses and wiped the lenses on the tail of her shirt. "We've had to make adjustments."

For your brother's child. Luna thought that her father was a poet named Winston, but Natalie knew the truth. And yet Natalie had always acted as if Glory had gotten pregnant from some negligent act like sitting on a dirty toilet seat. Glory had hated her for that. For treating her baby like a leper. Well, no more.

"I appreciate everything the sisters have done for us," Glory said, pressing on before she lost her nerve. "You know I love you and the sisters. You know I have always worked hard to support the sisters and the house. I'm the fastest cleaner you got here, and guests seem to notice."

Natalie squinted at her. "You sound kind of proud of yourself. You want credit for an ordinary job."

"No credit. I'm just saying, I do my best. But I know I've burdened the sisters. And I'm wondering if it might be time that Luna and I left the house."

"Why would you do that?"

"It's time I took responsibility for Luna. It's against the rules to have a child in the house," she said, parroting the scolding she'd heard for years, "and now I understand why. Children have different needs than adults, and now that Luna's getting older the confinement is difficult on her. I'm sure Leo mentioned he's had to lock her in the attic, more than once, because she went next door to visit with her friend."

Scowling, Natalie folded her arms over her chest. "You know I can't abide a child who doesn't obey the rules."

"All the more reason that Luna needs to leave the house. I don't want to burden the sisters anymore. But I know I have a lot to learn about making ends meet. I'm wondering what the two of us get in food stamps and what my weekly earnings at the hotel amount to?"

"That is all confidential information." Natalie closed a

binder that had been open to a chart of numbers and turned toward Glory. "And it's a moot point, because you're too late. Ten years ago I would have gladly cut you loose with her. It's been difficult having her in the house, sucking away our resources. Children are parasites, all of them. But now, after I've invested in this girl for a decade, now that she's close enough to the age where we can put her to work, you want to take her away. You'd be robbing me of thousands of dollars, Glory. And you know I don't like to lose money."

Glory was frozen, stumped by the money issue. She had hoped Natalie would see the savings in letting them go. "But I'm trying to save you from further grief. She's moving toward adolescence. Problems ahead. And then there's school. She needs to go to school before you can put her to work."

"She's gotten excellent homeschooling. She was reading Harry Potter when she was nine."

"But she needs to get out for social development. She's entitled to that, isn't she?"

"What school is going to enroll a kid who has no documentation, no record of immunizations?" Natalie asked quietly.

"But . . . but she was born in the house. I'm sure that's happened before. There must be a way she can get a birth certificate."

"That's the least of your worries. You see, she has a birth certificate." Natalie rolled her chair over to a dark wood file cabinet, pulled out a drawer, and extracted a folder. "Soon after she was born, I went through a midwife to let them know there was a home birth. She was kind enough to help us get a birth certificate for Luna. I knew I would need one to add her as a dependent on our taxes, not to mention increasing our food stamps."

The crisp piece of paper was embossed in the corner with a seal. Across the top was the banner: CERTIFICATE OF LIVE BIRTH. "She has a birth certificate!" Glory was tickled by the discovery as she read over the document. Name: Luna Petrov. So Leo had given his daughter his name. Leo was listed as the father, and as the mother . . .

Annabelle Clayton.

"Wait. There's a mistake here. It lists Annabelle as the mother instead of me."

"That's no mistake." Natalie's slash of a mouth curved in a smile. "I figured if I was going to invest in this child, Leo and I had to have ownership of her."

"Ownership? You can't own a child. And I'm her mother. You can't take that away from me."

Natalie shrugged. "What's done is done." She plucked the birth certificate from Glory's hand and dropped it back into the file.

"You need to change it. Put me down as her mother."

"Can't be changed. And we're not doing anything that will bring attention to our house. We can't have social workers and cops knocking on our door. You know what happens when you bring in outsiders."

Annabelle had contacted the police . . . she had paid the ultimate price.

Natalie waved Glory off. "Now go. Back to work or wait in the van. Out of here before you ruin my afternoon, which you've already done."

Glory walked stiffly down the hallway, nearly numbed by the prospect of servitude for the rest of her life. Slavery. And her daughter was being dragged into the mire behind her. She'd been a fool to think they could make a smooth exit. Now, even if she managed to sneak Luna out, Natalie could come after her with a kidnapping charge. A genetic test would prove that Luna was her daughter, but that didn't guarantee that she would get to keep her once Natalie got involved.

This was going to be difficult, but Glory and Luna had to do it. Glory was going to find a way, a man, an opportunity to get away . . . far, far away.

She had been sure Tyler Engle was going to be the answer to all her problems. But now the patina of pleasure was wearing off the bar scene as the server announced that it was last call, and Tyler declined.

"I'm going to miss you, Glory," he said. "Can I give you a ride home?"

"To your home?" she said sweetly, knowing he would take her there and hoping, hoping that she could persuade him bit by bit.

"Fine with me. As long as we stay in the moment."

She slid off the barstool and linked her arm through his, knowing she had nowhere else to go. The past and future were closed off to her. The moment was her only choice.

It was after 4:00 A.M. when he dropped her off a block away from the house. Climbing back up was always more challenging than sliding out, especially after a few drinks, but she had figured out a way to climb the woodpile, using the stacked layers as a ladder. Her bad knee ached as she climbed, and she looked forward to falling onto her bed and sleeping for a bit. Standing on top of the wood stack, she was high enough to reach the edge of the shed roof to pull herself up. The storage building was tiny, a six-by-four-foot rubber-coated shed that Leo used to store the lawn mower and garden tools. The fake-shingled roof was a bit slick with early-morning dew, but she managed to get some traction under her boots as she hobbled over to the side of the house and pushed up the un-latched window. After that, it was easy to hoist herself up a few feet, slip inside, and land on her bed. She had to wiggle on her back with her feet in the air to keep her boots off the comforter.

"Good morning, Mama." Luna's head popped out of the covers from the bed across the room like a sprite prairie dog peeking out of its hole. "Is it morning?"

"Not just yet. Go back to sleep, love bug."

"Did you have a good time with your friend?"

"Yes, I did." But not good enough. Tyler was not a hero. No one wanted to be a hero.

But maybe that was her mistake, looking for a savior when she should possess the courage to save herself. She removed the cell phone from her jacket pocket and stared at its shiny surface in her palm. What if she called the police right now? If the dispatcher believed her emergency and the police came to the house, would she be able to get herself and Luna to the door and talk to a cop? Would they believe that she was being held against her will? Would they believe that Luna was her daughter? And if they did, would they let her have custody of her own daughter once they had escaped?

She couldn't chance it, at least not right now. Too many times she had seen Leo smooth over things with the police. A few friendly anecdotes, a pitch about how he and his sister helped lost souls get back on their feet. Enter Natalie in a wheelchair, so respectful with her story of how their father had been a police sergeant in Idaho or Arizona or Oklahoma. A lie, but Glory had seen them use the story to woo everyone from the security guard at the mall to the cops who'd appeared at the door with lights spinning over the yard behind them.

The cops couldn't save her and Luna now.

There had to be another way.

CHAPTER 24

"She's waking up. Tamarind? Hey. Can you hear me? I love you. You're done with surgery, and you did great. The best patient in the history of medicine. Hey, *dilnashi*. Are you coming out of it? Maybe not. Take your time. We got time. Thank God, we got time."

Pete's voice came to her through cottony veils of anesthetics draped through her mind. Then the rhythmic beeping and whispering of the machinery, the monitors. She was in the hospital. Surgery. So afraid of dying, of leaving too soon on a cold metal table while the objects of her heart, her husband and daughters, her parents, were cut adrift in the void of her former life. So nervous, until she was not. Some drug mixed into the anesthesia to relax the patient, sending her off to the best sleep of her life.

Now the pain was raw and ever present, weighing on her chest, though it seemed separated from her—barely a problem—as her husband's voice flooded in through the symphony of hospital sounds.

"I'm okay?" The words came out like rusty barks from her burning throat. Damn, she needed water. She opened her eyes to see Pete leaning over her. Ruby was beside him, and Rima stood at the foot of the bed, crochet work in her hands as she observed, ever the mother hen.

"You *are* awake," Pete said, squeezing her hand. "How you feeling?"

"So thirsty."

"There's water here." Ruby produced a plastic white cup with a straw from the bedside table.

Tamarind's floppy hands were taped up and attached to lines, but she was able to hold the cup. She sipped cool, liquid heaven. The parched sensation eased, but her throat still felt pinched.

"I'll get the nurse," Rima said. "She wanted to know when you woke up."

"The surgery went well," Pete said, adding an explanation of the good things Dr. Hernandez had told him. As he spoke Tamarind's fog cleared enough for her to see their faces, her handsome husband and her thoughtful daughter, both of them at her bedside trying not to stare at her but unable to look away. Beyond the globes of their heads was a plant on the windowsill—a practical gift, no doubt from her mother—and a cluster of balloons anchored to some medical hookup on the far wall.

"Does it hurt?" Ruby asked.

"It's a good pain. It tells me I'm done with the bad part."

Ruby sniffed and gave a little laugh. "That's good."

"What time is it? Did you get something to eat?"

"We're going to get something in the cafeteria. We were waiting for you to wake up."

"That's sweet, but honey, you don't have to stay all day."

"I want to," Ruby said. "That was the deal."

Both girls had wanted to take the day off from school to be at the hospital for the surgery, which was fine for Ruby. When they learned that Aurora would not be able to play in that night's soccer game with a school absence, they had decided to send her to school and bring her to the hospital in the afternoon.

"Look what we brought you"—Ruby gestured behind her—"a bunch of balloons. You should have seen Dad trying to get them into the elevator. Some doctors got bonked."

Pete rubbed his forehead. "It would have been easier to corral a bag of marbles at Pioneer Square. You should have seen me trying to drive."

"I love them. They'll buoy my spirits," Tamarind said.

"Bah-dah-boom! Fresh out of surgery and she's making bad puns."

"I'm here every night. They've got me in stitches," Tamarind said, and Pete chuckled as he squeezed her hand.

Rima returned with the nurse, Hannah, who wanted to check Tamarind's vitals and the surgical dressing.

"This would be a good time for you all to take a walk, go grab some coffee or something to eat," Hannah said. "I'm going to give Tamarind some more pain meds, and she'll probably be sleeping for a while."

Tamarind just had time to finish her drink before she slipped down again into the bland world of hospital sleep. When she came up to the surface again, the buzz of voices was growing in her room.

The family was here. Pete's parents, her dad. Aurora in her soccer uniform. Ruby with her friend Maxi. Half the roster of Pete's very loud siblings, including Kaysandra, the sister who had seemed so argumentative at first, so strongheaded, until she had been unleashed as Pete and Tamarind's champion.

"I'm not supposed to be doing this, but I've been snooping around for you two, trying to get things going." Kaysandra's voice had boomed from the speakerphone when she called just a few weeks after they had completed the application to become foster parents. They had been asked to reveal financial information, their savings and debts, as well as personal information about how often they made love and whether they practiced a religion. A full shakedown, as Pete said. When was that? Twelve years ago? It seemed like yesterday.

"I can't be your caseworker, Pete. That wouldn't be right, with me being your sister and all, but I can push a few buttons if you know what I mean. And I saw those two little girls on the intake list, waiting for a foster family, and I thought, What the hell? Why not put them in a foster family that's interested in adopting? Foster parents like you two. An infant and her older sister who seems to be four, maybe five. We're not sure about her age, but we want to keep the sisters together, of course."

"Of course." Tamarind's heart was dancing in her chest at the prospect of an instant family. Two little girls. Daughters!

"Two children." Pete was hesitant. "We were kind of hoping for just one baby. One at a time, you know. Until we figure out what end is up." Tamarind smacked his shoulder and gave him a menacing look. "But two would work, I guess. You don't want to break up siblings."

"It's a dream come true," Tamarind said. "We are on board. Definitely."

"These little girls are mixed race, with dark hair and big ol' eyes. And Tamarind, I swear, the older one resembles you. Funny how that works out sometimes."

Tamarind pressed a hand to her heart and leaned into her husband's arms. Blessings were falling like rain from the sky.

"I'm going to have to call to find out more about their background. Not sure how these two landed in the system. And I'm going to connect with your caseworker, Lana, right? . . . Okay. Let me make some calls and I'll update you. . . . Okay, bye."

When Tamarind learned that the two girls had been placed in foster care after their mother abandoned them at a firehouse, the desire to pull them into her arms was irresistible. "The older girl, Ruby? I can't imagine what she's gone through. Abandoned by her mom, Pete. Her heart must be broken. My heart is breaking for her. And we can help her heal."

"How do we do that?"

"Love, you fool. We give her love and security, a forever home, a forever family."

He had kissed her, told her she was brilliant, and then they had driven to the other side of Portland to pick up the girls. At first sight Pete had been mesmerized by the demanding Aurora, a baby with smooth mocha-colored skin who wanted to be carried around when she wasn't trying to insert her fist in her mouth. The baby alone had been a handful, and Tamarind had been grateful that her mother had been willing to drop everything in Seattle and move into their guest room to care for the infant while Tamarind wooed Ruby. She had been determined to adopt a baby, but Ruby was the one who captured her heart immediately. The serious and methodical Ruby transitioned smoothly into the Montessori school but kept to herself most days, making up little games and role-playing with objects such as DUPLO blocks, Matchbox cars, crackers, and tub toys. That little girl could spend an hour just organizing rubber ducks in line to "visit" the closet. Most of the time Ruby was remarkably self-contained for a child that age, perhaps too self-disciplined. She seemed content when someone was reading to her, and she knew some children's books and poems by heart, which delighted Rima. But the little girl's resolve began to crack after a week or so, when she began to resist bedtime and positioned herself at the window each night after dark. Each night Tamarind asked her what she was looking for, but Ruby had no answer.

One night, she admitted she was waiting for her mommy.

Tamarind had suspected as much, though that didn't make it any easier to handle the situation. Pete looked up from his laptop and Rima looked over from the couch, where she bobbed her head over Aurora, making silly noises as the baby reached for her face.

Tamarind tried to be gentle without doting. "Your mommy isn't coming tonight."

"But she promised. She said soon."

"Sometimes mommies aren't able to take care of their children. That's why you're living with us."

"But I want Mommy," Ruby said softly.

"We understand that," Pete said. He came over and knelt in front of the little girl, her woeful blue eyes shiny with tears as she stared beyond her reflection into the night. "But since your mommy can't take care of you right now, we figure we're the next best thing. We'd like to take care of you and your sister. Do you think you could give us a chance?"

Ruby shrugged. "Maybe."

It was such an adult answer—noncommittal and evasive—that Tamarind had to smile. "That sounds hopeful."

Pete had offered to give Ruby a ride to bed on his shoulders, and suddenly he was a noisy elephant meandering through the apartment, using one arm as a trunk. Tamarind wanted to warn him to be careful, to hold on to her, but bit back her objections as Rima laughed and Aurora let out an animated squeal as her eyes lit on Ruby smiling down from Pete's shoulders.

The paperwork and legalities of adopting abandoned children required Pete and Tamarind to wage a slow and steady uphill battle. Giving up was not an option, but after a while anger burned brighter with each setback. Kaysandra became Tamarind's new best friend and champion of her girls, dismissing obstacles, saying, "This is nothing," or, "We can make this go away," or, "No worries. We got this."

And suddenly they were a family, juggling jobs, homework, day care, soccer games, and weekends at the coast just like other young families they knew. And suddenly they were finished with day care and sitters, done with Montessori school, and then all graduated from Bryant Elementary. Aurora was in junior high now, Ruby a sophomore in high school, and Tamarind had taken for granted how full and wonderful her life was until this cancer made her realize that it could end in the blink of an eye.

It was a good life, and according to the doctor, it looked like she'd be holding on for a little bit longer. She turned her head to scan the dozen or so people, her crazy, loud family, and joy bubbled up inside her. Wanting a better view, she tried to wriggle up higher in the bed, which made her wince. A reminder of what had brought her to this party. There was pain—oh yeah, searing, raw pain when the medications wore thin—but it was the suffering of life, the price all humans paid at one point in order to climb a mountain or birth a baby or sweat off the extra pounds dragging down a weak heart.

She was going to survive this. And she had so much to live for.

"How you doing, Tamarind?" Dressed in blue scrubs, the nurse emerged from the group and pulled some equipment closer to the bed. "I'm just here to get your vitals, and then I'll leave you alone." Hannah's dark ponytail bobbed as she glanced back at the crew. "Looks like you're a pretty popular person."

"Some people will do anything for a party," Tamarind managed to say before the thermometer was popped into her mouth.

Tears of joy sprang to her eyes at the sight of them all. Aurora showing something on her phone to her aunt Bernadette, her favorite. Ruby and her friend Maxi checking out the flowers on the windowsill. Pete's mom, Janeece, was admiring the print of Rima's dress, while Karim and Doc examined unlit cigars, Doc's evil hobby. Maisie was passing out candy, and Pete and James were sampling them all.

"You're doing great," Hannah said, removing the blood pressure cuff.

"Do you want some candy?" Tamarind offered. "Before my husband eats it all."

"No, thanks. I'm trying to be good, with the holidays coming. I'll be back later to check on you. I'm on until midnight."

"This one's a trooper," Kaysandra said, patting Tamarind's knee through the blanket. "She's got the McCullum fighting spirit."

Kaysandra and her husband, Ed, closed in to chat with the nurse, buttering her up to ease the offense of flouting the hospital rules of allowing only two visitors at a time in ICU.

Hannah smiled, insisting that she didn't work for Security, so emptying out the room wasn't her job. "Just ring the call button if you need me," Hannah said before slipping out of the crowded room.

Pete came over and put a box of candy on the table. "Save this for later, babe. It's supposed to be for you." He rubbed his jaw. "I think I cracked a tooth on that peanut brittle. But it was worth it. Damn good."

"We'll get your tooth fixed," Tamarind choked out, suddenly aware she was full-fledged crying.

"Whoa, whoa, whoa, what's up?" Pete lifted her hand, leaning close. "Are you in pain?"

"Tears of joy. I'm just so relieved to be okay, and to have everyone here. I'm so happy, Pete. So lucky to have our family."

"These crazy people are making you happy?" He kissed her hand, smiling. "Well, either you have a lunatic family that loves you, or you're still on the good drugs."

CHAPTER 25

"I feel a little bad, doing this while your mom is in the hospital," Maxi said as they waited for a light to turn green. They had driven to the East Center Mall from the hospital and started cruising down nearby streets in search of Ruby's former home.

"Don't guilt me, Maxi. We've already been through this, and you know this is the best way to keep it from my mom, who would only be hurt by it. And when else would we get a chance to go off together, no questions asked by either of our moms? This is the perfect time. I need the distraction, and since I saw Glory at East Center a few weeks ago, I know this is the right mall."

"How come we never shop here?"

"It's too far. And you know they've had those shootings."

Maxi opened her mouth in a wide O of shock. "You're serious?"

"They were gang related," Ruby said, working hard to keep her own resolve from chipping away. "We're good. It's daytime. I'll protect you."

"Why doesn't that make me feel better?"

They had driven in loops around the East Center Mall in search of the two-story house with a gated fence around the front yard. Ruby remembered funny things about the house where they had lived on the first floor. The morning light in the bedroom window that made the yellow wall shine. The fat rhododendrons that dangled at the front window, reminding her of a lamb's head, scaring her when they jiggled against the glass in the breeze at night.

"It's walking distance to the mall; I know it is. How hard could it be to find it?" Ruby asked in frustration when the road from the mall parking lot had sent them on a loop toward the interstate. When Maxi stopped short at a red light, Ruby lost it. "Oh my God, can we get off this road?"

"I'm trying. Don't make me crash."

"Sorry, I just want to find this place."

"Can't we just go look for her at the mall?" Maxi asked.

"I'm not sure she's there every day, and I want to find her house." *Our house.* Somehow, returning to the Cape Cod–style home was going to bring her closer to the little girl she used to be, closer to her biological parents. Especially to Winston Noland. She knew that he had died in Alaska. That probably added to Glory's reasons for giving Aurora and her up for adoption. But she wanted to be in a place where she could remember what it felt like to be his little girl.

"At least it's not raining," Ruby said as they took a wide curve on the dry roadway. She couldn't imagine trying to scout out the neighborhood in a dense November rain.

At last Maxi found a place to turn around, and they headed back toward the mall. They had spent another twenty minutes rolling slowly down residential streets when Ruby spotted it— the house with the dormers. Sunlight gleamed on the metal gate of the picket fence, as if it were a signpost. "There . . . I think that's it."

Maxi pulled up across the street and they both turned to stare at the tired but sturdy house. The olive green shutters, the patch of green lawn, the small painted porch where she had danced as she waited for Mommy to load the stroller. The fat leaves of mature rhododendrons blocked the bottoms of the front windows, though their summer blossoms had gone to seed.

"That's it," she breathed. "We lived on the ground floor—Glory might still rent it—and there was an old woman who lived upstairs. I think she owned the house. She kind of scared me, but then a lot of things scared me back then."

"Wow."

Ruby nodded. "Wow."

"So do you think your mother still lives there?"

"I guess we need to find out."

Maxi's dark eyes flared with excitement. "Are we going to the door? Oh my God, this is so out of the box. Delilah's going to be pissed that she's missing out."

"She probably won't even answer the door," Ruby muttered as she pushed open the car door and went to the sidewalk. Now that she was here, standing in front of the place of her fuzzy memories, the whole mission to find Glory seemed doomed. Best-case scenario, if she found her birth mother, what could Glory possibly do or say to make her feel better?

I was wrong to leave you and your sister behind.

My greatest regret in life is giving you up.

I'm so proud of what you've become.

Would any of those words be a salve to the malady that had brought her here? Ruby wished she could contain the curiosity that drove this search. She was usually such a rational person, but this was one part of her she couldn't understand or explain. Sort of like a bee sting that felt itchy, but then it hurt worse when you scratched it. She knew she was headed toward pain, but she couldn't stop the forward momentum.

The gate creaked as she pushed it open.

"Sort of like a horror movie." Maxi stayed close, her voice low.

They pushed forward through a yard that was green and claustrophobic. Thick cedars grew tall along the fence line on one side, overtaking the passage to the side of the house. The walkway and flower beds were lined by bushy plants—clumps of spider grass, dry heather, and lavender—that made Ruby think of aliens lurking, waiting for their moment to rise up and strike.

As the girls stepped under the awning of the cement porch, Maxi pointed to the NO SOLICITATIONS sign.

"We're in trouble."

"No," Ruby insisted. "We're not selling anything."

They decided to ring both bells, for upstairs and downstairs. There was no answer, of course, but Ruby could see into part of the downstairs living room. No one seemed to be home, but the little coffee table seemed familiar. She wished she could jump off the porch and press into the bushes for a better look through the window, but that would just be weird.

After a few minutes, Maxi sighed. "Nobody home."

"Figures." After one last try of the doorbells, they went back down the walk and pushed through the gate. "She probably doesn't live here anymore," Ruby said, looking back at the house.

"Or maybe she's at work. A lot of people aren't home during the day."

Looking beyond her friend, Ruby noticed a motion at the house as the front door was tugged open, a face appearing in the passage. It was an older woman, the age of Ruby's grandmothers, with short gray hair styled in a big puff around her head.

"No solicitations, girls," she said, moving down the walk with a slight limp. "We're not buying or signing anything."

"Sorry to disturb you, ma'am," Maxi said, "but we're not selling anything."

"We're looking for someone who lived here," Ruby said. "Maybe she still does. Glory Noland?"

The woman shooed them away from the gate, and Ruby stepped back, deflated, thinking it was over until she realized the woman was just checking her mail. "What do you want with Glory?" she asked, opening the door of the curbside box.

"It's nothing bad," Maxi insisted.

"She's my birth mother," Ruby said, getting to the core of the issue. "I used to live here."

"Is that so?" The woman tucked letters and flyers under one arm and peered at Ruby, as if seeing her for the first time. "Ah, I see it. Those blue eyes, and your father's cheekbones. You must be the older daughter. That was a long time ago, but I remember. You were little at the time."

"I was four when I was adopted."

The woman grunted. "Never understood that. She was a good mother till then. Got you and your sister out of the house every day, and she was patient. I never heard her raise her voice and I heard most everything. But when your father died, I guess it was too much."

"So you're the landlady?" Ruby asked. "The owner of the house."

"Ellen Carlucci. And your name is, no, don't tell me. Rosie?"

"Ruby."

"I was close." Ellen hobbled into the yard and closed the gate behind her, immune to the squealing metal.

"So Glory doesn't live here anymore?" asked Maxi.

Ellen shook her head. "She packed her clothes and hurried out of here after she gave up you and your sister. Left every stick of furniture, so I had to rent it furnished for a while. She owed me a month's rent, too, but I didn't go after her for it. Glory had enough problems. You know, when your parents first came to me, I was one of the few people in this neighborhood who would rent to a mixed-race couple. I thought, Here's a couple that needs a break, so I gave it to them. And they were good tenants until your father died. After that, I guess she just couldn't cope on her own."

Ruby's fingertips followed the peaks at the top of the picket fence. "Do you know where she went from here?" she asked.

"I don't have a forwarding address. She was out of here in a flash, and I ended up getting most of my information from Social Services. They came around here trying to clear up loose ends so you could be adopted after Glory disappeared. But I know she hooked up with that cult group led by Leo what's-his-name. Well, I'd call them a cult, but some folks say he's just a generous man helping out women in need. He and his sister own a hotel near the mall, and a lot of their staff are broken-down women who can't make it at anything except cleaning rooms. Maybe it's all charitable. I mean, it's not like he's trying to shove some religion down their throat. They're not exactly Bhagwan followers. But personally I wouldn't want to be beholden to any man. I'm no fan of the mall, but last time I was there, couple of years ago, I saw them buzzing around the food court and my radar went up. Way too cheerful, that band of sisters."

"The sisters," Ruby said, remembering. "That's what they used to call themselves, the women who met at the food court when I was little. Is that who you're talking about?"

"Probably. My friend Carol works at the mall. She chats with them when she's on break. Says they're delightful. But I have my doubts. I was never a joiner."

"Do these women live at the hotel?" Ruby asked.

"No. There's some kind of a group home, a house not far from here. But the other side of the mall, thank God. I don't think I could stand having a cult in my neighborhood."

"So maybe we'll check the mall," Maxi said.

"Thanks for your help, Ms. Carlucci," Ruby said, realizing she did recall being scared by a younger version of the woman before her. But back then, Ruby lived in a small world, uncomfortable with anyone beyond the small scope of her parents.

Ellen Carlucci nodded. "You seem like a good girl. Don't get mixed up with those people."

"We won't," Ruby promised as she and Maxi got back into the car.

"A cult." The situation made Ruby uncomfortable. "It's too weird."

"Right? I've never heard of this group. But a lot of people throw the word 'cult' around. Some people think sororities and fraternities are cults. Let's not judge."

"But I remember those women. It's definitely weird." Ruby pressed her fingertips to her temples. "I had to have the one mother who leaves her kids to join a cult. Maybe we shouldn't go—"

"Are you kidding me? It's right down the road, and we've got a hot lead. We are *so* going."

CHAPTER 26

Luna peered through the crack in the back fence, searching for signs of her friend at the house that sat catty-corner to theirs. "Hazel, where are you?" she said quietly, noting that Hazel's drapes were closed and her mom's car was gone from the driveway. Maybe she was still in school. Luna usually didn't come into the backyard until after three, but today she'd been impatient and annoyed, driven out of the house by Sienna and Leo, who were having an angry game of chase through the kitchen and up the stairs.

"I wish you were home." Luna sighed and looked at the workbook in her hands. *Oh, well.* With the sun out, it wasn't too cold. She decided to sit at the splintered picnic table at the back of the yard and do her assignments while she waited for Hazel. She opened the book to where the pencil was tucked inside and frowned. Long division. The opposite of multiplication. She understood how to do it, but it was so boring. Even interesting things could be boring when you couldn't share them with a friend.

The back door banged open and Sienna stepped out onto the porch. "Just leave me alone!"

"Sienna. Come back here, now!" Leo called, emerging from the house.

She wheeled around and stretched her arms out. "Stop. Just leave me alone."

Luna chewed the pencil, watching. She had never seen them fight before. Usually Sienna finished her chores and then disappeared into the big first-floor bedroom occupied by Leo and Natalie.

"I told you, I'm not in the mood." Sienna crossed the back patio, then spun around to face him. "Come close to me and I'm going to throw up on your shoes."

Throw up? That seemed kind of funny to Luna, but Sienna didn't seem to be joking. And neither Sienna nor Leo had noticed her sitting at the table at the back of the yard. She lowered her eyes to the workbook but listened carefully.

"I told you," Leo said, "we'll take care of it without Natalie. I don't want her to know."

"Damn right she doesn't need to know. It's my body, and she's got no right to inflict her witchy ways on me."

"She's not that way. It's her generosity that gives you food to eat and a roof over your head. You should be grateful to Natalie."

"Whah-whah-whah-whah!" Sienna snapped her hand at him as if it were a quacking duck. "Natalie this and Natalie that. That's all I ever hear around here. If you think she's so great, why don't you get her to suck you off?"

"Don't say that." Leo was on his feet, his voice an angry growl that reminded Luna of riled bears on a nature show. "Don't ever say that."

"Oh my God! I hit a nerve, didn't I? You actually mess around with your sister? That's so disgusting I—"

Before she could get the words out, Leo smacked her in the face. He hit her so hard that she was knocked to the ground, where she huddled in a ball, legs to her chest.

Luna scrambled up from the table and ran to where Sienna lay on the winter grass, hands cupping her jaw. At first she seemed like a rag doll, so limp and still that Luna wondered if she were dead. But then Luna got close enough to see Sienna's chest moving and hear her whimpering like a wounded kitten. Without a word, Luna stared from Sienna up at Leo. This was the monster that had killed Annabelle. Somehow, he didn't look any different from the everyday Leo.

There was sorrow on his face, but from the way his fists were clenched at his sides Luna wondered if he would strike again.

"What are you doing out here?" He squinted down at her. "Spying on us?"

As if it were Luna's fault. Standing her ground, she held up the pencil in her hand and pointed to the worn gray picnic table where her book was sprawled.

Leo took it all in with a sneer, as if the sunshine, the yard, and the blue sky disappointed him. When he turned away and went inside, Luna realized she had been holding her breath.

Sienna began crying then, sobbing into her hands.

Luna squatted down and tried to console her, touching her hair and patting her back, the way Mama did when Luna was upset. "Poor girl. What were you two fighting about?"

"I hate her."

"You mean *him*."

"No, that bitch Natalie. He doesn't see that she's using us."

"But he's the one who hit you."

Sienna pushed away from the ground and sat there on the porch, one hand still cupping her face as she glared at Luna. "You don't know anything."

This was the Sienna Luna knew: mean and cold. Still, Luna felt sorry for her. "Do you want some water?"

"Get me some milk."

"But I can't." Beyond a few cheap staples such as apples, oatmeal, and ramen noodles, they weren't allowed to touch food in the fridge or pantry between meals.

"You're so useless." Sienna stood up and headed inside. "I'll get my own damned milk."

"But that's against the rules."

Sienna did not bother answering.

CHAPTER 27

"We can't stay long," Ruby said as they pushed through the doors of the mall, entering the odd echo chamber of lame music, voices, and stale air in the vestibule. "If my dad gets home before me, he'll know something's up."

"You can tell him we stopped to eat. The rules are out the window today," Maxi said. "So what's the plan?"

"Those cult people hang out in the food court. If she's here, I'll introduce myself. If not, we'll head back to West Green."

"Wow. You're sounding brave again. I like that."

"I'm faking it." Now that she was this close to meeting Glory, a niggling sensation tugged at Ruby's conscience. Guilt over lying to her parents mixed with fear of being caught. "But I've gotten this far. I can't turn back now."

"You go, girl. But first I have to pee." Maxi nodded toward the restrooms by the entrance.

"All right. Meet me over by the fountain." The fountain in the center atrium had always been the focal point of the East Center Mall. Ruby hadn't thought much about it until a few years ago when she saw a photo of the Native American statue on a Christmas ad and a memory of pennies in a fountain had flashed in her mind. Had that been the place? The lines and angles of the man atop the rock seemed reassuring and familiar, like an old shoe. She'd suspected this was the place her mom had let her make wishes and throw pennies into the pool.

Now, as Ruby made her way to the fountain, she listened for the sound of rushing water but heard only the whine of drills punctuating the mall music version of a Nirvana song. Two men carried a flat board in front of her, blocking her view for a second as she tried to get her bearings. There he was, the Native American man atop the rocks. He wore cowboy chaps and a vest—not really the clothing of indigenous tribes like the Chinook or Clackamas people—but there was something cheerful about his demeanor, curious and wise and content. The Americanization of the West, as she'd learned in school. The statue and the rocks looked smaller than she remembered as they were being walled in by workers constructing a barricade. Ruby moved around the wooden fence and peered down the steps to the blue-painted pool. It was dry now, looking a little sad and moldy.

"What's happening with the fountain?" she asked one of the workers.

"We're covering it up. Too much of a liability. Putting in a garden area with a mobile stage. Should be done by Christmas. Gotta be ready for the mall's Santaland."

"But don't they have a stage over in the north wing, in front of J. C. Penney's?" Ruby said, recalling one of the few times she'd been here with her family, when she'd sung in the middle school choir for a holiday concert.

"That's right," the man responded, wiping his brow with his shirt sleeve. "They used to have a J. C. Penney's, too, but things change."

It was one of the stupidest plans Ruby had ever heard. Who needed a fake indoor garden when Portland was full of green spaces? "What about the statue?"

"He's staying for now. The designer wanted him out, but now people got a petition started. Who knows?"

Why it pissed her off so much she wasn't sure. Maybe she'd been hoping for a poignant reunion with her birth mother in a beautiful setting, one of those Hallmark moments when two people hugged and the picture blurred to soft focus. Good luck with that. Fountain or not, she sensed it was going to be sad and less than satisfying, if she and Maxi even found Glory at all.

Maxi joined her and they rode the escalator up to the second level, talking about the disappearing fountain. Maxi, who had never been to this mall, didn't have an opinion about the fountain.

"How could you not care? The Native American fountain is the signature of this mall," Ruby said.

"Don't pick on me. My mom doesn't leave her zip code. We don't come to the east side, and she hates malls, anyway. You know she's the Amazon queen."

"Sorry, I'm just . . ." Distracted, Ruby searched the area around the food court.

"Just freaking out?"

"Kind of. I don't see her. Those women at the table there? In front of Sbarro. That's them."

"Really?" Maxi squinted, assessing. "They look kind of normal for a cult. Old and boring, actually."

"Like zombie women. But no one ever said a cult was exciting."

"So. She's not here." Maxi scraped a bunch of dark curls behind one ear. "That's disappointing. So what do we do? I don't know cult etiquette, but I have a feeling we shouldn't ask her friends about her."

"Probably not." Ruby turned away from the food court, not wanting to be caught staring. "I guess we should go. Try again another time." When that would be she couldn't say. Their lives were jam-packed with school and all the extra things like music lessons and debate team and Model UN that were supposed to help get you into a good college.

"Okay, then," Maxi said, "but maybe, since we're already out, we should stop at Koi Fusion on the way back. I'm kind of starving."

As they headed toward the escalator Ruby noticed a woman with dark hair staring into the window of a teen clothing store. Dressed in jeans and a flannel shirt, she was the same size as Glory, but her face seemed older, her skin pale, her lips chapped, and the hollows of her eyes shadowed. Like a flower wilting in the dark, starving for sun and water. Ruby reached out for her friend. "Wait," she told Maxi, nodding toward the woman.

Maxi swung around and gaped. "Is it?"

"Think so." Her heartbeat accelerating as she edged closer to the woman, Ruby cleared her throat. "Excuse me. I'm just—" The woman turned to her and Ruby felt a stab of recognition as their eyes met. Those eyes, purplish blue, like cornflowers, were imprinted on her heart. "Are you Glory Noland?"

Glory's spine straightened as she looked around suspiciously, then nodded.

"I'm Ruby. I'm . . . I mean, I used to be—"

"My Ruby." She whispered the words as it sank in. "My daughter. Oh, my sweet girl, look at you." Tears glistened in Glory's eyes as she took Ruby's hands, opened them wide, and then brought them to her chest. "You've grown into a beauty, but that's no surprise. Your father was so handsome, and I see you've got his cheekbones. You must be a teenager now."

"Sixteen." Ruby's throat was tight with a ball of emotion, but she tried to swallow past it as she pulled back to gesture to her friend. "I just got my license, but my friend drove here today. This is Maxi."

"Hey there, Maxi. I'm Glory." She spared Maxi a look but then quickly turned back to Ruby, as if to prevent her from slipping away. "I'm just so glad to see you, after all this time. My heart's beating like crazy and I know I need to stop gushing, but I can't help myself."

"It's okay," Ruby said. Normally she hated when people made a fuss over her, but she didn't mind Glory's gushing in such a meek way. "I'm just glad you remember me."

"How could I not? A mother never forgets her babies."

And most mothers don't leave their babies at a firehouse, prodded a voice from a dark place in Ruby's heart. Even as Ruby longed to feel a connection to this woman, she felt guilty about being here, about lying to her parents, about needing more than her parents could give.

"I can't believe that . . . that you would just recognize me out of the blue," Glory said. "It's a miracle."

"Almost," Maxi said. "She's been trying to find you."

"I have," Ruby admitted.

"Aw. That's so sweet, but I'm a little pressed for time. Meeting some friends." Glory looked toward the food court, caution in her eyes. "Is there some emergency? Is your sister okay? You and Aurora got to stay together, right? I left instructions for them to keep you together."

"We were adopted together, and there's no emergency. I was just curious. I hope that's okay."

"It's wonderful," Glory insisted. "I don't have long to talk, but I'm so happy to see you. And your baby sister's doing okay?"

"Aurora's fine. She's not a baby anymore, except . . ." *Except when she's self-absorbed and snotty.* The words nearly flew out, but Ruby restrained herself. Somehow, that seemed like a betrayal of Pete and Tamarind, who had been loving but firm parents; it wasn't their fault if Aurora was a brat, but it would seem that way. "She's good. She's in junior high now."

"She's a great soccer player," Maxi said, "and Ruby is amazing at school. She's on honor roll every semester."

"Of course you are. I knew you were a smart one, the way you could entertain yourself for hours. You memorized books and poems and you could have fun with just about any object. Paper clips or crackers. You used to line them up, and then move them along. Very organized."

"She still does that with her collection of rubber ducks," Maxi said, evoking a scowl from Ruby, who wanted to hear Glory talk. "Just sayin'."

"I find them soothing," Ruby admitted. "Like stress balls. There are worse vices."

"That's for sure," Glory said. "I think, back then, you manipulated small objects as a way of controlling things. Sort of a comfort ritual. You were so cute."

A chill rippled up Ruby's spine at the weirdness of it all, this woman who knew a part of her so well but didn't really know the person she'd become. There was a huge divide between past and present.

"I am so sorry." Glory was glancing over her shoulder. "But I have to go. I'd love to talk more, but I can't. My friends . . . they're a very protective group. Overly protective, but I shouldn't complain."

"I understand," Ruby said.

"But I really want to talk more. Maybe we can meet again. One afternoon here?"

"I have school, but maybe after that?"

"Of course. I wouldn't want you to . . . to miss school. But I don't get here until two thirty or three, and we're usually leaving by four."

"What about weekends?" Ruby asked. "Would that be better?"

"Every day is the same. Work in the morning, and . . . and I need to be home in the evenings. But most afternoons, my group comes here after work."

"You guys should exchange cell phone numbers," Maxi suggested.

"Good idea. Here's my number." Glory pulled a flip phone from the pocket of her jeans and smiled at the surprised girls. "I know, my phone's a dinosaur, but it does the trick. Takes a little longer to text, but it works."

Ruby put the number in her phone while Maxi helped Glory add Ruby's number. *Thank God for Maxi.* Ruby's insides were now a ball of dough, mushy and flat from the crazy day, which started with Mom's early-morning surgery and brought her to finally coming face to face with her birth mother.

It was all over in ten minutes or so, leaving Ruby to mull over her new keepsakes. An awkward meeting. A sliver of the past. And a phone number that she would always keep hidden from her parents.

CHAPTER 28

On the short drive from the mall to the house, Glory tried to absorb it all—her first daughter, all grown-up now. Sixteen. And so beautiful, with Winston's high, strong cheekbones and Glory's blue eyes. It broke Glory's heart to learn that Ruby had been searching for her. She didn't deserve that kind of loyalty, especially after what she had done, leaving her two girls behind. She still winced when she thought of that day, that she had kept walking and not looked back. A million times over she tried to tell herself that she'd been run-down and grieving, her head not quite right, and a million times over she winced in guilt and shame.

The sight of Ruby at the mall today had sparked joy and fear, hope and anxiety. The wonder of seeing her firstborn had been wrapped in a determined sense that destiny was paving a way for them. Ruby had been brought back into her path for a purpose. Her oldest daughter was destined to help her youngest. Glory was beyond feeling guilty or mercenary for asking for help, especially after she learned that Ruby was a girl who took her responsibilities seriously. This was meant to be.

But she couldn't rush things. Glory planned to give it time: a few meetings to let their relationship solidify before Glory revealed that Ruby had another sister. And then Ruby would probably need more time to adjust after that before committing to helping them escape. Glory could tell that her Ruby was still steady and slow, not the impetuous type. If Glory pushed too hard, the thread of their tenuous connection might snap.

All the time they'd been talking, Glory had been afraid that Leo would come along and figure things out. These days he didn't make the trip to the mall very often, but if he got an inkling of this he might prohibit her from ever going to the mall again. That was the way he and Natalie ruled when someone was caught connecting with the outside world.

"When there's a tumor," Natalie always said, "you need to cut it out."

Leo and Sienna hadn't made it to the mall today. That was good news for Glory, who'd been able to speak with Ruby undetected, but she would have to be careful for future meetings. Maybe they would meet inside a women's clothing store or the ladies' room—a place where Leo wouldn't feel comfortable. But even in those places, there was the threat of being discovered by the sisters.

As they pulled into the garage, Glory had to snap back to reality when Natalie demanded help getting out of the van. "Glory, you can take one side and Kimani will take the other. I don't know what I did to myself, but both my legs feel numb."

Climbing out of the van, Glory wondered if the paralysis was real or just an attention-getting device. That was the mystery of Natalie's injury; some days Natalie got in and out of the van and moved in and out of the wheelchair on her own. Other times, she needed help with even small movements. Over the years Natalie had talked about the accident causing sciatica and a herniated disk, but Leo had also mentioned childhood polio. Glory suspected there was a medical reason for Natalie's complaints, at least part of the time.

"Maybe it's cramps," Kimani said as she reached into the car to lift Natalie out. Kimani didn't seem to mind that she was Natalie's unofficial caretaker. Her nurturing instincts and strength served her well in that role, a role Glory would have hated, despite the favors Natalie showered on her pet.

Glory helped lower Natalie into her wheelchair, her nostrils tweaked by the flowery scent of Natalie's hair. Definitely special shampoo. The rest of them had to use toiletries from the dollar store.

"Do you want a heating pad?" Kimani asked as she propped Natalie's shoes on the footrests. "It might help sciatic pain."

"I guess we'll start with that," Natalie said, a sour pucker to her mouth as she was pushed up the ramp. "The paralysis is back!" she called to Leo, who stood waiting in the kitchen doorway. "I hope it's just a virus."

"I hope so. You need to get better, Sister." Leo seemed so handsome and benevolent, standing there, greeting his sister. His beautiful façade. "Come on inside and we'll help you feel better."

Glory was relieved when Kimani wheeled Natalie to the master suite, allowing Glory to escape. As she climbed the stairs, favoring her sore knee, she allowed hope to bubble up inside her again. The possibility was thrilling. The girl who was linked to her past might also guarantee her future. Inside their room Luna looked up from the floor, where she sat cross-legged reading a slim volume of Dickens's *Christmas Carol*. "Mama, have you read this? Scrooge is a mean old man."

"It gets better." Glory kissed her daughter's forehead, pausing to smooth back feathery strands of auburn hair. "I have some very exciting news."

Luna rose to her knees. "Is it about Hazel? Did you meet her mom? Is Leo going to allow me to go over there? He was extra mean today. He got in a fight with Sienna and—"

"Hold on. I want to tell you my news, because this is something wonderful you'll never guess." Glory flipped open her cell phone and went to the directory to show her Ruby's number. "See this number? Her name is Ruby, and I saw her at the mall today."

Luna's eyes opened wide with expectation. "A new friend?"

"Not just a friend. She's my daughter. You, my darling girl, have not one, but two secret sisters."

CHAPTER 29

Thanksgiving with the McCullums was a crazy, loud mixture of too much food, too much pie, and a lot of hugging. The feast was always hosted by Janeece and Doc McCullum at their converted farmhouse out in Wilsonville, with a few acres of land, a spacious house, and double ovens for the cooks in the family. Ruby usually looked forward to the gathering, but this year she saw it as a chance to be herself again, a chance to re-possess the Ruby who worried about SAT scores and an annoying little sister instead of the guilt-ridden girl who was torn between one mom battling cancer and chemo and another one desperately trying to find a bond that wasn't there.

For a while her immersion worked. Gathered around the fire pit in her grandparents' backyard, she sipped on a bottle of soda pop—the grapefruit kind, Squirt—while she chatted with the cool cousins, Casey and Alice and DeShaun and Nayasia and Shark, about TV shows and music and places to travel. Alice had started college in August, and Ruby listened as she talked about what she liked (a whole new friendship pool and being able to stay out all night) and what she hated (dining hall food and community bathrooms in the dorms). Older cousins such as Jade, Keandre, and Bozie moved through their group, some staying to talk and others heading out to the fields out back to toss a Frisbee or football in the fading light.

At one point, Ruby noticed Aurora watching from the back deck, wanting to join in but knowing she didn't really belong with the high school and college kids. Ruby took a long drink of soda, considering the situation. Then, in a burst of generosity, she got up and went to her sister. "Come on over and hang with us," she said, putting her arm around Aurora and guiding her over to the circle. "It's warmer by the fire."

At first Aurora was quiet and uncharacteristically low-key, but then Casey asked her where she got her jacket and she asked DeShaun if he was playing football this year, and just like that Aurora was hanging with the older cousins.

You're welcome, Ruby thought, knowing her sister would never thank her. That was okay. They'd all been through a rough month with Mom's cancer and surgery, and it wasn't over yet. Everyone needed a little bit of lightness right now.

When they were called inside for dinner, Aunt Kaysandra clanged a spoon against a glass to quiet the group for a speech. For the toast, Aunt Bernadette and Grandma passed out champagne to adults and sparkling cider to the kids. Ever since Ruby could remember, her grandpa Doc, a retired physician, had always made the speech about the family tradition of kindness. Dad said that Doc hated public speaking, but that his father, Ernie, had always made a Thanksgiving speech and Doc needed to carry on that tradition. Although Ruby had never met Ernie McCullum, she had written a school paper about how her great-grandfather had served as a medic in World War II and gone to medical school when he returned home. He had learned how to blow the trumpet on an instrument given to him by one of his army buddies. Ernie sounded like a cool guy.

"We have so much to be thankful for." Doc's big bass voice filled the room, quieting the stragglers. "I'm grateful that we're here together as a family to celebrate another Thanksgiving. We are fortunate to have each other, safe homes, and a country that affords us the right to stand up for what matters to us. In the tradition of the late Dr. Martin Luther King, our family seeks to share the abundance of this holiday by performing good deeds for people outside our circle. I like to think that these acts of kindness reflect who we are as a family. . . ."

Family . . . Ruby scanned the people in the room full of fidgeting kids and smiling adults and wondered why she had ever wanted to look for her birth mother when she had a big, noisy, loving family right here. She'd caved to selfish curiosity, and now she was sick with regret and disappointment. After years of imagining a soul mate of a mother, Ruby had learned that her birth mother was simply an ordinary woman, somewhat tortured and worn down by time, work, and poverty. She could not expect poetry or song from a tired, nervous, discontent woman.

One of the most embarrassing parts of the whole thing was that Ruby had brought this all upon herself by searching for Glory Noland. And as soon as she had opened that Pandora's box, she could not stuff Glory back in and forget they ever met.

In the week since they'd first met, they had gotten together twice at the mall. The first time Glory had texted her to meet, Ruby's heart had sung with joy at the invitation. As if her birth mother wanted her after all these years. As if there were a connection between them, two complete strangers.

Ruby had realized her mistake when she'd driven back to the mall in Northeast Portland on her own and Glory had hustled her into the mall's game arcade, a dimly lit room strafed by the flashing lights and noise of pinball and video games.

"I'm sorry we have to meet here, but I can't be seen talking with you by any of the sisters. We reach out to strangers when we have space in the house, sort of a recruitment thing, but otherwise we're not supposed to be socializing."

"You recruit people to join your group?"

The uneasiness that had seeped in at that point had not been assuaged when Glory assured Ruby that she wasn't soliciting her to join. "I just want to get to know you again," Glory had said, but Ruby had sensed that there was something more at play. It felt like Glory wanted something from her, but Ruby couldn't figure out what.

"So it *is* a cult," Maxi had said when Ruby recounted the meeting.

"She says no, that there's no religious orientation. But to me it sounds like a tiny dictatorship ruled by the sister and brother team. She's locked into a strict schedule of cleaning hotel rooms every day and being at the house every night. Her only break is in the afternoon at the mall, when they give her a little money for food and small stuff. Otherwise, her salary goes directly to the house. And she thinks they're collecting food stamps in her name, too."

"It sounds like the black sharecroppers in the South during the 1930s. The black farmers didn't own their land, so they had to pay an unfair percentage of their profits to the landowners." Maxine spoke quickly, on one of her nerd rolls. "Or you could compare it to the collective farms in Russia or China, where people work all their lives on state-owned farms with no control over their profits and usually no salaries. It's a form of communism."

"That is so scary," Delilah said. "Maybe she's really trying to suck you into the vortex. I don't think you should see her again."

Ruby appreciated her friends' concern, but now that she'd found Glory she didn't think she could close the door. At least not yet.

Ruby was pulled back to the present when Grandpa Doc mentioned her mom in his thank-you speech. "And finally, we're grateful for the well-being of our own Tamarind," he said, nodding to the love seat where Mom sat with Nani Rima by her side. Tamarind's parents usually did not join in on McCullum family events, but Rima had already been in town, caring for Mom, and this year Mom had wanted to hold the people she loved close for the holidays. "We are glad you're with us, tonight, as well as the young lady at your side. We are grateful that you've brought us such good news, and we know you're a fighter." Grandpa Doc gave a thumbs-up. "And for all this we're grateful."

"Amen!" someone called out, prompting a chorus of "amens"

and applause as people turned away and began to line up at the food buffet.

Ruby went over with Mom and Nani, who were talking with Dad, Dada Karim, Aunt Rosie, and Cousin Maisie, explaining Mom's treatment. It had been one week since the surgery, and Mom was doing great, eating healthy and doing her arm exercises every day to avoid stiffness in her shoulders. She would start chemotherapy next week, but that was a precautionary measure, as the lymph nodes had shown no sign of cancer.

"An early Christmas gift," Mom told Rosie, who leaned down to hug her.

The air seemed to shift, and Ruby realized someone was standing behind her.

"Have you planned an act of kindness, young lady?" Grandpa had crept up on her, no small feat for a man his size, a former high school linebacker. As a little kid Ruby had been afraid of him, but then she'd realized he was like a smart, friendly bear. "Who's going to benefit from your good deed?"

"I know the person I'm going to help," Ruby said, looking up at him with earnest eyes. "I'm just not exactly sure how to help her yet."

"Hmm. Sounds complicated. And a simple act of kindness is supposed to be simple."

She shrugged. "I'm doing my best. You know how sometimes a person needs help, but she doesn't really know what she needs?"

He nodded. "All the time. You sound like a psychiatrist in the making. But don't overinvest. You could help your sister with her homework or do some extra chores around the house."

That would have worked for the old Ruby, but now she had graver responsibilities. "Sounds like a plan," she said. As he patted her shoulder and walked away, she felt like a traitor to the family.

Heads bowed at the table as the sisters ate without comment. No one dared to say a thing about the meager Thanksgiving meal, with rubbery turkey and gummy stuffing that tasted of salt and musky sage. *Everything is so gray,* thought Glory. She missed the color of her mom's table with shiny orange candied sweet potatoes, red cranberry sauce, bright green beans.

"Let's go around the table," Natalie said, sawing at a slice of turkey. "Everyone tell us what you're grateful for. Share your blessings."

"I'm grateful for my sisters, and for a chance to perform this evening," Rachel said.

"And I'm thankful that we'll be blessed with a concert tonight," Laura said with a giddy smile.

"Grateful for food and . . . and clean clothes," Georgina muttered without looking up from the table.

Soon it would be her turn, and she would have to say her usual line.

I'm grateful to have food to eat and a roof over my head. I'm grateful for all that you've given me.

This had been her mantra for a decade now, and though the words sounded right, the sentiment had worn thin. How can you be grateful to a master who owns your time, your body, your work, your future?

Your child?

But this year would be different, wouldn't it? Now there was Ruby, her hope, her savior. Next year at this time, she and Luna wouldn't be part of this going around the table spouting false praises.

It was her turn; all eyes were on her. "I'm grateful, so grateful, to be alive."

Their silent stares pierced the air. Natalie scowled at the notion, and Leo shook his head in disgust. From the chair beside her, Luna glanced up in confusion.

"How very selfish of you," Natalie said.

"I wasn't finished." Glory bit her lips to compose herself. Suddenly she had the urge to laugh, but she tamped it down. "I'm happy to be alive, so that I can appreciate your generosity, this wonderful meal, and this fine home."

The room seemed to exhale as Natalie nodded. "You're welcome. Next?"

"If you're nearly finished, listen carefully." Rima was amused by the eager faces of the teenage girls, teacups in hands, as they faced her at the kitchen counter. When they had learned that tea reading was a hobby of hers, they had lined up to have their fortunes told. "Drink most of the tea, but leave a little liquid in the cup, so that you don't swallow the leaves, you know."

"I'm done," one of the girls said. She was a little pudgy, with skin the color of caramel and liquid amber eyes that would one day make a man feel that she adored him. Casey was her name.

"All right, Casey. Now you hold the teacup in your left hand and swirl it round and round, clockwise. Swirl it three times. You too," Rima said, nodding at the other girl, a tall beauty who reminded Rima of her daughter, only Jade had very long hair that was bound into a hundred tiny braids.

"Now. Put the saucer on top of the cup and slowly pour the rest of the tea into this bowl. Use the saucer as a screen . . . that's right." As the girls followed her instructions, her granddaughter Ruby came over with a slice of pie and touched the china teapot.

"It's still warm. Okay if I have some of your tea, Nani?"

"Of course. Do you want your tea leaves read, too?"

"No, thanks. I just want some tea with my pumpkin pie."

"So pour yourself a cup," Rima said. "But it's no trouble to read one more."

"I'm good," Ruby said, placing a mug beside the teapot. "I'll just watch."

In the times Rima had read for Ruby she had seen that the girl was insightful. One day, Rima would teach her granddaughter the symbols, as she already had the intuition. In truth, Rima would have liked a peek at Ruby's cup. Something was going on with this girl, something more than the worry over Tamarind's cancer. But Rima didn't remark on it as Ruby joined them at the counter and listened in while Rima did readings for Ruby's cousins.

The younger one, Casey, had a lot going on. "So many leaves you have, all in a jumble," Rima said, showing her the cup. "This means you are busy. Lots of activities. A very full life."

"I'm on the debate team, and in January I'm going to Eugene for the Model United Nations," Casey said. "I want to go to be a lawyer, but I'm in theater, too. Do you see anything about law school in there?"

"Not law specifically, but this pyramid, do you see it? And pointing up. That's a very positive sign. It means you will have solid success. And these little grains here? I see a swarm of bees."

"Really? That's scary."

"But it's good for you, if you like to perform onstage. It means that you will be a hit in front of an audience."

"Really?" Casey's smile lit her face. "I'm auditioning for the next school production this week. I hope that means I'll get a part."

Rima nodded as she moved on to Jade's cup, which was not so busy, not so crowded, but also not so clear to her. "First I see a boat. See? Right there. You will receive a visit from a friend. Maybe a surprise visit."

"I keep trying to get my friend to visit from Spain. I studied in Barcelona over the summer. It was so hard to come home in September! I miss my friend."

"So it looks like she's coming," Casey said.

"No. This friend is a he," Rima said. "There's a cherry, a sign of love and luck. A secret love affair."

Jade covered her mouth as she giggled. "It *is* a guy. Mateo." She leaned toward the cup. "What else do you see, Mrs. Singh?"

Here was a case in which the tea reading was not something to be broadcast. Rima saw a rocket, the news of a birth. A baby. Would Jade be having a baby with this Mateo? Rima had a strong feeling that the answer was *yes*. Yes to marriage, too, as she saw a rose in the cup. Strong symbols, but since they were at the bottom of the cup, these events wouldn't be happening very soon. And maybe these were things Jade wanted. "I see that you or someone very close to you will marry and have a baby."

"Oh my God." Jade beamed a smile at the other girls. "That's amazing."

"But this is not today. I see it in the future."

"My destiny!" Jade flung her arms in the air. "I knew you would see love in my cup."

Rima frowned. "Love" was not synonymous with marriage and a baby, but clearly Jade hadn't learned that yet.

"I can't wait to tell Mateo," Jade said. "We're supposed to FaceTime later tonight."

"And I need to start reading over parts for the audition. Thank you so much, Mrs. Singh," Casey said, coming around the counter to give Rima a hug. Rima patted the girl's back briskly. Normally she didn't like to be squeezed by strangers, but Casey meant well.

"You are very welcome."

The girls took photos of their teacups, asked a few questions, and chatted on for a bit. Rima sipped her own cup of tea, patient, observant. Then the youth cluster wandered off, lost in their cell phones and dreams. Ruby went off with them, fielding their envy over having a grandmother who could read tea leaves.

Rima waited until the girls went out through the French doors, probably heading back to the fire pit. She carried her teacup and saucer over to the sink where Ruby had left her dishes. Yes, this was Ruby's teacup. She swirled it three times, clockwise, and then drained the excess liquid into the sink.

Peering into the cup, she let out a grunt. Bad omens, everywhere.

A pistol meant danger. A cat for deceit. An hourglass as a warning to be cautious.

A dancer leaping through the air. A sword. Both signs of disappointment.

And not far from the rim, a ball with a flaming tail arched across the side of the cup. A comet. A sudden event that would bring change, soon. And considering the other warning signs, this change would not be a good one.

What was going on with her granddaughter?

CHAPTER 30

Luna let her arms dangle as she bounced on a cushion and waited for Hazel to return from the kitchen. Bouncy-bounce. Luna was hungry, having slipped through the fence without lunch, but she just couldn't face more ramen noodles or oatmeal. Not even the peaches and cream kind. She had fled the house hungry for more than food. She needed friendship, and Hazel had been here for her.

"Luna!" Hazel had exclaimed, throwing her arms wide after answering Luna's knock at the side door. "This is so awesome! How did you know I just got home?"

Luna didn't answer that she could see Hazel's house from her upstairs bedroom and from the backyard if she peeked through the fence. Mama said it wasn't polite to spy on people, but she didn't understand that Hazel wasn't any old person. She was a *friend*. "I missed you," Luna said.

"Missed you, too. Come in! It's too rainy to play outside."

Stepping into the warmth of the kitchen, Luna felt a giant smile take over her body as she waved at Hazel's mother and followed her friend into the family room to help Hazel with her homework. She was breaking lots of rules, coming here, but being with her friend was worth spending time in the attic as punishment. She had waited until Leo and Sienna were in the downstairs bedroom, where they ended up every day after they finished chores. Mama told her to stay away because they were doing adult things in there, but she had always known to keep her distance from Leo and Natalie. They had never liked her, but Mama said it was their problem, not hers.

Usually, if she did her lessons, Leo didn't want to be bothered with her. He would have her help Sienna with chores around the house such as mopping or vacuuming and then do her lessons, which Rachel or Julia went over with her at night. Today she had been raking the last of the leaves when she heard Hazel's voice and saw her follow her mother in the side door. She couldn't resist! Leo would probably never notice she was gone, and if he did maybe he would see that her visits here would be easy for him. If she came over enough and showed Leo that everything was fine and there was no trouble, eventually he would change the rules and allow her to come here. He had to budge someday. She was ten years old and she needed to have friends her age. That was how it was in books and TV shows and movies. Of course, she would rather not get caught at all. She planned to sneak back into the yard in the late afternoon and no one would ever know.

First they did Hazel's homework together. Writing sentences was Luna's favorite part. Words always spilled out of her mind, and she could make up sentences faster than Hazel could write them. After that was math, which Hazel could do on her own. Still, Luna stayed at the table and mulled over the problems, making sure she could do them in her head. She imagined being in a classroom where the teacher smiled and told her she was doing a terrific job, just like the stickers from Hazel's past homework boasted. And all the other kids would like her because she was nice and smart, too. After Leo budged on some of the rules, maybe she could get him to allow school, too. That would be heaven.

Then they styled each other's hair. Hazel's thick brown curls tangled easily, but they held the flowered combs in place. Luna made a crown of flowers for her, and Hazel tied Luna's dark hair into three ponytails with glitter bows. Then they did Olympic tumbling, which made them hungrier, of course. That was when Hazel went to the kitchen to ask her mom for a snack.

"My mom is making us grilled-cheese sandwiches and to-mato soup," Hazel reported before diving into a somersault on the sofa cushions they had lined up on the living room carpet.

"Ask her if she has food allergies!" Hazel's mom called from the kitchen.

"What?" Hazel yelled back.

"Allergies!"

Luna's head pivoted from Hazel to the doorway and back as they volleyed the loud conversation in a joyous way that made her want to laugh. She wished the sisters called to one another that way, so full of energy, like popping corn.

"Do you have any allergies?" Hazel asked her.

"I don't know."

Hazel's mother, Nicole, appeared in the archway. "Are you allergic to wheat or gluten? Dairy? Lactose intolerant?" she asked.

Luna wrinkled her nose. "I don't know. But I'm not picky."

"Do you eat bread? And milk?"

"Yup."

"Okay then!" Hazel called to her mother in the kitchen, and then it was Luna's turn to do a shoulder roll.

"I wish I had a trampoline," Hazel said. "Then we could do flips."

"I can't do a flip."

"You could on a trampoline. It's easy, because you can bounce really high. If I get a trampoline for Christmas, I'll show you how to do flips. Maybe our moms will let us have a sleep-over after Christmas."

Christmas and a trampoline and grilled-cheese sandwiches with her friend . . . so many good things!

While they ate, Hazel's mom sat at the table with them, tug-ging on the wispy brown curls that sprang over her ears as she flipped through a magazine.

"Mom? Can Luna have a sleepover sometime?"

"As long as it's okay with her parents."

"Awesome!" Luna said, repeating her friend's word.

"As long as you get permission." Nicole looked up from her magazine. "I'm looking forward to meeting your parents."

"My mother will give permission," Luna said. "She knows that Hazel is my best friend."

"We love you, too, Luna. You're a delightful guest. But in the future I'd really like to get your parents' permission for you to come over. I know Hazel's dad tried to talk to your father last time you were here, but he scooted you off so quickly, Jeff didn't have the chance."

"Leo's not my father. My father was a wonderful man, but he died."

"Oh. Sorry about that. Is Leo your stepfather?"

Luna didn't know what that meant, but she wasn't going to lie to Hazel's mom, who had been really nice to her. "Leo doesn't want me to come over here, but my mom doesn't mind. She understands that it's important to have a friend. She has a friend, too."

"So maybe I could talk with your mom. What's her name?"

"Glory. She's at work now."

"I'll just give her a call. What's her cell number?"

Luna shook her head. She couldn't give away the number of Mama's secret cell phone. "None of the sisters have cell phones. But don't worry. Mama won't be mad that I'm here." It was sort of true. Mama would only be mad if Luna got caught.

"But I do need to talk with her. Would you tell her that, please? I'll give you our number and you can ask her to call. We would love to meet her sometime, but at least have her call."

"I'll tell her," Luna said, dipping a buttery sandwich crust into her tomato soup, the way Hazel did.

After they finished eating, Hazel turned on the television and Luna looked through her bookshelf while some Nickelodeon kids played a trick on the school bullies. Luna found a book about orphaned kids that looked spooky and exciting. "You need to start at the beginning of the series," Hazel said, telling her she should borrow the book.

Would she be allowed to have the orphan book in the house? Leo was strict about books. Reading was a good thing, but he needed to approve of everything the sisters read. For now, Luna stretched out on the carpet by the fire and started reading the book by the warmth of the fireplace. From time to time she looked up at the television and laughed along with Hazel.

The abrupt knock startled them both.

"I'm looking for Luna," came Leo's voice from the kitchen. Too close. In the past, he had rung the doorbell and waited in the driveway, pacing like a cat preparing to lunge.

"Hide me," Luna whispered.

But Hazel shook her head with a sad frown. "I can't," she whispered. "We'll get in trouble."

"Hazel?" Nicole's voice sounded tense. "It's time for Luna to go."

Was Hazel's mother face-to-face with Leo? Maybe they would talk, the way grown-ups did on television. Sometimes Leo liked to talk and win people over. He liked to be right. Sometimes Natalie called him King Leo, the Lion, and sometimes the sisters curtsied like he was a king. It always seemed like a little joke, except that Leo really liked it.

Luna pushed up from the floor, tucked the book under her shirt, and tucked her T-shirt into her jeans. "So Leo doesn't see," she whispered. Hazel knew that he had weird rules.

Leo stood at the side door, his eyes cold and stern, his arms crossed defensively over a leather jacket. "There's the little jailbird."

Hazel's mom forced a smile as she put her hands on Luna's shoulders. "Actually, Luna has been a great influence on Hazel. She's welcome here anytime. I hope it's okay with her mom."

"Did she tell you she has a mother?" Leo shook his head. "Poor kid's a chronic liar. But I guess violence can twist a person's sense of reality."

"I don't understand." Nicole squinted at him, confused.

"Luna is an itinerant foster child, a ward of the state. Her mother is dead, and no one is quite sure . . . Well, I like to think it was someone else who used the knife."

Luna glared up at him. "What are you talking about?"

"Sometimes the mind blacks out traumatic memories." Leo gave Hazel and her mom a sad look. "Sorry to scare you, but our girl is a killer. I hope you saw her good side. When she flips, it's a horrible thing."

"You're joking, aren't you?" Nicole frowned at Leo, her eyes skeptical. "It's a bit over-the-top for kids this age."

"He's lying! I would never hurt anyone."

"Come on, Luna-tic. Let's go."

"No!" Hands on her hips, Luna backed away toward the family room. "I'm going to stay. You can't make me."

Leo's eyes grew cold as stones. "You're just going to make things worse for yourself."

"No!" She turned and ran back into the family room, hugging the book to her chest as she scanned the room for a place to hide. Remembering a game she had played with Hazel, she ran to a window and stepped behind the long flowered drape. Tears stung her eyes and ran down her cheeks as a sob rattled her. Leo was ruining everything for her. Everything!

She sniffed, wondering if Hazel would still be her friend. A moment later, she heard Hazel's voice.

"Luna?" The curtain was pulled to the side and Hazel's sweet face tilted in sympathy. "Are you okay?"

"No." Her voice quivered. "He's lying about me. I never hurt anyone."

"I know." Hazel stepped forward for a hug. The book was a block between them, but Luna didn't care as she nuzzled her face against the soft shoulder of Hazel's fleece.

"Luna?" Hazel's mother called. "I think you'd better go."

"But you can come back," Hazel insisted. "Come back when we have our Christmas tree up. My mom will fix things with your mom."

Maybe, but maybe not. Not if Hazel's mom believed the horrible things Leo had said.

"Girls?"

Everyone was waiting for her to go. With an ache in her heart, Luna slipped out of her friend's embrace and plodded to the door.

CHAPTER 31

The post-holiday cleaning of hotel rooms had seemed never ending, as the smell of cigar smoke and spilled alcohol permeated half of the rooms on Glory's list, which had been booked for a bachelor party. It was disgusting work, but Glory muddled through in the hope of meeting up with Ruby at the mall today. She understood why they hadn't been able to meet over the long holiday weekend, but maybe today. There was so much ground she needed to cover with Ruby, but there was never enough time at the mall, especially with the possibility of one of the other sisters seeing them together.

She closed the windows of the last room on her list and gave an extra spray of deodorizer for good measure. It was better, but cigar smoke had a way of hanging on. Her feet were sore and her bad knee ached as she wheeled the vacuum to the door, pausing just inside to check her phone. There was a text, from Ruby, of course: *Sorry, but I can't meet you today. Super busy this week.*

Glory let out a sigh of disappointment as she bit her bottom lip. Was Ruby slipping away from her? She couldn't let that happen. She needed her, desperately. But if she seemed too clingy, she would lose Ruby for good. After taking a deep breath to push aside her worries, she wrote back: *No problem. Hope to meet up soon.*

She was going to leave it at that, but then she was taking a sculpted washcloth from her cart and she thought Ruby would get a kick out of the little duck-shaped thing. She used to like the ducks in the park, and she'd just told Glory that she had a big collection of rubber ducks. She liked to squeeze them to get rid of stress.

On a whim, Glory found the camera function on her cell phone, which she had used only once to take a photo of Luna, and snapped a picture of the origami duck. It was easy to send to Ruby. Then, inspired, she pulled out the other sculpted washcloths she kept in the cleaning closet—a teddy bear, a rabbit, a penguin, and a mouse. Moving fast, she snapped photos of each of them and sent them to Ruby. What fun! She was beginning to see why people were so attached to their cell phones.

"Thank you for driving me," Tamarind said as Ruby steered the VW into an uphill curve. "This saves your dad from having to take loads of time off from work."

"And it keeps Nani Rima off the road," Ruby said. "Which helps keep America safe."

Tamarind chuckled as she rested her head back against the seat. "Don't let her hear you say that."

"Of course not! I would never, Mom."

"Though Nani knows her own weakness. My mom never was a good driver. Her mind strays too easily, I think. Anyway, I've made the chemo appointments so that you can drive me after school. Which is such a big help."

Everyone in the family had played a role in Tamarind's recovery. Pete had put himself in charge of talking with doctors, researching the disease, the types of therapy, and the drug treatments doctors had prescribed. Rima had been cook and caretaker. Aurora was Tamarind's cheerleader, her bright star who shone a little each day with funny stories from school and a little snuggling. And then there was Ruby, rising to the role of big sister, driving Tamarind around. Staying on top of her own studies and trying to participate in every conversation about Tamarind's care. Suddenly Ruby, her rock, seemed like an adult.

The car went over a rise and Tamarind's right hand reached to steady herself against the door. Her chest, neck, and upper arms were still tender, though the last few days had been better. The arm exercises, which she'd done religiously, had definitely helped keep her from stiffening up, and she'd gotten off the pain medication, which had given her nausea and nightmares. She wasn't used to giving up the wheel to her daughter, but the doctors did not allow chemo patients to drive themselves home. Besides, she needed Rima at home to tend to Aurora's snacks, meals, lost items, and daily crises. Rory was not nearly as independent as her older sister.

"Are you scared?" Ruby asked as they waited at a stoplight.

"No," Tamarind answered, staring out the passenger side window. "Well. To be totally honest, yes. But not as scared as I was, going into surgery. I figure that it's worth the trade-off; I'm willing to feel like crap for three months if it means kicking the cancer's ass."

"Wow, Mom. Cursing now?"

"Only when I'm passionate about something. And I am. I'm going to beat this thing."

"It's just so soon after the surgery," Ruby said. "You'd think they'd give you some time to heal."

Tamarind's mastectomy had been less than two weeks ago, but she felt ready to go on to the next phase. "They want patients to start chemo within thirty days of surgery. They've found that immediate treatment helps keep the cancer from spreading." Tamarind glanced over at her daughter. "Bet you didn't know that."

"I didn't. I'm learning a lot of things I didn't know before."

"As we all are."

Just last night, Pete had closed the computer after hours of researching types of drugs used in chemotherapy, studying their effectiveness and side effects. He had wanted to be knowledgeable about the procedure Tamarind was about to undertake, but there were too many variables in the types of drugs and course of treatment. "Am I nuts to keep researching this?" Pete had called to her as she applied cream to her face and elbows—a nighttime habit that had become a soothing ritual for her.

"Are you learning anything that might be helpful?" she asked.

"Only that my head is going to explode if I don't stop."

Tamarind came over to the bed, sat beside him, and closed the computer. "Then stop, *dilnashi*. You've been my rock, and I love you, but there are some matters we need to trust to the doctors and the experts."

"Like whether they use a taxane drug or a cyclophosphamide?"

She squinted at him. "I love it when you talk medical to me. And that second drug makes it sound like I'll be glowing in the dark."

"With all the chemicals in those drugs, you never know." He touched her knee and leaned close to kiss her.

"There's a reason they call it chemo, Pete," she said before she pressed her lips to his.

The chime of Ruby's cell phone brought Tamarind back to the present. "You've got a message," she said as two other chimes followed in succession. "A few messages. Want me to read them for you?"

"That's okay," Ruby said. "I'll check them when we get there. Maxi and I are going to go over an English assignment while I'm waiting. Or it might be Aurora. She texts me all the time, to check on you."

"Does she? That's so sweet. And you've become a good source of support for your sister."

"She's not so bad sometimes."

Tamarind chuckled. "Such a rave review! Aw, Rubes. What's going on here? You taking care of me and your sister, too. The world's turned upside-down."

"I don't mind," Ruby said.

"No, I don't think you do, as long as you're in control.

You're a person who likes the patterns of ritual. You want to know that you can handle things, and I'm happy to say, you manage quite well, Rubes."

"Thanks."

Ruby's phone chimed again, a number of times.

"Your phone's blowing up! Sure you don't want me to check for you?" Tamarind looked down at the console, where the orange, sparkly cell phone was tucked into a rectangular compartment.

"I'll catch it later. You can turn on the radio and listen to your music."

"The music you hate?"

"Yup. Right now you get a free pass."

"Wow." Tamarind turned the radio on. "I'd better milk this thing for all it's worth."

CHAPTER 32

Luna couldn't stop crying. Sick with shame as she fled Hazel's house, she walked with her head down. In an effort to calm herself she counted the red paving stones in the Hansons' driveway as she retreated from the house. *Four, eight, twelve,* I hate you, *sixteen, twenty, twenty-four,* my heart is so broken it hurts. The rush of hot tears had embarrassed her, especially when Hazel's mom had taken her into her arms and hugged her close.

"Take care of yourself, honey," Nicole had said. As if they were never going to see each other again.

Had Hazel and her mother believed him? That crazy story about killing her mother, something about a knife? Luna wished that she'd had more time with Hazel, a chance to see if Leo had scared her away or if she realized he was lying.

What a stupid story!

She was furious with Leo and mad at herself for thinking he would ever come around, but she never expected him to come to the door and spout out disgusting lies about her. Her arms were folded across her chest, a gesture of defiance but mostly as a way to hold the book under her shirt as she marched down the driveway, rounded the corner, and walked around the corner to their house. The front door would be bolted from the inside; Leo always kept it locked tight, with the keys to the rows of locks on a ring that he clipped to one of his belt loops, but the back door from the kitchen was kept unbolted during the day when Leo was home. She paused at the garage door, waiting for him to catch up so she could distract him. They would have to go around the garage, and she didn't want him to notice the one window she had left unlatched in the garage. That was her secret way to return if she peeked through the fence and saw Leo working in the backyard.

She kicked at some stones at the end of the driveway and wheeled around. "Why did you do that? You made up a lie about me!"

He smiled as he closed the distance between them. "I was saving you. If that neighbor girl gets too attached, her nosy parents are going to start asking questions. And questions bring outsiders. Who will come and take you away and make you a ward of the state. You'll live in an orphanage and you'll never see your mother again. Is that what you want?"

"No! But you lied."

"I saved you, Luna."

"And you're wrong about Hazel," she said as they passed the unlatched garage window. She didn't dare look that way. "She's my friend. She's not going to report me."

"Ha. You're young, but you'll learn. You can never trust people on the outside. I'm the only one who cares for you."

She didn't believe him. She trusted the Hanson family. But telling Leo that would only make him madder.

"Did you hear me?"

"Yes, Leo." She traipsed across the backyard, careful to keep her distance from the shed that covered Annabelle's bones and the woodpile that Mama used to climb in and out their window at night. Two pieces of wood had fallen from the stack, but Leo didn't seem to notice as he followed Luna to the back door. It was Mama's secret—their secret. "I just want you to know so you won't be scared," Mama had told her. "If you wake up during the night and I'm not here, don't worry. I'll be back. I'll always come back to you, my Luna." She paused to bend down and pick up the wood. Leo glared at her as she tucked the split logs onto the stack.

"I feel like you're not really getting this," Leo complained. "It's not sinking through your thick skull." He rapped on her head with his knuckles. It didn't hurt, not really, but it made her feel like a stupid wooden puppet, like Pinocchio. "A day or two in the attic will give you some time to smarten up."

You're so mean! He led the way now, and she burned hatred into his back as he led the way inside. He paused to insert the keys that locked the dead bolts on the kitchen door.

With the door locked tight, he turned back to her. "Off you go. Up to jail."

She plodded up the stairs, arms crossed over her chest to keep the book in place. Dust motes swirled in the dim light from the outdoor vent at the top of the staircase. It glittered, a pretty sight, though it was only dust. She wished Hazel were here to see it. Then again, she wouldn't wish crazy, mean Leo on anyone.

She waited again while he unlocked the door, this time with a key to the knob. When the door had to be replaced after Annabelle scraped the surface away with her fingernails, Natalie had put her foot down on installing lots of locks.

"It's just the attic," Natalie had whined when Leo talked about installing three locks on the new door. "Not really a question of security. I'm not throwing hundreds of dollars into that door. One lock will do." Natalie managed the money for all the sisters, and she seemed to like reminding everyone that she was paying all the bills. Luna imagined her in her office at the hotel, counting gold coins and giggling, like Scrooge in the beginning of the *Christmas Carol* movie. Money, money, money was all she cared about.

That left Leo to be the boss of everyone.

Biting her lips to keep from saying anything else, she moved past him toward the dim attic.

"Hold on a second," he said. "What's that under your shirt?"

"Nothing." She let her hands fall away from the shirt, hoping the book would stick into the waistband of her jeans. It remained suspended there but flattened her sweatshirt, one of her favorites that Mama had gotten from Goodwill. Big red letters spelled out: SOU Raiders. Rachel told her it was the name of a university team, and that made her feel really smart wearing it.

"Seriously?" Leo knocked his fist against her chest, banging on the book. "You really thought I wouldn't notice?"

She clutched the book closed but didn't dare defy him when he told her to take it out.

He squinted at the front cover. "*A Series of Unfortunate Events.*"

"Hazel loaned it to me. It's the first one in a series."

"It's a ridiculous story."

"Hazel loved it."

"Hazel is getting a mediocre education based on dreck like this. You read adult books, classics."

"I've read the Harry Potter books."

"They're classics now. In this house, we don't read garbage like this." He opened the book to the middle, scowled at the pages, and then ripped it in two.

"No! Leo! That's Hazel's book and I promised to give it back."

"She can have it back. Both the beginning, and the end."

Tears were rolling down her cheeks again, as he taunted her with the two torn chunks, then tossed them into the attic space behind her. There was something different about Leo today, something scary. He had always been mean to her, always a strict teacher, but today he seemed to have a new interest in taunting her, teasing her. It was as if he were seeing her for the first time, and she didn't like being visible in his world, a prized rose budding in his garden. She turned away from him, grateful for alone time in the attic without him.

"Wait a second," he said, tugging on her hand. "Let's make sure you're not smuggling anything else in. Lift up your shirt."

Her lips hardened as she turned back and lifted the sweatshirt, grateful that she now had something to wear underneath. "See? It was only the book." As she started to pull the shirt down his hands were on her, pressing the fabric up higher as he pressed his palms against her.

"Look at that. Like ripe plums." He rubbed his thumbs

over the panels of the bralette, tickling the spots in the centers of her breasts. Nipples, Mama called them. It caused a sensation that tingled but made her step back.

"Don't," she said.

"Feels good, doesn't it?"

"No." She twisted away. "Stop it." Touching was against the rules; even hugs were forbidden among the sisters. Mama was the only person in the house who snuggled with Luna or kissed her, and only when they were alone. It was another reason Luna liked being with Hazel, who had taught her that friends could hold hands and sit next to each other on the couch, snuggling close while they watched television. Luna had always liked to be touched...until this...this touching in a personal place on her body.

He dropped his hands and cocked his head to one side, giving her a sleepy-eyed look. "What? Not ready yet?" He smiled. "It'll happen soon. What are you, eleven? Twelve?"

"Almost eleven."

"You look older. I guess because you're on your way. It won't be long until you're a woman, full-grown and ripe like a juicy apple."

He made it sound weird. She was a girl, not a piece of fruit. But she couldn't argue. She could feel the danger; the Lion waiting to pounce.

"You don't get it yet, but you'll come along." His voice seemed kind, almost like a friend, and it scared her. Sugar-coated poison. "Once you grow and the hormones kick in, you'll want me to touch them. You'll be begging me."

No. His touch wasn't friendly like Mama's or Hazel's. It was greedy. His touch would cause her pain. She folded her arms in front of her chest and stared down at the floor, wishing he would leave her alone.

"And now you're embarrassed," he said. "That's sweet, but you'll grow out of that, too." He let out a sigh. "Sweet, good girls always grow into bad, naughty women. I guess it's my curse to have to deal with you."

After a long stare, he let her go into the attic alone, and she felt the strange relief of someone who'd just missed death by a sliver of a moment, like a character in a movie stepping off the train tracks a second before the locomotive plowed by. She went immediately to the sleeping bag, fell to her knees, and lowered the zipper with trembling hands.

Was he watching? Had he gone? She hadn't heard the door.

She wriggled in between the flannel-lined panels and sank down, into the darkness, letting it swallow her completely as she imagined him gone, not just from the room, but from the house. *Go away,* she wished silently, *far away.*

At last, she heard him moving: the click on the knob as Leo locked her in. The creak and tap of his feet on the steps, growing softer as he went down, leaving her. She peeked out through the top to make sure, then breathed in the good stale air. She was alone.

She stared at the door of her prison. Yes, it kept her trapped here, but right now it also kept her a little safe from him. The door was newer than the rest of the house. Boring brown, made of cheap wood. Leo had decided it needed replacing after Annabelle had damaged the previous door.

"She tore down to the wood with her bare hands," the sisters had whispered. "Did you see it? I saw the blood. A terrible sight."

Having been a little kid at the time, Luna had been spared the graphic details of Annabelle's end until later. Mostly she remembered her funeral, a festival held in their backyard, where Leo and three of the sisters had lowered her body into a hole using blankets to ease it down. It all took place under blue tarps Leo had strung up in the backyard, making it seem even more secretive and special. For Luna, the funeral had been a creative time, as Mama had shown her how to weave crowns out of yellow dandelions, and she'd worked voraciously gathering the bright flowers and crafting a crown for each sister to wear for the funeral. She'd made a bigger one for Leo, too.

"King Leo, the Lion-hearted," Natalie had said when she

saw the crown on his head, and all the sisters had smiled and complimented Luna on her hard work.

For the grave Mama had cut some pale purple lilacs and leaves from the bush in the corner of the yard. Luna had wanted to place them on the grave once Leo and the sisters were finished covering it with soil, but in the end the dirt had seemed too soft and she was afraid she might sink in and go down, down into the moist earth, swallowed up like an explorer trapped in quicksand. So she'd handed the lilacs to Mama, watching curiously as they were tossed atop the soil and left to die like Annabelle.

The things that had seemed so important at the time—dandelion crowns and the blue tarp awning and a lilac bouquet—all were gone in a few weeks.

Luna went to the small, grubby attic window and wiped at the grimy glass with her palm. Below her, in the backyard, she could see only the edge of the shed that now covered Annabelle's grave. Over time the tarp awning had been replaced by the small storage shed and the woodpile, which had worried Luna at first.

"Do you think Annabelle feels the weight of all that wood on her bones?" she'd asked Mama after a day in which the sisters had helped Leo unload, split, and stack a cord of wood over the backyard grave.

"There's no pain at all," Mama had told Luna. "That's the beauty of death."

How did Mama know that if she had never died? And how could death be beautiful? And where was Annabelle, actually? Was she still down in the dirt below Luna and Glory's bedroom window, still trying to moan and cry for help as she'd done from the attic? Annabelle's moans had scared the sisters. Georgina had wanted to bring her soup. "She just needs a hot bath," Kimani had said. A bath and a good night's sleep, most of the sisters agreed.

But Leo wouldn't allow it. "She'll come out when she's learned her lesson."

Luna, who had been memorizing her multiplication tables at the time, couldn't imagine a lesson that would take that many days to learn.

When the moaning seeped through the walls into their dreams, Natalie had sent Leo up to the attic to "make it stop." After that the moans had softened to sighs. And then one day Leo told the sisters that Annabelle had passed. A hunger strike, he had said. Her choice.

Luna had never understood that.

Although it had been years since Annabelle died, sometimes when Luna was in bed at night she listened for her. She heard something moving, but it was only the creaking floors or roof vents shifting in the wind. Here in the attic, she thought she could feel her ghost. Sometimes she ran her fingers over the rough edges of the brick, convinced that the warmth of the chimney brick came from the glow of Annabelle, a friendly ghost who understood how cold and lonely this attic could be.

Now she pressed her palm to the grimy glass of the windowpane as she looked to the darkness below where Annabelle's bones lay mingling with the soil. The cold of the glass brought the greedy touch of Leo's fingers to mind, and suddenly she understood.

"Annabelle," she whispered. "You didn't mean to die. You just had to get away. From him."

CHAPTER 33

Although Ruby had been nervous about accompanying her mother to chemotherapy, her tension eased when they arrived on the infusion floor, where they were greeted by a friendly nurse named Jessica. "Come on down." Shorter than Ruby but big on personality, Jessica motioned them down the hallway as if she were flagging in a jet plane.

"Don't I need to check in?" Mom asked.

"We'll get you set up in a bay first, and then we'll take care of the boring stuff there." Jessica smiled up at Ruby. "I know Tamarind is the patient. Who are you?"

"I'm her daughter." Ruby was trying not to stare as they passed windowed cubbies with reclining chairs and medical equipment. Some of the cubbies were closed off by curtains. Most of the others were filled by reclining women and men, though she noticed one teenage boy being treated.

"Do you have a name, daughter?"

"Ruby McCullum."

"Okay, Ruby Dooby. You and Mom can get settled in here, bay number five. You've got your own recliner, a window, TV, and internet access."

Ruby eased onto the smooth reclining chair and leaned back. "This is comfy. I could settle in here and get some homework done."

"Pretty swell, huh?" Jessica smiled. "You can stay there.

But in half an hour or so, I'm going to be treating the person sitting there, so you may want to give it up."

Ruby slid out of the chair. "It's all yours, Mom."

"Gee, thanks."

"So this recliner is for the patient," Jessica said, patting the chair, "since it's got all the doohickies, bells and whistles. Emilio will be around in about an hour with the dinner cart, in case you guys need food. If you're desperately hungry, we can send Ruby on a reconnaissance mission down to the cafeteria on the first floor. But first, let me get your information so that I can order your chemo cocktail from the lab."

"Do you want me in the chair?" Tamarind asked.

Jessica waved her off. "You'll be there soon enough. Right now you can hang out wherever you want."

Mom perched on the windowsill as the nurse went over her information and history. Jessica entered her responses on an iPad and sent an order down to the lab. As they talked, Ruby went over to the television, muted it, and began to search to see what selection of channels they had. She wasn't a soap opera fan, but they had a few good movies and sitcoms on demand, including Ruby's most recent addiction, *Parks and Recreation*. Mom usually liked to watch that with her.

Keeping the television on that channel, Ruby took out her cell phone, sure that her friends had been bombarding her with messages. But no, just one message from Maxi. And six . . . six from Glory.

Glory. Ruby pressed her forehead to her hand, trying to think straight. She had opened this Pandora's box; yes, it was her fault. But there had to be a way to shut the trouble back inside. What did Glory want from her? She had told Glory no . . . and now what? Was Glory stalking her?

Ruby glanced over at Mom, who was engaged with Jessica. She hadn't noticed Ruby's minor freak-out. With a strong sense that she shouldn't be messing with this while she was here, Ruby angled her phone so that it was shielded from Mom's view.

Sick with guilt, she read Glory's cheerful text message and

scrolled through the photos she'd sent. Pictures of washcloths sculpted into animals. *What? Kind of weird, but wow.* What was it going to take to get Glory to stop hitting her up, especially at times like this, when she was in the middle of something with her family?

Ruby closed the messages, went to the home screen, and turned the ringer off. She had promised Dad that she'd keep an eye on Mom while she was here with her, and she didn't need any distractions right now. She looked over at Mom, who was pacing now, hands in the pockets of her baggy black print pajama-style pants. Comfortable pants.

"So when was the last time you ate, and what did you have?" Jessica asked.

"Red curry with basmati rice, and it was lunchtime, just after noon."

"Ooh. Sounds spicy." Jessica squinted at Mom. "Usually we instruct patients to stick with bland foods before chemo, just in case they get nausea from the medication."

"Well, the rice is bland, but I grew up eating curry, and it's never been a problem for me. My stomach is rock steady."

"My grandmother makes amazing Indian food," Ruby explained. "She grew up there."

"So it's authentic cuisine. You guys are so lucky. Love me some vindaloo and dal."

"My mother makes a delicious vindaloo." Mom nodded. "And her tandoori chicken is to die for."

"Ach! You're making my mouth water. But let's see how things go with you and spicy food during chemo," Jessica said as she typed something in on the pad. "I just want to make sure you know that the chemo medication can cause nausea and vomiting."

"I'm well aware, but I've never had a shaky stomach."

"Then the odds are you won't get sick, so fingers crossed. Also, I see the doctor has an anti-nausea medication in your premeds. That should help ward off nausea."

Although Ruby had been pretending to check out programs on the muted television, she'd been following their conversation carefully, worrying that something like this would go wrong. But Mom never got sick. Maybe she would be a kick-ass patient today.

"What other medication did Dr. Hernandez prescribe?" Mom asked.

"Let's see. In the premeds there are steroids, which would help reduce an allergic reaction to the chemo drug. She's got the anti-nausea drug I mentioned, and also an anti-anxiety medication. That one might make you feel sleepy, but most people don't mind it, since they're here already, in a comfort-able space. Good time to fit in a nap."

"Maybe," Mom said. "Ruby brought her backpack with homework, and I have my Kindle."

"Whatever you like. We've got cozy heated blankets that lull many of our patients to sleep. Let's get your IV line going, and then I'll let you two get situated."

With the IV line connected to a saline bag on a rolling cart, Mom could still move around. She took a photo from her purse and set it on the table beside the reclining chair.

"Aw. It's us. But Aurora and I were kids," Ruby said. The photo of the four of them was cute for its time, but it had been taken in the pre-braces days of crooked and missing teeth.

"I love this picture, and it's a good thing. It's so hard to get you guys to a photo shoot these days." Mom dug in her bag and took out a ring with a blue-green stone. "You probably think I'm nuts, but my friend Sadie, who went through chemo a few years ago, told me I should bring a few precious things so that I can focus on the people I love if the pain gets bad. So I brought our family photo and this turquoise ring. You've probably seen it before."

Ruby nodded. "But you don't wear it much."

"I'm not a big jewelry person, but my mother gave me this ring when I had that miscarriage years ago. Turquoise is a healing stone," she said, rubbing her thumb over the blue-green stone. "I like to think that it helped me heal back then. And it's a good thing, because it wasn't long after that that you and Aurora came along." Her dark eyes, bold and strong, caught Ruby as she looked up. "That was a wonderful time. A turning point for your father and me."

Ruby cocked her head, teasing. "And for Aurora and me."

"I like to think so." Tamarind smiled as she touched Ruby's cheek. After a moment, she reached into her bag again, dug around. "Here it is." She removed a chit of tarnished silver; it was the size of a large coin, but rectangular.

"What's that?"

"This is an amulet from Delhi, in India. It shows a warrior, going into battle. My father wanted me to have it before I went into surgery. He thought it would help give me the strength to fight this battle."

"Dada Karim? But he's not superstitious." Karim Singh was a college professor who only tolerated things like Nani's tea leaf reading.

"My father is a man of letters and science, but he has a soft spot in his heart for his family." Tamarind admired the dangling amulet and placed it on the table beside her. "He knew this would have meaning for me."

"Did Dada go to India to buy it for you?"

"No. The charm came from India, but your grandfather bought it on Etsy. Do you know Etsy?"

"Seriously?" Ruby laughed at the idea of her mother explaining the online store for one-of-a-kind items to her. "Of course, I do. It's so millennial, Mom."

"Then you know it's special, and think of how it must have pained my father to do something so sentimental. Especially when his scientific mind probably suspects that it's not authentic."

Ruby held up the amulet, running her fingers over the raised lines of the warrior on a horse. "It looks real to me. But the most beautiful part of it is that your father moved out of his comfort zone to do something for you."

"I think you're right." Tamarind leaned her elbows on her knees as she stared at the photo, the ring, the amulet.

Jessica stepped into the bay, two bags of liquid in her hand. "I've got the liquid treasures."

"Perfect." Tamarind scooted back in the recliner. "Bring it on."

At first they talked. Mom got really chatty, suddenly energetic, which Jessica said was probably from the steroids. "Just don't go jogging down the hall without your IV pole," Jessica teased. "Eventually the other drugs will take effect and balance things out."

A few minutes later, Mom got quiet. "Mmm." She closed her eyes and took a deep breath. "I think things are happening now."

Ruby leaned closer to her mom as the nurse disappeared. "Are you getting tired?"

"Tired and woozy."

"That's okay." Ruby took Tamarind's hand. It was ice-cold. She gave it a gentle squeeze, trying to pass on some warmth.

Jessica reappeared with a bright pink blanket, which she unfolded on Tamarind's lap. Ruby helped tuck it around her mom. "It's nice and warm."

"We have a great warmer on this floor. Let me know if you need another one."

While Mom dozed, Ruby put on *Parks and Rec* and pulled out a packet of history readings she'd downloaded. Everything was calm and quiet here, but lingering guilt kept Ruby from concentrating. She felt bad about turning Glory down, but Mom needed her now. Although getting in touch with her birth mother had been a mistake, it had solidified things about the here and now. Ruby belonged with her family. She'd been an idiot to look over her shoulder.

After a quiet twenty minutes, Mom woke up coughing and threw up all over the pink blanket. Tamping down the urge to freak out, Ruby pressed the call button and went to Mom's side.

"I'm sorry," Mom said, her eyes shiny with tears.

"It's okay. I'm here. It'll be fine." Ruby pushed her mother's hair back and gave her some tissues to wipe her mouth. "Here's a bucket in case you get sick again. Just ride it out, Mom."

Holding her breath against the smell, she folded the blanket over the mess and set it on the floor. "See? Not a problem."

"I'm so stupid," Mom said. "I should have stuck with bland food."

"So now you know," Ruby said in a soft voice. "Next time will be better."

"What's up, ladies?" Jessica appeared and immediately took in the situation. "Good job cleaning up. I'll get rid of this and get you a fresh blanket."

As her mother moaned and drifted off again, Ruby stared at the little end table containing symbols of Tamarind's future. Their family. Healing. A warrior. These were Mom's visions of the things she needed for herself. And yet they spoke to Ruby.

Everything she needed was right here.

CHAPTER 34

On the ride home that day, Glory smiled as she thought about the photos she'd sent to Ruby. She hadn't been so spontaneous in years, and it made her feel kind of bubbly inside. It was dark that November afternoon when the van pulled into the garage, where Leo stood in the doorway, arms folded and jaw set. Something was wrong.

"It's been a difficult day all around." Leo's gaze found Glory. "Your daughter is in the attic, and Sienna is in the master bedroom. This is a big house, but I'm running out of punishment spots for bad girls."

"I'm sorry," Glory said quickly as the other sisters filed around her, heads down as they made their way to their rooms. No one wanted to be caught in the cross fire. "What did Luna do this time?"

"She went next door again. Look, the neighbors seem nice, but you know we can't trust anyone. If she gets reported living here, you know she'll be taken away. Do you want to lose Luna?"

"No! Of course not. I'll talk to her. I'll go now."

"Not yet," he said. "I want her to bask in her own shame."

"When can I let her out?"

"She'll come out when I'm ready to deal with her. Just go. Talk to me at dinner. I've got to get Sienna out of Natalie's way." He seemed distracted as he headed off toward the master bedroom.

Upstairs in her empty bedroom, Glory felt like a dry, hollow husk of a person as she changed into a clean flannel shirt and gathered up the laundry. Unballing one of Luna's socks, she fought the silence roaring in her ears. She couldn't do this life alone. Never again. Her visits with Ruby had given her a sense of the rich, full life she might have had if she had not left her girls at that fire station. A steady, even life outside the shadow of fear. That was what she saw in Ruby. Glory had no one else to blame for that terrible mistake, but ... never again. She could no more abandon her fledgling girl than live in a world without the colors and sounds and delights of Luna. As soon as they could arrange it, they would leave here, together.

With her back pressed to the door to ensure no one would walk in and catch her with a cell, she took the tiny phone from her bra and composed a text asking for Ruby to meet her at the mall tomorrow.

Dinner was a miserable half hour, with Sienna moping in silence, her eyes pink from crying, while the other sisters pushed through their fat carrots and tried to talk cheerfully about the weather and Georgina's "tasty" stew. Georgina's talents in the kitchen were limited by the hours she had to work at the hotel. Consequently, the Crock-Pot seemed to be rattling most days when they came home, the steam giving way to a gray chicken or pork or meatballs, disintegrating in a watery mix of onions and carrots. Dinners added to the sense of sameness in each day, the nights that gave way to a new workday, capped off by a gray dinner followed by another night.

"We are going to make some changes," Natalie announced as she ladled stew onto sticky white rice. "We're going to start sending Sienna to work at the hotel, and we'll get another sister to do the chores here."

Sienna bit her lower lip but did not look up.

Glory let her spoon drop into the bowl as the reality sank

in. Sienna was being pushed aside for another pet, another plaything for Leo. Who?

"Does that mean we're recruiting?" Laura asked. "I've seen some very promising prospects at the mall lately. But of course, I don't say a word. Not unless you want someone new."

"Not just yet," Leo said. "We might not be bringing in a new sister. We'll let you know."

What did he mean, and why was Sienna so upset? Luna had told Glory of a fight she had witnessed between the two of them, an argument about Natalie. Whatever the circumstances, it was clear that Natalie had won this round.

After that Glory had to force down the carrots and sinewy meat. She waited until a few of the sisters had left the table to ask him. "Can I let her out of the attic?"

He held his water glass aloft, considering. "Not yet. Give it time."

A coldness seeped into her chest. Although Luna had been locked in the attic for hours at a time, Leo had never deprived her of dinner. "Can I bring some stew up to her?"

"Why do you always baby her?" Natalie said out of the blue. "You've spoiled that dirty little thing. Since you can't control her, we will."

Laura and Julia quickly cleared their plates from the table, leaving Glory alone to face Natalie and Leo.

"I'll talk to her," Glory offered.

"It's going to take more than talk," Leo said. "She needs to be broken. It's time to break her in."

A wariness tingled up Glory's spine as she tried to absorb his meaning. Luna was too young to begin work at the hotel, but the alternative—the notion of grooming her to be his pet—chilled Glory to the bone. That couldn't be what he meant. And yet his smug smile seemed to say it all.

"I'll get her to listen this time," Glory said breathlessly. "I know she's made mistakes, but—"

"Our little Luna has developed a bad attitude. So smug." Leo put his spoon down. "She needs to be broken."

"That's not necessary." Glory was losing ground. "I'll talk to her. I can work with her."

Leo bounced the bowl of his spoon on the table. "I don't think you can."

"She'll listen this time. Please . . ." Glory couldn't help the thickness in her throat, the panic that made her voice crack. "Just let me talk to her."

"Stop being so emotional." Natalie rolled her eyes, pressing her fingers to her temples. "You are giving me such a headache. The smell of someone else's desperation always gives me nausea."

"Just let me take her down to our room," Glory begged. "Please . . ."

"Nothing's going to happen to her up there, unless she dies of boredom," Natalie said, pushing back from the table. "It's clear that Leo wants her in there for the night, but we're not going to torture her. Take the key from the hook and check on her. You can take some food and water up to her and change the bucket before you go to bed. But that's going to be all on you." She was wheeling herself out of the room before Glory could answer again.

Turning to Leo, she searched for a way to appeal to him.

"Don't even try," he said.

She closed her eyes as he pushed away from the table and left the room.

The minute Glory opened the attic door, she sensed that something had changed. Luna stared up at her, a stormy look in her eyes as she was huddled reading under the tent of the unzipped sleeping bag.

"What happened?" Glory asked.

Luna rose to her knees, held up two halves of a book, and burst into tears. No amount of rocking her in her arms could calm her enough to get the tears to stop, but Luna did manage to speak. "He scared me, Mama. He touched me."

Something snapped inside Glory, but she quickly tightened her arms around Luna to hide the fear and panic.

"Oh, my dear girl! You need to tell me. Tell me everything." Holding her daughter close, Glory stroked her hair away from her face as she coaxed the details from her. So her fears had been founded. He was targeting Luna, grooming her to be his next pet.

His own daughter.

"I'm sorry, Mama," Luna whispered. "I should have listened when you warned me. I should have listened."

"Shh," Glory soothed. "The walls have ears." They would talk another time. For now, she needed to keep Luna safe. "He won't let you come to our room tonight. He wants you to stay up here."

"Please, take me with you!"

"We can't openly defy him."

"But I'm scared. What if he comes back?"

"I'm going to be nearby to protect you. Here's what I'm thinking. . . ."

In the eerie glow of the flashlight, they sat close on the sleeping bag. While Luna worked on a bowl of stew, Glory whispered her plan to watch over her daughter. It would work for tonight. Tomorrow . . . she would face that when they got there. While Luna washed up with a warm cloth, Glory dumped the contents of the bucket in the second-story bathroom and returned it to the attic.

"Are you warm enough?" Glory asked as she helped Luna get settled in. "I can bring you a sweatshirt."

"I'm shivering because I'm scared."

"Try to relax. I'll be watching and waiting. He won't get past me," Glory promised. She kissed her girl on the forehead and helped her nestle into the sleeping bag before leaving the attic. She paused in her bedroom, then opened the door and listened. The second floor was quiet, the house settling in for the November night. A muted conversation lilted through the walls: the voices of Laura and Kimani, who shared a room and were the least emotionally isolated of all the sisters. In a few hours there would be Georgina's chronic snoring, punctuated by the occasional cry of Julia, a poor wounded bird who could not make it through the night without recalling the torture of her mother.

Glory washed up with the bathroom door cracked open so that she could see any movement in the hallway. Then she quickly changed into her nightgown and thick socks and huddled under a blanket to wait.

From Luna's bed in the corner, she could see the bedroom door. After a long day of cleaning, it would be hard to stay awake. But she must. Leaning against the wall, she pulled a fat book into her lap but didn't have any real interest in cracking it open. It was one of many biographies of Leo's hero, Karl Marx, from the library downstairs, one of the "approved" volumes for reading in the house. Socialism, social change, and revolution had been Leo's passions when he was younger. His intentions had seemed pure—wanting to make the world a better place for all people, a fairer world. Now she wondered if the real attraction had been the thrum and chaos of rebellion.

She was staring off in space, her vision a blur, when she heard the creak of the door, then his footsteps. He paused at her open door. His hair had grown long on top, and it jutted out in different directions, as if he'd been raking his hands through it.

Her senses were on alert. She felt ready to pounce, scream, kick, and scratch—anything to protect her girl—but she dialed it back, trying to act normal, hoping she could fend him off with reason. "Are you going to let her out?"

He shook his head. "Just going to check on her."

"I went up there after dinner. Brought her some stew." She kept her voice steady, respectful. She knew he was lying, but it wasn't wise to challenge a lion in his den. "She's probably asleep already."

"Then I'll wake her up."

"Please, don't." She pushed off the bed and motioned him into the room. "Let's talk. I don't want to disturb the sisters."

He came inside and closed the door. He was wearing his gray glare, that dejected stare that had once made her want to soothe him. "You know, you and your daughter are becoming a problem."

"Me?" She blinked. "I'm sorry about Luna breaking the rules, but I usually keep her in line, and I work hard at the hotel. I do my part for the sisters."

"Always faithful to the sisters." He closed the space between them. "So loyal that you want to leave us."

"What are you talking about?" She backed away from him until she was pressing against the bed.

"Natalie told me you want to take Luna and leave." He shook his head, disgusted. "Did you really think she wouldn't tell me?"

"Don't be mad."

"At first I was hurt. Stabbed in the back, after all I've done for you. Then I got mad, especially when I realized how big your ego has grown. You really think you can survive in the big bad world? And with a snot-nosed kid to tote around, too? I thought you had more sense than that."

"I wanted to help. . . ." She sat down on the bed, her mind scrambling to come up with the right words. "I didn't want to be a burden on the sisters, especially with Luna getting older. Sneaking out of the house and eating more food. I thought I could spare everyone the annoyance."

"Well, you thought wrong. Doesn't this family mean anything to you? After what . . . twelve years sharing our home?"

Sharing? While he and Natalie collected all the money and doled out small bits for a slice of pizza at the food court or a used pair of jeans at the Goodwill store? And what kind of a home had doors that were alarmed and triple-bolted? "Alarmed with magnetic darts," Leo always bragged. "You know how magnetism is invisible? That's the theory behind the electronic weapon I've installed on the doors. You tamper with the locks, you'll have thousands of volts of invisible rays passing through your brain." She suspected it was all a ruse, but sisters such as Laura and Julia hung on every word.

"After all I've done for you, you stab me in the back? You sneak around when you think we're not looking?"

She wanted to cry at the injustice of it, but she forced herself to play the game. This was a rare chance to talk alone with Leo. "I'm sorry. I really was trying to help."

He seemed weary and older as he rubbed his eyes and raked back his hair.

"You're tired," she said. "You should get some rest. Things will look better in the morning."

"I've got too much on my mind. Too many problems, like you and your daughter."

"You don't have to worry about us. Luna finally understands that she can't sneak out. See? One problem solved."

"Fantastic." His voice was sour with sarcasm, but he seemed to be calming down as he sat beside her on the bed. "Next you'll be telling me what to do about Sienna."

"What's wrong with her?"

"She's not fitting in. Too surly and resistant to the rules. She won't melt the way you used to. Like butter." He put a hand on her bare knee and ran his fingertips up over her inner thigh, his intention unmistakable.

Glory had to force herself to stay calm, compliant. Years ago she had believed there was a magic in the two of them joining together. Now she knew that the only magic of that time had been the creation of Luna.

"You could let her go," she said, trying to stay on topic.

"That's not going to happen. Nat and I never fail. One way or another, we'll break her." He slipped his hand under her nightgown, his fingertips grazing her thigh.

"You keep talking about breaking her, as if she were a wild horse. She's not. She's a girl, Leo."

"A whiny girl. Not like you," he said, sliding his hand higher on her thigh.

Glory wished she could turn to smoke and rise up from her body. He hadn't touched her this way for years—not since he had learned she was pregnant. It made her sad to recall how she had craved his attention for years. Just months ago she would have gladly curled around him.

But something had changed inside her. Sneaking out of the

house like an adolescent, she had found her independence, and she couldn't go back to being the property of a man who alarmed and locked the doors, a man who threatened to track down and punish anyone who tried to escape the house. A man who killed rather than lose a woman in his possession.

A man who made advances on his own daughter.

No. You don't own me . . . not anymore.

Time to fend for herself and her daughter—time to break free of this place.

She pushed his hand away and rose from the bed. "We can't," she said, breathless with fear. "The sisters will hear. Sienna will hear." She opened the door, then turned to face him. "Then she'll be too angry to melt for you."

In truth, Sienna and Rachel's room was at the other end of the hall, but the seeds of shame had been planted.

He rose from the bed with a sigh. "You know, we had a good thing, you and I. Until you went and got pregnant and ruined it all."

As if it were her fault. They'd been careful, mostly because Leo had been afraid that his sister would find out he was having sex with one of the sisters. (As if Natalie didn't know how he and his pet spent most afternoons!) Most times they had avoided intercourse to be extra careful. But Leo had been game for just about anything else. He'd been voracious, a lion.

By the time Natalie had noticed Glory's weight gain, it had been too late to terminate the pregnancy. "I should send you packing, belly and all," Natalie had growled with a withering fury.

The threat had fed Glory's worst fear, to be once again alone and penniless with a child—and she took on the cleaning job at the hotel and dove in with a fury. She had thought it was so important to be allowed to stay with the sisters. Fool that she was. If she had pressed the point, maybe Natalie would have allowed her to go back then. A clean escape.

"Tell me, Glory." He paused at the doorway. "Do you still dream about me?"

"Sometimes," she admitted, though she didn't tell him the whole truth, that those dreams were nightmares.

Glory watched him go, waited ten minutes, then gathered blankets and a pillow to take up to the attic. Although she wouldn't break Luna out of her prison, she wouldn't take the chance that Leo would visit her during the night.

In a nest of blankets on the attic floor, she lay snuggled with Luna, plotting their escape. This time, she would do the right thing. This time, she wasn't going to let her daughter go.

CHAPTER 35

Shivering from the cold and damp, Ruby clicked on the seat heater and maneuvered the Passat out of its spot on the street. The black pavement, wet with rain, glistened in the headlights of the car as she drove through West Green toward the freeway. The town seemed empty, the shop windows dark except for strings of holiday lights that twinkled in the night. A few hours earlier, these streets had been congested with Saturday night traffic, with people gravitating toward restaurants, bars, and the town's old two-screen movie theater.

Now the empty streets reminded her of those quaint little snow villages along the tracks of a train set. Yeah, she and her friends complained that West Green was a dead spot on the planet, but after learning about the stuff Glory Noland had been through, trapped in the house and forced to follow the rules of the cult, Ruby had come to realize that West Green wasn't so bad at all. It was as if overnight Ruby's eyes had opened to the luxuries in her life. Her smooth lavender bedsheets. Her legion of rubber ducks. Mochas at Starbucks with her friends. This car.

Guilt tightened in her chest, a sharp blade under her breastbone as she sped up on the highway radiating out of their cozy town, aiming for the entrance ramp to I-5. Her parents would have a fit if they found out about this. Dad would be the morally righteous one, disappointed by Ruby's betrayal, while

Mom would be wounded, upset, and desperate to understand what Ruby had been thinking when she constructed a web of lies and ventured into East Portland on her own on a rainy December night.

Mom would be wounded that Ruby was curious about her birth mother, but also that Ruby hadn't told her about her mission to find Glory. If Mom managed to get beyond being hurt, she would be surprised to learn that this crazy meeting with Glory was more of a charity mission than a well-thought-out plan. Sure, Ruby had concocted a plan to cover herself, spending the night at Delilah's rambling house, always a zoo of girls and their friends. She and Delilah knew that no one would be the wiser when Ruby went out the back door and took off in her car, which she'd parked down the street, so that Delilah's parents, Ruth and Seth, wouldn't hear.

Ruby could barely believe she was doing this, but Wednesday's text message from Glory had sucked her back into it: *Can we meet at the mall today? I have a surprise for you.*

In the times they had gotten together, Glory hadn't figured out that Ruby was not a person who liked surprises, which so often were the opposite of good news.

Surprise! We're having a pop quiz.

Surprise! Your front tire is flat.

Surprise! Your mom has cancer.

Surprise! I'm leaving you and your sister here at the firehouse.

Ruby had texted back that she couldn't meet Glory, that she was really busy. So sorry. Maybe in a few weeks they could get together.

Please, Glory responded. *Let me explain.*

Explain what? Ruby had been about to tell her to explain in a text, but then she remembered that Glory had one of those old flip phones with no keyboard. Even a short message would take forever to type.

I can't drive over to East Portland this week, Ruby had texted. She had made the excuse of schoolwork, not wanting to tell Glory that Tamarind was sick. She felt a new sense of protectiveness toward her adoptive mother, and it seemed wrong to tell Glory that Tamarind was anything less than perfect.

Need to talk, Glory had texted back. *Please.*

Of course, Ruby wrote back, because that was the kind of person she was: polite and accommodating. She just couldn't say no when someone needed help.

They had set up a phone call for Thursday. Timing was tricky, as Ruby was in school during the time when Glory was free to call while working on her own at the hotel. They decided to do the call at 11:40, during Ruby's lunch period at school. She knew a quiet place where she could hide out to make the call.

During Thursday's lunch period, Delilah unlocked the door to the stairway at the back of the school auditorium and led the way up. "I wish you weren't doing this," she said, plodding up steps that had been carpeted to muffle noise of the stage crew. "I don't feel right about this. A grown woman contacting you."

"I got in touch with her first." Ruby followed her up the stairs to the lighting booth, where the girls gathered when they wanted a quiet place to talk at school. As tech director for the theater department, Delilah had keys to everything in the theater, where she spent much of her time working the lights and audio for shows and assemblies. Delilah's parents were glad she'd found a paying job, and Delilah liked having a place to hang out away from home. "It's not like Glory is a predator," Ruby said as they emerged into the control booth at the top of the stairs. "I started the relationship."

Delilah flicked on the low lights and the girls plopped into chairs. "I know, but it was natural for you to feel curious, to want to meet her. But after a few chats, she should have the grace to back off. I mean, it's not like you're going to become best friends, and you already have a mother."

"True," Ruby said. Delilah was blunt, unfiltered, and uncensored, but it was so much better than dancing around the issue. "But I only agreed to a phone call. Look, I'm already spread thin between school and driving Mom to chemo. I don't have the time to sneak away and play catch-up with Glory. But she was so persistent, I couldn't say no."

"Just be careful." Delilah stretched like a cat over the sound board to reach the switch at the back, then moved down the counter to also turn on the light board. "Sometimes you're way too nice."

"I can be a bitch. I know how to stand my ground."

"Okay, then. There's a class coming onstage in next period that I need to set up for. But do you want me to give you privacy until then?"

"Stay. Please. I may need support."

Delilah smiled, half-twirling in her chair. "Okay, bitch."

They were chatting over a bag of SunChips when the call came.

"Hi, Glory." Ruby wiped her salty fingertips on her jeans.

"You knew it was me!" Glory seemed pleased. "Thanks for taking the time to talk."

"No problem." Ruby sounded a lot more enthusiastic than she felt. "My next class is in half an hour, so we need to make it quick. What's going on?"

"I need your help. I need to escape. There's too much to explain, but if I don't get out soon, I'll never make it out. Please, Ruby . . . I don't want to die in that house like Annabelle."

"Whoa. Wait. Who's Annabelle?"

"One of the sisters. She was killed up in the attic."

Ruby was stunned. "What? Who killed her?"

Delilah turned away from the light board to gape at Ruby.

"It was Leo." Talking fast, Glory launched into a story of a young woman locked in the attic, dying of thirst. She had died in the house, and now another sister was in the attic and Glory would be next when Leo found out she was talking to Ruby.

Ruby was stunned and confused. "So Leo killed this Annabelle?"

"Yes, and he's furious now because Sienna isn't following orders and Luna is locked in the attic and . . . please, will you help me? Please. I need you to help me get away."

"I think you need to call the police. They'll be able to help you."

"They've been there many times, but Leo always manipulates them."

"Did you tell them about the girl who was killed in the attic?" Ruby asked. "That should get their attention."

It got Delilah's attention. She mimed a shrieking expression. Ruby waved her off.

"They don't want to listen to a damaged woman like me," Glory said. "They think Leo's doing a community service, lodging all those women. They think he's a hero. By the time Natalie rolls out in her wheelchair, the cops think those two are saints. They don't ever notice the broken women in the house, and they don't take complaints seriously. I need your help, Ruby. You're my only hope."

"What can I do?"

"Meet me outside the house at night. Late at night, after everyone has gone to sleep. I need your help getting away from here to a safe place."

"How are you going to get out if the house is locked up tight, with all those alarms and stuff?"

"I'll figure out a way. If you can get me out of his sight, I only need a safe place to stay, just for a few days, until I can find a job."

"Even if I picked you up from there, where would I take you?"

The silence on the line told her that Glory didn't have that part of the plan mapped out. "I can't . . . I can't bring you to my parents. They wouldn't understand."

"I would never do that," Glory insisted. "But there's got to be a place. A homeless shelter in Portland. One that's safe for women."

"I don't know anything about that."

"Could you, maybe, find out?"

"I guess I could look online, but I'm not sure how much I can help. I mean, I'm only sixteen."

"I'm sure some sixteen-year-olds are homeless and need a place to stay," Glory said pointedly.

"I guess." Ruby felt like she was tethered to a boat and struggling to stay afloat as she was being dragged out to sea. This all felt wrong, but she couldn't say no. Glory was desperate for her help.

"So you'll help me? You'll come for me tonight?"

"Not tonight. I have to be somewhere, and I have school tomorrow."

"Then tomorrow night. Tomorrow is Friday."

"But there's no time to figure things out. Can't it wait until next week?" Ruby asked.

"It can't. I can't even tell you the worst of it now, but later. I'll explain it all when I see you. One thirty or two."

"Like, after midnight?"

"We have to be sure people are asleep. I'll meet you out on the street, but park a block or two away so that Leo doesn't hear you."

Ruby wrote down the address, though her mind was already skipping ahead to obstacles like what to tell her parents and what to do with Glory once she was free from Leo and the sisters. After ending the call Ruby slapped her phone down and rested her head on the counter by the light board. "I can't believe I just agreed to that."

"Oh. My. God." Delilah gave her shoulders a shake. "Someone is dead in the attic, and you're driving out there after midnight to . . . what? Bury the body?"

"Not exactly," Ruby muttered, "but pretty close."

"Stay right toward Waterfront Drive," the electronic voice from her GPS instructed. *Thank God for that.* Ruby hated driving to strange places, and she would never have figured out where to go in the dark without the navigation system on her phone.

The look and feel of Portland changed once she crossed over the bridge, leaving behind the more institutional faux skyscrapers for converted warehouses and shops with signs and storefronts that were dated and stodgy enough to be considered retro now. She knew kids at school who came to East

Portland all the time for awesome Thai food or pizza or thrift shops with hidden treasures. *But not me,* she thought. Ruby had never been adventurous until she'd sought out Glory. She should have stayed true to her cautious nature, content in her bubble.

Once she turned right, off the commercial street, the roads seemed to shrink into smaller lanes dwarfed by houses that hunkered close together, like overgrown mushrooms sprouting in the flatlands. As she approached the "destination" she slowed down for a look at the place. The grass seemed dead and the bushes under the windows could have used some clipping, but it wasn't so different from any other house on the block. It was unremarkable. Hard to imagine that more than a handful of women lived under that roof as willing prisoners. Glory had warned her to park out of sight, just in case the awful man was awake and looking outside.

She continued down the street counting off two more blocks before she turned the car around and parked in front of a one-story cottage that seemed sleepy and dark behind two giant gumdrop-shaped hedges. She killed the lights, wondering if she'd be able to see Glory coming from here. Probably not. Then rain clouds had blotted out the moon, and the street-lamps were widely spaced, their light muffled by the bare branches of trees clawing at the sky.

I'm here, she texted to Glory. *About two blocks away. On Sequoia near . . .* She squinted through the watery windshield. struggling to make out the sign . . . *Plum Lane.* Making sure the doors were locked, she searched for a good song on the radio and then finally turned it off. The GPS on her phone was already programmed for their next stop, a motel near the airport. The room was cheap, and it was on a bus line Glory could ride to the long-term shelter, which she would need to apply to in person. Ruby had learned that you couldn't stay even one night until you had a "TB Card," which certified that you weren't suffering from tuberculosis. Even with that, Glory would need to meet with counselors and fill out forms and wait for an opening in the long-term housing. "It will be three or four days, minimum," one of the volunteers had told Ruby when she called. Four nights in a hotel was going to do some damage to Ruby's savings account, but she didn't have much choice.

She scratched at the back of her neck, picked at a little bump there, and then let her head loll against the headrest. She would be glad when this was all over.

CHAPTER 36

The buzzing phone between her breasts stirred Glory from a light nap. She hadn't planned to sleep, but in the lag time between lights-out and now there'd been nothing else to do, so she'd climbed into bed, pulled the comforter over her clothed body, and shut her eyes to meditate on the beautiful life Luna would have once they were free.

She removed the phone from her bra and flipped it open beneath the covers. The message from Ruby said that she had arrived and was waiting just blocks away.

It was happening. At last, it was really happening. They were going to be free.

Glory sent a text saying that she was on her way, then closed the phone, tucked it back into her bra, and sat up on the sloped mattress. In the bed across the room, Luna lay, breathing softly as she hugged her pillow. Glory had thought she'd never fall asleep after Glory had told her about the plan.

"Tonight?" Luna had spread her arms wide in surprise and joy. "We're leaving tonight?"

"Just me, but that's only because I don't want you tumbling out the window." Glory had spoken quickly, never breaking stride as the glee fell away from Luna's face. The details of the plan had restored Luna's hope. Just a day or two and Glory would be back. With the police, if necessary. Soon Luna would meet her sisters! And she would be allowed to leave the house, shop in a store, walk to the park. And school...five days a week, she'd be attending school with kids her age.

Luna had pressed her hands over her mouth to suppress a delighted squeal. "I can't wait!"

"Quiet, you." Glory fought to keep from laughing as she kissed her daughter's cheek and watched her struggle to contain her excitement. Luna had missed out on so many things. Soon her imprisonment would be over. Glory had fantasized about their new life for years.

At last, Luna would be able to attend a real school and get a proper education. School would also give Luna a chance to make friends with other children her age and develop some social skills. The budding friendship with the neighbor girl had been sweet, but the penalties had been so harsh and unfair.

And in her fantasy, she took Luna miles away from Portland to a country town similar to Roseville. Even if Leo and Natalie were thrown in jail, the city would be fraught with memories and fears that Glory couldn't escape. Maybe she was getting old and sentimental—in her thirties!—but she wanted to give Luna the freedoms she'd had as a child. Berry picking on a summer day. Chasing through the corn maze in the fall. Ice skating with her friends in the winter. Girl Scouts and cheerleading and soccer. For all of her differences with her mother, Glory realized that she'd had a good childhood in Roseville, and Winston had felt the same way about small-town living. Glory looked forward to the day when she and Luna could get in a car and drive until they rumbled into a quiet rural town.

Her only reservation was that she had to leave Luna behind tonight, but she would be back soon. Maybe she'd come with the police tomorrow while most of the sisters were off at the hotel. Or maybe she would bring them at night so that the other sisters would have a chance to speak up for themselves and ensure their own escape. She would need to break the news about Luna to Ruby, and she worried that revelation might hit the girl in the wrong way. And then there was the challenge of convincing the police that Leo and Natalie were holding some of the women against their will, but if she couldn't do that on her own she would get someone from the shelter or Social Services to help her. She was just one badgered woman, but she would make her voice be heard.

"Things are moving fast," Glory had told Luna. "I know that, but now is the right time, the only time for us to make the break."

"I'm fine with it, Mama." Luna had linked her fingers through Glory's and swung her hand back and forth. "This is going to be the best thing that ever happened in my life."

The truth of that statement had caught Glory's heart with a twinge of regret. She couldn't change her daughter's past, but she could change her future.

"Can I help you pack, Mama?" Luna asked. "We can bundle up your things in a plastic bag."

"There'll be no packing. I'm going with the clothes on my back, and you will, too, when we come back to get you. Don't worry. I'll take you shopping for some new things."

"Shopping . . ." Luna whispered the word with balled fists as she struggled to keep quiet. "My life is going to be a Nickelodeon show."

"Even better," Glory had said, hugging her girl. "But not a word of this to any of the sisters—and no visit to Hazel. And when Leo asks about me, tell him that you simply woke up and I was gone." Glory had to trust that Leo wouldn't hurt Luna in retaliation. He was not a good man, but his malice was a cautious, festering evil, slow to move. Before he targeted Luna, she would be gone.

Now Glory longed for one last hug, but Luna was in a deep sleep and she didn't want to wake her. They'd be together again, soon enough.

Moving quietly, she put on her sneakers and jacket and then blew her daughter a kiss good-bye. She transferred her cell phone to the jacket's pocket and then zipped up. Kneeling on the bed, she moved the gritty old curtain aside and unlocked the window. Water flew in and filled the sill as she opened the window on the miserable, damp night. The sky was dark with indistinct clouds of gray on gray, and visibility was poor. It was as if she were about to descend into the jaws of a monster, like the Jabberwock, in one of Winston's favorite poems. He'd taught it to Ruby, and now Luna could recite it too.

" 'Beware the Jabberwock ...' " The poem rolled through her mind as she turned around and eased her feet and legs out over the windowsill. " 'The jaws that bite, the claws that catch!' " She'd once thought it was a nonsense poem for children, but she had come to see it as a poem about conquering your fears. " 'Beware the Jubjub bird, and shun the frumious Bander-snatch!' "

Her feet slid down, seeking the shed rooftop as she held on to the wet windowsill. For some reason her toes weren't touching the shed, and she wriggled her legs, searching for a foothold but finding nothing.

What the hell ... why wasn't she feeling the roof underfoot?

The muscles in her arms were beginning to ache with the stress of holding on to the windowsill as her body dangled in the air. She shifted slightly to look down and spot the shed, but the motion made one hand lose its grip on the slick, wet windowsill. She was slipping, but she kept her hands pressed to the side of the house, knowing she would land on the little rooftop eventually.

She was wrong.

A quick glance down revealed that there was nothing to hold her up, nothing to stop her from falling into the darkness. A frantic cry escaped her lips as she scrambled and flailed and scratched at the siding in an attempt to save herself from falling. In the end, there was the quiet explosion of her life, the solid slam of the earth, the unnatural sound of bones breaking, tissues erupting, a searing flash of pain, and finally the dark sleep of escape.

What was that sound? Luna turned her face away from the pillow to listen. Something bad had snapped her out of sleep. Someone shouting? Some animal pouncing in the backyard? Another raccoon foraging among the dead plants in the garden?

There was only silence as Luna stared across at the rumpled

bed beneath the open window. A damp chill was penetrating the room, and she realized Mama had left the window wide open when she went out. That was weird. Usually Mama pushed it down, leaving it open just a crack.

Scrambling out from under her quilt, Luna scooched onto Mama's bed on her knees and saw that the lights were coming on across the way at Hazel's house. Two dogs started barking, the gruff sound echoing through the yards. Peering over the wet windowsill, Luna glanced down into the yard and gasped.

The shed! It was gone and . . . was that Mama? A clump of cloth, still and round as the big sack of rice Georgina kept in the pantry. She must have fallen. "Mama?" Luna called down, her senses on high alert now as Mama didn't move.

Like a wild animal running on instinct Luna bolted from her room and down the stairs. She skidded into the kitchen, her socks slippery on the linoleum floor, but there was no getting out the kitchen door with all of Leo's special locks and alarms on it. She threw open the door at the side of the kitchen and went into the garage and pushed the button to raise the big door, not caring anymore if the whole house woke up. Mama was hurt! She ducked under the rising door and plunged into the fog. Cold bit at her, soaking her socks as she sloshed through the squishy grass to get past the garage and into the yard where everything was wrong.

In an instant she took it all in: The shed that now sat on the far side of the house. The unevenly packed earth of Annabelle's grave where Mama lay sprawled in an awful position, her left leg twisted under her body, her torso twisted in another direction. The sight brought tears to Luna's eyes. She buried her face in her trembling hands, then dared to look again at her mother's broken body. "No." She held her breath as she went to help Mama.

Gathering her nightgown, Luna dropped down to her knees and gingerly touched her mother's cheek. "Mama, can you hear me?" She wanted Mama to wake up and say that she was fine, just a little bruised. And then Luna could help her around the garage out to the street to meet Ruby. Or they could duck through the hole in the fence to Hazel's house and go inside and have some hot cocoa while Hazel's mother gave Mama an aspirin. And then maybe they could stay there. Forever.

But Mama wasn't moving, and the part of her pants that was torn and bloody seemed to have bone showing through. A wave of sickness washed over Luna, and she forced herself to look away from the blood before she threw up.

Luna swallowed back a whimper, not sure what to do but knowing she had to stay calm. Help Mama. As she leaned back on her heels to take her mother's hand, she noticed something shiny in the grass. Mama's cell phone. She rested Mama's hand in her lap and reached for the phone.

When she flipped it open, it lit up. Still working. Her first time using a phone, but she'd seen kids with them on television. She pressed the numbers 9-1-1 and waited with the skinny part pressed to her ear, the way kids held it when they used it to talk. She wasn't sure what to expect, using a phone, but the burring pulse she heard there didn't seem helpful. Had she done it wrong?

"Nine-one-one operator, what's your emergency?" The woman's voice sounded stern.

"My mother fell out the window and she's hurt. I think she needs a doctor to take her to a hospital." *Off to a hospital. That would get Mama out of here, just as she planned.* "Yes. That's what she needs."

"Is she responsive?" asked the woman on the phone.

"I don't know. No. She's not answering me. She's not awake." Luna bit back a sob. Despite all of the books she'd read and movies she'd seen, she didn't know what to do in an emergency like this.

"Can you confirm the address? I have you at 4725 Sequoia Lane."

"I don't know." No one had ever told her the address of the house, but she had seen the street sign dozens of times when she stared out the front window. "Sequoia is right. That's it. Can you send a doctor?"

"We're sending an ambulance for your mom. How old are you?"

When Luna said she was ten, the woman told her she was handling things well for a girl that age. Then she asked her a lot of questions about Mama. Was she breathing? Did she have a pulse? Luna wasn't sure about the pulse, but she thought she saw her mother's chest rise and fall. The woman told her to talk to her mom until the paramedics arrived. "She might be able to hear you."

"I'm here, Mama," Luna said as she folded up the cell phone and tucked it into the band of her left sock. Lights were coming on at the back of the house, and she didn't want Leo to see the phone and take it away. "It's me, Luna, and I'm just going to hold your hand and tell you a story, so you can just listen or maybe try to wake up. Okay?"

As she spoke, she settled onto the ground next to Mama, ignoring the cold mud as she took Mama's hand and, one at a time, squeezed her fingertips. As if she could rub life into her. "What about the story of Harold? The kid with the purple crayon? You know that was my favorite when I was little. It was your favorite, too, right? So I'm going to draw you a picture of a doctor with a big medical bag. And inside his bag he has a stethoscope and medicine and everything else he needs to help you feel better." Luna had never seen a real doctor, and the ones on television were a little scary. But Mama said doctors and nurses helped sick people, so someday Luna would have to give that a chance.

"And I would use the purple crayon to draw a blanket to put over you, to keep you warm. And some hot chocolate for both of us." Sounds rose around her. The snap of the locks on the back door. Barking dogs and footsteps on gravel. The distant whoop of a siren, still too far away. People were coming from the house, but she ignored them and talked on, reminding Mama of sweet things she always said and stories they shared.

When two sets of feet walked up next to Mama, Luna kept

her head down and kept talking, totally focused on her mother. *He* had moved the shed without telling anyone. He had done it. This was his fault.

"What happened here?" Leo said softly. As if he were a kind person. "She must have gone straight out the window. It's a nasty drop."

"That's too bad," said the woman.

Luna followed the legs up to see that it was Natalie, standing out here in the yard without a wheelchair or cane or anything to hold her up. How could that be? Had she been faking it, pretending to need a wheelchair? She was a liar, like her brother.

Luna hated them.

Enough with them! Luna huddled down closer to Mama, pretending the others weren't there. Mama's skin was pale, white as snow against her dark hair, and her lips had a bluish tint. *Oh no, oh no!* Luna knew she should be doing something to save her! Maybe blowing on her lips? "You know I love you eight miles high," she whispered, "and eight miles wide."

"Maybe we should bring her inside," Leo said.

"No," Luna muttered without looking up. She wasn't going to let them hide Mama away now.

"I hate to say it," Natalie said, "but she looks dead."

No, she's not! Luna wanted to shriek, but she kept talking to Mama, rubbing her hand to keep her warm. The siren was getting closer, louder. And then it stopped.

"Did you hear that? Someone called the cops on us." Leo went back toward the house to look in through the kitchen. "It sounds like they're just out front."

"They're here, Mama," Luna whispered. "They're going to make you all better."

"Luna?" It was Hazel, coming round the side of the house with two people in dark blue jackets with patches on the shoulders.

Luna jumped up and motioned them to come quickly. "My mother! She fell from the window."

One of the medics wheeled a stretcher over to Mama, then turned to the other. "Looks like we'll need the backboard," he said.

The woman opened a box she was carrying and got to work on Mama while the man set up some equipment.

"Her heartbeat is tachy, and she's not breathing normally." The woman placed a plastic cup over Mama's face and started pumping air into her mouth. "Let's try and stabilize her. Go on and get the backboard."

"Is she okay?" Luna asked.

The uniformed man leaned down and touched Luna's shoulder. "We'll take good care of her, okay? You just stand back, honey, and give us some space." He had warm, dark eyes, but the serious expression on his face made Luna want to shrink away as he ran back toward the front of the house.

Luna turned to Hazel and was swept into a hug that brought tears to her eyes. Nicole came over and stroked Luna's hair back and told her she was a brave girl. Luna sniffed and wiped her face on a sleeve of her nightgown. She didn't feel brave at all, but she was glad to have her friend here.

"I heard a noise and I woke up," Hazel said.

"We both did," her mom added, putting her arms around the girls and turning them away as the medics worked on Mama. "I'm so sorry this happened. It's good that the ambulance got here so quickly. Do you know how it happened?"

Luna's throat grew tight as she shook her head. She didn't know anything anymore. She was a foolish girl. Too stupid to save her mother. She didn't even know her own address. She sobbed into the sleeve of her gown while Hazel patted her shoulder.

When she looked back at Mama, she was all strapped into the red board, her face masked by the thick collar around her neck and inflated bag that the woman kept squeezing.

"Ready to transport," the woman said. She kept squeezing the airbag while the man began to roll the stretcher out of the yard.

Luna ran over and fell into step beside them. "I'm staying with her."

"Sorry, little girl." The man spoke without breaking stride. "We aren't allowed to have ride-alongs. But you can meet your mom at the hospital. St. V's."

"But I need to stay with her!" Luna wailed as Mama's stretcher wiggled in the muck of the side yard.

"Stop right there," Leo growled, clamping down on Luna's arm. It hurt, but she tugged at his grip. She needed to stay with Mama.

"Can we take Luna to the hospital?" Nicole asked, catching up to them.

Leo released Luna, turning his cold blue eyes on Hazel's mom. "Why would you do that?" he asked.

"We don't mind. I know she wants to be with her mother, and there's bound to be lots of waiting around. The girls could keep each other company."

Luna's heart lifted at the thought of spending the night waiting with Hazel and her mom. Mama would be free in the hospital, with time to heal away from Leo and the sisters, and Luna would be free to live with Hazel's family. This would be their escape! Mama would work everything out and make it all final once she recovered.

"I think we're good," Leo said. "Thanks, anyway."

"Can't I go with them?" Luna asked. "I've got to stay with Mama."

"This has been traumatic for all of us," Leo said. "Let our neighbors get some sleep, and we'll get you to the hospital."

Luna blinked back a new wave of tears as Hazel hugged her and headed out. As she and Nicole walked off, Luna noticed Hazel was wearing the red rain slicker, the cherry red color that helped Luna spot her from the window. She had tucked her penguin PJs into her matching red rubber boots. Totes adorbs. Luna looked down at her nightgown caked with mud at the hem and all down the front, and something snapped inside her and she started running after Hazel, her friend, her only hope of staying with Mama.

"Come off it." Leo growled as he snatched her, his brusque grip knocking the air from her lungs. "I've got enough problems without you acting out."

"Let me go," she choked out, trying to catch her breath as he carried her, legs dangling, back to the porch and set her down.

"Inside you go . . . up to the attic," he ordered. "And I don't want to see that face peering out any of the windows."

"But I need to be at the hospital. I have to stay with Mama."

"I'll take you after we're done with the police. They're always suspicious after incidents like this, and we don't want anyone thinking that you pushed her."

She squinted at him. He was talking crazy talk. She would never . . .

"Go on, now." He shoved at her, hitting her shoulder. "Up to the attic before someone else sees you and the police take you away."

To be taken away from here . . . it was exactly what she wanted. Luna crossed her arms over her chest, standing her ground. "I'm staying right here."

CHAPTER 37

The stark white lights on the ceiling of the truck were the only things she could make out around the dark mask pressed to her face. Someone was leaning over her, attending to a broken body that had known horrific pain but now was cocooned in a glaze of numbness.

A truck . . . an ambulance . . . the lights.

Go to the lights.

Luna had been at her side, pressing her hand, tugging on her to stay.

And Ruby . . . she was nearby. Close.

The girls were out there, hovering.

The two girls who needed to see each other were on the right trajectory, two pin dots on a map moving ever closer, closer.

The girls needed their sisters. They didn't know it, but Glory did. That was the whole point of it. It had taken her a lifetime to realize that it wasn't about her at all; it was about them, the ones you leave behind. And they were so close to finding each other. She could feel that in her soul.

Go to the lights.

The girls were hovering; she could feel them nearby. She recognized that she was hovering, too, looking down on the woman strapped into the collar and backboard. How easy it was to rise from that body. Neither good nor bad, it was the simple trajectory of life and death. Like hopping to the next cloud.

Living was hard, but dying was the easiest thing Glory had ever done.

Ruby opened her eyes and yawned. She hadn't actually dozed off; just a late-night meditation. She shifted in the seat of the cooling car, annoyed that Glory was taking so long. "Where are you?" She had turned the engine off so that she didn't disturb the neighbors, but now she turned it on again and pumped the heat up to the highest setting. As her eyes focused in the darkness, she noticed the glow of flashing lights ahead in the distance.

Crap. Were the police out, randomly stopping cars? She had nothing to hide, except that she was just sixteen, and maybe there was a Portland curfew for young drivers.

She grabbed the cell phone and checked for messages. She had missed the text message from Glory that said: *On my way,* because her volume was turned off. So maybe she had dozed off. She adjusted the sound of the ringer and checked the time. The message had come in more than thirty minutes ago, more than enough time for Glory to find her. Had Glory gone in the wrong direction?

She shot off two more texts to Glory and waited. It was a straight run down this street to her car. Glory couldn't have missed her.

But Glory wasn't answering now, and it had been a while since she'd sent a text. It seemed like hours now.

And those flashing lights ahead stirred the tension in her chest. Had Leo called the cops when he heard Glory sneaking out of the house? *Not likely. Glory said he tried to avoid the cops and kept things under the radar.*

So find out what's going on.

Not so easy. She hated confrontation, but this was the time to take action. If Glory was involved in some way, Ruby could support her, back her up. She groaned. She didn't want to do this! *But the woman gave birth to you. Have a little gratitude.* With a sigh, she put the car in drive and rolled forward.

The flashing blue and red lights of the patrol car were mesmerizing as they bathed the nearby yards in a shifting glow. An ambulance was in the driveway of the sisters' house. Bright lights shone from its back windows, though the turret lights were dark. She didn't see any cops, but a handful of people milled around on the sidewalk in front of the house. Was one of them Glory? Too hard to tell from this far away.

Ruby pulled over and parked a few houses away from the emergency vehicles. A tall man wearing a flat newsboy cap looked over at her as she got out of the car, but no one else from the group seemed to notice her. One of the bystanders was a little girl who fidgeted around with the look of a kid who had been waiting around too long. She hopscotched over the sidewalk to the ambulance and went up on her toes, as if she could peer in through the high windows.

"Hazel!" a woman called to her.

"I just want to say hello to her when she wakes up."

"Give some privacy. Come over here."

Ruby approached the group slowly. "Hey." She tried to keep it cool. "What's going on?"

"Our neighbor fell out a window," said Hazel. Dressed in a red slicker with matching red rubber boots, she shifted from foot to foot. "It was a bad fall."

"Wow. One of the sisters?" Ruby asked.

An elderly man there with his wife stared Ruby up and down, as if she'd said the wrong thing. "That's right."

Ruby shivered. The misty air was cold; so were the neighbors. She zipped her jacket up to the chin and shoved her hands into her pockets. "Is she going to be all right?"

"We haven't heard yet," said a petite woman who seemed to be the mother of the kid. She had a wide, animated face that seemed locked in an approving look. "The paramedics are still working on her. She was unconscious, but we're hoping for the best." She nodded toward the ambulance.

"It's very sad," Hazel said. "I hope she's okay."

"Are you neighbors?" Ruby asked the question of everyone. The men in the group nodded.

"Our yard borders theirs," the mom said. She was a young mother, the concerned kind who tried to get you to order apple slices instead of fries at a fast-food place. "In the back."

"We live on the side street. From my bedroom I can see over the fence to their house, and I play with Luna, her daughter," the girl explained.

So the woman had a daughter. Then it wasn't Glory in the ambulance. That was a relief, but where was she? Hiding out somewhere? Maybe Ruby should be driving around, looking for her.

The little girl tilted her head to stare at Ruby. "You have pretty hair."

"Thank you." It was curling up in the rain. The curse of curly hair, though Delilah thought it was so much better than her wispy, thin hair.

"Doesn't she have pretty hair, Mom?"

"Yes, Hazel, she does. And I can't believe you're up this late."

Hazel shrugged.

Suddenly the back door of the ambulance popped open and a paramedic climbed out of the van. Ruby tried to see inside, but she could only make out the figure of another attendant leaning over a stretcher as he closed the door behind him.

"How's it going there?" asked the man in the cap.

"Taking her back to St. V's." The paramedic went around to the cab and started the engine. Everyone watched as the ambulance drove off in silence, lights flashing.

"I hope she's okay," Hazel said, and her mom put an arm around her shoulders and pulled her close.

"Not to alarm your daughter, Nicole, but that's never a good sign," said the man with the cap. "No sirens means the emergency is over. She's probably DOA."

The mom shook her head sadly. "That would be devastating for Luna. For all of us."

The older man turned to Ruby and stared blatantly. "Young lady, do you know the sisters?" He had white hair and wire-rimmed glasses that were fogging up.

"Not really," Ruby said, then realized she would seem ghoulish without some sort of connection. "I just know one woman who lives here. I met her at the mall."

"The mall." He peered at her over his glasses, fixing Ruby with a hard look. "That's where they recruit. Are you one of them? Gonna join them?"

"No, I'm only—"

"Just a word of advice, you'd better be careful with these types."

"She can go to the mall if she wants," the woman said.

"Can't blame a man for trying to help. I don't wish anyone ill. What happened here tonight was sad. But it's just not right, these women all living with one man."

"It's what they believe, Hal."

"It's unnatural."

"I appreciate the warning, and I respect what you're saying, sir," Ruby said. "Don't worry. I have a great family. I won't be joining up anytime soon."

"Make that never. You never want to land with a lot like that."

Ruby nodded respectfully.

"Well, I'm going to call it," said the man with the cap. "I've got a race to run in the morning." He nodded and headed across the street.

"But the police want your statement, Joe."

"They know where to find me."

"Maybe Joe's right." Nicole closed her arms around her daughter and swayed from side to side. "It's late. We can do this tomorrow. Or I can call your dad to come out and get you. But I hate to wake him up."

"No way, Mom. I'm staying."

"I know. I'm tired, too," Ruby agreed, though she really wanted to hear more about the woman who'd fallen, and she was beginning to feel comfortable enough with the neighbor to ask if she knew Glory. "But at least Hazel and I don't have school tomorrow."

"We don't?" Hazel asked.

"Because it's Saturday," her mom said.

"Oh. I forgot that. Whatever."

"You're tired, sweetie," Nicole told her daughter, sounding so much like Tamarind it made Ruby bite her lower lip. "Are you going to have enough energy to go pick out a Christmas tree tomorrow?"

"I always have energy," Hazel said, jumping on and off the curb. "And I can't wait to decorate our tree."

Ruby wondered when her family would go cut down a tree. She wasn't really ready for Christmas, with all this drama with Glory and the constant fear with Mom's cancer. The little bit of money she'd saved for Christmas gifts was now going toward Glory's hotel bill. She wished she could go home and climb into her warm, dry bed right now. She could do it, but she'd feel guilty until she figured out what was up with Glory. Besides, the flashing red and blue lights from the police vehicle drew her in, promising some kind of answer or explanation. Wasn't that why they were all hanging out so late at night on a damp, misty street?

A few minutes later the front door opened, and two police officers emerged. Ruby watched the front entrance closely for a look at Leo, the cult leader, but the dark door quickly closed behind the cops.

"Thanks for waiting out here, folks." The older officer, a fortyish man with a shiny bald head, had the buttoned-down look of a retired soldier. "After something like this we usually canvas the neighborhood, but I wouldn't want to go door to door and wake people up this time of night." He motioned to the other cop, a younger guy with a crew cut who stood by with his thumbs tucked into the armholes of his vest. "Ray's going to talk to you folks over here," he said, motioning to the older couple, "and I'm going to interview this group so we can get these kids home to bed, where they belong."

Ruby realized he was lumping her in with Hazel and Nicole,

and she was fine with that. They seemed to have a better bead on what was happening.

"I'm Jake Swanson." Tucking his notebook under one arm, the cop leaned down toward Hazel. "And you must be the little girl who called nine-one-one? That was a good move. The dispatcher told me you probably saved your mom's life."

"It wasn't me." Hazel scowled up at the cop as she linked arms with her mother beside her. "This is my mom."

"Luna was the one who called you." Nicole nodded toward the house. "Didn't you see her inside? Ten years old. Blue eyes and reddish-brown hair."

"And totes adorbs," Hazel added.

He gave a gruff smile as he looked down at his notes. "There are no children living in this house, ma'am."

"That's not true." Nicole stood her ground, pushing off her hood to face the cop squarely. "The daughter of the injured woman lives there, in that house, with her mother. I know that because she hangs out with Hazel. Luna's been over to our house a few times. She says she's homeschooled, and she's smart as a button, but there may be some neglect there."

"I'm just saying that this little girl is not living there now. No sign of children in that house, so she must be living elsewhere. Maybe with her father."

"She doesn't have a father," Hazel said. "Just her mom and her."

"Right now my priority is the young woman who's been hospitalized," the officer said, smoothly shifting the focus of the conversation.

A slick move, Ruby thought. She could see that Nicole was annoyed with him.

"How is she doing?" Nicole asked. "Do you have an update on her condition?"

"I understand that she's in critical condition," Officer Swanson said. "Did you know her well?"

Nicole shook her head. "Not at all. Actually, I've never laid eyes on her before tonight. But I know her daughter, Luna. The mystery girl who plays with my daughter?"

He nodded, not taking the bait. "We're trying to locate the next of kin for her. Do you know if Glory Noland has any family in the area?"

Ruby's heart sank. Had he just said "Glory Noland"?

"I wish I knew more about her, but as I said, I never met Glory." Nicole shot an annoyed look at the house. "But Leo? He's come knocking on my door before to collect Luna. If you're conducting any kind of investigation, I'd start with him."

"Ms. Noland's fall seems to be an accident. So far this is a routine investigation." He clicked his pen. "But let me get your names so I can let you go. It's getting late."

Ruby didn't want to get herself in trouble, but when he asked for her ID—maybe because of her age, or maybe it was the color of her skin—she complied. She made up some excuse about dropping off a friend in the neighborhood and seeing the ambulance in front of the house. Yes, she had met Glory, a few times at the mall. No, she lied, she didn't know about next of kin.

Driving home that night, Ruby held it in as she maneuvered out of the little neighborhood, across the Willamette River, and south on the interstate. She told herself she was too tired to feel anything as she tried to sort through Glory falling or jumping from a window, and the little girl named Luna who claimed that Glory was her mother. Glory had another kid? That didn't seem right, because Glory had told her that children were not allowed to live in the house with the sisters. That had been the reason Glory had left Aurora and her behind all those years ago.

But it seemed to be true. Although the cop wasn't aware of the girl, Hazel and Nicole had vivid details about Luna, the girl in the house. It was all a big jumbled mess that couldn't be solved tonight. Tomorrow she would go online and see if there was any news about Glory's condition. She was so tired she wanted to cry as she pulled the car into the driveway and turned off the engine. Moving quietly through the house, she locked the door behind her and went downstairs to her room. Rolled up like a burrito in her favorite blanket, she tried to sleep. But every time she closed her eyes, she saw the flashing blue and red lights that raced and darted over the landscape like a chain of rogue waves.

Emergency. Emergency. Emergency.

A terrible accident.

A serious injury.

A failed rescue attempt.

And all the time Glory had insisted that she was in danger, Ruby had thought she was exaggerating.

CHAPTER 38

With her hands pressed to the tiny round vent in the attic, Luna struggled to hold herself up as she sucked in fresh air. It smelled funny, different, but everything smelled a little bloody since her nose was swollen and clogged up. After falling into a fitful sleep last night, waking whenever she rolled over and felt the throb of her head and face, she had spent most of the day crawling from her sleeping bag to the vent in the wall, where she tried to get fresh air. It was so hard for her to breathe, and her head felt as if it had been stuffed with cotton balls. The dampness of the air felt good on her swollen face, but she kept expecting Mama to come in with a Tylenol for the pain. Mama would make her feel better. But the only visitor she'd had was Sienna, who'd come in sometime before dawn.

"It was Natalie who did it to you," Sienna had told her as she'd dabbed at Luna's swollen cheek with something cold and stingy. "She had us all fooled. The bitch has muscle."

Luna's fingers had trembled as they moved over the swollen flesh of her cheek, her tender face. "What did she do?"

"Hit you with a frypan." She mopped at Luna's face and neck, where the cold cloth felt good. "You are just a bloody mess, but I'll get the wound cleaned and covered. You can clean yourself up when you get out of here."

Luna drifted, unable to answer. It seemed impossible that

Luna would ever lift her heavy body from the pallet on the attic floor. When she opened her eyes again, Sienna's face was softer than usual; her lips were not pressed into the slash of a sneer as she looked down on Luna and lowered something cold to her face.

"Ughh. . . ." Luna gave a low howl.

"I know, little girl, but the ice will make the swelling come down, and we need some pressure to stop your cut from bleeding. Kimani says you need stitches in that gash, but Leo won't allow it. After last night, he said no one's going to see a doctor for a long time. Except Natalie, of course. Queen bitch." She stroked Luna's hair back from her forehead. "See? Once it numbs up, it's not so bad."

"Why are you being nice to me?" Luna's voice was raspy from her dry throat.

"Because I'm pissed at him."

"When is Mama coming back?"

"I don't know. Go back to sleep."

The next time Luna woke up, milky light filtered in from the windows. Her face and head were still throbbing with pain, but that was nothing compared to her desperation to see Mama, to hold her hand and hear her voice and know that everything was going to be okay. She should have known that Leo was lying when he said he'd take her to the hospital. He'd never taken Luna anywhere in the car, even though she'd gone through a phase when she'd begged for a ride—just a ride through the streets of the neighborhood in the new van.

Instead, Leo had dragged her, kicking and screaming, into the house. Once inside the kitchen, Luna had finally broken free of his grip and started to bolt out the slider. She'd been planning to run to Mama in the ambulance. To Hazel and her mom. To anyone who would help Mama and her get out of this house forever. She had just pushed away from Leo when a crash exploded in her head, making stars and pain pop out in the darkness.

She had thought it was Leo, but Sienna had said Natalie.

Natalie. Luna hadn't expected that, but then she hadn't thought she'd see Natalie rise from her wheelchair and walk around the way she had last night.

Now Luna moved away from the vent and pulled herself up, smelling the caked mud and bloodstains on her night-gown. She wished she could take it off, but she didn't have clothes up here. One of her hands was bloody, too, the nails blackened from blood. *Gross.* She used the bucket and drank a little water from a plastic pitcher someone had brought up. There was also a sandwich sitting in a ziplock bag. Peanut butter. She didn't touch it.

It didn't hurt to stand, so she stood at the small window. For a moment she caught her reflection, the dried blood, the black eye, the bandage on her cheek. A wounded soldier girl. She hoped it would heal fast so Mama wouldn't be upset when she saw her. She peered out toward Hazel's house. What time was it? She didn't know if it was morning or afternoon, but she longed for a sight of Hazel in her totes adorbs red slicker and matching boots. Right now there was nothing but the empty backyards, gray sky, and drizzle that soaked the fence and grass.

But Luna could wait.

She had time.

Maybe, if Hazel came home while Luna was watching, she could get her attention.

My friend. I know you would help me if you could.

Luna wished she could squeeze her little body out through the vent and fly down to Hazel's yard. Hazel's mom would drive her in a car to the hospital. She'd take her straight to Mom's room, and Ms. Nicole wouldn't be scared that Leo was mad at her.

The Hansons were her way out. Mama had escaped. Now it was up to Luna to catch up. But she couldn't squeeze through the vent, and she couldn't fly.

She would have to wait for the right moment to fly away to Mama.

*   *   *

The damp air was layered with the smells of fresh-cut trees and woodsmoke as the family searched for the perfect tree. Following the others through the rows of green, Tamarind hummed along with a symphonic version of "Joy to the World" that flowed from the sound system. The season was here, and Tamarind, grateful to be breathing, wanted to dig in and savor every smell, taste, and Christmas carol. They had started with Sunday brunch at Le Metro, eating flaky croissants, eggs, and thick bacon under strings of blue and white lights that Aurora said made the restaurant look like a fairyland. No, Tamarind wasn't firing on all pistons yet, but she had pushed for this outing, knowing that the fresh air would do her good after feeling like she'd been riding a skiff in a storm since her chemo treatment. It was important to stick to their regular routine, especially one as important as picking out their Christmas tree the first weekend in December.

"Let's get that one!" Aurora said as the teenage guy with the watch cap and ruddy face twirled a tree for their family to see. "It's so grand, like in *White Christmas.*"

"We need something to fit our family room," Pete said, "not the Dusky Pine Lodge. Something shorter."

"We can always trim the bottom for you," the kid said.

"Thanks, but I'm looking for eight feet," Pete said.

"But Ruby and I want a big tree this year," Aurora insisted.

"I didn't say that."

"You said we had a twig last year," Aurora insisted.

Ruby shoved her hands into her jacket pockets. "I was just kidding."

"But isn't a bigger tree more work to do?" asked Rima, who had never been shopping for a Christmas tree before. Tamarind's family had always celebrated the Hindu festival of Diwali and over the years had taken on many Christmas traditions, such as gift giving, joyful music, and festive dinner gatherings. But never the tree. Rima didn't like the idea of bringing pine needles and animal nests into her home.

Now a woman sang "Hark! The Herald Angels Sing" with

a country twang, and Tamarind sang along, causing Aurora to roll her eyes.

"We're looking for an eight-foot tree, girls." Pete turned to the teenage boy. "Do you have anything shorter?"

"Sure." The kid scanned the church parking lot, squinting. He didn't seem so sure. "Let's try over here."

As the family traipsed after the young man, Tamarind fished her cell phone from her pocket and took some photos. The cancer had taught her that it was always time to make memories and grab a few pictures for posterity. She was capturing a rare shot of Ruby and Aurora together in front of a wreath when her phone chimed.

"Who is calling me on a Sunday?" She saw that it was Ruth Thorn. "Delilah's mother." She tapped the button to answer. "Hi, Ruth."

"Tamarind, I'm sorry to bother you, just knowing what you're dealing with. I hope you're feeling okay."

"Feeling good today. We just went for a little family brunch."

"Wonderful! Are you able to talk? I hope this isn't a bad time."

"It's fine," Tamarind lied.

"I'm so sorry to bother you, but I just thought you should know. Ruby's a great kid and we love her, so this is probably nothing. But the other night, Friday night, when Delilah had Ruby come for a sleepover? Ruby left sometime after midnight and didn't return."

"Oh, really. She didn't?" She glanced at Ruby, who was facing away from her, inspecting trees. "No, I didn't know about that. I appreciate you telling me."

"Honestly, I don't know what these girls are up to, but with my girls there are usually some shenanigans involved when they disappear."

Tamarind chuckled. "Shenanigans. I haven't heard that word in years, but yes, it sounds like something's going on."

"I just thought you should know."

"I appreciate that. I'll let you know if anything pops on this end." When Tamarind ended the call, Ruby and Pete were nowhere in sight, but Aurora had edged closer, listening in.

"Where's your sister?" Tamarind moved down the aisle, her boots clicking on the pavement as she passed a family with little kids, the youngest ones hopping in glee.

"Is Ruby in trouble?" she asked.

Tamarind gave her a withering look.

"I'm just asking."

From the end of the aisle Tamarind spotted Ruby, Pete, and Rima lingering near one of the checkout counters. "We're having hot apple cider," Rima said, lifting a minicup. "It's very good. Plenty of cinnamon."

"Would you like some?" Pete offered.

She shook her head, her gaze trained on Ruby, who seemed to watch from a million miles away. Traces of the old Ruby, who'd been haunted by anxiety, by the sad sorrow of longing for something she could never have. "I just got a call from Delilah's mother. She was concerned." Tamarind recounted the call, watching Ruby retreat further away, until she was left staring at the ground. The reaction scared her. There was something going on, and it seemed a lot weightier than typical teen shenanigans.

"Wait a second." Pete straightened and squared his feet, the papa bear instinct emerging as he faced Ruby. "You snuck out of Delilah's house?"

"I couldn't sleep. I just drove around, and then I came home. Remember? I was home before breakfast."

"You drove around alone? In the rain?" Pete balled up his empty cup and shot it into the can. "I don't like the sound of that."

"I would have been out of my mind with worry if I'd known that was going on," Tamarind said. "Not a good choice, Rubes. We trust you with your friends. We let you use the car. We do that expecting you to make responsible choices."

"I'm sorry. I just . . . I needed to work some things out."

"Well, pull something like that again and you'll be doing your thinking on a bicycle." Pete lifted his chin in that authoritative gesture that reminded Tamarind of his father, Doc. "Don't make me start watching mileage on the car now."

Tamarind wanted to stop him from coming down hard, but she bit her bottom lip and kept quiet. Discipline was a good thing, in the right doses. And if he was going to be the hard guy, she could offer a sympathetic ear.

"I won't do it again." Ruby's voice was hollow, zombie-esque.

"All right. Sheesh. Let's move on, all right?" Pete went over to the first row of trees and tugged at the branches of a noble fir. "There's got to be at least one Doug fir on this lot that isn't twelve feet tall," he said as he disappeared in a flurry of green.

"If you ever want to talk . . ."

"I know, Mom," Ruby said, staring at the ground. "I'm sorry, especially now, with your treatment and everything. This is my screw-up, but it's not about you or Dad. I love you guys, okay?"

A screw-up? Oh, God, that sounds bad. "Honey, what happened? Are you okay?"

"I'm fine. I'm just really sorry. I won't let it happen again, okay? I promise." Ruby's eyes were shiny with tears, but she turned away, ending the discussion as she went off and disappeared into the maze of trees.

Fighting a wave of nausea, Tamarind stifled a burp as she held on to the counter. She didn't want to lose her delicious breakfast. She glanced over at her mother, who had remained quiet during the encounter. "This isn't good," Tamarind said. "Do you think it's drugs? Opioids . . . or heroin? Or maybe she's pregnant." She braced herself against the counter as the deluge of horrible possibilities washed past her. "We've always given Ruby a lot of latitude because she earned it. But now, I feel like she's fallen into something awful while I wasn't paying attention."

"I don't think so. This is not Ruby's big crisis, but someone else's. I saw it in her tea, many bad omens. Disappointment everywhere. But that was the worst of it."

"You read her tea? You never mentioned it."

"I was reading for some of the teenage girls at Thanksgiving. Ruby didn't participate, but I took a look in her cup after she turned away. It worried me for her, but I didn't see a great evil. But there were omens of disappointment, and there was a warning—the hourglass—and the cat of deceit."

"I hate that damned cat."

"Ha! That's right. It came up in your tea when you were a teenager, too. Going to parties with your friends when you said you were at a sleepover. Like mother, like daughter."

"Not exactly how I remember it, but that's not Ruby. She's a straight shooter. Has she fallen in with some bad kids?" Tamarind wanted to kick herself for not paying closer attention to her daughter. "I've been too self-absorbed to keep an eye on her."

"You have to take time to heal. I've kept my eyes on her. On both girls. I don't know what's going on with Ruby. We're not getting the full picture. We're not meant to see everything. Not yet."

"I can't stand by and not do anything. What can I do?"

"You watch and wait. She's handling it. Didn't you listen to her?"

"What sixteen-year-old knows how to handle a difficult situation?"

"Your daughter." There was steel in Rima's voice, the confidence of someone who stood on solid ground. "Your Ruby. Because you taught her well."

CHAPTER 39

All through her Monday classes Ruby dreaded driving her mother to chemo that afternoon, knowing that Mom would prod her for more information during the awkward ride.

"Tell her you don't feel well," Delilah suggested when they met in the control booth at lunchtime.

"But there's no one else to drive her," Ruby said, "not at the last minute."

"What about an Uber?"

"What's wrong with you?" Maxi flicked the air toward Delilah. "She can't let her mom take an Uber to chemo."

"Thank you," Ruby told Maxi, who understood Ruby's dilemma but couldn't think of a way out. Because there was no way out.

"I'm sorry my mom called your mom." Feet propped up on the sound board, Delilah was eating cafeteria mac and cheese, one of her favorite lunches. "She doesn't usually butt in that way."

"She was concerned," Maxi said, "and her radar is on track. I mean, you drove to East Portland in the middle of the night and found a shit show when you got there. I'm kind of freaked for you. What do you think happened to Glory?"

"I know she went out the window. I don't know why or how." Her friends knew the story from start to finish; to pick through the details would only highlight all the things she didn't know: the cause of Glory's injuries and the story of the little girl, Luna.

"What if Leo tried to kill her?" Maxi said. "She said he killed that other sister, Annabelle. Maybe Leo pushed her from the attic."

"Maybe. I just can't stop thinking about the little girl. If it's true that Glory had a kid, she was about to leave the house and abandon her. I was going to help her abandon another daughter."

Maxi jostled her shoulder. "But you didn't know that."

"I was going to help Glory repeat the worst thing that ever happened to me."

"But was it the worst thing?" Maxi asked. "I mean, you're here now. You're good."

"You're great," Delilah agreed. "So we're talking about parallel universes here? We'd be screwed without you."

"I don't feel great. I feel very small and ineffective."

"I'm so relieved that nothing happened to you Friday night. That house isn't safe. I wouldn't go near that place if I were you," Delilah said, pointing her plastic fork in the air for emphasis. "And that leader of the group, Tony the Tiger? He's trouble."

"It's 'Leo the Lion,' " Maxi corrected her.

"It's just 'Leo,' and don't worry. I'm not going back there." She had no reason to, now that Glory had gotten out.

Although Ruby braced herself for an honesty assault, once they got in the car after school Tamarind asked about SAT review courses, and the trip was filled with talk of college prep. Ruby had a handful of schools she was planning to apply to. "Nothing Ivy League. Three in Oregon, and then Seattle and San Francisco."

"Fun places for us to visit you."

"I'm down with that. I just don't have any idea what I want to study. And if one more person asks me what I'm going to pursue in college, my head is going to explode."

"That would be messy. But you're a solid student and you work hard. You'll get to where you want to be."

"But what if I never feel passionate about any profession? I know people who have it all figured out. They're going into microbiology to study genetics. Or they're premed or business. They know where they're going."

"Mmm. But not really. None of us can see that far ahead. It's like when you read your tea leaves and you tell the story in the cup. But that story only goes so far. You can't get an entire novel in one glimpse. Just a few hints, the occasional signpost."

"You remind me of Nani Rima," Ruby said, "in a good way."

"That's so sweet." Tamarind touched Ruby's shoulder.

Ruby kept her eyes on the road, not wanting her mother to see the budding tears.

This time the infusion ward wasn't frightening, but as they passed by occupied bays Ruby once again felt the weight of hope and suffering for the patients here. A young woman wearing a pink bandana on her head. A man with a blue beanie napping with his eyeglasses propped on his chest.

"My good friends are back for more fun on the fifth floor." Jessica greeted them with a smile and assigned them to a bay.

"You'll be glad to know I stuck to a bland diet today," Mom told her. "I hope it helps."

"Most patients find that it helps control the nausea," Jessica said. "You might have a better go of it today. Let me order up your cocktail and get your vitals."

While Jessica was taking Tamarind's blood pressure, Ruby excused herself. "I thought I'd check out the cafeteria," she told her mom. "Do you want anything?"

"I'm good."

"They've got killer chicken Santa Fe soup." Jessica removed the Velcro cuff from Mom's arm. "Just saying."

Ruby rode the elevator down four floors, walking past the cafeteria to the big, donut-shaped information desk that dominated the hospital's main lobby. The woman working there wore a Christmas sweater with a grinning Rudolph. His nose was made of a shiny glitter tassel. "How can I help you?"

"I'm looking for a patient. Her name is Glory Noland." The paramedics had mentioned that they were coming here. Maybe Glory was still here.

" 'Noland' with an *N* as in 'Nancy'?" Rudolph's nose glimmered as the woman typed on her keyboard and studied the screen. "We have Glory Noland on the sixth floor. That's Intensive Care, so they're strict about visitors. Are you family?"

Ruby nodded. "Yes." A stretch, but it was true.

"Okay. So you want to take those elevators up to Six, and talk to the nurses there. They allow visitors one at a time, so you'll have to wait in the reception area if someone else is with her. Okay? Good luck."

The Intensive Care Unit had more than a dozen individual rooms that surrounded a central workstation with screens monitored by two attendants. When Ruby asked about Glory, a nurse asked her if she was one of Glory's sisters, too.

"No. I'm her daughter."

"Finally, a more plausible connection." The woman asked her to sign in and show some form of ID. "Our rules are one visitor at a time, so you'll need to wait your turn. One of her sisters is with her now, and there are a handful of the others in the waiting room. Your aunts? You can visit with them in the waiting room at the end of the hall."

Ruby nodded and thanked her. On her way to the waiting room, she wondered if she'd really have the nerve to look in on Glory. She would have to wait until the sisters were done, and in the meantime she didn't want them knowing who she was.

One half of the waiting room was taken up by a family of seven, one of them a sobbing grandma who spoke rapidly in Spanish as a younger woman patted her back. Two little kids sat at a kiddy table staring beyond the toys while a toddler kept trying to pull himself up on a table of fanned-out magazines. There were a few other couples and singles waiting patiently and three women who sat talking in firm but quiet tones.

The sisters.

Ruby caught a glimpse, then turned away before she was caught staring. A petite woman with thin glasses and hair somewhere between blond and white seemed familiar, and Ruby wondered if she had been one of the sisters who'd doted on her at the food court when she was a kid. Ruby lifted her chin. If so, the woman dunking a tea bag in a paper cup would never recognize the young woman Ruby had become. There was a stern, stiff woman with the air of a drill sergeant, and a softer, pudgier woman with a curtain of amazing dark hair. From the doorway Ruby couldn't hear what they were saying, but there was tension in the air. She moved toward them, grabbing a magazine on the way and landing in a seat near the tea drinker, who was being scolded by the prim one for having too much caffeine.

"Another cup of tea, Laura?" The brusque woman with stiff posture and graying hair pulled back in a ponytail was definitely a bitch. Something about her manner reminded Ruby of a server in a fancy restaurant. Or maybe it was her white blouse and prim black skirt. "You are going to be buzzed all night."

"It's decaf tea," said Laura, the birdlike woman with short blond hair. "Chamomile. But that's not what's making me sad. I'm worried about Glory."

"I am, too," said the one with the beautiful hair. "It's not good to be unconscious for so long. I hope she can make her way back."

"I thought you used to be a nurse, Kimani?"

"A nurse's aide." Kimani shifted her hair over her left shoulder. "There's a big difference."

"Glory's not going to recover." The stern sister seemed annoyed with the other two. "Didn't you hear the doctor? The scans aren't showing any sign of brain activity. For all intents and purposes, Glory is gone."

The other two sisters stared at her for a moment; then Laura started crying. "She's going to die."

"Technically, she's already dead," muttered the stern sister.

Ruby's heart was beating hard in her chest as the news fell over her. *Glory is dying. It sounds like it's just a matter of time.* Ruby turned the page of the magazine, trying to keep a neutral expression when she wanted to shriek.

"Leo should be here," Laura said, sniffing. "He would know what to do."

"He won't come. Leo doesn't deal with messes. You know what he says: 'Focus on the good.' And leave the bad for the rest of us to clean up." Kimani shuddered. "He should have mentioned that he and Sienna moved the shed. He should have told Glory, at least."

"Why? So that she could find another way to sneak out?" asked the stern one.

"Listen to yourself, Rachel." Kimani's voice was soft now but serrated with anger. "You admit he killed her. You're saying that's okay, that she deserved to die because she occasionally climbed out the back window and met people while we were sleeping."

So that was Glory's means of escape—out the back window and onto a shed?

"Wait." Laura held her hands up to pause the momentum. "Deep breath. We can't change what happened."

"But Leo knew she was using that shed to sneak out. Everyone knew it." Kimani raked her hair back, clearly anguished by the situation. "It's just so over the line. We need to help, not to hurt."

Ruby liked this woman, Kimani. Despite whatever situation had led her to join the sisters, she seemed to have a moral compass.

The prim one, Rachel, sniffed and turned away. "I'm not going to have this conversation right now. Not when Natalie is due to join us any minute. I did nothing wrong. I came to visit my injured sister, that's all."

"I think it's important for us to visit, even if Glory doesn't know we're here. It's so sad," Laura said in a small, childlike voice.

"That's true," Kimani said. "They say the sense of hearing

is the last one to go. That's why I think we should be allowed to bring Luna to visit."

Luna? So the little girl is real.

"You're right, Kimani. The girl should have a chance to say good-bye to her mother."

"Say good-bye to a shell of a person?" responded Rachel. "Why can't you two accept scientific fact? Even if Luna was allowed to come visit, Glory is unconscious. It would be like talking to a sack of potatoes."

"Rachel . . ." Kimani glanced toward the other people in the waiting room as one couple rose and headed toward the door. "Have some respect."

Off on her own flight of whimsy, Laura clasped her hands together. "I'm hoping for a miracle. Maybe Luna will bring her out of it!"

Kimani patted her shoulder. "That's probably not going to happen, but it can't hurt to give it a shot."

"There will be no miracles!" Rachel snapped. "You heard the doctor. Glory is in a vegetative state. There's no brain activity. She was deprived of oxygen for too long and her brain is dead. That's science, plain and simple."

"But at least it's worth a try, bringing Luna in," Laura needled the stern woman. "Oh, what could it hurt?"

Rachel clasped her hands to her cheeks in frustration. "Did you not hear anything I said?"

"My hearing is perfect, sister."

Their squabbling was halted when a shiny wheelchair came rolling into the waiting room. Their queen bee.

Ruby remembered.

The sisters had fawned over this woman, and apparently, Natalie still ruled. As a kid, Ruby had admired her chair with big, shiny wheels. Bigger than the stroller Ruby had shared with Aurora.

"We can go," Natalie announced. The sisters rose quickly to meet her halfway as she wheeled the chair closer. "I've signed the papers."

"And we didn't even know there was something to sign. Was that about the medical bills?"

Natalie looked up at her over slender glasses. "No, no. We're not responsible for that. I signed the DNR."

"What's that?" Laura chirped, childlike, though she seemed to be the oldest of the sisters here.

Kimani reached out and clasped Laura's arm, seeming to need support. "It stands for 'Do Not Resuscitate.' It's an order to let Glory die."

"Good," Rachel muttered. "Someone had to do it."

"I thought papers like that needed to be signed by the next of kin." Kimani seemed uncomfortable with the situation.

Right on, thought Ruby.

"I'm her sister," Natalie said. "That's close enough. I was able to provide the hospital staff with sufficient documentation. There's something to be said for keeping your paperwork in order; isn't that right, Rachel?" Backing up her chair, Natalie ran over the toe of Ruby's boot. It pinched a little, but more upsetting was Natalie's bland expression as she felt the obstruction, glanced at Ruby, and rolled forward without an apology.

A few miles away, Luna lay in bed staring across the room at the empty single bed. Mama's slippers were lined up neatly at the foot of the bed, and her robe hung on the hook next to Luna's.

The empty bed seemed enormous tonight, and Luna felt the loss of her mother keenly. Leo had let Georgina bring her down here this afternoon, with the message that she had better behave because no one wanted the task of dumping the bucket from the attic. At first Luna was relieved to return to her room, take a bath, and change into clean clothes. But now that night was here, this room seemed to stretch and warp around her, too cold and empty.

Above Mama's empty bed, Luna saw the bedroom window,

wide open and blackish blue with star clusters twirling in pin-wheels. How did that window get open? And it was so odd, because she knew that stars didn't move that way. The sun didn't move that way; it was the Earth that orbited the sun. She sat up on her bed, wondering if it was the end of the world—stars dancing in the sky and the Earth swinging out of its regular orbit. That would be an okay way to end.

Then the darkness expanded from the window like racing floodwaters, reaching into the room, snaking over the floor to clutch her in its bulky fist. Its massive black coils surrounded her waist and flung her across the floor, dragging her over to Mama's bed, to the black hole, the void, the end of time.

She tried to resist, holding on to the bed frame until she was yanked loose. The windowsill was her last chance. Her fingers gripped the white ledge, turning blue from the pressure. Then, the black tide peeled them loose, easy as tapping the keys of a piano. *Plunk, plunk, plunk,* ten times, and she was wrenched away and falling out the window.

Luna woke up screaming and writhing on the floor of the attic. She had rolled out of the sleeping bag to the dusty, rough wood, moving only two feet or so, though she felt as if she had fallen for miles. Some sisters stood over her, Georgina and Julia, staring down, telling her to calm down, but she batted their hands away. Covering her head, she rolled over to the bedpost and sobbed against the comforter.

"I need Mama. Mama . . ."

She was surprised to hear comfort in Georgina's gruff whispers. "It's all right now. Quiet down. You can go back to sleep." The meaty fingers of the sisters' cook were gentle as they nudged Luna back over to her sleeping bag. Patting Luna's shoulder absently, she sang the nonsense chorus to "Tura-Lura-Lural."

Rolling over onto the swollen side of her face, Luna let out a cry, which made Georgina sing louder. She didn't get it. No one got it. The world was hopeless.

*   *   *

The next day Ruby found the online obituary for Glory Noland. It seemed like significant news for an unremarkable Tuesday in December, too early in the month to be Christmassy. Just another gray, wet December day.

The short blurb reported that Glory Noland broke her neck and sustained a traumatic brain injury in a fall from a second-story window. She died Monday night at St. Victor Hospital.

She had probably died after Ruby left the hospital with Mom. Ruby could imagine the nurses of that ward methodically doing their job, turning off life-support machines and making sure the patient had enough drugs in her system to die without pain. She also imagined that Glory had died alone, since the sisters had exited when Natalie gave the order.

After the sisters had left, Ruby had gone to Glory's glass-walled room, edging cautiously toward the beeping monitors and the silent body wrapped in tape and tubes and a neck brace. It was hard to feel a connection to the person fading away under the scary equipment, but she found one of Glory's hands, a little cold, and held on to it. She had read that when people were dying sometimes they needed encouragement to move on.

"It's Ruby," she said. "I just want to let you know that everything's going to be okay." Glory didn't respond, and Ruby didn't cry. Her head was too full with the antiseptic smells; her memories of the barbs of the quarreling sisters; the cold blips of the medical monitors. None of this seemed real; it was like stepping into an episode of *Grey's Anatomy*.

The news account said that the preliminary investigation pointed to suicide. Investigators were trying to locate surviving family. *Me*, Ruby thought. *I'm her daughter.* And what about the mysterious girl who played with Hazel? If Hazel's mother was right, the girl, Luna, would be Ruby and Aurora's half sister. At least by blood.

But Ruby already had a sister—a sister and a father and a mother. Digging around to find her birth mother was a horrible idea. She'd opened a Pandora's box. She lived in fear of her parents learning of the betrayal, but she couldn't bear to tell Tamarind and Pete McCullum about it. Ruby wasn't sure that she would ever shake loose the mantle of shame and guilt.

She closed the news website, erased the computer history, and promised herself she would never dig again.

PART 3

GLORY'S GHOST

CHAPTER 40

Middle of December

Sitting cross-legged on Mama's bed, Luna watched out the window for signs of movement at Hazel's house. It was Luna's first day out of the attic since Mama had fallen from this window, and all that time Luna had not been brought to the hospital to see her mother.

Not once.

It made her so mad at Leo and Natalie. Burning mad at them. "All I want is to see my mother," Luna had said constantly since the night Mama had been taken away. "Why doesn't anyone listen to me?" she would bellow as she rattled the attic door against its hinges.

But Leo and Natalie couldn't hear her shouting from their room on the first floor, and her demands had fallen on the ears of her prison guards: Sienna, who had told her to stop being a spoiled little monster, and Georgina, who was so afraid of everything and everyone that most of the time her hands quivered like Jell-O. After five days of shouting, tantrums, and banging on the attic floor to bother the sisters below, Luna had paused halfway through a bowl of lukewarm, salty ramen noodles to think over her plan.

No one was really listening to her demands.

And no one would tell her when Mama was coming back.

That did it. By the time she finished the bowl, she had a new plan. She would behave and follow orders so that she could get her freedom back. If she could start visiting Hazel's house again, she might talk Hazel's mother into giving her a ride to the hospital. And once she was in Mama's arms, she would never, ever come back to this place.

It took a few days for things to sink in, but this morning Sienna had come up to unlock the door and walk her down to the second floor. "Get yourself cleaned up," Sienna had said. "Leo will come up and talk to you later."

Stepping into a hot bath, Luna had wanted to cry, maybe from relief. But she'd just leaned her head against the tub, studied the familiar cracks on the ceiling, and wondered why Mama hadn't come back to get her. Did that mean she was still badly injured? Or was she trying to save up money to arrange a ride or a place to stay? There had to be something, something that had gone wrong that Mama was trying to fix so that they could be together.

Afterward she got dressed and went down to the kitchen to find some breakfast. Luna liked being able to pick what she wanted—peaches-'n'-cream oatmeal. She mixed the packet with water and added some milk to cool it down, being careful not to spill on the table. Leo got mad when she spilled things.

From the quiet house she knew Natalie and most of the sisters were long gone to the hotel, and she sensed that Leo and Sienna were gone, too. Probably to the grocery store.

Or maybe they were visiting Mama at the hospital.

It made her so mad that no one would tell her how Mama was doing while she was locked in the attic. That had made her bruised face and lumpy sleeping bag a thousand times worse. In the times Leo sent her up to the attic, Sienna had talked more than ever to Luna. Those first few days, she had been a little like Mama, taking care of Luna, cleaning out the gash on her face, trying to make her feel better.

Other times Sienna complained bitterly about the disgusting part of attic duty. "It's too much for me, lugging water up the stairs. And this piss bucket is disgusting."

Luna didn't like the bucket, either. "It's not my fault."

"Leo should take this over during the day. He would if that

bitch would let him. I think she's trying to make me miscarry. That would make her day! So she could save money on the abortion."

"What's abortion?"

Sienna squinted at her as she wiped her hands on her apron. "How old are you again? It's when you make a baby go away."

Luna didn't understand this, and when Sienna started crying she knew she'd said the wrong thing. "I'm sorry."

"It's not your fault. It's just that . . . I want to have this baby, but they're making me get rid of it. Natalie's making me."

A baby? Luna's eyes opened wide. "I can help you take care of a baby."

Sienna swiped at the tears on her cheeks with the back of one hand. "What do you know about babies?"

"I can learn, and I'll be so gentle. Mama's going to get me out of this house, and we're never coming back. Mama will save you, too. You and your baby can come along."

"You don't get it. I don't want to leave," Sienna whined. "I want to stay and have my baby and be Leo's wife. I love him."

"You want to marry him?" Luna blinked, unable to understand why Sienna would want to stay with Leo. "But we could help you. Mama can help. She's coming back as soon as she can. How is she? Have you heard?"

"You think they tell me anything around here?" Sienna took the empty plastic bowl from the wooden crate. "I'm not in with the sisters like that. I'm not part of the popular crowd." She had given a sour laugh, revealing a crooked tooth that reminded Luna of a pebble from the yard. "The ones that went visiting her at the hospital. Laura and Rachel and Kimani. Well, Kimani makes sense, since she used to be a nurse. But Rachel and Laura, they would wrestle each other to lick Natalie's boots."

That was the thing with Sienna: No matter what she talked about, she was never far from complaining about Natalie.

While she'd been locked in the attic, Luna's only other contact had been Georgina, who had never been a source of information about anything. Georgina had trouble forming words, and even when she managed it, talking seemed painful. She didn't seem to pay much attention to what people were saying, but she understood the power of food. The first night, Georgina had clopped up the stairs, struggling with her arthritis, to bring Luna a cup of applesauce she'd smuggled home from the mall! Tears of joy had rolled down Luna's cheeks at the cool, tart sweetness. It made Luna feel bad about how she used to complain about Georgina's sloppy joes and gray rice pilaf. After that there'd been a treat every night. Sample chocolates from the mall candy shop. A pretzel stick. A mini cinnamon bun. And saltwater taffy that had blue and purple flecks in it. Wonderful treats, though nothing topped that first night. "Can you get more applesauce?" Luna had asked, and Georgina had nodded in her gruff way. Luna couldn't wait to tell Mama about Georgina's good deeds, and she'd even saved some saltwater taffy to share with her.

After cleaning up her dishes, Luna went back to her room and sat on Mama's bed to stare out over the backyard at Hazel's house. She refused to think of the distance Mama had fallen or the bones of Annabelle rotting in the soil below the window.

Her eyes were on the Hanson house. Waiting and watching for Hazel.

It was a gray afternoon, but the Hansons' Christmas tree was lit, their back window aglow with dots of red and green and blue and yellow. Those colorful lights gave Luna hope.

She was going to find her way to Mama.

She was just waiting for the right moment, a clear shot over to Hazel's house, where she would beg for a ride to the hospital. Then she'd catch up with Mama, and they'd be together in a much better place than this. Maybe a house like Hazel's.

Her chance came a few days later, when she was left alone in the house.

Something was wrong with Sienna. She was curled up on the floor of the parlor, her head resting on the love seat as she moaned in pain.

"I've got to get her to a doctor," Leo said. "You keep on

with the vacuuming. I expect everything to be neat and clean when we get back."

"Are you going to the hospital?" Luna asked. "I could come along and help." *And go find Mama.*

Leo had squinted at her as if she'd sprouted wings. "No. Just the clinic."

A few minutes later there was a car and driver waiting outside for them. Luna stared out the front window, wondering how Leo had made that happen. She knew it was called a cab or Uber, but how did it all work? She heard the click-clack sounds as he bolted the series of locks on the front door, and then watched as he put his arms around Sienna to help her down the front walk.

And then they drove off.

Luna walked past the vacuum cleaner strewn like a sick robot on the living room floor and went upstairs to wait. Since Hazel wasn't home yet, she took the time to change her shirt to the pink T-shirt Hazel liked. Then she pulled up the corner of the bedding on Mama's mattress and checked inside the little slit Mama had cut on the side. The cell phone was tucked safely inside there. Luna flipped it open and closed a few times, but the little screen wasn't lighting up anymore. Luna's heart sank. Was it broken? It probably didn't matter much, since she couldn't use it to call Mama. Still, it was a shame. She tucked it back into the mattress, determined to take it with her when she went to join Mama.

When Hazel and her mom walked up the driveway at the usual after-school time, Luna's heart soared. Her friend!

She made it down the stairs and out through the unlocked garage window in no time. Hazel was still waiting for her mom to unlock the door when Luna called to them through the fence.

"Luna! Oh, my gosh, I've been thinking about you!"

Squeezing through the loose fence boards, Luna was greeted by a splash of red—her friend's rain slicker—as Hazel pulled her into a big hug. "Come inside," said Hazel. "My mom made Christmas cookies."

After a week in the attic, Hazel's house seemed sweeter and warmer than ever. There was the pine scent of the tree and the smell of butter cookies that Hazel's mother had made, and the tree itself, like a fairy's home in the forest.

"It's good to see you, Luna." Nicole put a hand on Hazel's shoulder, then tilted her head. "That must have hurt," she said, gently touching a fingertip to Luna's cheek. "What happened?"

"It was an accident." Luna went over to the cookies on the counter.

"I see. I'm sorry about your mom."

"I know. She was hurt bad. She's still at the hospital." Luna turned back with a cookie in hand. "Ms. Nicole, can I ask you something?"

"Of course, honey."

"I need to visit my mother and no one will take me to see her. Can you drive me to the hospital?"

"To the hospital?"

Hazel lifted her head from the cookie she was licking to extract the sprinkles. "She could drive you, right, Mom? She drives me everywhere. And I could go with you. We could visit your mother together. Right, Mom?"

"I . . . I'd love to help," agreed Hazel's mother, though she was staring at Luna in a funny way.

"Does that mean we're taking a road trip?" Hazel asked. "Road trip! Road trip!"

Luna felt thrilled and frightened at the prospect of riding in a car. It looked like an amazing way to go from point A to point B, but she knew that accidents happened on the road, too. Her father had been killed in an accident up in Alaska when she was a baby.

"A short trip. But not today. You've got an appointment with Dr. Kerr in forty-five minutes. The orthodontist."

"That's right." Hazel broke off a corner of the star cookie and confided in Luna, "I might have to get braces."

"What's that?"

"You know. On my teeth? Some kids hate them, but I think braces are sexy."

"What are you talking about?" Hazel's mom called from the pantry.

"Nothing." Hazel leaned close to whisper in Luna's ear: "You're not supposed to say 'sexy.' It's a naughty word."

Luna nodded. There were so many things to learn, so many things to know, things that weren't covered in the books she'd read. How did people learn everything?

Hazel poured two cups of milk, and they went in to watch a holiday show on television before Hazel had to leave. Luna savored the creamy milk, but it was hard to enjoy herself, knowing she wouldn't be seeing Mama today. She would slip back into the house and then sneak over here another time when Ms. Nicole could give her a ride.

The pounding noise at the kitchen door made Luna jump. When she heard Leo's voice a second later, she knew she would be in trouble. Peeking into the kitchen, she saw Hazel's mother talking with Leo.

"Really, we're happy to have Luna over anytime," Ms. Nicole insisted.

"She's not supposed to be here, and she knows it."

"Still, it's not a problem for us. And she's so smart. I think she might benefit from attending the local school. I'd be happy to walk you through registration, and I could drive her to and from school. I have to take Hazel, anyway."

Ms. Nicole was being so nice, Luna wanted to hug her! But Leo stared at Hazel's mom, his eyes cold as ice. "Luna is homeschooled, and she needs to learn to follow the rules. She needs to stay on our property. If she leaves, she'll be punished."

"No offense, but it's not healthy for a kid to be cooped up that way."

"No offense, but I don't remember asking your opinion." Leo turned and caught Luna watching. "Let's go, Luna. You're wasting my time."

Luna plodded forward reluctantly as Hazel made a little fuss, saying how much she had missed Luna and giving her a hug. Luna tried to hug her back, but her heart was iced over with fear, making it impossible to be a good friend.

"I know you think you're helping," Leo told Ms. Nicole as he directed Luna toward the door, "but you're not. Keep interfering like this and you'll leave me no choice but to take action against you and your husband."

"You would sue us for having your girl over for a play-date?" she asked in disbelief.

"I won't wait around for law enforcement. I'm proactive. I like to take things into my own hands." He opened the kitchen door and pushed Luna out. She moved off the stoop, tears stinging her eyes.

"Wait. There's something else." Hazel's mom came out the door after them, her arms crossed against the damp cold.

Leo grinned, liking the attention from her.

Hazel's mom frowned at him. "You haven't told her yet, have you?"

He squinted at her. "What are we talking about here?"

"Her mother. She wants to go to the hospital to see her mother. She thinks Glory is there. You haven't told her."

"Told me what?" Luna asked.

"Nothing." Hands on her shoulders, Leo pointed Luna toward their house and gave her a push.

CHAPTER 41

Tamarind was sitting on the living room couch, sipping tea by the Christmas tree, when Ruby came in with her laptop.

"Homework finished?" Tamarind asked.

"Almost. I just wanted to sit by the tree." In the past week Ruby had been spending more time in the family room with her mother and grandmother, who probably thought she was having some teenage freak-out.

The freak-out part was true. But she couldn't tell them the reason for it, that she was being haunted by her birth mother and the only way to escape the guilt was to surround herself with people. As she'd mulled over her last moments with Glory, Ruby had realized that her final words to Glory had sounded like a promise. A vague promise, yes, but Ruby had told her things would be okay.

Now Ruby felt responsible for the little girl. With Glory gone, it was up to Ruby to make sure Luna was okay. That was all. The kid was probably fine, but it was worth checking.

Her friends disagreed.

"It's not your responsibility to take care of someone else's kid," Delilah said, "even if she is your half sister."

"I'm not taking care of her; of course I can't do that. I just need to make sure she's okay living with the sisters."

"And how would you do that?" asked Maxi. "You can't go

near that house again. Glory told you they killed a woman there. That makes two women killed at that house."

"We can't be sure what happened to Glory," Ruby said.

"You know," Maxi said. "You know it's true. I won't let you go back to that house."

"Believe me, I don't want to go," Ruby told her friends. She wasn't even sure that she would find the little girl there. The police had found no sign of her.

So really, there was nothing she could do.

Really.

But that didn't stop the guilt from seeping into her consciousness every time she was alone in her room or driving in the car. Guilt had amazingly invasive qualities, the ability to penetrate glass and steel, the ability to find you anywhere like a signal beamed from a satellite in space, the ability to sour the sweetest moments. Guilt was making Ruby squirm. She was coming to realize that she would eventually have to rise from her shell, like the Venus in that famous painting. She couldn't cower in her room squeezing rubber ducks for the rest of her life. One of these days, she was going to have to step up.

Until then, she tried to elude Glory's ghost by nestling into conversation with her family and friends. She typed a few sentences on the English assignment and then glanced at the tree. Dad had switched to white and blue lights from their usual assorted colors, and there was something peaceful about the cool tones. "Looks like someone added some presents under the tree," Ruby said.

"Nani and I went shopping this afternoon." Tamarind cocked one brow as she lifted her teacup. "You can always find plenty of things to wrap at the dollar store." She took a deep sip. "I remember your first Christmas with us, how you loved having gifts under the tree. On Christmas Day, after all the presents were opened, you begged us to wrap them up and put them under the tree again."

Ruby winced. "I was such a dorky little kid. I don't know how you and Dad had the patience to deal with my phobias and issues."

"Are you kidding? It was such a huge victory every time we figured out what was bothering you. Like working a puzzle, piece by piece. And we were deeply motivated because you were a fascinating little girl. You still are. Not so little anymore, but we love you anyway."

"Aw. I love you, too. I gotta say, you really scared us there."

"Keeping you on your toes." Tamarind took another sip of tea and then rose from the sofa. "But my last numbers were really good. Looks like I'm sticking around."

"Yes, yes, you will live a long and happy life, my daughter." Rima entered the room with an armful of small gifts wrapped like candy twists. "Here's the last of the dollar store goodies."

"That's a lot, Nani." Ruby leaned over to pick up a small package and check it out. "Got any rubber duckies in there?"

"Don't ask, and I won't tell you," Rima said. "So what shall we have for dinner? It's too late to start from scratch. You want the pizza from the 'Papa' place?"

"I was thinking of some quick spaghetti with jar sauce," Tamarind said, swirling her cup. "But I'll do it, Ma. You've been on duty every night."

"We're going to miss you when you go back, Nani."

"I know. You've never had so much home cooking. But I need to return home. Your grandfather has had enough with bachelor life."

"Here, Ma." Tamarind used the saucer to drain the rest of the liquid into the sink, then set the cup on the kitchen counter. "You can read for me while I get dinner started."

"Of course." Rima peeked down at the cup, then went around the counter into the kitchen and filled another cup from the hot-water spigot. "And here's a cup for Ruby. I need to read your tea leaves, my dear, before I go back to Seattle."

Feeling trapped, Ruby looked up from the computer. "You don't need to do that, Nani. But I do want to hear about Mom's."

"I'll do both. No need to waste my talents."

"I'm just not in the mood," Ruby said.

"I insist." Rima handed her a steaming cup. "When it cools, sip slowly. Thoughtfully."

Ruby had no choice but to accept the cup. Staring at the sparkling tree, she blew on the hot cup and wondered how far her grandmother would be able to see into her tormented soul.

"Now, my dear daughter, let's see your leaves. Mmm. As I said, you have many good omens. I knew that good things were coming for you. Here is a bird, a sign of good news, and I think that will be about your medical outcome. And let's see . . . a fat jug for your health. This is all very good, Tamarind."

"Fantastic, Ma." Tamarind flung her arms wide and then pulled a wooden spoon from the jar on the counter.

Ruby took a sip of the tea and set it aside to return to her work as her grandmother searched for other patterns in Mom's tea leaves. She found a donkey as a reminder to be patient, and a tiny ant for perseverance.

"Are you sure it's not a real ant in there, Ma?" Tamarind teased.

"I am sure it's only tea. And here, my dear daughter—the five-pointed star. This is very good." Gratified by the sight, Rima waved Tamarind over to the teacup to take a look. "It's the sign of good fortune, at last. I think the worst of that cancer is behind you now. One look at you and anyone can see it's true. Not even a month since your surgery, and getting that terrible chemo, and yet you are making dinner for your family."

Tamarind returned to the stove to lower the fire on the tomato sauce. "It's only spaghetti and jar sauce, Ma. And the star's a little wimpy. One of its points is sagging."

"Still, it's a star, most definitely, and you are up and moving around, on the road to recovery." Rima turned to Ruby. "Do you want to see it?"

Dutifully, Ruby brought her laptop to the counter and peered into the cup. "I see it. Reminds me of Patrick on *Sponge-Bob*. A little misshapen."

"You two are birds of a feather." Rima tried to sound disapproving, but she was smiling. "Now, on to Ruby. Have you finished drinking?"

"Not yet." Ruby took another sip from her cup, hoping her grandmother would lose interest.

"Leave her be, Mom. She doesn't need us intervening with tea leaves. She's got a lot on her plate, and I think she's juggling it well."

"Sometimes not so well. I see the dark circles under her eyes, and she's always tired," Rima said.

"She works hard in school. Teens are typically sleep deprived," Tamarind said.

"Um, guys? I'm right here in the room."

"Tell us, Ruby, and maybe we can help. We can advise. This is what mothers and daughters do. Tell us, what are your secret troubles?"

Ruby frowned. "Well, if I tell you, they won't be secret anymore."

"Let her be, Ma."

"Do you have a boyfriend?" Rima asked.

The surprise question almost made Ruby spit out her mouthful of tea, but she gulped it back. "No?" Ruby snickered as her mom's cell phone began to ring, "Pete" lit on the screen's surface. "It's Dad."

"Hello?" Tamarind turned away from the kitchen as she spoke. "All good. I'm making pasta for dinner. Yup..." She disappeared down the hall.

"Perfect timing for a phone call," Rima said, looking down into Ruby's cup. "One more sip. Good. Perhaps you don't want your mother to see beneath the surface. We all have secrets." She took Ruby's cup into the kitchen to strain it.

"Do you ever worry that you're going to see something horrible in someone's cup?" Ruby asked. "Like, somebody dying, or a terrible accident?"

"I've always found that the tea leaves give us only as much as we can fathom. And even the most dire predictions are tempered by some positive signs. Now, let me see what we've got here. There is such a big clump of leaves here. That's trouble. But it's across from the handle, so the trouble is not caused by you. It's not your fault."

Ruby scraped her hair back. This was what she'd been dreading. "What kind of trouble?"

"Some sort of deception. I see this bad, bad cat. It means you'll encounter a false person, a trickster. He is not what he seems. But you say there is no boyfriend."

"Nobody on the radar now."

"Then it's someone else who will cause you trouble. A bad influence."

"Really? That's creepy."

"Do you know who this is?"

Ruby shrugged.

"If you do, be on guard. You have good common sense. Watch out for the tricky cat."

Ruby frowned. "What about good news, Nani? Do you see any birds in there? Hearts and flowers?"

"No, none of that. But I do see a shoe."

Ruby hoped a stiletto heel. Or wedge sandals. "And that's good?"

"It means you can expect change for the better."

"Finally, something good." Ruby went around the counter to the stove, where the saucepan was spitting tomato sauce. She stirred it, lowered the heat, and turned to her grandmother. She hoped that the tea leaves meant that Ruby wouldn't be haunted by Glory's ghost forever. "Thanks, Nani."

"I know you will be doing the right thing." Rima patted her on the shoulder. "But just in case, I'll be keeping my eye on you."

She swung the axe into the ground, breaking up the hard crust of the garden bed. It was a cold day, not cold enough for the ground to freeze, but cold enough to see your breath. When she swung again, with all her might and sorrow, dirt clods and pebbles flew into the air and bounced down. The impact of the axe blade on the earth was so hard, Luna thought it might fracture her arms. Mama would never let her touch the axe. But Mama was gone now.

Dead.

How many days had they kept it from her? They'd finally told her yesterday after she'd gotten back from Hazel's house. From Ms. Nicole's burning looks, Luna had known something wasn't right. But she'd had no idea it could be so awful.

Natalie had been the one to tell her. "Listen, kid. Your mother was badly hurt in that fall. She was deprived of oxygen for too long. Once she got to the hospital, the doctors told us she was brain-dead."

"That's ridiculous," Luna said. "A human body cannot survive without a brain."

Silence gripped everyone in the room. Julia stopped her knitting needles clicking. Rachel stopped setting the table. Over in the kitchen Georgina stopped clattering pot lids.

"Glory's passed," Natalie said, breaking the silence. "I'm sorry to be the one to say it, but at least now you know."

"But she was coming back for me," Luna said, swiping at the tears in her eyes. "She promised."

"Well, you can stop waiting on that, and stop asking everyone about her," Leo said. He stood at the kitchen counter, restlessly clicking a pen in and out. Luna hated him. She hated the way he acted around Hazel's mom. The way he ruined her fun at Hazel's. The way he treated the sisters when he snapped. He thought he was Harry Potter, a wise and brave prince. But really he was Voldemort. He was evil incarnate.

She hoisted the axe high and swung it through the air, aiming at a spot near Leo's feet. It cut into the crust, cleaving the packed dirt.

"Careful," Leo said, pointing toward the fence. "Why don't you work over in that direction. We don't want any accidents happening."

Part of her felt that an accident would be perfect. What if she went too far over and chopped into one of his feet? The dark, evil dream brought a sour taste to her throat.

But Leo would get back at her. She took a few steps away from him, watching as he searched the soil with a spade. He sifted through one of the holes she'd opened up, shoveling dark soil and shiny earthworms into an old bucket. Mostly he wanted the worms, reddish gray tentacles looping and flailing to escape into the dirt. Luna had read about earthworms in one of her textbooks. She knew they were both male and female and that they could usually regenerate if you lopped off one section of the worm. Interesting, but yucky.

"You're not going to kill the worms, are you?" Luna didn't like worms, mostly because she thought it would be an awful life living in the dirt, alone most of the time. It made her think of Annabelle. But she didn't want to be a part of killing them. She didn't like killing any living thing—even the spiders in the attic.

"Why? Do you want them as pets?" he teased.

"No. I just want to know why we're collecting them."

"You'll see," he said. "Just keep digging."

He kept her out there working, pounding away with the axe, through much of the afternoon. Finally, he sent her inside, told her to go upstairs and get cleaned up. "And don't track dirt inside!" he called after her.

Luna took her shoes off outside and left them neatly lined up on the patio. On her way to the stairs, she passed Sienna, who was curled up in a chair in the parlor with a mug of tea.

"You didn't do the vacuuming today, and I'm too sick to do it," Sienna said.

"Leo told me to work in the garden."

"Well, then, I guess it's just not going to get done." Sienna rolled her eyes and then sighed. "I don't care about stupid chores, anyway. If Natalie wants shit done, she can get out of that chair and do it herself. Ha."

"Are you still sick?" Luna asked. Sienna seemed to be a little sick all the time now, and when she couldn't do her house chores Leo pushed most of them onto Luna. But Luna didn't mind a few extra chores if it made Sienna like her more. With Mama gone, Sienna was the only person who really talked to Luna.

She nodded. "Killer cramps."

"Aw." She touched Sienna's arm. "I hope you feel better soon."

Sienna stared at Luna's hand. "Your fingernails are filthy. What were you doing out there?"

Luna pulled her hand away. "Just digging. Leo wanted worms."

"That's disgusting. What for?"

Luna shrugged, heading up the stairs. It took a while to get all the dirt out from under her fingernails, especially since the bristles on the old nail brush in the shower were nearly flattened. She quickly got dressed in a T-shirt and old sweat pants that were baggy, but her tights were dirty from working in the garden. Brush in hand, she sat on Mama's bed, missing her as she tried to work the tangles out of her hair. Mama had always done that for her and Luna didn't know how to do it without pulling and yanking. Every day, every minute, she missed Mama.

With most of the tangles out she tossed the brush aside and reached under the pillow for her *Harold* book. The books for her lessons were stacked on the dresser, but she would do them later. She read through the familiar book, reciting the words in her head as she let her index finger follow the purple line of Harold's crayon.

If she had a magic crayon right now, she wasn't sure what she would draw. She had longed for a car to take her to the hospital to see Mama, but now that Mama was gone, where in the world could she go? To Hazel's house? It seemed like a lot to ask the Hansons to save her from Leo and the sisters.

She looked out the window at Hazel's house, where the colored lights of the Christmas tree glimmered in the back window. The car door slammed, and a moment later the car backed out of the driveway. Ms. Nicole was probably headed off to pick Hazel up from school.

Leaning back, Luna saw her reflection in the window. The bruise around her eye was fading, but the scar on her cheek was an angry sliver like a crescent moon. Luna felt bad about lying to Hazel's mom about her scar, but she hadn't wanted anything to get in the way of getting a ride to be with Mama. That was yesterday. Today none of that mattered anymore.

The clatter of breaking glass made her turn to the window again. Someone was in Hazel's backyard. Leo! He'd broken one of the windows.

He swung the axe again, popping the rest of the glass from the frame.

"What are you doing?" she yelled at the closed window, then raced down the stairs. The slider was unlocked, and she swung it open and ran across the yard. "Leo! Leo, stop." In a few swift moves she was through the fence and rushing up to him.

He had dropped the axe to the ground but was hoisting a bucket up to the window frame. The window was over his head, but he managed to tip the bucket and shake the contents into the house.

"Stop it! Stop!" Luna pounded on his back with fisted hands. "You're wrecking their house!"

He glared down at her, pushing her away. "That's the point." She pummeled him again as he reached down for the second bucket. The worms! He was throwing the worms she'd dug up inside Hazel's house. Their back room with the television, their Christmas tree, the little sofa where the girls sat to watch Nickelodeon, would all be ruined.

"Why are you doing this?" she cried as she jumped, trying to knock the bucket out of his hands.

He smiled, lifting it out of her reach. "The Hansons need a reminder to mind their own business." Taunting her, he pretended to hand her the bucket, then shoved her back with an elbow and hoisted it up to the window. She yelped as he dumped the second batch of worms and dirt into the room.

"No!" Defeated, Luna sank back onto the winter grass, mindless of the shattered glass around her as she started to cry.

This was her fault. She had brought this trouble on Hazel's family. And now she could never visit here again. If she did, Leo would torture them even more. It broke her heart, but she knew she had to give up her best friend before he ruined her life. Luna could never visit Hazel again. She sobbed into her hands, not noticing as Leo slipped away through the fence, leaving her to cry over her shriveled world.

CHAPTER 42

One Month Later

Jets of warm water buffeted her feet, so soothing. Ruby sighed and settled in as the hidden fingers of the massage chair rumbled up her spine. A pedicure definitely helped to chisel away the stress, and it was great to be here with her best friends. But still, Ruby was having trouble shaking off the lingering guilt that clung to her like a tiny crab clamped on to her toe. Right now, pleasures like this made her feel greedy.

"We should make our next appointment while we're here," Delilah said. "We'll need mani-pedis before winter formal next month."

"Wow. I wonder if last year's dress will still fit me," Maxi said.

"That's the beauty of having sisters. I get to raid the closet of abandoned dresses." Delilah turned to Ruby. "Are you getting something new?"

Ruby frowned. "Winter formal? Meh."

"Oh, come on," Delilah said. "We agreed that we would go together again. Three silly singles? We had so much fun last year."

Last year had been a blast. The winter formal, also called MORP for backwards prom, was supposed to be a girls' choice event, though Ruby and her friends thought that was hopelessly old-fashioned and demeaning to women. "If I want to ask a guy to a dance," Maxine had insisted, "I am going to ask."

The truth—none of the girls had a guy to ask. Maxi was close with Tyler and Adam Capeci, senior twins who were family friends and seemed like brothers to Maxi. Delilah had a lot of guy friends in the theater tech department, but she wasn't really into any of them. Ruby admired the way Delilah dealt with the guys—some of them tall, low-voiced seniors who were more men than boys, seeming to have crossed a line that Ruby and her friends hadn't yet approached. Delilah was totally comfortable giving them instructions and working beside them for hours in the control booth during a show.

For Ruby, interaction with guys was kind of awkward right now. Sometimes she felt them staring. Sometimes they made flirty comments, and sometimes the comments were so blatantly misogynistic she gave the guys a scalding glare. But she looked forward to a time when guys weren't such alien creatures, incapable of intelligent communication. And to be honest, part of the communication deficit was her own lack of experience.

"Hello?" Delilah prodded. "Don't tell me you're thinking of bailing on us?"

"Thinking about it," Ruby said. "But when I mentioned it to my mom, she kind of freaked, too. She said there are certain opportunities that only come along a few times in life. I guess winter formal is supposed to be one of them."

"That's so funny." Maxi wriggled her shoulders, adjusting her neck warmer. "My parents could care less if I go. Actually, I think they'd prefer to save the money for the ticket and everything."

"Listen, guys, I have to pay for my own ticket, and I think it's worth every penny." Delilah was getting annoyed. "We are so going. End of story."

"I'll go." Ruby sighed. "It's just so commercial. Materialistic. Capitalistic."

"Nothing wrong with that!" Delilah said, and they laughed.

"It's just that, recently, I've become aware of how advantaged we are. I guess I got woke."

"We know what's going on, Rubes," Maxi said. "You're worried about the mystery girl."

"I just wish I knew that Luna was okay. If I could make sure she was fine, maybe Glory would stop haunting me."

"I don't believe in ghosts," Maxi said. "Science is the only thing that's real. But if it really bothers you, call the police and tell them what you know."

"But I don't know anything, not really." Maybe the stories Glory had told her were lies, fabrications to convince Ruby to help her.

"You've been through a lot. You deserve to feel better about this. Nothing to do but move on. You'll feel better soon."

Ruby hoped she was right.

Back and forth, Luna pushed the vacuum over the parlor rug, leaving long trails in her path. When she got close to the chair, Sienna lifted her feet up so that Luna could vacuum underneath them. Luna smiled at her, wondering if she was really her friend.

Sienna ran hot and cold. She still had bad cramps; that was what she said every day in a low, whispery voice that seemed sad. She had lost the baby a few weeks ago, which made Luna even sadder. "I stopped taking the abortion pills, but it was too late," she had explained. "That bitch Natalie."

Luna had bitten her lips and patted Sienna's arm in sympathy, but she didn't understand all of it. She felt sad about the baby, sad for Sienna and for herself. A little baby was going to be the one thing that made her smile in this house, and she had been looking forward to rocking it in her arms and changing stinky diapers, just like she'd seen on television at Hazel's. The one thing that was clear was that Sienna didn't like Natalie. At first, Luna hadn't completely understood that. Then, one evening when she'd been doing a lesson at the kitchen table with Laura, Luna had overheard Natalie talking about her.

"This one has become a problem," Natalie had said. "Didn't I always warn you about having a child in the house? She's a liability we can't afford."

"What choice do we have?" Leo had answered. "Where could she go?"

"Put a hood on her head and drop her on the other side of town. The girl's a goldfish; she'll die once she leaves her small world. She'd never find her way back. End of problem."

The image was horrifying to Luna. Being blinded and dragged out to a strange place, a strange world, frightened her more than anything else right now. She hoped that the other sisters would stop Leo and Natalie from sending her away. She hoped Sienna or Georgina might step in and speak up for her. If they dumped her somewhere, like Natalie said, she would die out there. Luna never realized how tiny her world was until the night her mother went out the window and she'd been unable to really help her, unable to give the lady she talked to on the phone her address. Natalie was right. Luna lived in a tiny world, and she was deathly afraid of falling off the edge.

But she had learned that if she did her chores and Sienna's without complaining she was usually left alone, a ghost girl who swept through the house to blow away dust and scrub toilets. So she vacuumed and scrubbed and dusted.

When she leaned down to move the footstool, her sock slipped down and something thumped against her leg. She looked down and saw that Mama's cell phone had fallen from Luna's hiding place and bounced onto the rug.

Suddenly Sienna was on her feet and leaning over to switch off the vacuum. "What's that?" she asked.

Luna was already scrambling to pick it up. "Nothing."

"It's a cell phone. The ancient kind." Sienna held her hand out. "Give it to me."

Luna handed it over. "Don't tell Leo. Please."

"Where'd you get a cell phone? Leo took mine when I came to the house." Sienna flipped it open and shut. "Ha. It's an old flip phone."

"It was Mama's. It used to light up, but it's broken now. But I keep it because it reminds me of her."

Sienna turned it over and flipped it open again. "It's not

cracked or chipped or anything. It probably just needs to be charged." She looked up at Luna. "Where's your charger?"

Luna shrugged. "What's that?"

"A cord that plugs into the wall. Wow, you really are stuck in the bubble."

Lifting her chin against the dig, Luna answered, "I think there's a black cord upstairs."

"Well, let's go see if we can get this dinosaur working."

Up in Luna's room, she found the cord in the bottom of the bin with her papers and the stories she'd written with Mama. She had seen Mama use it before, but she hadn't understood that the little battery inside the phone needed to be plugged into the wall every few days.

After a few minutes, the screen lit up again. "There we go. See? It still works." Sienna pressed different buttons, making messages and names appear on the screen. "I can show you how to work it, since you're such a newbie."

"I know how to make a call," Luna said.

"Okay. Not that you have anyone to call, but whatever. Let's see who's in your phone book. Ruby. Shawn. And a Tyler Engle." Sienna squinted at her. "You holding out on me? You got secret friends out there?"

"I guess they were Mama's friends."

"And let's check your history. The last call was made to . . . nine-one-one back in December. Wow. That's creepy. And before that, a call to Ruby."

Luna leaned in to peer at the little screen. "I think I know who that is. Mama said Ruby is my sister, except we've never met." Mama was going to meet Ruby that night. That awful night.

Sienna's face lit with interest. "Wait! No. You have a sister—a real one? You have to call her."

"I don't know her." Although Luna had thought about Ruby and the other sister, Aurora, a few times since she'd learned of Mama's death, they were like puffy clouds floating out of sight, nice to think about, but unreachable.

"You have to call her," Sienna insisted. "I want to know

what she says. Does she even know that your mom is dead? I mean, Glory was her mom, too, right?"

"I guess." Luna hadn't really thought about that much, and right now she just wanted her phone back from Sienna so she could get it out of sight before Leo and the sisters returned from the hotel.

"How old is this Ruby?"

"I don't know. Can I have Mama's phone back?"

"Fine." Sienna held it out.

"You're not going to tell Leo, right?"

Sienna's dark eyes shone like those of a squirrel who had just stolen a nut. "I don't have to tell him anything. You just keep up with the house chores and things will be fine."

Ruby knew it was a stupid move. Her parents would freak if they found out, and her friends would have been so against it that Ruby didn't even tell them what she was doing. For the early release from school—a teacher conference day—Ruby had made up some excuses, and then driven to Northeast Portland to check on her half sister.

The logical part of her mind kept reminding her not to get her hopes up. She might not find out anything, and there were definitely risks involved in poking around. She suspected that this part of Portland held the danger Nani had seen in her teacup.

All signs pointed to Ruby being an idiot, but she had to do this.

Years ago, that firefighter with the funny mustache had saved Ruby and Aurora. What if Luna needed saving and had no one to give her a hand? That neighbor had mentioned that she suspected neglect.

Ruby couldn't let this go until she knew the kid was okay.

When she pulled up it was just after one and the neighborhood was quiet. Turning off the engine, she tried to remember all that Glory had told her. The sisters would still be at the hotel, cleaning rooms, before heading to the mall for a late lunch. But a kid Luna's age couldn't be put to work—not in such a public place. People would wonder why she wasn't in school. No, they would leave her at home.

In this house.

Ruby stared up along the façade of the two-story building and found no sign of an attic up top. *Great.* Had Glory been lying to her? *I'll be so burned if the story about that girl dying in the attic is a ruse.* Getting out of the car, Ruby realized she'd become coldhearted, wishing for confirmation of a girl's death. She was so mired in drama. Did she really want to find evidence that Annabelle was killed, or did she want to make sure Luna was living in a safe situation?

There was no doorbell, but she banged the door knocker, waited, and then banged again.

It seemed like no one was home. That would be a relief.

She stepped off the porch and looked at the front windows. The shades were cracked open a few inches, but it seemed dark inside.

Was the house empty, or was Luna inside, following instructions not to answer the door? Ruby was studying the house, trying to extract information from its tired gold paint and overgrown bushes, when the door opened and a man leaned out. Probably in his thirties or forties, he had blue eyes and sandy hair and the glow of a celebrity.

"Hey," he said casually, as if she came to the door every day. This had to be Leo. He had beautiful eyes and a big presence.

"Hi. I didn't mean to bother you, but I'm looking for someone." When she had rehearsed in her mind, she'd decided to play it as straight as possible without giving up too much information about herself. "A little kid named Luna? She's nine or ten years old."

"Nine or ten. Which one?" He had a smile that made you like him. "I'm kidding. No kids living here. None of any age. How old are you?"

Ruby didn't expect the question. "Sixteen."

"I thought so. That's why I opened the door. I don't talk to reporters or Bible beaters or salespeople. But you, you're different."

He seemed so honest, so genuinely interested in her. "I'm just looking for a friend."

He chuckled. "A nine-year-old friend?"

"It may seem strange, but it's not a joke." Ruby knew he was lying, that Luna was probably inside, and she struggled to come up with a way to get through to her without pissing him off. "Is there a better time for me to visit her? I can come back."

"Who are you?"

"I knew Glory."

"Then she probably told you what we're about. My sister and I, we take in young women in need. But you don't look so needy. Is that a VW key I see in your hand?" He looked beyond her to her Passat, which she had stupidly parked right in front of the house. "A shiny, new one. A pretty black car for a pretty black girl. Or are you mixed race?"

The question was too personal, his way of getting under her skin. "I have to go." She turned and started walking.

"So soon? And we were just getting to know each other."

As she got into the car he stood on the porch, watching. She knew he wouldn't come after her, and yet she couldn't wait to get away. He wanted her to know that he could and would hurt her if she crossed him. Leo was one scary dude. Shaken, she fumbled with her seat belt under the burn of his scalding gaze. There was no time to check her phone or program her GPS; with clenched jaw, she started the car and drove away from his laser sights.

Two blocks later her hands were still shaking as she pulled over and reached for her phone. She was going to check her route home when she thought of the neighbors, the woman and her kid who was around Luna's age. Would the mom even be home? It was iffy, but since she was here, it was worth a shot.

"We're not buying anything today," the young mom said.

Ruby struggled to recall her name but drew a blank. "I'm

not selling. I'm sorry to bother you, but I'm wondering about the little girl who lives in the house on the cross street. Luna?"

This seemed to make the woman tense even more as she pushed her daughter back away from the door. "I'm sorry, but I really can't help you."

"My name is Ruby McCullum. I met you and your daughter out on the street the night that . . . the night that Glory fell out the window next door. Please. I need to talk to you about Luna."

The petite woman shoved her hands in her jacket pockets. "Are you one of Leo's sisters?"

"No, I'm here for personal reasons. Glory Noland was my mother."

The woman stepped closer to the door and peered through the glass. "Are you an investigator?"

"I'm just trying to make sure my half sister is going to be okay."

The woman let out a deep breath and pushed open the door. "Then you'd better come inside and talk; I can't let that sociopath get wind of this. I'm no expert, but anyone can see that child needs help."

CHAPTER 43

After Sienna showed her how to charge the cell phone, Luna kept it nearby all the time now, rubbing it like a lucky charm and popping it open and closed to see it light up under the covers at night. Most days she kept it tucked in the folded-over band of her sock, and most nights it was at home under her pillow, right next to her worn *Harold* book. Luna knew that it was silly, as she had no one to call, but the phone reminded her of Mama in those last months, when she had seen it as a way to connect with people outside the house.

Falling asleep had been a problem in the empty room with that yawning window over Mama's bed, the one that had sucked her out in her nightmare. But now, with the light of the cell phone, Luna was able to melt a little part of the darkness.

One night, in the middle of the night, something pulled her from sleep. As she rolled over in bed, the air felt different. She opened her eyes and found Leo sitting on her bed, stroking her hair back. He wore a dark T-shirt and jeans, and he had a strange, sleepy expression on his face.

"Is it time to get up?" She scratched her nose. "It's dark outside."

"Quiet." He put his finger on her lips, reaching into her safe cocoon. "I was too cold to sleep. Is it all right if I get under the covers with you?"

"No." A sense that this was wrong jolted her completely

awake now. Her hands found the quilt and held it tight to her chin. "Go away."

"Come on, Luna-tic." His voice was a low animal growl, reminding her of the neighbor's dogs. He yanked the covers hard and ripped them out of her hands.

"Get away!" she shouted, scrambling toward the wall.

"Shut up!" he hissed as he lunged toward her, pressing his hand to her mouth and yanking her by the neck with his other hand.

"No. No!" A shrill cry tore from her voice as she tried to wriggle loose. She didn't know what he wanted to do to her; she just knew she had to make him stop. He growled again, pressing on her throat, choking her, pinning her down. At last, she managed to squirm loose and shift on the bed, pushing him away with her feet.

"Leave me alone! Get out of here!" Trapped by the wall, she used it for leverage as she kicked at him, her legs flailing as he tried to grab at them. She was crying out and struggling against him when the door opened, and suddenly there were sisters streaming into the room, bringing tears of relief to Luna's eyes.

"Why are you making such a noise in here when we're trying to sleep!" Rachel marched in, ready to pounce on Luna until she saw Leo. He released Luna's legs but continued to glare at her.

"I didn't do anything." Luna's voice was shaky as she gathered the quilt around her and huddled back against the wall.

Laura blinked, still half-asleep, but Sienna seemed fully awake as she whirled on Leo. "What the hell? What are you even doing up here in her room?"

He scowled back at them. "What do you think? I heard her shouting. A nightmare or something, and I tried to get here before Natalie was disturbed."

"Really? You heard that?" Sienna shoved at his chest. "From all the way downstairs?" She pushed him again. "When I didn't hear anything till just a minute ago."

"Well, it's over now," Laura said, placing a hand on Sienna's shoulder. "Let's quiet down and get back to bed. No harm done. Oh, I'm so tired."

Still huddled on the bed, Luna was afraid they had forgotten her, afraid they would leave her here to be punished by Leo.

"I'm glad it was nothing," Laura went on. "Let's get back to bed before we really do wake Natalie and everyone else up."

Refusing to settle down, Sienna kept poking Leo. "I don't give a shit about Natalie. I know what you were doing up here . . . the two of you." She shot a scowl at Luna, who shook her head, as if all the bad things could be flung away.

"But I didn't do anything wrong," Luna said.

"Stop saying that." Sienna wheeled around and lunged toward the bed. She was ferocious—an attacking tiger—until Rachel grabbed her by the shoulders and held her back. "Stop whimpering like a baby and acting all innocent."

Leo gave a sick laugh, enjoying the fireworks, but Rachel was clearly losing patience. "We can't have this going on here, with all of us trying to sleep." Rachel nodded at Luna as she gave a tug and the attic door squeaked on its hinges. "You. Grab your blanket. Up to the attic you go."

"Ha! Like he's not going to find her up there." Sienna sneered at Leo. "You're such a liar. I hate you."

While they were arguing, Luna scrambled to grab her quilt and cell phone. At least no one seemed to notice.

Her head was cloudy and her heart was still beating fast when Rachel opened the attic door and walked her up. She stood at the door, watching as Luna hunched onto the sleeping bag.

"Go to sleep," Rachel ordered.

"But wait." Luna was scared. Didn't Rachel understand what had just happened?

"What do I do if he comes up here?"

Rachel closed her eyes and drew in a breath. "Just don't make any more noise."

For a long time after Rachel left, Luna stared at the door, frozen in a spell of fear and dread. Her wild mind tried to sort through what had just happened, what the sisters had said to

her. Her new friend, Sienna, was mad at her, and now Rachel
had told her to keep quiet.

Did that mean that no one would stop him?

No one but Luna.

Sometime after she dozed off the tread of footsteps on the
stairs jolted her awake.

Someone was coming.

He was coming.

She sat up and hugged herself, squinting as the door swung
open and Leo stood in the rectangle of light. Even from across
the dusty attic, she could sense his simmering anger. He was
going to destroy her.

"I told you to keep quiet."

"I am." She rose to face him, pulling the quilt around her
shoulders. "I'm quiet when you're not here. So go."

The tunnel of light seemed to follow him as he took one,
two, three long strides toward her. "You think you're smart?"

She held her breath as he swooped over her, grabbed her by
the shoulders. "Leave me alone," she squealed.

He dragged her over to the fireplace, her feet barely sweeping the floor as he moved her like a rag doll. It was like a
dream, being dragged and tossed without control. Luna knew
she couldn't stop that, but she couldn't let him get inside. She
squeezed her eyes shut, wincing to keep him from cracking her
invisible shell as he pressed her to the brick, his breath hot on
her cheek.

She escaped in her mind, summoning Annabelle, who had
fought him up here. She called for Mama, who had warned
Luna about him. She imagined Annabelle and Mama floating
around her like angels, coaxing her to look away, hold her
breath, brace herself, and it would pass. "Mama, Mama," she
whispered. She pretended it was the angels who were holding
her up in the dark.

With all her focus on shutting her eyes tight as a fist, Luna
wasn't aware of what came over Leo as he suddenly let her go
and stepped back.

He stared at her, still angry. "You're going to need a lot of work. A lot. But you'll come around."

She cringed when he stepped toward her again, but this time he was bending down to pick something up—one of her books. He straightened as he glared at it. As if the book were all wrong.

In a flash of motion he flung the book across the dim room. Shards of glass sprayed onto the floor as it hit the window.

His eyes flared with satisfaction.

Luna remained frozen in place, waiting for the next attack. But he turned and left, slamming the door behind him.

The next morning, Georgina was her first visitor in the attic. She set down a bowl of oatmeal and an apple on a box and clapped her hands softly. "Wake up, wake up."

"You'll never believe what Leo did last night," Luna said, nodding toward the window. "He actually broke the glass."

Georgina's face fell at the sparkling disarray of glass on the floor. "A mess. Leo's bad temper."

"If you bring up a dustpan and broom, I'll sweep up," Luna said.

"Mm." Georgina looked down at her watch. "Maybe quickly. Off to work."

"Or maybe Sienna can bring it up," Luna said. "Have you talked to her? Is she still mad at me? She was so angry last night, but it wasn't my fault."

She shook her head, her graying brows moving toward each other. "Sienna won't come." Shoulders hunched, she went to the door.

"Tell her it's not my fault!" Luna called after her, though she knew Georgina probably would not find the words and even if she did Sienna wouldn't listen.

The oatmeal was still warm, and Luna tried to eat it, knowing that she'd be hungry later. When someone came up the stairs a few minutes later, she didn't know what to expect. Georgina paused, leaning a broom against the wall and holding up a cardboard box and tape. "For the window. Cover."

Luna nodded. "I'll cover it later. Thank you. But I kind of don't mind the fresh air right now."

"Cold will come in," Georgina said, patting her arms. "And bugs and birds. Flying everywhere." She shook her head. "No . . . no bats in the belfry!" For some reason Georgina found that incredibly funny.

But Luna didn't laugh. She didn't think she would ever laugh again. Sienna had been her new friend, but Leo had ruined that, just like he'd taken Hazel from her.

He wouldn't let her have a friend. He wanted her to himself.

She couldn't let that day come.

After she was sure the van of women had departed, Luna took the cell phone from her hiding place in the sleeping bag. She'd been waiting to dial the number. Now, finally, she took a deep breath and gave it a try.

The blast of cold air that had moved into the Northwest had brought a dry spell that meant Ruby and Maxi's aerobics class could go outside and walk the paths that ran through the park next to the school. The chilly air smacked their bare legs, but Maxi contended that they'd be fine once they started moving.

As they walked together and Maxi talked about a quiz they had taken that morning in Ms. Pfenning's algebra class, Ruby's mind fell back to the day before. To the meeting that had left a sour taste in the back of her throat all night. She had never met anyone with that blend of charisma and menace.

The woman next door to the sisters, Nicole Hanson, had painted a picture of a cruel, possessive man. "I'm trying not to upset you," Nicole had said, "but when it comes to a man like Leo, a healthy amount of fear is a good thing. I can tell you that Luna always had to sneak over here because she was not allowed to leave her yard. She says she's homeschooled, and as far as I can see, she never leaves that place. I doubt she's been to a doctor or dentist. The few times I saw Leo, he told demeaning lies about Luna and ordered her around like a servant. And recently, when I offered to help get her into the local school, he punished our family by breaking the window of our family room and tossing debris onto our furniture."

Ruby's chest muscles clenched. "Did you see him do it?"

"He did it while we were out of the house, but my neighbor Molly witnessed it."

"And the police didn't do anything about it?"

"The police weren't notified. Molly and her husband are elderly. They're afraid of what Leo might do to them, and I can't blame them. Everyone in the neighborhood steers clear of him."

She shook her head. "My daughter's heartbroken, but she knows she can't have Luna over anymore. We can't predict what Leo might do to us."

Even after Ruby had left that neighborhood she'd been scared of what Leo might do if he figured out who she was. It made her feel sorry for Glory, living under his power all those years.

"Hello? Have you heard anything I've said?" Maxi prodded her. "How'd you do on the quiz?"

"Okay, I guess." She hadn't been listening. "Radical expressions are fine if you remember to keep the sign positive."

"Exactly," Maxi said as they started up the hill path that led to the tennis courts.

Just then Ruby's phone buzzed in her pocket—the long buzz of a call. It had to be a solicitor, since anyone who knew her would text during the school day. She looked around to make sure no teachers were watching, and then took it out.

The caller's name on the screen brought her a stab of fear.

Glory.

"Oh, shit. Oh, shit, oh shit."

"What? Who is it?" Maxi demanded, and when Ruby showed her the phone her mouth dropped open. "Is that some sick joke? I mean, are you afraid it's really her?"

"Of course not. But it's creepy."

"Are you going to answer it?"

Ruby stared at it, then looked at her friend and shook her head. She could only guess who had gotten Glory's phone, and it chilled her to the bone to get this call now, the day after her visit.

It was him. Trying to rattle her.

When it finally stopped ringing, Ruby scowled and texted back: *Who is this?*

She sent the text, but nothing came back immediately. As the girls walked on, Ruby wished she could tell Maxi what she'd done yesterday. About how creepy that Leo guy had been. How he was terrorizing the neighborhood. And the mystery girl. The neighbor had shown her a photo of Luna, describing her as a good kid. She was the one who needed saving in the center of this dysfunction.

Luna was the one. But no one could get close to her, because of Leo.

And now Ruby was just another useless bystander, aware that something was wrong, but unable to fix things.

CHAPTER 44

That day there was no lunch at eleven or twelve and Luna went back to her apple core from breakfast and nibbled every last bit, except the stem. She knew it was okay to eat the entire apple, but there was something about eating the seeds that made her imagine an apple tree taking root in her stomach and eventually poking twigs out her ears, nose, and fingertips. It wouldn't be terrible to be a tree girl. She could stand in the yard and let birds land on her.

She stood at the window, peering out through the square of missing glass. The cold, damp breeze on her face made her feel closer to the outside world. As if she were part of it, instead of just someone watching from the outside.

She didn't expect any visits until the sisters got back from the hotel. Sienna was mad at Luna, and Leo always refused to bring food or water or lug the bucket, saying he was no one's servant. But at one forty-three—Luna knew the time because she was snapping the cell phone open and closed—there were footsteps on the stairs. Luna buried her phone as the door locks clicked. It opened to Sienna.

"Hi!" Luna jumped up. "I didn't think you'd come."

Sienna put a plastic cup of water down on one of the boxes, then flung something at Luna. A banana! Luna caught it, then ducked as a bagged sandwich whizzed past her.

"Hey! Don't do that. It wasn't my fault."

"I'm not speaking to you," Sienna said. "I only came up because he made me. He wants to fatten you up, so he can push you in the oven and roast you!"

Luna stared at her in horror. "What?"

"That's right, you little butterball." Sienna rolled her eyes. "Jesus, you are so naïve."

So that meant she was lying. Luna understood the meaning of "naïve." But it was a nasty joke. Who was she supposed to believe now? Without Mama, there was no one she could trust.

Sienna left just as quickly as she'd breezed in, leaving Luna to gulp down the water and feast on her food. The sandwich was peanut butter, one of the frozen ones that was made every Friday and stacked into the freezer for the sisters to take to work. It was still frozen, but Luna savored it, licking it like an ice pop.

As she nibbled, Luna wondered what was going to happen to her. She didn't mind doing Sienna's extra chores, and she could even put up with the sisters until she was old enough to go work at the hotel. Then, once she got out and got a look at the world, maybe she would escape, like Mama had wanted.

But that was years away, and right now she had a problem with Leo. She didn't ever want last night to happen again. To wake up and find him close, touching her.

Never again.

She mulled over the torn book Hazel had loaned her. The orphans didn't give up. It was up to her to try. She dug her cell phone out from its hiding place in a box of Bubble-Wrapped cups and called Ruby a second time.

The buzzing phone in Ruby's pocket pulled her attention away from a lecture on Odysseus that grabbed her interest a lot more than the actual passages. Normally she would have dismissed the call without looking, but after she'd heard from Glory she'd been on edge.

She flashed a look.

Glory.

Her whole spirit sank.

But this time, she wanted to know.

Slipping quietly from her desk, she grabbed a bathroom pass, went into the hall, and took the call.

"Who is this?" she snapped.

"My name is Luna." The voice was young, almost chirpy. "I'm Glory's daughter. I'm locked in the attic, and I'm afraid of what Leo is going to do to me."

Ruby left school as soon as English ended, which wasn't an easy task. She had to print a fake excusal note on one of the library computers, then forge her mother's signature. Even then, Ms. Gina, the office monitor, was annoyed at the late notice.

"Ruby, you know we need excusal notices at the beginning of the day."

"Sorry," Ruby said, spreading a lie on top of another lie. "Dental emergency."

Begrudgingly, the administrator handed her an exit pass.

The sick feeling of dread that had clung to her since Glory's death began to lift as Ruby steered her VW out of the school parking lot and headed toward Portland. This was crazy, but at least she was doing something. About to break the deadlock.

It had been almost ten years since she had been to her aunt's office. The GPS directions took her through unfamiliar neighborhoods in Portland, but when the low-slung, square building housing the Department of Social Services came into view, she remembered it.

The rows of windows and the long hallways, like her preschool.

The smell of cleaner on the shiny floors.

And cubicles of desks in rows. As a little kid, Ruby had wondered why a place that was supposed to help children had so many desks. Children didn't need desks. And the building didn't have televisions to watch or cribs for babies like Aurora.

She laughed. Back then, she used to think that all the foster mothers and fathers were stored in one big room, like bars of soap ready to come racing out on a conveyor belt. She'd learned a few things since then.

The woman at the front desk seemed determined to send her packing until she learned that Ruby was family. Then she sent her down to room 132.

The open door led to a room that housed five cubicles with desks and computers. Four of them were occupied at the moment. Aunt Kaysandra recognized Ruby first.

"Ruby McCullum, is that you?" Kaysandra rose from her desk and drew Ruby into a big hug, then pointed at her. "Hey, guys, this is my niece Ruby. My brother Pete's daughter."

Ruby turned awkwardly, nodding to the other people in the room, two women and a man with a black-on-black shirt and vest who reached out to shake her hand. "Wassup, Ruby. Are you a crazy Seahawks fan like your aunt?"

"I haven't really gotten into football yet."

"But you will. Can't avoid it when you're a McCullum." Kaysandra used two fingers to bend the curl of hair at her chin. She looked young in a short, straight bob that curled in at the bottom. Probably a hairpiece, Ruby realized, but it looked really nice. "What are you doing here, child?"

"I wanted to talk to you. In person."

"Well, okay, sure." Kaysandra squinted at her, sensing that something was up. "Come on over to the conference room. You want a soda or water or something?"

"I'm good."

They walked down the hall to a room with a large table and enough chairs for ten people. "So sit yourself down and tell me what brings you here. 'Cause it makes me nervous not knowing what the hell is going on with you. Is this about your mother's cancer?"

"Mom's doing well with the chemo," Ruby said, rolling her chair in under the table. "I'm here about someone else's problem. Someone you've never met. Sort of a friend of a friend."

Kaysandra tapped a scarlet fingernail on her chin. "Um-hum. Tell me about it."

"It's about a little girl whose mom died. And the girl is still living with friends of her mom. But I think they're neglecting her. Maybe abusing her."

"Really? And who's got custody?"

"I don't know. I'm not sure anyone does."

"Somebody has to have custody. Usually it's a parent, grand-parent, aunt, or uncle. Unless she's been in the foster-care system."

"This kid isn't on the Social Services radar. I think she's an anomaly. She was born in the house, so she has no birth certificate, and they've never let her out. So she's, like, off the grid."

"That's impossible. How old is this kid?"

"Nine or ten."

"How would she get her shots and medical care? Parents want their kids to have education and social development."

"Not this kid. She was homeschooled, at least, but she's been living in the dark. And now she's afraid to come out. Not that the people keeping her captive are going to let her out."

"Okay." Kaysandra took a notepad from the stack at the center of the table and slid it over to Ruby. "You need to give me her name and address, and I'll run her information. If I come up empty, I'll do a welfare check on her."

"How does that work?" Ruby asked as she wrote down Luna's name and the address she had memorized.

"We call the police and ask for a welfare check. Anyone can call, and the police are compelled to come out. They visit the house and check on the child. When it's my case, I always go out there."

"But what if the police have been called, a few times, and they never found anything?"

"Child, are you talking about a real case or an episode of *Grey's Anatomy*?"

"She's real. I've talked to her."

"This friend of a friend. Well, I hope you didn't promise her anything, because she might be yanking your chain, you know? It might not even be a little girl that you talked to. There are a lot of weirdos out there. Did you happen to meet this person online?"

"No, it's not like that." Ruby longed to open the floodgates and let the circuitous, complicated story of her reunion with her birth mother, her discovery of Luna, and her scary brush with Leo pour out. She needed Kaysandra to know that this was real, but she wasn't ready to confess her part in it. "This is a real kid. I've talked to her neighbors, and they're worried about her, too."

"Really? Okay, then." Kaysandra tore the top sheet from the pad. "You want me to step in and check on the kid?"

"That would be great, except I don't think you'd find her. The police have been to their house more than once, and the child is always hidden away. They lock her up."

"Ha. You've never seen me do a search. No stone left unturned."

"So can I go with you?" Ruby asked.

"Sorry. That would be so unprofessional of me, my ass would be fried. But I'll let you know how it works out."

"I wish I could go," Ruby said. "I'm done with my classes for the day." Another lie, but she was in too thick to count at this point.

"Today? Oh, honey, I can't squeeze in any more fieldwork this week. Maybe next week. I'd have to check my calendar."

Ruby closed her eyes as she saw herself tumbling back to the bottom of the mountain. This couldn't wait. That was clear from Luna's call. "But what if it's an emergency?"

"From what you tell me, this thing is so far from the norm that it's probably all trumped up. I'll reach out to this girl, but chances are, it's just a ruse. But you did your part, honey. You done good, girl. Go home, and let me take it from here."

CHAPTER 45

Although she knew her aunt meant well, Ruby didn't take her advice. Instead, she found the address of the sisters' house in her GPS and started the direct route.

This could not wait.

It was suddenly clear that the danger Nani had seen was not to Ruby, but to her half sister, Luna, who had given Ruby chilling details during their phone call that afternoon. A violent attack. Seclusion in the attic. And no defense. Ruby was her only lifeline.

"You should call the police," Ruby had told her. "As soon as we finish this call, dial nine-one-one."

"The police won't do anything. They've been here before, but Leo hides me away in the attic, and they leave. And then Leo stays mad at me for days."

"Then leave. Can you get out of the house? Get out. I'll come get you," Ruby had said, her heart thudding in her chest.

But Luna was locked in the attic, and even if she was released, the doors of the house were locked and alarmed. She was trapped, the house her prison.

And yet the girl had seemed calm, bracing for a coming storm. When Ruby asked how she could help, the call ended. Abruptly. And she hadn't been able to reach Luna since then.

Forced to take action, Ruby was now so out of her comfort

zone. Her hands gripped the steering wheel so hard, her knuckles were pale. This was crazy. But it was the only choice.

This time when Ruby arrived at the house she drove past and parked near the side street, a bit out of the way but close enough to see the house. Her nerves were buzzing as she picked up her cell phone and called 911. Just as Kaysandra had said to do, she requested a welfare check on a child at the sisters' house, saying that neighbors had witnessed neglect and abuse. When the woman started asking questions, Ruby dodged them, stressing that it was an emergency.

She waited for more than an hour. During that time the gray sky turned to pewter and a van rolled up and entered the garage of the house. The sisters were home.

Hope began to dissolve as dusk pinched the sky. Maybe the cops would take days to respond.

It seemed like ages had passed, but it was just before five o'clock when a police car pulled up in front of the house and a single officer went to the door. Watching him, Ruby made a quick call to Aunt Kaysandra—an insurance policy.

She was relieved when her voice mail kicked in. "Aunt Kaysandra? It's Ruby. I'm at the house, Luna's house in East Portland. Just wanted to let you know, I called the police and I'm going to try to get in there. And I am not leaving until she's free."

With a deep breath, Ruby went to the front porch. The main door was open. Through the glass of the outer door she could see Leo talking to the cop in the vestibule. It was the same cop who'd been supervising the night of Glory's fall.

Ruby waited, listening as globs of their conversation swelled through the door. "Welfare check ... take a look around ... sorry to bother ..." Leo seemed gracious, clapping the cop on the back and guiding him into the house.

Once they left the vestibule, Ruby stepped inside and eased the door silently shut behind her. The house was thick with the smell of boiled grains and old shoes, and it seemed that no one had thrown the windows open and aired the place out for years. She followed the men, edging slowly behind them. This sort of aggression was so alien to her usual manners, but she couldn't back down. No one seemed to notice her as she hung back in the archway leading to the kitchen area.

The back room was a kitchen attached to an eating area with a good-sized table, where a few sisters were congregated. Leo introduced them to the cop. Laura, the petite faded blonde Ruby had seen at the hospital, sat knitting beside the imperious Natalie, who seemed to be filling in some sort of ledger at the head of the table. A graying woman filling a pot at the sink was introduced as Georgina, and a young woman with thick, slightly matted hair who sat at the table, peeling potatoes with a vengeance, was Sienna.

Leo's girlfriend. Ruby had pieced that together based on information from Glory and Luna.

Laura stood to offer the cop some tea, but he declined. "No, please just do what you're doing. I've been here before. I think I know the lay of the land." He turned to Leo. "So the caller said you have a child here. A ten-year-old girl."

"We've been through this before." Leo scratched his jaw with the knuckles of one hand. "They must be thinking about the neighbor girl. Lives over on the side street." He pointed toward the backyard. "Are they the ones who called?"

"I can't say, though I don't really know. The dispatcher didn't get a name."

Leo nodded. "A lot of disgruntled people around here. They don't understand what Natalie and I do. The service we provide to the community. These women here? Without us, they'd be homeless. Out on the streets."

The cop nodded. "Believe me, I've seen plenty of that. You're doing a good thing here, Leo."

"Thanks, Jake. I guess you want a look upstairs."

"I need to do that, and then I'll get out of your hair."

"No problem." Leo chose Sienna to take the officer up. From the way she threw down the potato peeler and pushed away from the table, she didn't seem too happy about it.

"Just make sure you knock before you open any door," said Leo. "A few of our sisters are up there. They worked a long day at the hotel, and I like to give them some privacy."

"Understood."

Ruby moved aside and pressed herself to the wall of the archway just before Sienna came traipsing through with the cop. Thank God they didn't notice Ruby. Although she was medium height and willowy, Sienna's feet were heavy on the stairs, as if she were throwing a tantrum.

"I don't like her attitude," Natalie said, loud enough for Ruby to hear her. "You need to control her."

"She's getting better," Leo said. "She'll learn that sulking won't get her what she wants. I'm grooming Luna to take over her chores. In a week or so, I'll be sending Sienna over to the hotel to work with you."

"Oh, goody. Make her my problem now."

"You're so good at fixing things. That's what big sisters do."

They switched topics to something about "SNAP" and losing resources, which wasn't making Natalie happy. She was determined to fix that, too.

The noise of movement on the stairs sent Ruby cowering back into the shadows of the recessed wall until Sienna and the cop moved past her, back into the kitchen.

"All clear up there," Officer Swanson announced to everyone in the kitchen, and it occurred to Ruby that none of the sisters had said a word since he'd arrived. Were they not allowed to speak? It seemed that way.

"All right, ladies. My apologies for interrupting your evening." Swanson emerged into the hallway, Leo at his side. "I don't know who called this in, but the complaint is unfounded."

"Thanks, Jake. Take it easy out there," Leo said, walking him to the door.

"Wait. Officer Swanson!" Ruby called after them.

The men turned, both surprised to find her there.

Leo did a double take. "The pretty little rich girl. What the hell are you doing here?"

"I'm the one who called in the welfare check," Ruby said, forcing herself to stand tall, chin up. "I talked to Luna this afternoon, and she's scared. He's locked her in the attic."

"That's BS. Luna doesn't talk to anyone." The malice in Leo's eyes was cutting. "How did you get in here?"

"The door." She turned to the cop. "Officer Swanson, have you checked the attic?"

"She's not one of your sisters?" the cop asked Leo, who shook his head.

"No, I'm the complainant. And I told the dispatcher to make sure you check the attic," Ruby repeated.

The cop turned to Leo. "You said there's no attic."

"Nothing that we use." Leo shrugged. "There's some space above the eaves. The door's been sealed off for years."

The cop seemed to accept the answer. "I'm not here to break down doors."

"He's lying. It's not sealed off," Ruby pressed on. "Luna is locked up there whenever they want her out of sight."

The cop rubbed his lined forehead. "How hard would it be to unseal this door?"

"I can't really say."

"Please, Officer Swanson, you need to take a look; you need to talk to her," Ruby pleaded. "My sister is up there. My half sister, and I'm not leaving until she's released."

"You're Glory's daughter?" Leo's eyes seemed to bore into her, getting in her personal space. "I should have known, those blue eyes. Just like her."

"Stop it." Ruby stepped back. "I want to see Luna, now. I came here for Luna."

"Whoa. A little sensitive, aren't we? I mean, you push into my house and demand to see my daughter, and I'm supposed to produce her?" He scanned his audience: Ruby, the sisters watching from the kitchen, the cop. "As her father, isn't it my job to protect her?"

"So there is a child?" asked the cop.

"She's very shy," Leo said. "And I don't see why she should be exposed to any of this."

"I see your point, Leo." Officer Swanson rubbed his knuckles against his jaw, considering all this. "You know we'd hate to scare the kid, but when we're called in for a welfare check, it's for the child's own good. If we can just get eyes on her, talk with her a minute, that should be satisfactory."

"It's not right," Leo said, appealing directly to the cop. "Invading a man's home, making demands."

Ruby was relieved to see that the cop wasn't backing down. "It's for the sake of the child."

Leo looked over at Natalie, who nodded. "All right," he said. "Georgina, go on up and ask Luna to come down."

The oldest, grayest woman of the group went up the stairs. Ruby wondered if he'd chosen Georgina to make the whole interview slow and awkward. The men chatted as they moved into the kitchen, the cop trying to reassure Leo that everything would be fine, that his rights weren't being violated, that laws were in place for a reason.

Ruby edged into the kitchen, aware of fleeting glances from Sienna and Laura, who mostly kept their heads bent to their work. Were they slaves here? Ruby wondered what was keeping these women together here.

The little girl entered with measured steps, hesitating once she made eye contact with Leo. He was controlling her, Ruby realized. Playing mind games. Ruby recognized her from the photo the neighbor had given her—a petite kid dressed in ratty tights with a baggy hoody that she pulled her arms into, as if she wanted to retreat like a turtle. Her face was dominated by big blue eyes and a crescent-shaped scar on one cheek. A fresh wound.

Ruby wanted to lean in and introduce herself. In a normal world she could say, *Hey, we're sisters!* and they could hug, but this was the weird, twisted world of dysfunction, and any connection between them could get Luna in trouble. Ruby wasn't sure if Luna had even noticed her standing in the shadows a few feet from Leo, the sun.

"This is Luna," Leo said. "Officer Swanson wants to ask you a few questions."

"Hey there." The cop leaned down, resting his hands on his knees. "I'm surprised we haven't met during my past visits. How old are you, Luna?"

"Ten."

Swanson nodded. "A lot younger than my daughter. She's in college now. Do you go to school, Luna?"

"She is homeschooled by some of our excellent sisters here," Natalie answered. "Rachel, an accomplished cellist, is highly skilled in math and music. Kimani teaches science. She was a nurse. And Laura covers language arts."

"That's me," Laura said, looking up from her knitting. "And I just want to say that Luna has strong reading and writing skills. She used to write a series of short stories with her mother."

Swanson nodded, then pointed to Luna's cheek. "Got a little honker on your face. What happened there?"

"It was an accident." She looked past Leo to Natalie, who presided over things from the head of the table. "I bumped into something."

"It happens. Were you playing sports? Soccer or dodgeball?"

She shook her head.

"Some people have been worried about you. I'm just here to check and make sure that you're okay. But I see that you've got a home, with lots of people to take care of you. You're getting an education."

"An education, a roof over her head, and plenty to eat." Natalie counted off the benefits on one hand. "You may inspect our pantry if you like, Officer."

"I don't think that's necessary. I have everything I need." The cop turned toward the door, clapping Leo on the shoulder. "Thanks for cooperating, buddy."

"No problem," Leo said, smiling at Ruby.

"No, wait." Ruby couldn't let this one chance slip away. "That's it?" she asked the cop. "She says things are fine, so you just leave? Can't you see she's intimidated by them? Don't you see the cruelty and the underlying threats here?"

"There's nothing cruel here. I see a little girl who's respect-ful of her parents. I'd like to see more millennials who treat their parents that way."

"You didn't ask her if she's ever seen a doctor. If she's ever been allowed out of this house. Can't you see she's trapped here? She's never been outside this house?"

He held a hand up to stop her stream of questions. "Take it easy. She goes next door to see the neighbor girl. I heard that myself from Nicole Hanson. Leo and Natalie are good people, doing all right by this kid."

"But what about the mark on her face? And what happened to her mother, Glory?"

"Glory's death was ruled an accident," Natalie piped up. It was eerie, the way she was staring up at Ruby. "I spoke to the coroner last week. It's sad, the way she fell. We miss her. But life goes on."

"But wait. She wasn't the first woman to die here," Ruby said, desperate to keep the cop here. "There was someone else."

Natalie looked up at Leo. "Who is this young woman?"

Arms folded, Leo smiled as if Ruby were mildly amusing.

He doesn't take me seriously, Ruby thought. *He thinks I have no power. That will change.* "Officer, are you aware of the other woman who died here?"

Frowning, Swanson ran a hand back over his bald head.

"What was her name?" Ruby scanned the blank faces watching her—Luna, Georgina, Leo, Sienna, and Natalie. "She died up in the attic. She died of thirst. Is that cruel enough for you? Annabelle! That was her name. And it was Leo who killed her. Leo."

"No!" Sienna jumped in. "It wasn't Leo! He's a good per-son. He's kind and loving. It's Natalie! She's the cold bitch who can't stand to see anyone else happy. She killed Anna-belle."

"Says the woman who never even met her." Natalie shook her head, sneering disapproval. "You don't even know what you're talking about."

Sienna's eyes flared with fury. "I will never forgive you for killing my baby." Sienna linked her arm with Leo's. "Our baby."

"Stop with the drama," Natalie said. "Abortion is legal, and you signed the consent yourself."

"You forced me." Sienna's voice was a low growl. "You killed my baby, and you killed that girl in the attic, too. You killed Annabelle! You're a killer." Leo held her away from Natalie as the cop stepped between them.

"I understand you're upset, young lady," Officer Swanson told Sienna. "But I have to consider facts. How would Natalie get up to the attic in her wheelchair? It's two stories up, right?"

"She can walk." The small, chirpy voice belonged to the little girl.

Luna was now the center of everyone's focus.

"Sometimes," said Luna. "I've seen her walk."

Natalie shook her head. "Oh, little girl, you are such a liar."

"She's not lying," Ruby said. "They killed Annabelle because she wouldn't conform, she wouldn't follow orders, and . . ." She tried to remember the things Glory had told her. "They buried her body in the backyard."

Luna stepped up to the cop. "I can show you where she's buried."

"That would be helpful," Swanson told her. "Let me just call this in and get some help out here." This time, when the officer looked toward Natalie and Leo there was concern in his eyes over the mess that was unraveling at his feet. There would be no smoothing over the situation.

An investigation was under way.

CHAPTER 46

After that, the house became chaotic as Leo tried to corral all the sisters upstairs to their rooms while Officer Swanson overruled his plan, insisting that they remain downstairs until the police could get statements from them. Two other cops had arrived quickly, one taking equipment up to the attic while the other talked with Natalie. While Leo argued with Sienna and Natalie yelled that no one was listening to her, Ruby went out the back door with Luna, who was determined to show Swanson where Annabelle was buried.

"We gave her a funeral," Luna said. "But it was very sad. Mama said Leo killed her. Is he going to get in trouble?" she asked.

"It appears that way," the cop said, photographing the rectangle of mossy earth in the dying light.

"Will you excavate her bones?" Ruby asked.

He nodded. "Forensics might want to x-ray first. And we'll revisit the death of Glory Noland, which was never really solved."

"I can tell you about that, too," Luna said. "It was an accident, sort of. Mama used to sneak out at night and meet people by climbing down to the shed under our window. Then Leo and Sienna moved it over there." She pointed across the yard, and Swanson shone his flashlight on the rubber shed in the corner of the yard. "Sienna said Leo moved it to stop Mama from sneaking out. He didn't know he was killing her."

"It was all about control," Ruby said aloud, thinking of the patterns of abuse she'd read about.

Swanson put his flashlight back in his belt and touched Luna's shoulder. "I'm sorry about your mom, Luna. We're going to have someone from Social Services come round to pick you up, okay? Someone nice."

"My aunt is on her way. She works for Social Services."

"Is that right? Okay, then. For now, let's get you girls in the front yard. Not sure I want either of you subjected to the chaos inside. Let's go this way." He walked them around the garage door to the front of the tired house. "Are you going to be warm enough out here, Luna?" Officer Swanson unzipped his jacket and propped it over her shoulders. "There. That should help for now."

While they were talking, a third police cruiser pulled up, the lights of its roof rack flashing. Two cops came up the walkway. They went inside with Swanson and returned with Leo traipsing between them, his hands cuffed behind his back. They shuffled him into the patrol car.

"He's under arrest?" Ruby asked Swanson.

He nodded. "They found blood in the attic. A good amount. And two of the sisters are corroborating the homicide of Annabelle Clayton." He pointed to Luna. "You mind staying with her?"

"I'm good."

Ruby was left facing the mystery girl, her sister.

"So I'm Ruby. We talked on the phone earlier."

"I know." Luna stared at the ground. "I didn't expect you to come here. And now, I'm in so much trouble." A tear slid down her cheek. "Leo's really mad."

"Don't worry about him. You won't have to deal with him, ever again. He's the one who's in trouble." She pointed to the street. "Did you see the police take him away? He's going to jail, probably for a long time."

Luna sobbed. "It's my fault."

"You did the right thing. You needed help and you reached out to me. You're a brave kid, Luna."

"I don't feel brave." She swiped at a tear. "What am I going to do now?"

"I know it's hard. Like you, I lost my parents when I was a kid." As Ruby sat beside her on the porch and put an arm around her shoulders, she thought of herself so many years ago, sitting in a big chair at the fire station, dwarfed by all the brawny men with furry mustaches. And then the foster home with a round, dark-skinned woman who was so good at keeping Aurora from crying. And then the McCullums, both of them getting down on the floor and playing with her the way her daddy used to play. All through those first weeks, she'd been waiting for Glory to return, waiting and losing patience and watching as her familiar world slipped through her fingers like water down a drain.

And now here was Luna, watching the thread of her life come untwined in much the same way. "I know it's really hard," Ruby said. "But my aunt Kaysandra is a social worker, and she's going to make sure you have a safe place to live, with people who love you. And one day, you'll wake up and realize that you love them, too."

"I want my mama."

"I hear you. I get that. But our mother is gone. And you're going to need to open your heart to someone else. Someone who wants to help you and teach you things. So it's okay to feel sad and confused. There's going to be a lot of that. But you need to keep your heart open for the family who really loves you. 'Cause you can't miss out on love."

As if on cue Aunt Kaysandra's minivan pulled up, with Tamarind in the passenger seat.

"Mom!" Ruby flew across the lawn and hugged her mother, shivering with relief that she wasn't alone in this anymore. "How did you know?"

"I've known you were up to something, but when Kaysandra called I was floored," Mom said. "You are so courageous and so grounded."

"We were on our way when my office was notified of a child to pick up," Kaysandra said, her gaze alighting on the girl hunched over on the stoop. "There she is, God love her. And here I thought you were getting sucked into some internet scam." She hustled over to the porch and bent down to be eye to eye with Luna. "Hey, little miss. My name's Kaysandra. Can you tell me yours?"

"Luna."

"Hey, Miss Luna. You and I, we're going to talk and talk and talk, and I'm going to listen to you. We are going to become good friends."

Luna lifted her head. Her blue eyes were shiny with tears, but she swiped them away with one sleeve. "I like having a friend."

The tremble in her voice tore at Ruby's heart, and in that moment she vowed to protect this little girl, her sister.

It was late—after nine—when Tamarind got behind the driver's seat of Ruby's VW to head home. Her daughter sat beside her, looking just as overwhelmed as Tamarind felt. At first, Tamarind let the radio play on Ruby's station, letting the Bruno Mars tune rock their minds back to the safe and normal. The Northeast Portland neighborhood was quiet as Tamarind steered east, deciding to take the 205 expressway, a longer but smoother route that would give her a chance to talk with her daughter and clear her head.

Tamarind was only a paralegal by profession, but from the stories she'd heard tonight she suspected that Leo and his sister would be charged with kidnapping, child abuse, and neglect. There was also the possibility of homicide charges for the deaths of Glory Noland and the mysterious Annabelle and fraud for Natalie's creative bookkeeping, as explained by a strikingly pretty sister named Kimani, who had emerged as an excellent possible witness. Ultimately, Leo and Natalie were turning a profit on the backs of their houseful of women.

"What will happen to them?" Ruby had asked Kaysandra, who promised that she would work with the sisters on job placement and life skills. Still, it had been upsetting to see a few of the sisters sitting at the kitchen table, sobbing over the news that the Petrovs would not be returning to the house that night.

"Leo is our protector!" one of them had cried. A tiny blonde who reminded Tamarind of a fragile bird. "We need him."

No, sisters, you don't. Tamarind had wanted to counsel them, to reassure them, but she had been warned to stay out of it: "Don't taint the witnesses or get involved with the clients." She had come to the scene as Ruby's mother, and that, she realized, had been an honor and a blessing, as her daughter seemed to have gotten everything in control by the time Tamarind and Kaysandra arrived.

So Tamarind had observed. The run-down house, linoleum worn through to the previous layer in spots, and walls with blistered, yellowed paint. The women, who had an odd way of avoiding eye contact—a gesture of submission, she suspected. It made her sad that this had been the final destination of Ruby's birth mother, Glory Noland. Even sadder that this had been the only world the little girl Luna had ever known.

"Do you want to tell me how it started?" she asked her daughter. "How you traced Glory to that house? Because that had to involve a nifty bit of detective work."

"It was mostly luck. I was curious about my birth mom, but I didn't want to hurt you and Dad, especially after you found out about the cancer. So I went looking and I found her. And then . . ." She bit her lips, taking a moment. She swiped at her eyes. "And then I lost her. She died, and I think it's because she was trying to escape from the crazy cult she joined when she left Aurora and me behind."

"Oh, honey, I'm so sorry that—"

"Please, let me finish. I want you to know that I tried to find her because of my own stupid curiosity and not because I don't love and appreciate you and Dad. Because I do. You guys are great, and I love you. And I knew you were uncomfortable about me searching for my birth mother, and I respected that. But I always wondered, so I was doing a little research, and then I got lucky when I took Aurora over to the East Center Mall and there she was."

"Did your sister meet her, too?"

"No. I never said a word about it to Aurora."

"That's good. I guess she'll need to know now. Luna is her half sister, too. I'm sorry, Rubes. I should have been more honest about the reasons I didn't want you to be in touch with your biological mother. It wasn't about Glory Noland at all. She seemed like a good person. Well intentioned, but the deck was stacked against her. I think she tried, but when your father was killed she couldn't dig herself out. Penniless with two babies and no family support, no resources. I think she knew you and Aurora needed more than she could give. And I admire that clarity of thought. I think Glory had a lot of good qualities. It was the cult that stopped me in my tracks. Based on what Kaysandra had seen from her limited contact with Glory, Leo Petrov and his sister were unstable people with a crazy amount of power over their followers."

"So you'd heard of Leo and the sisters? How did you know?"

"Mostly through Kaysandra. When we took you and your sister in as foster kids, a big part of Kaysandra's job was negotiating with your birth mother. Glory had left a note with you at the firehouse, signing over custody, but of course, Social Services has laws and regulations to conform to. Kaysandra was able to find Glory at the sisters' house, and that got her looking into Leo and Natalie. Their cult was a bit controversial when they hit the neighborhood some twenty years ago—a young, attractive man, surrounded by young women—but the Petrovs were never accused of breaking any laws."

"Leo is really scary, the way he sucks you in. And Natalie is just a bitch."

Tamarind let out a breath. "It scares me to think of you tangling with them."

"I never planned to, but when I found out about Luna, that there was this little kid living there without her mom after Glory died, I had to make sure she was okay."

"And of course she wasn't."

"She was in danger, Mom. Leo was targeting her. She called me using Glory's old phone. Mine was one of the few numbers in there. But she almost didn't speak up when I barged in today. I don't know if it was fear of Leo or fear of the unknown world beyond her back fence, but it's crazy that that kid's never gone past the house next door. Never ridden in a car or plane. Never seen the ocean or the mountains."

"Well, she's in good hands now. Kaysandra is a strong advocate."

"That was such a moment, seeing Luna get in Aunt Kaysandra's car. The look on her face. Her first car ride."

"You're really brave," Tamarind said. "And a risk taker. I never expected that of you."

"Same."

"You could have told me. You can tell me anything."

"I know that now, but you had the surgery, and then chemo, and I couldn't heap one more terrible thing on you."

"That's considerate, but too kind. Don't you know you're supposed to be a burden to your parents, kiddo?"

"I guess I made up for lost time tonight," Ruby said. And they laughed together, letting go of the strange house and the lost sisters and the wide-eyed little girl. Letting go, at least for now.

EPILOGUE

August

Ruby placed the cake with Harold and his purple crayon on the kitchen table and followed her family out to the Hansons' backyard. Luna had held fast to her friend Hazel as a source of security during all the changes, so the Hansons' house had seemed a good, familiar place for a celebration.

The backyard gathering with purple and blue balloons, a bouncy castle, and party lights could have been any eleven-year-old's party. But today's birthday girl was a special kid, not just for Ruby, but for most people in Portland.

The trial had been hot news for a few weeks that summer, with headlines like "Pdx Man Keeps Sex Slaves: The Cult Next Door" and "Orphan Imprisoned in Home 10 Years." Ruby had been glued to the news coverage, as had much of the country, though she and Luna hadn't needed to testify. *Thank God.* Ruby had gotten sick of shaking off hero status. She'd been glad when people had begun to forget her role in releasing Luna and let her slide into being just Ruby again.

Ruby was glad that Luna didn't need to know all the details of the trial until she was older. The way Leo had brought in broken young women, grooming each woman as a sexual partner and then sending her off to work in the hotel after he had tired and moved on to another young woman.

At least two of Leo's "pet" women had gotten pregnant. Glory had kept her pregnancy a secret from Natalie until it was too late, and Luna had been born in the house, unattended by any medical professionals. Undocumented, Luna had been raised by Glory and the sisters in the small, dysfunctional world of the cult. Glory's attempt to leave had resulted in her death.

Most of the sisters didn't even try to leave. By targeting damaged women, Leo and his sister had collected women too insecure to leave once they were assured of food and shelter. And for those who wanted to escape, they were stopped by doors secured by multiple locks and alarmed with fictitious lasers.

"Leo and Natalie kept us captive through a system of psychological control, threats, and occasionally physical violence," testified Kimani Adams. A former nurse's aide, she had joined the group when she'd hit rock bottom with opioid addiction. During her time with the cult, she described a process of her own cognitive healing that had helped her recognize the Petrovs' accelerating control of the sisters. The prosecution's star witness, Kimani described how she learned of Leo's schemes to kill Annabelle Clayton and Glory Noland when she heard him bragging about it after the fact.

Kimani had also led the police to investigate Natalie's bookkeeping practices, leading to charges of theft and fraud. It turned out that Natalie not only had collected money through the SNAP program to feed the sisters, she also had allocated payroll to them for their services to the hotel—money that the women never received for their work.

Passing by the fat hydrangea blossoms in the Hansons' backyard, Ruby said hello to Hazel's father, Jeff, then went over to join Mom and Aurora at a table with Nicole Hanson, who was pouring everyone lemonade.

"Have a seat, girls. We've got more chairs if we need them."

Taking a seat in a wicker chair, Ruby sat back and realized she was looking straight in the direction of the sisters' former house. The tired façade hadn't changed, and she could see the small attic window where Luna used to peer out at the neighborhood when she was trapped. For a moment that window held Ruby's gaze, like an instrument of dark magic. *Creepy.* Then, with a deep breath, she got up and angled her chair so that she was facing the other side of the yard.

"Where's Marigold?" Mom asked.

"Monitoring the bouncy castle," said Nicole. "Or playing inside it, knowing her."

Marigold and Charles were the amazing foster parents Aunt Kaysandra had found for Luna. Quirky, loving, and down-to-earth, the former schoolteacher and archeologist had brought Luna the balance of playfulness and social grace that she needed.

Even Aurora, who had begged her parents to adopt Luna, had been won over by Marigold and Charles, but it hadn't been easy. The first time Aurora met her half sister, she had wanted to move the little girl into their home. "She is so stinkin' adorable! I could hug her every day, all day. And have you noticed how smart she is? This kid has read *War and Peace!*"

"She's definitely a bright kid," Ruby had said. "But she's missed so much socialization. Don't you notice her insecurities about social interactions, and how clingy she can be?"

"That's so unfair after what she's been through," Aurora insisted.

"I don't mean it as a criticism," Ruby said softly. "It's just that she needs to do some catching up and our house isn't the best place for a little kid anymore."

"I agree with Ruby," Dad said. "Luna is a quick learner, but she'd be better served by a nurturing environment that's completely tailored to helping her grow."

Then Aurora had pulled the family card. "Mom, Dad, come on. You always talk about how important family is. This is a time when we have to keep the family together."

"Luna is part of our family," Ruby said.

"That's right," Tamarind said. "But because we love her, we want her in the most suitable home for an eleven-year-old girl who's been through hell. And we are going to take every opportunity to spend time with her and drag her to our crazy McCullum family functions."

"Hey." Dad squinted at Mom. "You calling my family crazy?"

"Absolutely."

Although Luna was in a wonderful home now, horrible details of her treatment in the sisters' house had emerged during the trial. Ruby had turned to Aunt Kaysandra, who wasn't supposed to talk about details of the case but sometimes guided Ruby on her developing relationship with Luna. "Did Leo abuse her?" Ruby had asked. "Sexually?"

"He was beginning to target her," Kaysandra said, "but from what we can tell, he did not sexually assault her. And I'm only telling you this because you're her family. So not a word to anyone, you hear me?"

It had been an easy promise to make, as Ruby would never have done anything to hurt Luna. Since their dramatic first meeting they had spent time together, along with Aurora, trying to find common ground. Ruby learned that Luna also adored *Harold and the Purple Crayon,* and they talked about things they would draw to make the world a better place. At the spring show in her new school, Luna went onstage and recited "Jabberwocky" and Ruby, seated in the audience, cried at the realization that this poem about conquering evil was their legacy, like a family crest. They attended Aurora's soccer matches and spaghetti nights hosted by Marigold and Charles. Disney movie dates and ice skating. Ruby loved the way Luna clung to her on the ice, holding on to her jacket and hand while Ruby pushed off on the ice, showing her how to glide in an easy stride.

It was nice to be needed in the purest way. To be able to keep Luna from falling, to be able to help—that just made Ruby's heart soar.

The pace of the party was picking up now. Aurora had helped Hazel's dad choose some music on his iPhone, and the noise level was rising with the whir of the bouncy house compressor, the music, and the shouts of kids.

"How many kids do we have here?" Tamarind asked.

"Eleven, plus Luna," said Nicole. "Luna and Hazel planned it—one guest for each year for the birthday girl. We're so pleased that Luna wanted her party to be here. I know we're right next door to the black hole, but the neighborhood has already begun to change, and I think the aura of the house will change once the new owners get their hands on it."

"I hope they give it a beautiful facelift," said Mom.

"Or bring in a wrecking ball," said Ruby, craning her neck a bit to take another look at the old house beyond the fence.

"Honey, that's a little extreme," Mom said.

"But I've felt that way myself at times," Nicole agreed.

Even after the Petrovs had been jailed, some of the sisters had wanted to stay at the house, but lawyers for the Petrovs had ordered that the property be sold along with the hotel, which had ceased operation. Laura and Julia had been on television crying in court, lost without their caretakers. Rachel had been whisked away by her wealthy parents, who had negotiated a way to make her testimony by deposition. Later in the trial it came out that Rachel's family had been paying Leo and Natalie a generous monthly stipend for Rachel's room and board, as if they had been running a care home.

Sienna Johnson, a runaway from Idaho, had testified against Leo and Natalie but later sobbed at the guilty verdict, telling a TV reporter that she loved Leo and that he was "a good man." Hearing that Sienna had been Luna's friend at times, Ruby had felt bad for her, still deluded, still thinking she was in love. Just eighteen, Sienna wasn't a lot older than Ruby, but she still had a lot of stuff to figure out. She refused to return to her conservative family in Idaho, but she didn't seem to have any immediate plans beyond waiting for Leo to be released from prison.

It looked like she would be waiting for at least twenty-five years.

The music switched to the "Happy" song, and Hazel led the kids out of the bouncy castle to dance around in a line. So corny, Ruby thought. She had been that age once, though she and her friends had been way too self-conscious for something like that.

The song ended and Luna came bounding across the yard to give the McCullums hugs. One magazine had called her the "miracle girl," but to Ruby the real miracle was that she was quickly learning to be a normal kid.

"I've never had a birthday before!" she exclaimed.

"Well, you've had birthdays," Ruby said, "just not parties."

"You're a stickler for accuracy," Luna said, making Ruby laugh. "Did you see your gift? Where is that box?"

"A gift for us?" Aurora teased. "But it's not our birthday, silly."

"It's just your lucky day," Luna said, finally spotting a box on the back of the deck. She slid it onto the table and opened the lid. "Kaysandra said you guys might want to read some of these. They're not as good as Harry Potter, but they're stories Mama told me, and I wrote them down to practice writing and spelling."

Ruby and Aurora lifted stapled packets of handwritten work from the box. "Aw, look at these cute little drawings!" Aurora exclaimed. "Here's a man throwing a football and a cheerleader with pompoms and a sweater with a red R on it. What does the R stand for?"

"Roseville," Luna said. "That's where Mama went to school."

"I didn't know that." Aurora turned to Ruby, who shrugged. She had never heard it, either.

"So you and our mom wrote these stories?" Ruby asked, intrigued to find this treasure trove of information. These stories might be her final glimpse into the heart and mind of her birth mother.

"Mama made them up, and I was her scribe. It was part of my homeschooling in the house. My favorite part. A lot of the stories were about my father, Winston."

Ruby looked up from the story she was skimming. "Wait. That was our birth father's name, too."

"I know that now. I mean . . ." Luna hesitated, flustered. "I used to think he was my dad, but now I know that Mama told me stories about your dad and pretended he was mine."

Ruby nodded, trying to encourage her. Leo had claimed to be Luna's father, and most people assumed that it was true. But Kaysandra had mentioned that Luna often mentioned a mythical father—a rapping, poetic football player who was uncannily similar to Winston Noland.

"I think Mama told me about your dad because she thought it would hurt me to know Leo was my father. Marigold says he mistreated me and that's never going to happen again. But if Marigold and Charles can adopt me, I'll have a new dad soon. It'll be official."

"I know. Isn't it great?" Ruby gave her a friendly nudge. "You and Aurora and I, we've got a second shot at being part of a family. Some people barely get one, but we get a second chance. We're lucky girls."

Squinting against the brightness of the candle flames on her cake, Luna let her eyes sweep over the faces gathered around her. She was supposed to make a wish, but how could you know what to wish for in a world where things changed overnight?

Last August, she would have probably wished for a candy bar or permission to visit Hazel. Now those wishes were easily granted, but she would never have Mama again, brushing the tangles out of her hair or tucking her in at night.

Back then she might have wished for a chance to attend a real school, though she couldn't have realized how tired she would feel from having too many eyes on her all the time, how she would have longed to go in the coatroom and hide behind the backpack suspended from a hook and listen to the teacher's lessons through the filter of darkness, just for a few minutes.

Wishes and sorrows seemed to be rolled up together, like the beans and chicken and cheese in a super burrito from Marigold's favorite Mexican place. And now Luna was on the spot to make a single wish until next year. Impossible.

"Make your wish," Aurora prodded her. "The candles are dripping."

Sucking in a breath, Luna blew out the candles and cast her wish for love.

Everyone clapped and cheered, and Luna was happy to melt into the group again, one of many children being served purple and brown cake in Hazel's backyard. She loved having friends and being free to be a kid, but sometimes she got tired of having to listen and be enthusiastic. Friendship could be draining. She pasted on a smile and let her mind wander as her gaze rose beyond the fence at the house that had contained her world for most of her life.

Had she ever really stood at that attic window, feeling safe and bored and trapped, wondering about the other side? The old attic seemed so far from where she was today, surrounded by friends and new family.

I wish for love.

Her wish had been a last-minute thing, but at least it wouldn't hurt anyone like those wishes that went awry in fairy tales. Now more than ever she worried about bad things happening to herself and to people she loved. Falling from a window. Getting killed in a car crash. Eating the wrong thing and getting worms or cancer or food poisoning. *Ick.* The more you learned of the world, the more there was to fear.

Still, a person needed to keep on learning.

She had learned that carrot sticks and apple slices were the healthier choices, but French fries always tasted better. That seemed unfair.

She had learned that emotions could be labeled and it was important to care about what other people were feeling in their hearts. Sometimes kids were mean because their hearts were hurting. She wished that Cara Farrel would stop being mean to her just because they were computer partners and Luna was a "computer weenie."

She had learned that Charles made the best spaghetti and meatballs in the world and Marigold was a terrible cook but a very good listener. Luna could be herself with Marigold. Quiet or loud, shy or curious. Somehow, this woman could make the right amount of space for who she needed to be.

And she had learned that her sisters, Ruby and Aurora, were there for her. Ruby with her smart ideas and quiet strength, Aurora with a gush of surprise and joy and sunshine.

I wish for love.

From the other side of the table Marigold caught her eye, observing, smiling, drinking in Luna's mood like a mama bird tending a nest.

Luna pressed a hand to her mouth as a random giggle slipped out. Just like that. It was crazy, but her wish had already come true.

Please turn the page for a very special
Q & A with Rosalind Noonan!

What inspired you to write this novel?

The initial spark came from a 2016 article in *The New Yorker* called "Thirty Years in Captivity: One woman's escape from a London cult" in which Simon Parkin tells the story of Katy, a young woman born into a South London cult and imprisoned in the compound until she managed to escape at the age of thirty. Katy's plight in captivity was worse than the one I crafted for Luna, as Katy was regularly beaten and emotionally abused. Katy's birth father and cult leader, "Bala," denied her contact as a baby, and Katy grew up without nurturing. The women in the household helped educate her, but the environment was so riddled with strife that Katy used to escape to the bathroom, grateful for a toilet that flushed upon command—one of the few reliable things in her life. Ultimately Katy manipulated other women in the house to finally help her escape at age thirty. Her new life had to include real-world lessons like learning how to cross the street, how to make a purchase in a store, and how to respond to social cues.

Katy's story made me realize how the dynamics of a cult could render a person helpless. In *The Sisters,* the captive Luna manages to escape at a younger age, but that is only because Luna has allies in the story—her mother, Glory, and eventually Ruby. Of course, once I get my hands on story material I push and pull it in different directions, crafting it into something far different from the source of inspiration. The *New Yorker* story turned out to be that little glimmering gem that winked at the possibilities: What if *this* happened? And then . . .

Are these characters based on real people?

The characters in *The Sisters* are 100 percent fiction, though some of their struggles and sweet moments have been based on my life and my family's and friends' experiences. The idea for a mom like Glory to leave her children at a fire station came to me when a family member who went into early labor saw signs at the hospital maternity ward proclaiming it a safe haven. It was incredibly upsetting for my cousin, worried about losing her baby after infertility issues, to imagine a mother dropping off her healthy newborn a few feet away. That experience led me to contrast Glory's desperation to give her girls a good life and start over herself with Tamarind and Pete's struggles to have a baby and start their family.

When I was imagining how the cult house might fit in a neighborhood, I recalled the transformation of a house behind us a few years ago when the owners got a divorce and the woman, who took possession of the home, turned it into a boardinghouse. That brought a lot of cars and one quite unsavory character to our otherwise friendly suburban neighborhood. The figure of a man with the sound of a clicking camera appeared in the house window when my daughter and her friends were in our backyard. A man was overheard arguing that he knew how to get revenge on someone. The same man was seen lingering on his bicycle at the school playground, talking to kids. None of these activities was illegal, but we're talking crazy creepy. It doesn't take much to menace a neighborhood.

Did you have a favorite character as you were writing the novel?

When writing any scene, I worked hard to get under that character's skin. Ruby brought me back to that pretend confidence of a sixteen-year-old girl who worries about the future. Glory required persistence through the exhaustion of being a young, single mom. I had to do some research to pinpoint the behavior of Ruby at age four and Luna at ten. The blatant, unfiltered voice of Aurora was a lot of fun for me, as was the defiant Sienna. Why is it so easy for me to write for a whiner? Hmm.

Do you worry about readers believing in your characters?

That's always a concern, as a character is the vehicle that takes you through a story. Whenever possible I draw from real people, biographies, and experiences. Sometimes it seems like we are living in a world where truth has become stranger than fiction. As I was writing this novel the news broke of a seventeen-year-old girl who escaped from the family home and called for help to rescue her siblings from captivity. The thirteen children of the Turpin family were allegedly being starved and tortured by their parents in their California home. Hard to imagine, but having considered Luna's circumstances, I could relate to the thrill of these children at learning how to use a toothbrush and having a chance to choose their own reading material. And their mixed feelings toward the parents who alternately fed and tortured them show how reliant we are on each other.

THE SISTERS

Rosalind Noonan

ABOUT THIS GUIDE

The suggested questions are included to enhance
your group's reading of Rosalind Noonan's
The Sisters!

DISCUSSION QUESTIONS

1. Early in the novel, Glory Noland makes a difficult choice giving up her children in the belief that they would have a better life being raised by adoptive parents. Do you think a child's birth parents are inherently more fitting caretakers than a stranger, or are there cases when adoptive parents are the best choice for the emotional security and well-being of a child?

2. Although Glory doesn't dwell on her mother's prejudices, Katherine Halpern is angered by her daughter's involvement with a black man from the time Glory starts dating Winston in high school. What external factors in Katherine Halpern's life might have played a role in her rejection of Glory and her children?

3. In what ways is the title *The Sisters* threaded through the story?

4. What qualities attract women like the sisters to Leo Petrov? How does Leo benefit through the nonsexual relationships he has with these broken women?

5. What is Leo's sister, Natalie, gaining by taking in women and putting them to work?

6. Is there a certain quality or flaw in a person that would make her more likely to join a group like the sisters? What do Laura, Rachel, Kimani, Georgina, Sienna, and Julia have in their pasts that make them vulnerable to controlling people like Leo and Natalie?

7. Crockett Johnson's children's book *Harold and the Purple Crayon* is mentioned throughout the novel. Discuss how Harold's ability to use a crayon to draw his way

out of a fix might have played in Ruby's fantasies. How does this imaginative skill help Luna?

8. Do you think Leo is morally and legally responsible for Glory's ultimate fate?

9. Throughout the novel, women reveal different methods of mothering. Glory wants the best for her children at any cost. Rima is quick to give advice and checks the barometer of the lives around her through tea reading. Tamarind works to keep channels of communication open, but gives her daughters space. Nicole is protective of her daughter and tries to protect the girl next door when there are hints of abuse. What quality do these women have in common? Which woman would you choose as a mother?

10. Ruby's friends Delilah and Maxi are quick to tell her what to do. Do you think their advice was wise or foolish? Do you think teens are more likely to take advice from their friends or parents?

11. Why is Luna so forgiving and tolerant of Sienna in her attempt to become friends later in the novel?

12. If you were choosing a cast for the novel, what actors would you pick to play Glory, Ruby, and Tamarind?

Connect with U(s)

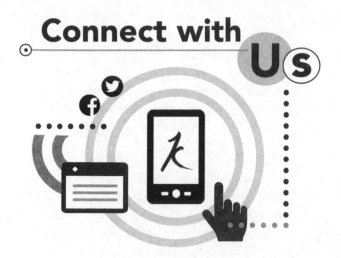

Visit us online at
KensingtonBooks.com
to read more from your favorite authors, see books
by series, view reading group guides, and more.

Join us on social media

for sneak peeks, chances to win books and prize packs,
and to share your thoughts with other readers.

facebook.com/kensingtonpublishing
twitter.com/kensingtonbooks

Tell us what you think!

To share your thoughts, submit a review,
or sign up for our eNewsletters, please visit:
KensingtonBooks.com/TellUs.